TOTALLY FOLKED

GOOD FOLK: MODERN FOLKTALES BOOK #1

PENNY REID

WWW.PENNYREID.NINJA/NEWSLETTER/

COPYRIGHT

DEDICATION

For any and all people who consistently fail to make a good first impression.

CHAPTER 1

JACKSON

"Look your best—who said love is blind?"

— MAE WEST

"*B*ad day, Jackson?"

"Not at all." I nodded once at Genie Lee, unconcerned that my smile resembled a grimace. She probably couldn't see much of my mouth seeing as how I currently wore a lemon meringue pie on my face. I hadn't taken the time to wipe much of it off, wanting to keep my hands as clean as possible should I have need to employ them. I figured I'd either wipe it off once I finally made it back to the truck or just take my shirt off at some point and use it as a towel.

But not right now. Right now, since I was downtown, too many folks milled around. I'd worked hard on changing my reputation. Last thing I needed was stories circulating back to the station and beyond about me running shirtless through downtown.

"Anyone I should keep an eye out for?" Genie asked my back as I jogged past and scanned Walnut Street for Deveron Lawrence Stokes Jr., or as his momma and everyone else called him, DJ.

"No, ma'am. Have a nice day."

Her chuckle followed me down the sidewalk, and I shook my head, momentarily lifting my eyes to the heavens. When I'd come upon the trio of eleven-year-olds behind Bob's Bait and Tackle, they'd clearly panicked. I suspected the stolen pie had launched out of DJ's hand on instinct. That kid had one hell of a pitching arm and a mighty good aim.

I didn't mind the pie to the face, the discomfort temporary, hardly a blip on my radar. As far as embarrassing situations I'd experienced, this maybe ranked one point five out of ten.

My grimace had been inspired by the fact that they'd stolen the pies in the first place. Stolen pies necessitated a third call this month from Daisy Payton—local business owner and community heavyweight—complaining about a group of kids sneaking into her diner's kitchen during business hours to swipe fresh baked pies. This time they'd made off with six. Last time they'd only taken two.

Understandably, Daisy Payton wasn't pleased. And when Daisy Payton wasn't pleased, she called the sheriff, who also happened to be my father. And when my father wanted to make a show of taking action, he called either Deputy Monroe, Deputy Boone, or me. But if the complaint originated with a Payton—especially Daisy—I was always tapped for the job, regardless of date or time, regardless of whether or not I was on duty.

"I've got Jackson on it, Daisy," he'd say, and that always made her feel better, settled ruffled feathers long enough for the situation to be handled.

But back to now and spending my rare Saturday off chasing down eleven-year-olds wielding stolen pies as though launched by trebuchet.

"Jackson! What happened to your face?" Bonnie Linton called from across the street.

I tipped my head in her direction while power walking, a blob of meringue falling to the steamy sidewalk in front of Big Ben's Dulcimer Shop. "Just trying out a new beauty regimen, Ms. Linton."

"Having a bad day, Jackson?" Karen Smith taunted from where she stood next to Bonnie Linton. I imagined she enjoyed this, probably considered it "just desserts" for her DUI arrest last year.

Keeping my eyes forward, I inspected a line of overgrown azalea bushes while slowing my steps. The second bush back from the sidewalk rustled, and it seemed to be having a heated, whispered argument with itself. I heard a harsh *Shhh* and a *Stop pushing!*

I stopped, placing my hands on my hips. "I know you're behind there. I hid in those bushes too when I was a kid. I need you to come out."

"With our hands up?" came a defiant little voice I recognized as belonging to Mac Hill.

"Sure, if you want. Unless one of those hands holds a pie. If you've still got those pies with you, just keep them safe." I glanced to my right and took a step closer to the bush. A few folks—some I recognized, some I didn't—had halted their Saturday window-shopping to watch.

"Are you going to arrest us?" Kimmy Mitchell squeaked. I was uncertain if she sounded worried or excited by the prospect.

There was no way I'd be arresting Kimmy Mitchell. Exhibit A, she was eleven. Exhibit B, arresting anybody for pie thievery without violence or breaking and entering didn't make much sense. At least it didn't make sense to me. Exhibit C, I was in the process of courting Kimmy's momma, Charlotte Mitchell.

Although, had Charlotte and I not been courting, even I—a perpetual rule non-bender —would've given the law a wee little flex for Charlotte Mitchell and her kids. Around town and among the deputies, it was just understood as fact, different rules applied to Charlotte, a single mom of four kids.

Regardless, I couldn't come right out and say *No, Kimmy. I'm not arresting you 'cause your momma has enough to deal with* because Kimmy wasn't alone. If Kimmy had been alone, I definitely would've reasoned with her by bringing up her momma.

So instead, I said, "Now that depends," while wiping at my left eyebrow with a knuckle. Tossing a fair bit of lemon curd to the pavement, I brought my hand back to my hip. "If y'all come out now, agree to apologize, stop stealing Ms. Daisy's pies, and figure out a way to make things right, we can avoid a trip to the station."

"What about my momma?" DJ asked, fear tinting his words. "Are you going to tell my momma?"

I sighed again, noting that the number of spectators had grown. "Can y'all come out so we can talk man-to-man?" The back of my neck prickled. I shoved the heightening discomfort aside, determined to focus on reasoning with the three kids rather than worrying about the good or bad opinions of a crowd.

"Hey! I ain't no man," came little Kimmy's voice just before she stepped out of the tall azalea. Her eyes fierce, she balanced a pie in each hand. From the looks of it, she held a blueberry and an apple.

"Fine then, man-to-woman." I crouched down on my haunches so that we were now eye level. "And I see Miss Mitchell is the bravest among you."

The little girl lifted her chin proudly as the two boys still hidden in the bush grumbled.

"Having a bad day, Jackson?" JT MacIntyre's blustery voice sounded from somewhere behind me. "You need any help?"

"No. Thank you, JT," I said without turning, keeping my eyes on Kimmy. "It's a fine day, and we're just having a conversation."

In my peripheral vision I saw that a person I didn't recognize had pulled out their phone, probably a tourist, which was fine. It wouldn't be the first time I'd been filmed while trying to de-escalate a situation, but it would be the first time I'd done so covered in pie.

I licked my lips to keep from laughing my frustration, the lemony sweetness and eggy meringue not at all tasty in the heat of a June afternoon. Funny thing, I'd eaten this very same kind of pie off the breasts of a naked woman a few years back, and it had been damn delicious. I reckon dessert tasted different when worn involuntarily.

Mac climbed out of the azalea next, followed by DJ. As soon as DJ appeared, I locked eyes with him. His cheeks were bright red—maybe from the earlier chase—and he wore a scowl that reminded me of his father. I'd arrested Deveron Stokes at least ten times over the last decade and seeing the familiar petulant expression on little DJ didn't sit right with me.

"I don't see what the big deal is," DJ spat, holding a chocolate pie of some sort in his right hand and nothing in his left. "Daisy has plenty of pie. Why can't she just give us some?"

This statement also reminded me of DJ's father. Deveron was always playing entitled victim, thinking everyone else owed him what he hadn't earned.

Narrowing my eyes, I gestured for the pie thieves to come closer so I wouldn't have to raise my voice to be heard. They shared looks with each other and then shuffled forward as a group, looking sour. Between them, they still held five pies. *Well, that's something at least. Five out of six isn't too bad.*

When they were close enough to hear my whisper, I spoke. "Here's what we're going to do. We're going to return these pies to Ms. Daisy. Then we're going to ask her if she has any work that y'all can help with."

"You mean you want us to do chores," Kimmy supplied, her face scrunching up.

"In my line of work, it's called reparations," I said gently. "But yes. Y'all took property that didn't belong to you, and so now you need to make that right."

DJ stepped closer. "But Daisy has—"

"It doesn't matter if Daisy Payton has a thousand pies. If you want one of those pies, you work for it or pay for it."

Fire flashing in his eyes, DJ shook his head. "No. No way. I ain't doing no chores."

My eyebrow lifted at his defiance, and I had to tilt my head back to keep an avalanche of lemon and meringue from falling into my eyes. "If you have another idea on how to make things right, go ahead. Tell me."

DJ glanced from side to side and then focused on the crowd gathered behind me. "You can't touch us, cop. Not now, not here. We're just kids, and that guy over there is filming everything. You'll get in trouble. So how's about you let us walk?"

I felt my mouth curve into a sad smile, my heart sunk, and my thoughts oscillated between *This poor kid* and *You little shit.*

"You stole those pies. That means I *can* touch you." I kept my tone relaxed, still hoping—despite the crowd, despite the clown filming us, despite the distrust and insolence in DJ's stare—that I could diffuse his temper. "Here's the truth, DJ. I don't want to put my hands on you. I don't want to force you. I want you to do the right thing, and I think you want to do the right thing too."

"Fuck off, cop."

Ignoring that—likely something he'd heard his daddy say—I pulled in a deep breath. "So, the way I see it, y'all got two choices: either you come with me now, on your own, making it your decision, or you spend the rest of the day running while I chase you around town."

DJ scoffed. "You're gonna spend all day running after us?"

"As you can see, I'm in my running clothes. I was getting ready to go on a run when I got the call about these stolen pies." I shrugged. "I need the exercise. Either it's running on a treadmill or running after y'all. It doesn't matter to me either way, and I need to get in thirteen miles. You wanna run thirteen miles?"

"Don't you wanna go chase other bad guys?" DJ eyed me, like he hadn't yet made up his mind whether I was serious.

"First, you're not a bad guy. You're making some real sketch decisions, DJ, but you're not bad. Second, today is my day off. So, no. I got nowhere to be, nothing to do. I'm happy to spend my whole day chasing you." The first part of what I'd said was true, but the second part was mostly a lie. I did have somewhere to be this evening, namely taking Charlotte Mitchell out on a date.

Rebelliousness and irritation glittered behind DJ's eyes, his mouth forming an unhappy curve. He looked at me. I looked at him. I waited.

"Fine," he bit out. But before I could feel relieved, he lifted the pie in his hand. I saw the intent in his eye and ducked to one side just in time for the pie to whiz by my head and miss my face by a scant few inches.

That. Little. Shit.

I bit my lip, doing my best not to glare at the kid. I understood why—in his mind— he'd done it. He didn't want to spend all day running and he needed to save face in front of his friends. That said, the action, though it might've felt good in the moment, was only going to make both his life and mine harder.

Meanwhile, Kimmy Mitchell gasped. "That was the chocolate mousse with chocolate cookie crust, you dummy!"

Mac Hill made a sad grunting sound. "Why'd you have to do that? I still have the pumpkin pie right here. If you were going to—"

"Let's just go." DJ held out his arms, as though he expected me to cuff them.

I'd cuffed kids before, not many times, but I'd done it. It was always the last resort and always when the minor was in the process of physically hurting themselves or someone else. Neither of those scenarios were true at present.

"Come on." I stood, ignoring his outstretched hands and gesturing in the direction of my parked truck. I hadn't brought the cruiser, not wanting to be the one to give young DJ Stokes his first official ride in the back of a law enforcement vehicle. "Y'all can practice your groveling on the way."

"What about my momma?" DJ asked, sullenly stuffing his now empty hands in the pockets of his dirty jeans.

"I already called your momma. She knows what's up, and she said whatever Daisy decides is fine by her."

His shoulders slumped as he walked in front of me, and I could guess why. His momma was a sweet lady who'd had a hard life, but she was also a screamer. I suspected he didn't want to disappoint her, but I thought maybe the imminent screaming fit was the true reason for his bowed posture. In my experience, folks screamed and cussed when they felt powerless.

I nodded to JT MacIntyre, Genie Lee, and a few unfamiliar faces as we approached. "You're in the passenger seat, at the front of the truck, DJ. Kimmy, I got a booster seat for you in the back."

"You mean you don't have your cop car?" Mac sounded regretful.

"I didn't think I would need it today." Out of the corner of my eye, I saw the same stranger from before still recording. As soon as we were buckled up in the truck, I was going to wipe my face off.

"That's too bad," Mac said on a sigh.

I split my attention between the kids and the man with his phone as we walked closer to my truck. "If you want to do a ride-along, I'll call your momma and get one scheduled."

"Oh!" Mac sent me a quick grin.

"Can I come too?" Kimmy turned to walk backward. I took one of the pies from her grip.

"I'll ask your momma next time I see her." Charlotte hadn't told her kids about us dating yet. I'd always been in Charlotte's life—and their lives—as a friend. We were still just friends as far as they knew.

Charlotte and I had been together for a while, but we'd only managed three official dates so far, if you didn't count grabbing a quick bite for lunch every so often. I understood her hesitation. She needed to be certain of a man before taking that kind of step, and I was determined to be someone she could be certain of.

My eating-pie-off-naked-ladies days were over. Unless, you know, Charlotte brought it up if we eventually got married.

"Y'all are traitors," DJ grumbled. "He's not cool, he's a pig."

"Hey, the only reason I got food on my face is 'cause y'all put it there," I said, hoping to lighten the mood. "Once we get in the truck, I got a towel in the back to wipe it off." Unable to stand it anymore, I used the back of my hand to push globs of pie from my forehead and chin.

Kimmy abruptly stepped closer to me, peering at the onlookers who hadn't yet dispersed. "Why are so many people watching us?"

"They're looking at me." I patted her shoulder, making sure I sounded unconcerned. "Ignore them."

"This is so embarrassing." She lowered her face, her hair falling forward. "Oh no. There's Mrs. Smith. She's so mean."

"Is that guy still filming us?" Mac was looking over his shoulder at the stranger in sunglasses we'd just walked past. The man was now following us, still holding his cell out.

I opened the passenger side of the cab and handed the pie I'd taken earlier back to Kimmy. "Here, get in. I'll go talk to him. And be careful with the pies. The more we can return to Daisy, the better."

Giving the man filming us a hard look that was likely disguised by the remaining sticky residue, I strolled the short distance over and ignored the phone he held. "Hello, sir. Can I help you?"

"Where are you taking those kids? You a cop? What's your badge number?" He thrust the phone forward and into my face.

Genie Lee, standing nearby, lifted her voice to holler, "Put that phone down, you fool. That's Jackson James. He's having a bad day."

"No worries, Genie. Day's been just fine, thank you." Working to make my smile appear more natural, I lowered my voice so only the man—and his phone—could hear me. "I don't mind if you record me, sir. But these kids are underage, and you shouldn't be filming them."

"Is that a threat?" The stranger straightened, peeling off his sunglasses to glare at me. "I know my rights."

"Nope." I shook my head. "And it's not against the law to film in a public place, so I'm not gonna do anything other than point out that you're scaring them. So, if you could stop scaring the kids, I'd sure appreciate it."

That done, I turned back toward the truck as a bystander in the slowly dispersing crowd called out, "Bad day, Jackson?"

I lifted my head to offer a friendly retort when something—or rather, someone—caught my eye.

Doing a double take, I spotted Jethro Winston standing among the remaining crowd, his movie star wife next to him, and his three boys. But their faces hadn't been the source of my surprise or stunned focus. Breath whooshed out of me like I'd been punched in the gut, and my heart hammered between my ears. I stopped mid-stride. I stared.

Raquel.

Raquel Ezra.

Holy shit.

The woman who, for the last handful of years, had never been far from my thoughts.

Unreachable.

Untouchable.

Holy fucking shit.

Here.

Now.

9

Looking right at me.

And I'm covered in pie.

"Jackson?" A heavy hand on my shoulder brought me back to reality. Shaking myself, I stared at the arm, shoulder, and face connected to the hand, finding Fire Chief McClure giving me a paternal smile. "You got a little something on your face, son."

I glanced down at the handkerchief he held out. I blinked at it.

"Bad day?" he asked.

I nodded, dumbly accepting the folded square. "Yes, sir." I spoke around a sudden roughness, my mind wild. "You could definitely say that."

CHAPTER 2

RAQUEL

"Avoid popularity. It has many snares and no real benefit."

— ATTRIBUTED TO DOROTHY DANDRIDGE (BUT MAYBE
ALSO WILLIAM PENN)

*W*hen my friend Sienna and her husband paused to watch a man in exercise clothes talking to three kids, all of whom were holding pie, I automatically craned my neck to see over the crowd, wondering why the scene held such interest. The man's back was turned to us, and he was crouched on the sidewalk, yet a spike of heat pierced my chest at the sight. The broad shoulders, blond hair, and something about how he held himself felt familiar.

Murmured conversations surrounded me, but I didn't hear them, my thoughts a tangle of *Does he have kids? Are those his kids? They look really tall for*—I did some mental math—*four-year-olds.*

Eventually, he stood and turned, and I sucked in a breath because it was definitely him, Deputy Dreamy from my one night in Green Valley. I thought maybe he wouldn't spot me, and that was preferable. I wasn't ready. I wasn't prepared. I told myself to turn away to ensure he couldn't see my face in the crowd. Perhaps one or more of those children were his, and here I was, a hussy staring at a married DILF of three exceptionally tall four-year-olds. It shouldn't matter, I wasn't in town to see him.

. . . Really? Then why are you here?

GO AWAY VOICE!

Rae, you are a mess.

I didn't get a chance to argue the case with myself before Deputy James stalked back over and spoke to a man who'd been recording them with his cell phone. He didn't like that the man was recording the kids and he told the man so. The sound of the deputy's voice—all growly with polite, disdainful authority—made my stomach do backflips, and I could not look away.

Then our eyes locked.

He saw me. His face may have been covered in what looked like whipped cream and some kind of yellow-ish goo, but I know for a fact Deputy James looked right at me. Our eyes locked, held, and a million questions whizzed through my brain.

I hadn't expected to see him so soon. Honestly, I wasn't sure if I'd actually expected to see him at all. My heart tripped all over itself, and I couldn't quite gather a full breath. Even covered in frosting and goop he was just so . . . *sigh.*

And then, Deputy Dreamy left. He just up and left. He blinked, looked away from me, talked to an older man briefly, walked to his truck—the same old truck he'd been driving that one night we spent together—climbed inside, and shut the door. My body deflated.

"What does Jackson James think he's doing? Making a scene like that." A woman nearby spoke with salty conviction, her words cutting through my daze. Too absorbed by the oddly queasy feeling in my stomach, I didn't—couldn't—spare her a glance.

"Are those his kids?" I croaked, wondering at the intensity of my reaction to the unexpected sighting of Deputy Dreamy—my nickname for him—and my disappointment. *It's been years, Rae. Years. Of course he has kids.*

"That'll be the day," Sienna's husband Jethro said, his voice tinged with humor. "Jackson James has no kids."

Another woman nearby tacked on a mumbled, "That we know about."

The sudden knot in my stomach eased, and I mentally chuckled at myself. What was wrong with me? Why should I be so relieved that a guy I'd spent a few hours with years ago had no children, which reduced the chances that he might possibly be in a committed relationship? Although, by no means did lack of children equal not being married, or in a relationship. Plenty of marriages and committed relationships were completely and totally fulfilling without the addition of—gah! You know what I mean.

Whatever. He probably didn't even remember our night together. Besides, I really wasn't here to see him.

Suuuure.

I MEAN IT, VOICE. NO MORE OUT OF YOU!

"Those three hooligans are the pie thieves who've been stealing from Daisy Payton." The first lady made a sniffing sound, adding to her friend, "About time they were caught. Menace, all three."

"Must've been pie all over his face." Jethro ignored the nearby women as Jackson James's truck pulled away. "And I bet it was that little sh—uh—" he hesitated, glancing at his oldest son and then back to Sienna "—I bet it was DJ Stokes that got him."

Sienna also laughed. "Did you hear what he said to Bonnie? Said it was his 'new beauty regimen.' Hilarious. That line is going to show up in my next script."

Jethro shook his head of shaggy brown hair, chuckling lightly and taking his youngest son out of Sienna's arms, then bending down to give her a kiss. "Okay, enough excitement. Nap time. See you pretty ladies later."

"Thanks, honey." Sienna tossed her long, glossy hair over one shoulder, her dark brown eyes warm with obvious affection as she gazed at her husband. "We'll be back after lunch."

"No rush. Take your time. Take all day. I'm sure y'all want to catch up."

"Are you sure this is okay?" I twisted my fingers, glancing between the two of them. "I know I showed up unannounced."

Jethro's grin was friendly and easy, and his brownish greenish eyes twinkled. Then again, they always seemed to twinkle. Whenever I saw Sienna and Jethro at industry

PENNY REID

events, the man rarely left her side, his hands were all over her, and his eyes twinkled.

He opened his mouth as though to respond, but the oldest of their sons tugged on his cargo shorts before he could. "I'm hot. Can we get ice cream?" The little boy pointed to a sign I recognized from my first visit here, *Utterly Ice Cream.*

The fat baby/toddler in Jethro's arms grabbed his dad's beard with both hands, fisting it and grinning.

"No." Jethro tried to extract his facial hair from chubby fingers as he steered their three sons down the sidewalk. "We got ice cream at home. And your uncle is coming over."

"Which one?" the oldest asked, automatically reaching out to hold his middle brother's hand.

"They'll be fine," Sienna whispered at my side, giving me a wink. I sent her a look of uncertainty and noted that her eyes were also twinkly. Perhaps people as in love as they were had perpetually twinkly eyes.

"Does it matter which uncle?" Jethro's voice carried to us as he juggled his three boys and pushed them toward the parking lot where we'd parked earlier.

I heard the middle son say something like, "Can I drive the tractor this time?" just before they were out of earshot.

Sienna sighed next to me, then whispered urgently, "No one approaches when Jet is around, and I'm not saying anyone will. But just to be safe, don't make any eye contact with the locals if you can help it. Otherwise, we'll be swarmed."

I flinched back in alarm. "What?"

"I'm kidding!" Her wide grin returned, and she nudged me in the ribs with her elbow, laughing. "Totally joking. Everyone here is great, super chill. No one really cares that we're movie people. I haven't been asked for an autograph since before Jet and I were married. Tons of friends have visited—Tom, Eva, Juliette—no one pays any attention. So as long as you didn't bring any paparazzi or stalkers with you, we're good."

"Oh." Relief flooded through me. "Okay." I hadn't thought about being recognized by moviegoers, or swarmed by fans, or being approached by one of my stalkers when I decided on a whim to come visit.

14

Admittedly, leaving without at least one guard had been reckless. But I hadn't given much thought to anything except escaping Los Angeles. A light application of makeup, baggy clothes, and a hat pulled low had been enough of a disguise in the airports.

"What I'm saying is, you can relax. No one cares you're here. I mean, except for me. I care. Obviously." Her hand came to my upper arm, and she gave it a little squeeze. "Feel free to be yourself."

I laughed at that, and I'm sure it sounded weird and sad. Sniffling, I closed my eyes against a rush of tears.

Rae, you are a mess. A. Mess.

"What? What's wrong?" I felt her move closer, and she dropped her voice. "What did I say?"

"God, Sienna. If I knew how to be myself, I would. I would be her." Opening my eyes, I compelled my lips to form something like a smile. "I just feel so lost."

Ugh! I hadn't meant to say that. I needed to pull myself together. If Aristotle was right and knowing yourself is the beginning of all wisdom, then I was the dumbest person on the planet.

Concern wrinkled her forehead and her eyes darted over my face. "What's going on?"

Gathering a deep breath for boldness—*be bold!*—I planned to make some joke about their twisty unmarked streets and the backwoods roads my taxi had navigated to her house, but instead I blurted the words I'd been thinking for over a year, "I think I want to retire."

Sienna stared at me, her eyes wide. "Retire?"

"You know, *retire*," I whispered, like it was a secret. Which, I supposed, it was since I hadn't confessed this to another soul until just now. "I'm sorry."

"Why are you sorry?"

I rubbed at my forehead, feeling ridiculous. "I'm sorry because I dropped in without warning on your doorstep today and ruined your plans with your handsome husband and adorable children. And now you're not having the day with your family that you planned."

She continued staring at me, like she was trying to figure me out. "I told you it was fine when you arrived. I mean, I was surprised when you showed up, and especially without some sort of a security detail—that seemed odd—but I would much rather you show up on my doorstep unannounced than continue to ignore my calls."

"Oh yeah, speaking of, I'm sorry about that too." Acutely, I became aware that we were standing in the middle of the sidewalk, blocking traffic, and forcing people to walk around us. I pulled Sienna to one side and into the nook created by the window display of an antique shop and the corner of the adjacent building. "But I wasn't technically ignoring your calls. I'm ignoring everyone's calls."

She gave her head a little shake. "What is going on with you?"

I watched her, my brain in a riot. *Get back on the rails, Rae. Your champagne problems are not Sienna's problems. They're not even real problems.*

She stepped closer at my silence. "Rae, are you okay?"

"Yes. Yes, I'm fine. Totally fine." I laughed, working to slip into the character I usually played at industry events. I hadn't come here to make her worry. I came here to . . . "I'm not even sure why I'm here, honestly." Still struggling to smile, I infused a lightness I didn't feel into my words. "I guess I just wanted to see how country life is treating you, take in the sights, have myself a hoedown."

Have myself a hoedown? Really? Could you be any weirder? Had I been this inept at conversation the last time I was here, five plus years ago? I didn't think so.

But a lot had changed. I'd gone from rising Hollywood star who was good at faking bravado to an A-list celebrity with a team of people to manage my money, and a team of people to manage those people, and a team of people to manage me.

Which brings me back to Sienna. We hadn't engaged in more than a quick conversation at a red carpet event since before her wedding. In order to avoid severe-conversation-flail, maybe I simply needed to think of Sienna as a professional colleague instead of as a . . . what? Friend? Were we even still friends? We used to be.

"I see." Sienna seemed to give my words intense scrutiny, her eyes narrowing. "I had been thinking we could grab some lunch, but based on that odd series of statements, I think we should skip straight to the wine portion of the day. It's only eleven thirty, but I get the sense we need to have a wine conversation."

"Oh! Wine. I could do wine. Hey, maybe we could make it a whiskey conversation." I was only half joking.

"Sure. There's a whiskey distillery just outside of town." She pulled out a cell from her little purse. "I'll call a car and we can just go. Then we'll have somebody pick us up after so we can drink without driving. You can get drunk if you need to."

I made a face like *whaaaa?* and an uncomfortable laugh tumbled out. "Why would I need to get drunk? I'm fine. I'm so fine. I've never been finer."

Lifting the phone to her ear, Sienna's eyes skated over me shrewdly. "Don't worry. I won't let you get too drunk."

CHAPTER 3

RAQUEL

"I've always just simply seen myself as an actor. And I believe that it serves me well to just think in terms of my craft. If hypothetically, I saw myself only as a sex symbol, or as some other limited stereotype, I think I would feel like a complete failure."

— VIOLA DAVIS

*S*ienna took me to a distillery not five miles outside of town. As soon as we entered the brewery, she'd greeted the woman behind the counter like they were old friends, introduced me, then asked for two whiskey flights. The place wasn't technically open for customers this early in the day, but they were open to her. Unsurprisingly.

Sienna Diaz was a household name, America's sweetheart, gorgeous, funny, fun, kind, generous, and sublimely happy with her former-criminal-turned-park-ranger-turned-stay-at-home-dad husband. She was the most with-it and together person in Hollywood. And the most genuine. By far.

"Shoot the first shot, sip the rest." Sienna pointed to the first in a series of shot glasses.

Presently, we sat at a table outside on a flagstone patio overlooking a summer garden of tall wildflowers, tomato vines, and the remainder of spring vegetables.

"Bottoms up." I picked up the first of the shot glasses in front of me and swallowed its contents in one gulp. Setting it down on the wood serving plank, next to the other full glasses, I breathed out fire and shook my head. "Damn."

"Whew. Okay. Now we can talk." Sienna, her nose still wrinkled with post-alcohol burn, leaned forward. "So, tell me, what's going on? What do you mean you want to retire?"

Reaching for the pitcher of water in the middle of the table, I poured myself a glass, concentrating on it rather than giving my eyes to her. "Just exactly that. I think I want to retire."

"What? Like a dance move? You're retiring your dance moves? What do you mean?"

"I want to retire from acting."

"At twenty-seven?"

"I'm twenty-eight, and yes. I feel like—like maybe—like, yes. I think it's time."

I felt her gaze inspecting me. "Are you thinking about getting into directing? Producing?"

"What? Me?" I snorted. "Like I could do that." I couldn't even make my own lunch. And if the lunch came in a paper bag, I probably wouldn't be able to find it. I'd needed a map of my own house when I first moved in.

"Did you just scoff? It was a serious question. I think you'd be great behind the camera. You basically rewrote the entire *Tabitha Tomorrow* script, and everyone knows you were in the cutting room for *Starlight Express*—and that movie swept the award season for editing."

"No." I waved my hands in front of me.

But she wasn't finished. "AND! You have a great eye for picking projects with universal themes, ones that connect with wide audiences. Any studio would be lucky to have you on the development side."

"No. I want to retire from the business. I want out."

Her face fell, dropping right into a frown. "Should I say congratulations? Or should I push you to tell me what's really going on?"

"Nothing is going on." I twisted a finger in my long hair and looked out over the raised garden beds. They needed to be weeded. "I'm just bored, you know?" If I were Pinocchio, my nose would be a mile long after that statement. "And besides, what am I doing with my life?"

"Let's put a pin in that last question," she said almost primly and mimed placing a tack in an imaginary corkboard. "First, do you feel good about this decision?"

"Yes. Of course." *Ope.* There goes my nose again. Liar, liar, pants on fire.

"Hmm." She looked me down and then up. "So, uh, what does Harrison think about this?" The way she said his name told me that Sienna didn't think much of Harrison.

"This is not about Harrison." I picked up the second shot glass, its color a lighter brown than the first, and brought it to my lips. I meant to take just a sip but ended up drinking half.

"Yeah, but what does he have to say? Does he know you want to retire?"

"I haven't talked to him about it."

"You two are engaged and you haven't talked to him about it? What am I missing?" Sienna touched her second glass but didn't pick it up, she was too busy interviewing me.

I squirmed in my seat, drank the rest of my shot, and then picked up the third.

"Rae."

"Fine!" I set the whiskey back down but didn't release it. "It's fake. It is fake. It's all fake. We are big fakers. We've been faking it." I drank the third shot. It didn't burn at all. "Sorry, was I supposed to sip that one?"

She ignored my question, her mouth dropping open. "You and Harrison are fake engaged?"

"Yes. We're not really together. It's all a ruse, which is a word I say but don't know how to spell but feel like I should. Does it have a *z*? R-O-U-Z?" My mother had always been horrified by my lack of spelling skills. Sometimes, before I sent her text messages, I typed them out in a word processor first, to check for grammar and spelling errors. True story.

"Spelling lessons later. How long have you been faking it?"

21

"Since we publicly got back together during the filming of *Hard Nights End*."

She shook her head like this made no sense. "That was over four years ago. Why would you—what—whose idea was this? Was this Domino's idea?"

Domino Bing was both Harrison's and my publicist and manager. "No. It was Harrison's idea, and my agent's, John. Do you know John?"

She nodded.

I continued. "They approached me about it before filming started and then we went to Domino together. Only the four of us know—not even Harrison's agent knows—except now you know." And I couldn't believe I'd just told her.

My face must've displayed my flare of panic because she held a hand up. "I'm not going to say anything."

"Thank you." I believed her.

I . . . trusted her. I didn't know why I trusted her so much, but I did. *Which is ultimately why I'm here, isn't it?*

"But I don't understand." She leaned back in her seat, crossing her arms as her gaze skated over me. "Why would you agree to this? With *Harrison*?"

"It made sense at the time. And it did help me get that part in *Tabitha Tomorrow*. Our ruse has definitely helped." Furthering my career was why I'd agreed to do it in the first place and was the excuse I used—like a chant—whenever I felt shitty about the situation.

"You don't need Harrison to get film parts. You're hugely talented. And you're stunning, I can't think of anyone close to your age that looks like you. Maybe Eva Mendes? A little? You're what would happen if Raquel Welch and Sophia Loren had a baby. And your eyes give me goose bumps. The pinnacle of Italian and Bolivian beauty."

"My dad is Cuban." I fiddled with the azabache bracelet on my wrist, a gift from my dad's mother, and one of the only things I had from that side of my family.

"Oh. My mistake. I'm sorry. For some reason I thought your dad was Bolivian."

"My grandparents were Cuban, both sets of great grandparents came over from Cuba." I'd had a better relationship with my grandparents than I did with my father, especially with my grandmother. Every summer before they died, I would spend two weeks in Miami with them. He'd married someone else by the time I'd reached ten months, and they welcomed their first baby one year later.

I don't know if his wife didn't want me to visit them, or if my father resisted imposing his illegitimate daughter on his perfect family, but during all the visitation time he'd been given in the custody agreement I'd stayed with my grandparents.

"Why did I think your dad was Bolivian?"

"Raquel Welch is Bolivian—well, partially—and we share a name, so I think that's why there's confusion. And it's okay. I don't talk about my dad much. No biggie." I shrugged, mentally sidestepping around the tenderness I felt about this subject, which was why I rarely talked about it.

It's hard to talk about something you don't even want to think about.

"My point is still valid. You're brilliant. So I'm confused why you'd consent to this arrangement with Harrison."

"Why are you confused?" I fingered the fourth and final shot of whiskey, glancing between her remaining three full glasses and my three empty ones. Was it too late to pace myself?

"Harrison cheated on you—for real—when you two were actually together. I know he hurt you."

"That's all in the past." I waved her statement away. "And we're—I'm not angry or hurt. I'm not at all angry with him about it anymore." Finally, a truthful statement.

"This sounds complicated." She sipped her second shot of whiskey, but *actually* sipped it. Not like me and my sudden insatiable thirst for lowering my inhibitions.

"It's not that complicated." I threw my hands in the air for some reason, the big movement feeling good. "We're friends. We love each other as friends. The end."

"Rae. He cheated on you, and now you're friends? You came home early from shooting halfway around the world, found him in bed with two men, and you're telling me you're over that?"

Hmm. Maybe I trusted Sienna so much because she was the only other person—other than me, Harrison, and his two boy toys—who knew the truth about that night, and she hadn't told anyone. His cheating being the reason for our split was well and widely known, who(m) he cheated with was still a secret. The debacle had happened when Sienna and I were shooting our one and only film together, and she had been the person I stayed with that night after walking in on the threesome.

"I am over it because, in retrospect, I can see now that I loved Harrison only as a friend. We were—are—friends." God, it felt so good to discuss this with someone who wasn't Harrison. I'd been keeping this secret for years, and it just *felt good* to talk about my ex, our non-relationship, and my thoughts on the subject.

"You think he prefers men?"

"Yes. I do. Sexual orientation is a spectrum of course, but I think he prefers peen and pecs, and I get it. *I* prefer peen and pecs. What do I want with boobs and beavers? So many parts, so many holes. Why do we have so many hills and holes? Women are basically golf courses."

Sienna made a short snorting sound of both humor and surprise, her shoulders shaking with laughter, and she lowered her attention to the table. After a moment, no longer laughing, she cleared her throat and asked, "Okay, but you didn't answer my question. Why do you think he prefers men?"

"Perhaps I'm wrong? Perhaps it's just me? I do think he wasn't super attracted to me. My breasts do nothing for him, they never did. It was actually one of the reasons we got together in the first place. He looked at my face when we spoke." Despite our table being shaded by a mighty oak, I felt hot. I started to unbutton the linen shirt I wore over my tank top.

"You started dating him because he looked at your face when you spoke? That's as high as you've set your bar?"

I gave her a flat look. "At the time, it made him special, unique. He was different than everyone else and seemed genuinely interested in me and my career. We shared the same goals, we wanted the same things. Plus, he's Harrison. Funny, charming, sexy Harrison."

"If tall, dark, and handsome do it for you." Her admission sounded reluctant.

"Since we're in a fake relationship there is no actual cheating anymore. I mean, other than sanctioned cheating, which I guess is what he does now. But it's my turn to cause a scandal and I just—I'm just out of energy." I plopped both of my elbows on the table and released a noisy breath.

"Cause a scandal? What do you mean sanctioned cheating?"

"All right, so per the agreement, to ensure we stay in the public spotlight, we're engaged, right? But it can't be smooth sailing. We're back together, on again, off again, on again, off again. Everybody loves it, they follow it, constantly trending everywhere. Hashtag Harriquel, hashtag TeamRaquel, blah, blah, blah. And so he created the last scandal. Now it's my turn."

"You mean when he was photographed last month making out with Sabina Ureil?" Her question sounded salty, like she'd been harboring resentment on my behalf. It warmed my heart.

"Yes, the soccer player. And it's fine because I knew about it. I guess we have an open relationship, except we can have sex with everyone but each other." I hadn't been with anyone, but I knew Harrison had. "We're not romantic or touchy-feely at all unless we're in public."

"Now you have to. . . ?"

"Oh! Yes. Now it's my turn to cheat and get photographed 'accidentally.' We got a guy who'll tip off the right paps whenever I decide to give the go-ahead." I used air quotes around the word *accidentally* because, apparently, I'd had enough whiskey to use air quotes. "But time's a tickin' and Domino is worried that if I'm not photographed being sexy with someone soon, then I will look pathetic getting back with Harrison yet again. I forgave him for the soccer player, therefore Harrison should forgive me for something. You know how it is."

"I don't." She shook her head, her eyebrows pulled together in a frown. "I honestly do not know how it is."

"Well, this is how it is. On and on." I stared at my last whiskey, still untouched. "Now that I explain it out loud, you're right. It sounds twisted."

"I didn't say it sounded twisted."

"But it's crazy, right?"

She took another sip of her second whiskey, saying nothing, her expression giving nothing of her thoughts away.

My brain felt warm, fuzzy, which made me inclined to add, "It's like we're playing these roles for the public. And I didn't mind at first. I mean, it's just like playing another part, right? But that means my personal life has become another acting job."

"Rae—"

"And I should be fine with that, as long as it gets me to where I want to be in my career."

"Where exactly are you wanting to go with your career? You're already at the top."

"You're right. My career has never been better since we've done this." I smacked the table. "And I'm considered for roles I wouldn't usually be considered for, even though I'm tempted to turn them down."

"I find this hard to believe. Last I heard, you're considered for every role."

"Not every role."

"Name one."

"The new Scortez film."

"Oh! I wanted to read that script. I heard it's excellent."

"Depends on which character you play. I think the male part is great, strong."

"But yours isn't?"

"It's. . ." I made a face. "See, the whole angle is that I, Raquel Ezra, actual woman scorned by the 'love of my life' Harrison Copeland—" more air quotes "—am pouring my heart and real feelings of betrayal into the role, leaving a man who is no good for me, only to come full circle and have an affair with said cheater at the end. Like, we can't escape who we are, we can't escape our destiny, even if our destiny is bad for us. It's a whole tragic *the heart wants what it wants* theme."

"And you're taking the role?" She eyed me over the rim of her shot glass. "Or are you retiring?"

"I have no idea. I'm just—my agent wants me to take it, so does Harrison."

"What do you want?"

"It would be good for my career."

"That's not what I asked. I asked what do *you* want."

"I have no idea. God, I'm a mess." I released a tremendous breath, Sienna blurring in my vision.

If I were being honest, I didn't actually want the Scortez part. Yes, it was more serious and artier than my usual projects, but nothing about the role felt new or interesting to me. I used to enjoy the work I was offered, grateful for any chance to improve my craft. Making an actual paycheck from acting felt like hitting the lottery.

And yet, after playing the victim of circumstances and/or bad choices over and over again, just once I wanted to be someone who made their own destiny and knew exactly who they were—good, bad, didn't matter. My heart twisted, lodging itself in my throat as I released an aggrieved sigh.

I'd actually found the perfect part six months ago. Over the objections and concerns of my agent and basically my entire team, I'd signed on to an indie film that paid peanuts with a location shoot in Cuba!

I couldn't wait. I was excited about a role for the first time in ages just to have the part taken away from me at the last minute and recast with my best friend—*scratch that, FORMER best friend.*

Sienna and I sat quietly for a long moment and my mind went blank, which might've been why when I broke the silence, random thoughts gushed forth. "I feel like I don't have anything real in my life. My relationship with Harrison is fake. Obviously my LA friendships are fake. My career is real. But then again, it's not. I play the same part over and over, and it's not what I want anymore. Plus, how am I helping people? What am I doing that's making any kind of difference? And I need a new bra. This one itches."

"Let me ask you this." Sienna patted the table, as though to get my attention. She waited until I gave her my gaze before continuing, "If you could pick one real thing that you want—just one thing—what would it be? And I don't mean a career goal, or a part, or an award. I also don't mean something you can buy. What is something real you want, maybe even something selfish, just for you?"

I bit and chewed on my bottom lip, staring at her and considering the question. "I guess. . ."

I have no idea.

None of the typical responses applied in my case. Not a vacation. Who would I go with? Not a spa day. In LA, I had a team of people who took care of my skin and hair, gave me massages, guided me through meditations and yoga, directed my daily workouts, dictated and prepared what I ate whether I wanted them to or not.

I was so tired of their company, of being watched, of being told what was best for me, of being surrounded by colleagues and employees and yet isolated because none of them were truly my friends. And the answers came to me all at once: Privacy. Freedom. Anonymity.

But more than all that, I wanted a real friend.

A friend who wasn't using me—like Harrison—or one who pretended to be my friend but wasn't—like my role-stealing ex-BFF, Lina. A person I could talk to without worrying my statements would end up in a gossip magazine, provided by "a source close to Raquel Ezra."

"Something obtainable," Sienna pressed, cutting into my sad thoughts. "Something you've wanted for a while."

Wanting to ask Sienna to be my friend and feeling utterly pathetic at the thought, I shrugged. "I don't know, eating a whole chocolate cake?"

She gave me a patient smile. "We can do that while you're here, I know of an excellent bakery. But I'm trying to get at something else. Something good, something healthy."

"Healthy," I parroted, leaning back in my chair and crossing my arms under my chest.

While I debated how to address her question without giving the real, pitiful answer, a server approached. He placed his hand on the back of a vacant chair at our table and grinned down at Sienna first and then I felt his attention move to me. "Hey ladies, how are we doing?"

I tilted my head back to look at him and found his gaze resting on the neckline of my tank top and the swells of my girls. *Ah, girl power.*

"Hey Damon. We could use some privacy." Sienna's tone sounded unmistakably wry with the barest dusting of irritation. "I'll come get you if we need anything."

"Sounds good." He licked his lips, his eyes still on my chest. "Please, do not hesitate."

I righted my head as he walked away, looking at Sienna and finding her wearing an apologetic expression. "I am so sorry about that."

"Uffda, I'm used to it. I developed at ten. By the time I was twelve I'd learned to ignore men's stares." Lifting my heavy hair off my neck, I shrugged. "It's also a good way of weeding out assholes. If a guy makes lasting eye contact, they've passed the first test, ya know?"

"Yes. I know." Sienna chuckled, flashing her winning smile. "But I'm sorry all the same. I know you didn't come here for that."

"Actually, I kinda did. Remember? I need to be photographed making out with someone." I groaned inwardly at the thought. The last time I had to "cheat" on my "boyfriend" for the benefit of a camera, the random guy I'd chosen had been incredibly grabby. I'd ended the short encounter with bruises all over my arms and sides, and a super painful hickey on my neck.

"Hopefully, you'll be doing this with someone you're actually interested in." Concern flickered behind her gaze.

"Hopefully." A vision of Deputy Dreamy from our night together years ago flashed through my mind, him sitting on the couch just before I'd straddled him, just before we'd kissed. My neck heated and a twisting warmth curled low in my belly. He'd given me plenty of eye contact that night, and he hadn't been at all grabby. I tried to recall the last time a man had looked me in the eye longer than in the chest.

Deputy Dreamy was the last.

As though poking around in my thoughts, Sienna asked, "When was the last time you were with someone you were actually interested in?"

I worked to make my small smile look sincere, but knew I failed when Sienna's neutral expression became a frown.

Wanting to disarm her worry, I let the whiskey do the talking, "It's actually a funny story."

"Is it?" She sipped her second shot, finishing it, her gaze direct and disbelieving.

"Remember your wedding?" I asked, and then rolled my eyes at myself as soon as the words were out. "Of course you remember your wedding. Sorry. Anyway, there was a guy at the wedding, and we kind of hooked up."

She sat up straighter. "What? Who?"

I picked up the last whiskey shot and sipped it, rolling the liquid around on my tongue to delay responding. According to Sienna and Jethro, Jackson didn't have any kids, but that didn't mean he wasn't married or in a serious relationship with someone.

"Rae. Why am I just hearing about this now? Who was it? Do I know him?"

Nodding, I took another sip. *Please oh please let him be single.*

"Oh my God. It wasn't one of Jethro's brothers, was it?"

"No! No, it wasn't."

"Oh, good. That might've made things awkward."

"Why?"

"I've decided you're staying with us in our carriage house, and you're staying as long as you want—hopefully two weeks or longer, if you can spare the time. Jet's brothers stop by pretty frequently."

I forced a smile to hide the abrupt pang of bitterness. "I can stay two weeks, thank you." The truth was I could stay months if Sienna wanted. The movie I was supposed to begin filming had dropped me a mere three days ago, replacing me on the project with my once and former BFF. I now had a gaping hole in my schedule for the first time in years.

"Good. It's two bedrooms with tons of privacy, you'll love it. Now, who is he? Who is the guy?"

"Ah, yes, the hookup."

"Who was it?"

"He's—uh—the deputy. From today." I braced myself, watching her, holding my breath.

Why are you holding your breath, Rae? And why is your heart beating so fast?

Sienna didn't frown, but her eyes grew impossibly large. "Jackson? Jackson James?"

All pretense of self-control lost, I drank the rest of the fourth whiskey and smacked my lips together. "Yep. That's the guy."

"Are you serious?"

"As serious as a Botox shortage in Beverly Hills."

"Wow." Her gaze lowered to the table, losing focus. "Wow."

"Do you know him?" I picked up the last shot glass, but then I remembered it was already empty. "Is he a bad guy? Is he married?"

"No, he's not a bad guy. He's a good guy, I think. I like him! Though I honestly don't know him as well as I should. Sometimes he babysits for us, when we're in a crunch."

"He babysits the boys?"

"Yes. They love him. What I know about Jackson's personal life is mostly just what I hear about him from others when I'm in town between location shoots. Small-town gossip, that kind of thing. And he's *definitely* not married." She said the word *definitely* funny, with a strong intonation that made me think maybe there was more to the story. "And he doesn't date."

"Wait, what does that mean? Is he gay?" My heart sunk while my brain raced to and then jumped off the cliff of hasty conclusions.

"No, no. I mean, as far as I know, he's not. But I didn't know Harrison liked men until he cheated on you that first time. And it's not like I'm going around asking people where on the sexual orientation spectrum they fall. But, if I had to guess, I'd say Jackson is firmly and vigorously heterosexual based on his—uh—history. With women."

Selfish relief mixed with suspicion, and I narrowed my eyes at her. "You're babbling. Why are you babbling?"

"Sorry." She laughed, looking like she wanted to say so many things. "You just caught me off guard." Sienna picked up her shot glass and sipped it, watching me closely.

I glanced down at my shirt to make sure I'd hadn't spilled something on myself. Finding my tank top free of liquid, I asked, "What?"

"Jackson."

"Yes. Jackson." *Jackson James.* I'd always liked the way his name sounded. He had a great name.

"You know, I'm kind of related to him."

"Does that make him off-limits?" I blurted.

Another smile curved her lips, a slow, sneaky looking one. "No, no, he's definitely on-limits. My husband's brother Duane—one of the twins—is married to Jackson's sister, Jessica."

"That's a lot of *J* names."

"Indeed. Duane and Jessica just had a baby last year."

"Let me guess, Jarvis?"

"No. Liam. Anyway, I guess Jackson is my brother-in-law, in a roundabout way."

Parched, I reached for my water glass and took a big gulp. Sienna fiddled with her whiskey shot, her stare what I would call speculative, that secretive smile still on her lips like she had *thoughts.*

She was making me nervous. "What? What is it?"

"Nothing." She shrugged, clearly lying. "So, what happened? Did you two keep in touch?"

"No. It was just a one-time thing. You know me."

"Yes. I know you."

"What is that supposed to mean? I'm feeling judged."

"You shouldn't. It's not like it's any secret that you don't take home your leftovers. I've never seen you with the same guy twice, except Harrison."

Blah.

"Hey, so." Sienna shrugged, her tone excessively casual. "If you want me to set something up with Jackson or help you figure out how to approach him, I will."

"You will?" I couldn't keep the enthusiasm out of my voice. Oh man, this was great. So great. I had no idea how to approach him. What does one say to a man that one wishes to snog after five plus years of silence?

Hey, so, I know I said I'd never contact you again after our one night together, but do you maybe want to play golf. . . with my holes?

"Yes." She inspected me for a quick second before asking, "Is he why you're here? You need to be photographed with someone—to continue the Harrison ruse—and so you thought of Jackson James?"

32

I opened my mouth to respond, but no words arrived.

Be honest, Rae, if only with yourself. Is Deputy Dreamy the reason you're here?

Looking toward the garden again, I tilted my head back and forth as I debated how to answer and ended up speaking the truth out loud. "Partly, yes. It's been impossible these last few years, meeting someone, and I know that's my fault. I used to not care. Work came first, always. But recently, I don't know. It would just be nice to have a person who I didn't have to pretend around, someone trustworthy who didn't go running to the tabloids to sell an insider story. I meant what I said, I'm tired of having nothing real in my life. It's . . ."

"What?"

"Exhausting. Pretending all the damn time." I peeked at her, gauging how weird I might make things if I continued talking and were actually 100 percent honest.

As I've mentioned, Sienna was, by far, the most genuine, *real* person I knew in the business. She never faked anything. Or if she did, she was just that good an actress and she made her life look authentic. Since her wedding, I'd seen her with her husband at red carpet events and they always looked so happy, so in love, and they stood out from the crowd because of it. Where others—like me—were airbrushed and arduously determined to exude effortless perfection, Sienna and her Jethro *were* effortless perfection.

"You came here so you wouldn't have to pretend?" she said after a while, her smile faint and shaded with concern. "And you think, with Jackson James, you won't have to?"

"Why do you look worried?"

"It's just—" she sucked in a breath, her eyes moving between mine "—he has a reputation in this town. He is a good guy, but he's not . . ."

"Boyfriend material?" I pressed my lips together to keep from grinning because this felt like good news for me. "I'm not here to go steady with him, remember?"

"Yeah, well, then Jackson is perfect." She chuckled. "What happened that night? Between the two of you? He must've made a big impression."

"More like, he's the last guy I've felt any actual attraction to and with," I hedged. "If I have to get caught making out with someone, it would be nice to enjoy the experience."

"I see." Her eyes moved over me and narrowed, grew thoughtful as her smile flattened.

"Don't worry, I won't mack down on him at your house. It has to be public. And I promise, I'll be out of your hair by next Friday."

"Stay as long as you like, I mean it." She sipped her whiskey, but her eyebrows told me she was troubled. "I'd be more than happy to host you all summer, if you want."

Oh man, I wanted to accept her offer. But I wouldn't. I wasn't a freeloader. That said, I couldn't remember the last time I'd been as tempted to break my own rules as I was right now. Whatever Sienna's secret for happiness was, I wanted it. But I couldn't say *that* either. I didn't want her to think I was needy.

So I said, "Thank you, you are very kind, but I probably should get back to LA," because it was the truth.

Just not all of it.

CHAPTER 4

JACKSON

"Spock was the sex symbol. A lot of people think it was Kirk. But, no, it was really Spock."

— JOLENE BLALOCK

*M*y father and I had breakfast together on the first Tuesday of the month, usually at Daisy's Nut House. This was partly because the food was always so good, partly because it was so close to my parents' house, and partly because Daisy expected us. And my father never did anything to disappoint Daisy.

"Daisy here?" he asked by way of greeting the moment he arrived at the booth, taking off his hat and glancing around the diner. "I don't see her."

"I haven't seen her yet." I took a sip from my coffee, my second cup since arriving thirty minutes ago. My father was on time, I'd been early.

After catching that quick glimpse of Raquel downtown on Saturday, I'd been early to every appointment and meeting since. *But there's no use thinking about that.*

Moving on.

I typically only drank coffee brewed at home, so much cheaper than buying it elsewhere. This was especially true around Christmastime when local businesses sent the station heaps of gifts. The cafe on Main Street roasted their own raw coffee beans. They sent the station a pound for each deputy and ten pounds to the sheriff. My father didn't drink coffee anymore, so I'd end up with eleven pounds to start the year.

"What're you having? Green tea or water?" I lifted my hand toward Rebecca, signaling for her to come over.

She never came over unless we asked her to, convinced my father and I were discussing secret sheriff's business. Little did she know, we never discussed work during our monthly breakfasts. He didn't believe it would be right or fair giving me, one of his deputies, extra face time with him every month when he didn't—and couldn't—do the same for everyone. I agreed with him.

"Your mother watched me drink the green slime this morning. Water, please." He wrinkled his nose in distaste. He'd always hated tea—all tea, even sweet tea—but he drank green tea with ginseng every morning because it made my momma happy.

"Hey, Rebecca." I gave her a smile as she approached, and she glanced between us, eyes wide. "My father will have an ice water, and I think we're ready to order."

She withdrew her writing pad silently, and I sighed. I'd known this woman my whole life, and as far as I could remember, she'd always been skittish with my father. Maybe she expected him to arrest her at any moment. Who knows what went through her brain?

"I'll have the egg white omelet with four eggs instead of three, spinach and tomato. Instead of hash browns, could you ask chef to cut me up a bell pepper? Red or orange if y'all got it." This was my regular order, but I always asked since it wasn't on the menu.

She nodded, and I met my father's eyes. Even after over a decade of me abstaining from meat, dairy, refined sugars, and processed grains—except on holidays, dates, and special occasions—he still looked at me with sympathy. But he hadn't grown up with cystic acne, asthma, and chronic cluster headaches. Me eating picky meant I felt good.

"I'll have the number three, please," he requested gently, sending a warm smile her way even though she never looked directly at him, if she could help it.

With that, Rebecca dashed off, returning to the safety of the diner counter and then the kitchen beyond. I didn't know if these kinds of interactions with folks bothered him or not. But I did know he never stopped trying to be friendly with anybody.

"So, what's the news?"

"Nothing much to report," I said, my throat tight with the lie. But it wasn't really a lie, because there truly wasn't anything to report.

What could I say? *Oh, you know that woman I've been pining over for the last five or so years? The one I never told you about? The reason I haven't seriously dated anyone until just recently? Well, I saw her in town on Saturday with Sienna and Jethro Winston. I was covered in pie and looked like a fool. She looked stunning. We didn't speak. I'll likely never see her again except in her movies.* And that was that.

Besides, the woman was engaged. My blood pressure spiked every time I thought about Raquel with that scumbag, cheating loser . . . *rich, famous, sex symbol.* I grit my teeth.

Moving on.

Rebecca returned with my father's ice water, and he muttered a *thank you,* taking a sip before asking, "Are you and Boone running that marathon next month?"

"We are. Are you sure you don't want to join us?" Boone was another deputy, real smart guy, and my roommate. He'd moved in about eighteen months ago, to save on rent and expenses he'd said, but I also suspected he'd done it to create some distance between himself and his family.

Don't get me wrong, the Boones were a great family. But when he'd been living on his own, I got the sense they felt free to come and go from his place whenever they wanted. Now that we bunked together, they'd become more circumspect.

My father chuckled. "Yeah, right. My marathon running days are over. How about the boat? You taking her out yet?"

I'd bought myself a Scout 380 LXF at auction. The weekender fishing boat had been abused and neglected by its original owner, a business mogul from Knoxville who'd gone bankrupt, but not before taking a shotgun to his cars and boats, destroying an entire fleet of luxury vehicles before the bank claimed them. I wasn't too angry about it, I couldn't have afforded the boat otherwise.

It had taken over four years, but I'd completely renovated her, teaching myself how to upholster, replace fiberglass and epoxy-infused carbon fiber, lay teak decking, add custom motorized awnings, install a shower surround, and rebuild a few Yamaha motors along the way. I'd also made a lot of early mistakes and had been forced to redo and redo and redo work until I'd done it right. But she still wasn't ready yet.

"No, sir. The rudder system still doesn't have full radius, so I ordered some parts, and they'll be in next week."

His eyes narrowed even as he smiled. "Jackson, is this a hobby or a boat?"

"A bit of both."

"You ever planning on using that thing? Why don't you just call Shelly or Beau to help you with the rudder? They'll get her fixed up right quick, save you the hassle. Rely on the experts."

Because I want to do it myself.

Forcing my jaw to unclench, I shrugged, saying lightly, "Oh, I know. If I can't get it worked out this time, I'll give Shelly a call."

He looked me over, shaking his head like I amused him. "You're stubborn like your momma, even when it serves no purpose other than causing delays and increasing your own frustration. Would you expect Beau Winston to do a better job at being a deputy than you?"

"Course not."

"Then why do you think you'll do a better job at fixing a steering system than a mechanic?"

"I don't. I'm not stupid—"

"No. You're not."

"—but I still want to do it myself."

He sighed, a smile still lingering around his mouth like he didn't know what to think. "Fine. Just promise me you'll have her ready by the time I retire."

I grinned. "That gives me three years? I think that's plenty."

"Speaking of which, did Eugene reach out to you?" Eugene had been my father's campaign manager the two times he'd run for sheriff opposed. But for the last four elections, my father had run unopposed. Sixteen years without a single contender. I reckoned it made sense. No one enjoyed losing by a landslide.

"Eugene did reach out. We spoke." I eyed him, reluctant to discuss my potential run for sheriff in the next election cycle. As mentioned, our conversations never ventured near work issues during these breakfasts. I didn't know if me running for sheriff in three years counted as a work issue.

"It's okay. We can talk about it."

When I still hesitated, he lifted up his hands. "Jackson, talk about it. I'll be your father, not the sheriff. Can't a father talk to his son about plans for the future?"

That was a good point. "He said my chances are good."

"Did he?"

"Yep."

"Then why do you look like that?"

"Like what?"

"Like you just ate the bait instead of the fish."

I glanced at the ceiling while reluctantly confessing the truth, "He said my chances are good because we share the same last name and first initial. Most folks will see J. James on the ballot and assume they're voting for you."

"I see." A glimmer of something that looked like both sorrow and pride shone from his eyes. "And this is frustrating for you."

"It is."

He grinned in that quiet way of his, leaving his assumptions unspoken. But I could see he understood, I wanted to win on my own merit, not his.

"So, what are you thinking?"

"Maybe not run in the upcoming election? Maybe wait until the next cycle?"

His shoulders rose and fell with a sigh. "You want my honest opinion?"

"Always."

"I think that would be silliness, Jackson."

I breathed a laugh. He did too.

"You've always had a peculiar perspective about right and wrong." He didn't say it, but I knew he'd always wished I'd included more shades of gray in my outlook. "But consider this, you're not-not m-married. You're not a-a family man." My father's discomfort with the subject was obvious as he spoke. He only stuttered like this when he didn't quite know what to say, which wasn't often.

And what he didn't say—what he didn't have to say because I understood the implication of his words—was that I had a reputation for being a *ladies'* man. Eugene, the campaign manager, had said as much when we'd talked. Eugene also wanted me to keep "cleaning up" my reputation and "settle down as soon as possible."

"I'm sure Eugene brought this up?" My father cleared his throat, another something he did when venturing too far into any subject that made him uncomfortable.

"He did. We came up with a plan."

"Good. Because no matter where you are, how liberal or conservative the county, most folks—not all folks, just most—prefer a candidate who is settled, especially the sheriff. You having no spouse, no kids, it'll hurt you in an election. You'll be at a disadvantage even though it shouldn't matter."

"Right."

"So why not run in 2026 and use the advantage of your name? Something else that shouldn't matter."

"Are you suggesting they'd cancel each other out?"

"Something like that. Just think about it. Also think about your momma's offer to get the ball rolling on a campaign fundraiser. It's never too early." Looking harassed and ready for a subject change, he took a gulp of his ice water and then asked, "How's Charlotte?"

A pang of guilt twisting in my stomach, I took another sip of coffee to hide the reflexive tensing of my muscles. "Oh, she's fine."

I hadn't done anything to feel guilty about. Every time thoughts of Raquel surfaced in my mind, I'd pushed them aside. I didn't entertain hope for a renewed connection. I was committed to seeing things with Charlotte through, I was committed to her.

And yet, I felt guilty.

"How was your date Saturday? It was Saturday, right?"

"She had to cancel. We're going out tomorrow instead." I leaned back and moved my coffee cup out of the way as Rebecca approached, my breakfast in one hand and my father's in the other.

"Oh. That's too bad. You taking her to The Front Porch again? Thank you, Rebecca."

Rebecca nodded once tightly, then scurred away.

I picked up my fork. "Yes, sir. I switched the reservation."

"Y'all go there a lot."

"This'll be the third time." I didn't volunteer that this would also be our third actual date in the months we'd been together.

We'd tried going on a picnic, just the two of us, but her sitter canceled at the last minute and we'd ended up taking the kids along, choosing a park with a playground instead of the private, romantic location originally on the agenda.

I'd tried taking her on a hike three weekends ago and her momma—who was set to watch the kids—decided she wanted to come too when she'd heard our plans. It had become a Mitchell family outing ending with an extended family barbecue at the trailhead.

"Why not take her to Knoxville?" he asked, cutting up his eggs.

"The drive is too far. She only has the sitter for three hours."

"How about if your momma and I babysit? Then y'all could go as far as Nashville if you wanted. Take the whole day."

I perked up at that. "Really? That'd be great. I can certainly ask." I liked Charlotte. She was funny. Not many people are funny. Even when she was surrounded by her kids and family and all that chaos, she was always hilarious, positive, upbeat. And she did her best to try and make me feel seen and special. This troubled me.

Here she was, a single mom of four, worked full-time, managed her house and kids and everything all on her own, and she was worried about making *me* feel seen and special? That didn't sit right.

"A couple needs time alone, especially a courting couple," he said around a bite of bacon and fried eggs. "It's hard enough to woo a woman when there's no time limit on your evening out."

41

I knew my father liked Charlotte, so I knew he was commiserating with me, not complaining about her circumstances or lack of availability.

"But you're creative," he added. "I'm sure you're finding other ways to sweep her off her feet."

Finished chewing a slice of pepper, I nodded. "I am."

"Like what?" He peered at me, gaze suddenly sharp.

My hand halted, another slice of bell pepper halfway to my mouth. "Seriously? You want me to talk to you about this?"

He nodded. "Humor me."

Huh.

He had never—and I mean *never*, not even when Zora Leffersbee and I were faking an engagement, and he *adored* Zora—asked me about my romantic prospects other than how the woman was doing and wishing us well.

Well, that wasn't exactly true. After Zora ended our arrangement and ran off with the man she was actually in love with, he'd sat me down and asked me how I could expect the people of Green Valley and this county to take me seriously if I didn't take myself seriously. That's how he always made his point, he asked questions with only one right answer.

He needn't have asked the question at all. I'd tried returning to my previous habits, but they didn't seem to fit anymore, like trying on an old pair of shoes from high school. It all felt too small, and I'd felt . . . tired. Tired of pretending, tired of being passed around, tired of no expectations. I wanted something that at least felt real, something that felt deeper.

Something like the taste of that night I'd shared with Raquel.

Of course, I didn't tell any of this to my father. I'd just said, *Yes sir,* and left it at that. By and large, my father was more comfortable discussing the details of a gruesome crime scene than talking about anything related to feelings or emotions or relationships. He was very much a man of his generation.

And now he wanted to talk about me and Charlotte?

"Well, let's see." I placed a pepper back on the plate and scratched the short hair covering my jaw. "I went over on Saturday anyway, and we had a movie night with the kids."

"Then what?"

"Sunday, I watched the kids so she could run some errands. And then we went to Kimmy's soccer game together. I'd made dinner while she was out running errands, so we all ate that after the game, and I helped her put the kids to bed."

"And then?" He put his fork down and leaned forward.

"Well, then I left." Obviously.

"I see." His sharp look turned hard. "What else?"

"Yesterday afternoon we talked, and she told me she's been having trouble with one of the bathroom sinks, so I went over there late, after work, and—"

"She wanted you to come over late?"

"Yes, sir. I wouldn't have gone if she didn't—"

"Okay, okay." He waved away what I was about to say. "You fixed the sink?"

"I did."

"It didn't need any parts? You didn't have to wait and go to the hardware store?"

"No, sir. It was just a loose pipe. I tightened it and then I was finished."

"And did you stay? After?"

I stared at my father, getting the sense he was hoping I'd give him a particular answer. "No, sir. Course not. It was very late."

Breathing out loudly, he leaned back in the booth, wiping his hands on a napkin. "So?"

"So?" I stared at him, bemused. Had he been expecting—hoping for—a different response? "So she needed to get the kids up for school in the morning, and I had an early breakfast with you."

What was he fishing for? Did he want me to tell him I'd spent the night with Charlotte? For the record, we hadn't slept together. We hadn't even made it past first base, when

43

would we have had the chance? And I'd be damned if the first time we did anything other than kiss was at midnight during a weeknight when I was half asleep and exhausted after a ten-hour shift that had turned out to be thirteen once all was said and done.

Also, my parents hadn't raised me that way. They'd raised me to be a gentleman. I hadn't always been a gentleman, and my father had told me as much. He'd been right at the time, and I'd reformed. I liked that I'd reformed. I appreciated drawing these hard lines in the sand I no longer crossed.

And now he was disappointed that I was acting like the man he wanted me to be? *What the heck is going on?*

He sighed, then pressed his lips together in a grim line, glaring at the back of the booth behind me. "You know I love you, son."

"Yes, I know."

"And I'm proud of you. You've always been an exceptional deputy—and I mean that, though I don't often say it."

"Thank you. That means a lot." And it did. My father was a man of few words, he didn't often use them to compliment or praise.

"I see you're finally taking yourself seriously outside of work too. Using your time wisely, building something lasting with a fine young woman. But . . ."

A short laugh erupted out of me. "There's a but?"

"You're a good son. You're a good man too. But women—most women—don't always w-want a-a man to be-to be good."

I let him see how confused his words made me. "What does that mean? Should I. . . Are you saying Charlotte didn't want me to fix her sink? Should I have said no?"

He seemed to struggle. Eventually, he placed his elbow on the table and his forehead fell to his hand. "Your momma and I, we should've had more kids."

I flinched at that, dropping my eyes to my coffee cup and trying my best not to see his words as a reference as to how I might be lacking. This wasn't the first time he'd mentioned wanting to have more than just me and Jess, but he'd never elaborated, and I'd never asked.

A saying my momma favored—and one I'd learned well over the course of my life— was, *Never ask a question if you don't want to know the answer.*

CHAPTER 5

RAQUEL

"If being a sex symbol means you have lots of sex, then I am glad to be a sex symbol. But in real life I'm not. That doesn't happen."

— DIEGO LUNA

he "carriage house," as Sienna called it, was awesome. She'd described it as a two-bedroom cottage, but it had an enormous chef's kitchen, a huge family room with a fireplace, and a substantial living area lined with shelves, every inch of which were stuffed with books and magazines. Set back, as it was, from the circular driveway and the main house, it was the first time I'd experienced anything resembling real privacy in ages.

The easily defensible twelve-room mansion I'd bought in Hollywood Hills felt more like a high-security dorm than a home on most days. The only place where I had any privacy was in my bedroom, and not all the time. Someone was always knocking, asking me a question, needing me for some reason.

After two lazy days on Sienna's property spent in virtual solitude, reading books, ignoring my phone, social media, and email, taking walks in thick wildflower fields and green forests, I debated asking if she'd been serious about me staying all summer.

But if you stay longer, then you will have to return Sasha's calls and ask her to bring more clothes.

I didn't want to do that. I couldn't explain the depth of my aversion to the idea but inviting my personal assistant or any member of my team to visit here—even for a brief afternoon—felt wrong on a visceral level. Like an invasion. Or an infection.

I made do with the three outfits, three pairs of underwear, and one pair of pj's I'd hastily shoved into a backpack before leaving California for Tennessee three days ago. That meant only two clothing options existed for Operation Deputy Distraction, which was what Sienna eventually nicknamed our plan to approach Jackson James. One that would hopefully end with him enthusiastically agreeing to being photographed making out with me.

Convinced he would agree to my proposition, Sienna originally proposed Operation Flaxen Action as the code name for our plan, I guess because he had blond hair?

"Or what about Operation Saxon Angler? Because you're trying to catch him and reel him in, and Jackson rhymes with Saxon. You know he's got to be of Saxon ancestry with his coloring."

I made a face even as I laughed. We were sitting on her porch after a delicious dinner she'd cooked, the first meal I'd shared with anyone since the whiskey flight on Saturday. They'd stocked my fridge in the carriage house but left me alone until just this evening, sending their oldest over earlier in the afternoon with a no-pressure invitation.

"Saxon? If anything, he looks German." I poured myself a third glass of wine, thoroughly enjoying the looseness in my limbs, the mild summer evening symphony of crickets and frogs, and the fullness of my belly. I hadn't indulged in a real home-cooked meal in what felt like ages.

Don't get me wrong, my chef in LA made my strict plant-based diet more delicious than it had a right to be, but there's just something about home cooking, a meal made with love meant to nourish more than just the body. And then there's the actual eating of the meal, gathering around a table, saying grace, asking someone to pass a dish, listening to chaotic conversation, being a part of something so simple and mundane, and yet so wholesome and authentic. *Something real.*

"That's what I said. Anglo-Saxons are descended from three different Germanic tribes—the Angles, Saxons, and Jutes." Sienna took the bottle of wine from me and refilled her own glass.

I laughed harder, looking at her like she was crazy. "How do you even know this?"

"My sister-in-law's sister-in-law knows all the random facts. Hey, how'd you like to hail from the Jute peoples? That's a fun sounding word. *Oi! Jute!* Oh, wait. That rhymes with flute! We could call it Operation Jute Flute, because a flute is sorta shaped like a long—"

"No!" I erupted with more laughter, the intensity of which was likely aided by the two glasses of wine I'd already finished. "You have to stop. I'm going to pee my pants." God, it felt so good to laugh. I'd needed this.

We spent the next forty-five minutes debating the name while her husband did the dishes and worked on getting the boys down for bed. Sienna had waited until we were alone to bring up Jackson and didn't want me to ask Jethro his opinion, nor did she want me telling Jethro that I was interested in Jackson.

"It's a long story," she said, sipping her wine. "I don't even know the whole thing, but Jackson and Jethro have never gotten along even though sometimes I think they do. Maybe?"

"They don't? Why?"

"Eh." She shrugged. "I like Jackson, but Jet only sporadically likes him. Jackson has babysat for us before, and he did a great job. I don't understand the dynamic there."

"Jethro doesn't like Jackson but is okay with him babysitting the boys?"

"It's hard to—it's a long story. Long, long story. Longer and more tedious than *The English Patient*, despite Ralph Fiennes living up to how his last name sounds phonetically."

I decided if Deputy Dreamy agreed to my proposition, I would ask him why he and Jethro didn't get along. They both seemed so laid back and nice. My curiosity burned like the Duke did for Daphne.

Ultimately, since Deputy James and Sienna's husband didn't get along all the time, inviting Jackson over for dinner was out of the question. We decided I would have to seek him out at the sheriff's station.

"You will wear those shorts"—Sienna gestured to the cutoff jean shorts I wore—"and your black tank top. It's supposed to be hotter tomorrow than it's been all week, skimpy clothes will be understandable."

"You don't think I'll look desperate? Showing up dressed like that?"

"Once he sees you, he'll be feeling too desperate to care."

I appreciated that Sienna hadn't responded with something like, *What's the big deal? Haven't you been topless in a movie?* That was the typical response I received whenever I expressed concerns about being less than fully clothed in any situation. Like, since I'd shown my breasts in a movie *once* I no longer had the right to cover myself. I'd somehow forfeited control over how much skin I wished to share and with whom and when.

If I'd known in my early twenties when I'd filmed my first and only topless scene how it would be forever after, I never would've taken the role.

"It's not unusual for members of the community to show up at the station with treats and goodies for a particular deputy. You should bring him sour cherry pie." Sienna nodded at her own idea.

"Pie? Really?"

"In Green Valley, pie is always the answer." She paused for a moment and frowned thoughtfully. "Or so I'm told. Anyway, we'll reserve one from Daisy's Nut House, you'll pick it up and take it to him tomorrow, just before dinner."

"How do you know he'll be at the station?"

"While you've been in your fortress of solitude these last few days, I called Jessica—his sister—and asked what Jackson's favorite kind of pie was, as well as if she knew his schedule this week. She said he has Wednesdays off but usually goes to the station to catch up on paperwork. He'll be there."

"He has the day off, but he works anyway?" Consistently working on his day off likely meant he didn't have a healthy work-life balance. So why was this news about him such a turn-on? *Hmm.*

Plan settled, I left Sienna's porch soon after and spent that evening and the next morning considering my perplexing interest in Jackson James. Why did I hungrily inhale every ounce of information Sienna had shared? Why was I so attracted to him, this responsible and diligent pillar of the community who clearly worked too much, a man I'd only met once? I mean, other than the obvious: body, face, voice, accent, the skill with which he wielded his kraken tongue.

But as I reflected (i.e. obsessed) on the issue, it wasn't just his exterior (or his tongue) that had elevated him to the level of man-legend in my mind. That night we'd been together years ago, Jackson had been . . .

A gentleman.

He'd been a gentleman. Thoughtful, considerate, unselfish. He'd given me his coat because it was a cold night, before I'd even shivered. He'd wanted to make sure I was fed since we'd left the reception before dinner. He'd opened my door. He'd said please and thank you. He'd asked me what I wanted, and he'd never asked for a single thing in return.

Had I ever met anyone like him?

A resounding *no* echoed between my ears as I pulled into the county sheriff's station Wednesday afternoon, the sour cherry pie Sienna had reserved from Daisy's Nut House on the front passenger seat of my loaner car.

Oh! Speaking of the loaner, I must tell you all about it. Sienna arranged a verra nice car for me to use in my quest. Verra, verra nice. A vintage, souped-up dark blue Mustang convertible with a white top and racing stripe down the hood and over the trunk. When I'd stepped out of the carriage house, I'd found it parked directly out front with a note on the windshield:

This is the loaner for Ms. Ezra, keys are in the ignition. Please return to Winston Bros. Auto Shop whenever you're done using her. By the way, she likes premium. Give her premium. –CBW

I figured the *W* at the end stood for Winston, and *CBW* had to be one of Sienna's brothers-in-law. Jethro had mentioned over dinner that two of his brothers owned an auto repair shop nearby.

Clearly restored with a great deal of attention and love, I felt uncomfortable using it without paying for the privilege and didn't like accepting freebies on principle. Staying at Sienna's carriage house without reimbursing her in some way felt squicky enough. I decided I'd leave an envelope of $5000 cash in the loaner Mustang's glove box when I returned the glorious car to the auto shop next Friday before my flight back to Los Angeles.

Ugh. I heaved a sigh at the thought, glancing at my reflection in the Mustang's rearview mirror and smoothing a frown from my face. Don't get me wrong, I loved Los Angeles. I loved Southern California. I loved the beach and water, the sun and the temperate climate. But I didn't—currently—love the idea of returning to my high-security golden cage, cloistered like a nun, and picking up my pretend life right where I'd left off.

You still have a week . . .

Technically, I had nine and a half days left in Green Valley. I intended to make each moment count, starting with this afternoon.

Resolutely picking up the pie from the passenger seat, I exited the car and pulled in a deep breath for courage.

Do you want to know something (perhaps) surprising? I'm a twenty-eight-year-old woman who has never asked out a guy, never initiated a conversation with someone I'm attracted to, never flirted with someone who hadn't already made a pass at me.

Jackson James would be my first.

I approached the double doors to the station and inspected my reflection in the glass. I looked . . . good. *I think.* My long hair was down and fell around to my lower back in glossy waves. It had taken me almost a full hour to dry and wrestle and arrange. I had my Italian and Cuban ancestry to thank for the dark brown color, wavy texture, and heavy thickness.

I also had them to thank for my every three-week waxing appointment, particularly the Italian in me. My Cuban grandmother never had facial hair issues—that I knew about—but my mother always had a faint mustache since I could remember. But she wore it proudly, along with the dark hair on her arms, armpits, and legs, and especially when she interacted with my dad. I think it was one of her big F-U's to his preoccupation with how women were supposed to look and act and behave.

My eyes moved to the makeup I'd applied around my eyes and then lower to the thin-ish black tank top and cutoff shorts. *Hmm.* I reminded myself that it was—indeed—quite hot. Sienna had promised me that the outfit did not make me look desperate. I'd decided to believe her at the time, but now I wasn't so sure.

Maybe because I feel a little desperate?

The door opened before I could debate the level of my desperation or the Converse sneakers on my feet, and a woman walked out, fiddling with her purse, and doing a double take as she passed me. I rushed forward, not wanting to be distracted from my mission. I struggled to silence my doubts and stop second-guessing the plan.

But . . . what if Sienna was wrong and Jackson wasn't even here? What would I do? Leave the pie? What if he was here but was too busy to see me? What if he didn't want to see me? What if he did see me and laughed at my request? What if he was insulted by it? What if he didn't remember me and—

"Raquel Ezra?" A voice that was somehow both sharp and breathless pulled me out of my worry cascade. An older woman with dark brown eyes and short graying hair stood behind a circular desk, her hands clasped beneath her chin. The desk was placed in the center of what looked like a combination lobby and waiting room.

I pasted a smile on my face, darting a glance to the empty chairs lining the far wall before settling my attention on the woman's expectant expression. "Hi?"

Had Sienna called ahead? Was Jackson expecting me? That wasn't the plan!

"Oh my stars, I'd heard you were in town, but folks thought you'd already come and gone. I cannot believe it's you." Sidestepping her chair, she scurried out from behind the desk and rushed over, her eyes and smile wide. "I am such a fan. I hope you don't mind my saying, and I know you aren't here to be mobbed, but I honestly love every single one of your movies. *Starlight Surprise* is by far my favorite." She grabbed my hand and squeezed it, her gaze dreamy and unfocused. "You brought me to tears at the end, when you lost y'all's baby."

"Thank you." I slipped into the character I assumed when chatting with individuals who hardcore enjoyed my work. "I can't tell you how much that means to me."

The woman's gaze grew more unfocused. "Good Lord, you are just too gorgeous to be real," she said on a croaky sigh, giving me the sense she was speaking mostly to herself. "You're like an angel."

"You are too kind." I found my smile growing more sincere, her words a boost to my faltering resolve and doubts. An angel never looked desperate, right? What could this woman possibly gain by lying to me? This was a compliment I could trust. "I don't suppose you could point me in the direction of Deputy James, could you?"

"Jackson?" She blinked, giving her head a little shake. "I'm sorry. Are you here to see Jackson James?"

Okay, so, good. Sienna hadn't called ahead, Jackson had no idea I was coming, the plan was still in play.

"I am." I withdrew my fingers from hers and supported the pie with both hands, lifting it up between us. "Sienna asked me to bring over the deputy's favorite pie while I was out today. Is he here?" This was the story Sienna and I had decided on, and a bold-faced lie. I had no reason to be out and about today other than buying pie for bribing and then propositioning the good deputy.

"Oh! Well, yes. Absolutely, yes." She nodded, turning suddenly and calling over her shoulder, "The big room is just through here. We don't usually let civilians inside—unless they're under arrest—but I think we can make an exception in your case."

I jolted into action as soon as she pushed through a set of swinging double doors, rushing to follow her inside. She hadn't waited for me but had marched halfway down the aisle around the perimeter of what she called the big room.

It was clear why it was called the big room, as it was a big room. Packed full of desks—some occupied by women or men in tan uniforms, some empty—the only way through the space without disrupting the buzz of movement and activity was to walk around the perimeter. Bringing the pie closer to my chest, I power walked to catch up to the older woman, and she sent me a grin once I pulled even with her shoulder.

"Jackson's over there, at the corner." She pointed to a desk that was the farthest spot from the double doors leading into the room, and I saw him, a fissure of nerves zinging through me as my eyes greedily devoured the sight.

He leaned back in his chair, a phone receiver caught between his shoulder and cheek, his elbows resting on the arms of an office chair while he. . . *peeled an apple?*

Yes. As I drew closer, I confirmed Jackson was indeed peeling an apple. He held what looked like a small paring knife in one hand and an apple in the other. His eyes were on the piece of fruit, absorbed in his task, and his movements weren't slow, but they were careful. The apple's skin dangled in one solid piece, a spiral below where his fingers worked.

"Look at that, he's finally got it," the woman next to me said, gesturing to Jackson. Two deputies—also on their respective phones—glanced up as we passed. Like the woman who'd been leaving the station earlier, they both did a double take.

I ignored them. My eyes were fastened to Jackson as heat spread through my body at the sight of his big hands and meticulous movements skillfully slicing through the apple skin. Unlike most of the other deputies in the big room, he wasn't wearing his uniform. I surmised this was because it was his day off. Instead he had on a plain black T-shirt and jeans. He didn't spare us a glance as we approached, clearly listening to someone on the other side of the phone, his brow furrowed in concentration.

"I understand that you're allergic, and I will certainly be glad to check on that, sir," he said as we drew within earshot. "But if the flowers aren't over the property line, you can't remove them. Mrs. Templeton is right, it's damaging property."

My stomach gave a little flutter at the deep timbre of his voice. I'd forgotten how wonderful his voice was. Somehow, the deputy sounded firm and reasonable and sympathetic. How did he do that?

My escort halted a few feet away from his desk, just out of his eyeline, and so did I. She clasped her hands in front of her and glanced at me, a creaky smile on her lips. "We'll just wait 'til he's finished. Shouldn't take long."

I nodded, thankful for the extra time, because I suddenly needed a moment. Swallowing convulsively, I repeated my lines in my head. I just needed to get him alone, flirt a bit, and then make my request. That's it. That's all.

Another deputy walked past us as though in slow motion, her mouth hanging open, and her eyes widened as she looked me up and down.

"Holy . . ." the deputy said on a rush of breath, a young-ish woman with her brown hair pulled back in a tight bun. She stopped, gaping at me, and whispered, "Are you—"

"She is," my escort whispered back harshly, straightening her spine. "And she's here to see Deputy James. Get back to work, Mable."

I gave the female deputy a friendly grin as I wrestled with my frazzled nerves and then ended up offering the same grin to three other male deputies who'd also stopped their work to stare at me.

Jackson's brows pulled lower, and his mouth formed a stiff line. His movements stilled, the apple three-quarters peeled. "Sir, if you can prove they're over the property line, I'll be happy to oversee the relocation myself. But you know those are blue ribbon roses and she makes a bundle on prize money during the season. If you touch, remove, abuse, or otherwise molest Mrs. Templeton's flower beds , she will be justified in pressing charges." His tone was firmer this time, deeper, tinged with a hint of anger.

My breath caught, a renewed spike of heat flared outward from my chest. God, he was so sexy when he was stern. I guess listening to Deputy James reprimand faceless civilians about the placement of roses really did it for me.

Chuckling a breathless laugh and gritting my teeth, I shook my head at myself, earning a curious side-eye from my escort.

"It's the reverend," the woman said in a lowered voice, like this would explain everything.

"The reverend?"

"He and the missus just moved next door to Mrs. Templeton and her acre of rose bushes."

"A—a whole acre?" My mouth fell open.

"Yes. They're blue ribbon every year *and* she supplies the lodge. Her husband planted the garden before his passing—may he rest in peace—and Reverend Seymore is allergic to all flowers. Roses, lilies, peonies—every single kind. Never has any in the church. He uses ferns and branches, I've heard." My escort leaned closer, her tone that of a person who was practiced in the art of gossip. "Why he bought the place, no one knows, but now he wants her to remove the roses and she near pitched a fit, showed up in tears earlier today, *inconsolable*." She lifted her chin and sniffed, her dark brown eyes shrewd. "If you ask me, Seymore is a bully. Jackson will put a stop to it."

"Just as long as we understand each other, Reverend." Jackson leaned forward and turned away from where we hovered, offering his strong profile. He transferred the knife to the hand holding the apple and caught the phone in his free palm.

My lashes fluttered as he gave us his back, my mind telling me without being asked that the deputy had been working out. He seemed bigger, bulkier, his shoulders broader than five and a half years ago, the sleeves of his short-sleeve shirt not exactly tight at his biceps, but nowhere near baggy either. My attention moved to his butt and thighs just as my escort cleared her throat.

54

I stiffened, shifting my gaze to hers. She'd narrowed her eyes, seemed to be watching me speculatively, and embarrassment bloomed thorny and hot around my neck. The woman had caught me ogling Deputy James's butt, and she didn't seem to like it.

Is this his mother? They were both white, but she didn't look like him—no cleft in her chin, her eyes were the wrong color brown, her upper lip was bigger than the bottom whereas the opposite was true for Jackson. Plus, her forehead was small, her face was heart shaped instead of oval, and the silver in her hair was mixed with black, not blond.

Unless he'd been adopted, this was not his mother. Nevertheless, her stare reeked of disapproval. Fan or no, this woman did not like me ogling Deputy James.

I offered a small smile, which she didn't return as she asked, "Why'd Sienna Diaz want to give Jackson a pie?"

I shrugged, shifting away from her sudden frigidity. "Oh, you know. Being neighborly."

The intensity of her squint increased, and perspiration trickled down my back. I looked away and meant to arrange my features in a neutral expression while pretending to benignly study the big room. Except, in the next moment, I found that everyone in the big room—except Jackson, who was still on his call—was currently studying me.

Also, the room had grown remarkably quiet. Crap.

Aaaaaand now we have an audience.

Having an audience didn't bother me once upon a time, back before I traveled every-where with a human wall buffer; back before I lived in a heavily guarded mansion with a host of people I paid; back before I never left my house for any reason other than to go from the gated environment of my house to another gated environment of filming locations and sound stages. I'd grown accustomed to living *separate*, and I hadn't felt or realized how much until right this moment.

"That's right, sir. Uh-huh. . . Uh-huh. . . R-right. Glad to hear it." Jackson leaned forward over his desk, and I didn't look at his butt, his voice virtually the only sound in the big space. "Okay. Bye now."

My heart thundered between my ears. I did my best to appear entirely at ease while I gave myself a hurried pep talk. If I could act like kissing Gardner Beatty in *Starlight*

Surprise was an enjoyable experience, then I could act calm now. I could slip into a character far removed from myself and my current discomfort. I could *pretend.*

Pretending is my superpower.

"Deputy James." My escort stepped forward and in front of me, his title and last name a sharp rasp, and basically blocked me from his view. "This woman is here to see you. I told her you were busy, but she said it would only take a minute or two. Do you have the time, or should I send her on her way?"

The older woman's misrepresentation of events shaved away some of my unease, allowing me to focus on a spike of irritation rather than the twenty or so sets of eyes staring at me.

Before he could respond, I straightened my spine and stepped around her, prepared to say hi or some other sort of greeting. But then his eyes—those dark bedroom eyes I'd been fantasizing about for *years*—connected with mine.

It felt like being slammed into. Or doing a flat belly flop in a pool. Words failed me. Everything failed me. *Oh no.*

Rae, you are a mess. And this was a huge, huge, HUGE mistake.

CHAPTER 6

RAQUEL

"Being a sex symbol was rather like being a convict."

— RAQUEL WELCH

*T*hose sexy bedroom eyes of his widened with obvious surprise. He shot up from his office chair and backed up a step, like the sight of me was a shock. Unfortunately, I didn't know him well enough to know whether the shock was a good one or a bad one.

Jackson breathed out, blinking rapidly. I sensed my escort look between us. I didn't spare her a glance, but Jackson did. Whatever he saw on her face seemed to sober his. Drawing himself up to his full height, he returned his gaze to mine, dark eyes now shuttered, his expression neutral.

"Ma'am." Jackson tipped his head toward me, not quite a smile on his lips. "How may I help you?"

I stared at him because . . . ma'am?

Ope! Did he just call me *ma'am?*

He wasn't supposed to call me ma'am! He was either supposed to say "Raquel!" as though surprised, or "Raquel!" as though excited to see me. I would then say something friendly and witty and ask if I could have a moment of his time in private.

He wasn't supposed to regain his composure so quickly, and he wasn't supposed to call me ma'am like we didn't know each other. And we weren't supposed to have an audience or a grumpy-interloper-disapproving escort.

And now I forgot my lines completely. *Dammit. What is my line?!*

As we stood there, the room near silence, Jackson's eyebrows ascended slowly while I merely stared at him, struggling to make the words and say the thing. His gaze seemed to grow less guarded and more *hey-crazy-lady-are-you-okay?* while he waited for me to do something other than look panicked and constipated.

Say something!

Tearing my eyes from his, I looked around without allowing myself to absorb the surroundings, gathered a deep breath, and opened my mouth because I absolutely had to speak, even if my words made no sense. That's when I noticed the pie in my hand. *Yes! Sienna was right, pie is the answer.*

I would hand over the pie and then I would promptly leave because this was a bad idea. Clearly, it had been crazy of me to think I could just walk in here without drawing attention and proposition the guy I'd been fantasizing about for over five years. I didn't proposition people, I didn't know how. And if I'd known how at one point in my life, I'd completely forgotten now. I was completely out of my depth because I'd spent the last several years of my life exclusively in shallow waters.

"This is for you." I held up the pie between us, trying not to cringe at the breathless quality to my voice. As soon as he took it, I would smile politely, wish him well, drive back to the carriage house, and hide under the covers for the rest of my days. *That's a good plan. Hiding under covers is approximately my maximum depth.*

His gaze shifted from me to the pie and then back again, one side of his mouth curving up. "You're not going to throw it at my face, are you?"

I breathed a surprised laugh and responded automatically, "I heard it was part of your beauty regimen, and I wanted to help."

He unleashed a grin and a laugh, his eyes bright. The room seemed to fade away, leaving only him as my stomach did a trapeze routine, swooping up and down. It was disconcerting to realize my memory hadn't overexaggerated how breath-stealingly attractive he was, especially when he smiled.

Jackson stepped closer, his gaze now significantly more open than before. "Thank you."

"What?" *Oh no.* I worried that I'd just told him how handsome he was out loud instead of just thinking it.

"Thank you for the pie." His lips twitched, and the look he wore told me he thought I was both weird and cute. The deputy's gaze traveled over my face deliberately, perhaps reacquainting himself with the shape of it, or committing it to memory, or simply just enjoying it.

"I was told it was your favorite," I said truthfully, disarmed by how he was looking at me as I handed the pie over.

He stepped even closer, not looking at the dessert as he accepted the container, our fingers brushing. The contact sent an aching, tingling thrill down my spine—*first contact!*

"Sour cherry? From Daisy's? You didn't."

"I did." For some reason, I hadn't yet let go of the pie.

He grinned, his voice dropping to a deep rumble. "How'd you know?"

"I have my sources."

"Sources?" His eyebrows ticked up. "Now I'm intrigued."

"You weren't before?"

"Oh, I was. But now I'm even more intrigued."

"Are you?" I was helpless against the urge to smile.

"I am. Not many people know what my favorites are."

"And now I do."

Those bedroom eyes seemed to heat and darken as they lowered to my lips. "Yes. You certainly—"

"Jackson James!"

I flinched, and so did he. We both turned our heads in unison toward the woman at my right. My escort. The woman who'd loved my movies and was a big fan until approximately two minutes ago.

That's when I remembered where I—where *we*—still were.

"I do believe you have an appointment with *the Mitchells* to prep for," she snapped, appearing to be . . . not exactly angry. Accusatory maybe? Indignant?

I felt Jackson retreat, the pie slipping out of my hands as he took it with him and placed it on the desk. By the time my eyes returned to his, he was looking everywhere but at me.

"Yes. I know that, Florence." He wore what could only be described as a grim smile, his eyes darting around the room while a faint hint of pink colored his cheeks above his close-cut beard. "Thank you for the pie, Ms. Ezra. It's also my momma's favorite, so I'll be sure to send her your regards."

Then and only then did he lift his gaze to mine. If I thought he'd looked shuttered and distant before, his stare seemed ten times more guarded and aloof now.

My stomach sank.

Oh no. I'd embarrassed him. At his job. In front of everyone he worked with. I'd made a scene. Me making unintentional scenes by merely showing up someplace was why my mother had asked me to stop visiting her. Absentmindedly, I rubbed my thumb over the center stone of my evil-eye bracelet.

You're a mess, Rae. And this was a mistake.

I managed to force a light tone—to pretend—as I shoved my empty hands in the pockets of my shorts, taking a step back. "Technically, the pie is from Sienna, so please make sure Mrs. James thanks the right person. Anyway, I'll be going. So . . ." I nodded to him and tore my eyes away, the act physically painful.

I nodded to the stern-looking Florence lady. "I'll just show myself out."

"I'll walk you," came her curt reply. "Don't want you getting lost."

"Absolutely. Thank you." My pretend smile increased for the benefit of everyone watching.

She marched me down the perimeter aisle, and I kept my eyes forward, a pleasant, unconcerned expression on my features. I nodded politely to the one or two deputies who were looking at my eyes instead of my chest. Soon we were through the double doors, and Florence stopped just in front of them, crossing her arms and standing tall as though barricading the way.

"I think you can see yourself out from here." There was no mistaking her snide tone as anything but disapproving.

I countered her attitude with another pretend warm grin tossed over my shoulder, and I unhurriedly walked to the exit, even though I wanted to run. "Thank you for your help. Have a nice day."

Maintaining the façade, I walked to my awesome loaner car, got in, and started the engine. I then turned my phone on, intent on pulling up Google Maps for directions so I could get back to the carriage house ASAP. And then I would hide under the covers until my flight next Friday afternoon.

That's a good plan. The other plan? The plan to approach, bribe with pie, and proposition Deputy Dreamy? That was a bad plan. That was a—

The feel of my phone buzzing along with the accompanying chimes announcing text messages had me frowning at the screen. I'd turned my phone off for most of my stay in Green Valley. Sasha had been texting me nonstop since Saturday, and I didn't want to listen to the cell chime every ten minutes. Frustrated and sad—yes, I was a little sad at how sublimely I'd crashed and burned with Deputy James—I prepared to fire off a text to Sasha, telling her to chill out, when my eyes snagged on the sender of the latest string of texts. *Sienna.*

Frowning, I unlocked my phone and read her text messages:

Sienna: Stop! I have information. Do not approach Jackson James, do not procure a pie, do not pass go. Call me!

Sienna: Please tell me you haven't gone to the station yet.

Sienna: PLEASE CALL ME ASAP. URGENT ALERT URGENT!

Sienna: Oh no. You've gone, haven't you? You've seen him. I'm so sorry. I am responsible. This is my fault.

Sienna: Prayers have been said. Call me when it's over.

I read through her messages a second and a third time, trying to make sense of them, then I hurriedly called her. Pushing the AC vent to blow more directly on my neck, I brought the phone to my ear.

Almost immediately she picked up. "Rae? Did you see him? Or did I stop you in time?"

"I saw him."

She groaned. "God, I'm so stupid. And I'm so, so sorry. I should've talked to Jet about it before you went over there, and that's my fault. I never know who is dating who, I can't keep up, but he's got the inside track on all the gossip in town. When I told him where you were, he told me about Jackson and Charlotte, and now I feel like I led you astray and—"

"Wait, wait. Stop. Charlotte? Charlotte who?"

"Charlotte Mitchell." Sienna's voice was small and apologetic.

Mitchell. . .

MITCHELL!

My escort had said that Jackson was late for a meeting with the Mitchells. She must've meant his girlfriend, Charlotte Mitchell. "Oh snap."

"But I swear I had no idea when I sent you over there. They've been together for a few months."

I stared out the windshield, the scenery beyond blurry while her words soaked into my brain. *Together for a few months.* He was dating someone. He had a girlfriend.

He's dating someone, and you brought him your pie to eat?!

"Ugh." I placed a hand over my stomach, feeling ill. "I am such a dick-twat." No wonder Florence-the-former-fan had looked at me like I was scum.

And no wonder Jackson didn't want my pie.

"No. You are not a dick-twat."

"Are you kidding? I went in there to proposition someone else's boyfriend! I am a dick-twat."

"No. If anyone is a dick-twat, it is me. I am the dick-twat. And I'll wear a vagina sash and a penis crown proclaiming my dick-twat championship status. You had no idea he was with someone because I took for granted that he was single. Jackson has been single *forever*, ever since his fiancée left him and—"

"He was engaged? When? When was this?"

He'd been engaged. He'd been in love. And she'd left him.

"I don't remember. I can't keep up with the Green Valley gossip. Years ago at this point. And before that, the man was a complete player, never with the same woman twice."

Never with the same woman twice.

The sick feeling in my stomach bubbled up my esophagus. I closed my eyes; my chest tight, aching; my forehead pressing against the steering wheel. That night we'd shared all those years ago, I'd told him our time together came with no strings, that I was never with the same man twice. I'd promised him I would never speak to him again after the night was over. I'd promised.

Now I was a liar.

I'd spent half a decade wishing I hadn't left, that I'd stayed one more day, even though he hadn't asked me to. And then the first thing (other than hermiting) that I did when I came back to Green Valley was seek him out and break that promise. A one-night stand, showing up unexpectedly and unannounced at his *work place* after no contact for five and a half years.

If he'd wanted to talk to me, he could've asked Sienna a million times. But he didn't. Seriously. What. Had. I. Been. Thinking?

"Rae?"

"Sorry. I'm here. I'm . . ." I took a deep breath, filling my lungs with the tepid air gushing out of the car's AC. It wouldn't cool down until I was on the road. "I'm coming back."

"To the house?"

"To the carriage house, yes."

"Come up to the main house. Spend the rest of the afternoon with me."

"I think I want to hide under some blankets for a while." Straightening in my seat, I checked the rearview mirror and buckled my seatbelt.

You're a mess, Rae. Normal people don't proposition people, especially when those people have nice girlfriends and live nice, normal lives with nice, normal coworkers in a nice, normal office.

And nice, normal people keep their promises.

Maybe I really did belong in LA. Maybe flying out here to escape my pretend life was the fantasy, and Hollywood was the reality. Maybe the sooner I made peace with my reality, the better.

"No. You will not hide under blankets. Hey, I'll get a sitter, and we'll go out to dinner. We haven't been out to dinner since you arrived. There's a great steak place called The Front Porch. They have cocktails."

I shook my head even though she couldn't see me. "Sienna—"

"It's settled. You, me, Jet. Maybe one of his siblings is free and can join us."

"Don't try to set me up."

"I wouldn't, I promise. Plus, all Jet's siblings are married or in committed, long-term relationships. They're just fun people, and I think what you need is an evening out with fun people."

I didn't agree.

But I didn't have the energy to argue either.

CHAPTER 7

JACKSON

"Nobody can understand what you're feeling unless they burn the way you burned."

— RIHANNA

I didn't allow myself to think too hard about why I took meticulous care getting ready for my date with Charlotte—trimming my beard, styling my hair, wearing my best suit, and using both aftershave and cologne.

Nor did I allow myself to think about Raquel's visit to the station today. Her unexpected visit. Or how I'd taken one look at her and forgotten where I was. Or how, when she'd left, I'd felt like the entirety of my life was walking out the door with her.

Because none of it made any damn sense.

My priorities were in order, I had my sights set on something and someone permanent, not on temporary or fun or easy. Not anymore. I would not think about Raquel. I had no reason to think about Raquel. So, I wouldn't.

"Look at you, Fancy." Charlotte, pulling open her front door, smiled and then frowned within the span of two seconds, glancing down at her jeans and red V-neck shirt. "Wait. Should I change?"

"No need, you look fine."

"Gee, thanks." She rolled her eyes. "But you're in a suit." Now Charlotte squinted at me, and her hands came to her hips. "Wait a minute. Is tonight a surprise? Are you taking me to a surprise?" Before I could answer, her eyes got big all of a sudden and she lightly hit my shoulder, looking excited. "Let me guess, is it a funeral?"

I laughed. She was so funny and weird. We'd been friends forever, and I knew not everyone appreciated her humor, it could be dark at times, hitting an off-note. But I thought she was hilarious.

"No. There is no surprise, I swear. We have reservations at The Front Porch, like we agreed earlier. I ordered ahead your favorite to cut down on time, so you can get back for the sitter. Now, come on." I motioned for her to get moving.

Charlotte looked torn. Glancing down at her clothes again, she sighed. "I want to change."

"Okay. Go change. I'll wait."

She grimaced and stepped closer, whispering, "My mother is here."

I understood her indecision. Charlotte's momma made a habit of inviting herself on our dates. "Then don't change and let's go."

She huffed. "But I really want to change. Why'd you have to wear a suit?"

"We can go to my place—"

"Really?" She perked up, looking pleased, but then wary. "Wait, is Boone there?"

"Boone is there, I think. But I can change real fast. If we leave now, we might still make it."

"Or, if Boone isn't there, we could just hang out at your place?"

"Charlotte, I called ahead. They're expecting us. The food will be waiting."

Charlotte's face fell and she made a low, grunting sound in the back of her throat. "Never mind. I'll go change. But—" she quickly glanced behind her "—you stay out here. In fact, go get in your truck. Don't let her see you."

"Are you kidding? I have to say hi to your mother."

"What? Why?"

"It'd be disrespectful not to."

Charlotte rolled her eyes. "It would be nice if you made more of an effort to be less respectful every once in a while."

I released a frustrated breath, her statement sounding suspiciously like what my father had said at breakfast.

"What ever happened to fun, flirty Jackson James? The one who used to sneak in Darlene Simmons's window for a quickie? Did you stop by her momma's room to say hi on your way out?"

"I'm not like that anymore, and you know it." Charlotte had been one of my friends who'd cheered me on when I'd stopped acting a fool. She'd been there when I'd drawn those lines in the sand, so why she was surprised and/or irritated with my manners now felt like a giant mystery. "Besides, where'd you hear that?"

"Women talk. But I'm starting to think Darlene made the whole thing up."

I sighed, backing away from the door. I didn't want to fight, not when we had so little time. "Fine. Fine. I'll stay out here. You don't have to change."

"Yes, I do. I can't have you looking prettier than me." She stepped back, winking, and promptly closed the door.

Dutifully, I pulled out my keys and walked back to the truck, careful not to make too much noise as I shut my door. If her mother knew I was still out here, she'd come out to say hi. I wasn't at all against saying hi to Ms. Mitchell, but I knew Charlotte didn't want to give her mother a chance to be a third wheel and invite herself—and maybe the kids—along on our date.

Sooner than I'd expected, Charlotte was dashing from her house and jogging to my truck, pantomiming "turn the engine."

As soon as she hopped inside, she said, "Floor it! The old woman is after me."

I chuckled, but I didn't floor it. Instead, I pulled out of the spot nice and slow, and only after Charlotte had buckled her seatbelt.

"What is wrong with you? I told you to floor it."

"I can't floor it. This truck is an antique."

"You need a new car."

"I love this car." I petted the dashboard. "Don't listen to her, baby. She doesn't know you like I do."

"I'm feeling a little jealous of this truck." She gave me a side-eye even as she laughed good-naturedly, then pulled down the visor to check her makeup in the mirror. "Which color? Rambunctious Red or Pernicious Pink?"

"Pardon?"

"I haven't put on lipstick yet. Which one goes better with what I'm wearing?"

"Uh . . ." I hadn't paid much attention to what she'd changed into, so I tried to sneak a look. "Sorry, let me get to a stop sign."

"Never mind. Pernicious Pink it is."

"Always a solid choice."

She snorted but said nothing. We drove for a bit in silence as she applied her lipstick. Charlotte didn't live too far from the restaurant, and before we'd settled into any kind of real conversation, I'd parked, taking note of the cars in the lot.

"I think that's Jethro Winston's truck," I said, not cutting the engine, my mouth suddenly dry.

"So it is," she agreed, sounding distracted. "And—uh—look at that. There's Ashley Winston's—I mean Ashley *Runous's*—car. They must be having a family dinner."

I struggled to swallow. "Maybe we should go somewhere else."

"What? Why?"

"It's probably crowded."

"I thought you 'ordered ahead and they're expecting us.'" She quoted my earlier words, infusing a good dose of Charlotte attitude.

I leveled her a flat look, and she stuck her tongue out.

"Real mature, Charlotte."

"What do you want? I'm surrounded by other people's children all day at the elementary school and my own at home. You're lucky my hands aren't sticky." She unclicked her seatbelt and opened her door, which made me frown.

68

"Hold on a sec." I cut the engine and hopped out, jogging around to Charlotte's side. "Let me get the door."

"You know, I can get my own door," she said, hiking up her skirt to climb down from the passenger seat.

"Yes, but I like getting the door."

"Instead of getting my door, why don't you give me something I really want?"

"Oh yeah, like what?" I offered my elbow, which she took.

"I don't know, a massage? I haven't had a massage in ages."

Oh. That's easy to fix. "Sure thing." I shrugged.

"Really?" She smiled at me, her eyes widening again like they had earlier when I'd suggested we go back to my place. "You'd give me a massage?"

"Yeah. There's that spa my momma likes in Knoxville. I'm sure they have massages. I'll get you a gift certificate."

Charlotte made a face, her shoulders slumping. "Oh. Sure."

"What? Is there a different place you want to try?" I opened the door of the restaurant for her, and she filed in, walking straight to the hostess stand to check us in, my question apparently forgotten. No matter. I added *Get Charlotte a gift certificate for a massage* to my mental task list.

While she spoke with Hannah Townsen, I did a quick sweep of the restaurant, spotting Cletus Winston and Drew Runous—Ashley's husband—almost immediately. They were standing near a cluster of benches where folks waited to be seated. Holding my breath, I searched the rest of their party, bracing myself for—

Long dark hair. Smooth, tan skin. Addictive, musical laugh and voice.

"Crap." My stomach stiffened. Actually, it was the area south of my stomach that stiffened.

"What?" Charlotte had come to my side without me noticing.

"Uh—" I shook my head to clear it, determined not to look over at Raquel again "—it's crowded. I think we should go somewhere else."

"It's not that crowded. And where else would we go? And we have a reservation. Hannah said our table is almost—" She cut herself off with a gasp. "Oh my gosh! Is that Raquel Ezra?"

Crap, crap, crap. "Appears to be."

"I'd heard she was in town. Marina Simmons said her brother said she was at the station today. I can't believe she's standing right there. She's so—gosh—she's stunning."

"Most movie stars are generally considered pretty." I plucked a menu from the holder by the door and studied it.

"What? No. She's not pretty. That word does not apply here. That woman is full-blown gorgeous. Striking, you know? Like she's so beautiful, she doesn't look real."

I grunted, staring at the menu I'd memorized when I was ten.

"Jackson, what is wrong with you?"

"Pardon?" I flicked my attention up to Charlotte and then promptly returned it to the menu.

"I know you're her biggest fan."

I opened my mouth. No sound arrived.

Charlotte huffed. "You used to drag me and Zora and all the other women in your harem to every one of her movies on opening night." She hit my shoulder and then slid her palm down my bicep, gripping my forearm. "You have to go over there and introduce yourself, say hi, say *something*. When will you ever get another chance?"

I dug my heels in, a flare of straight-up panic clogging my airway. "No, no. That's okay."

"What?"

I allowed my eyes to flick up for the barest of seconds. "She's here with the Winstons."

"So?"

"So, uh, you know. Jethro and I don't always get along—"

"Oh, come on, that's all in the past. And Cletus is there. I know you two are basically best friends these days. Here, let's go say hi."

"No."

Charlotte grew still, except her lashes, which blinked rapidly. "Is it because Ashley is there with Drew?" she asked, her voice gentle. "Does seeing them together make you uncomfortable?"

"What? No. I didn't even see her." I was so tired of folks thinking I had any residual romantic feelings for Ashley Runous. We'd been friends all through school, dated for a half minute when we were seventeen, I'd been an asshole, she left. Then she came back years later, and now we were friends again. End of.

"Then I'll go over by myself."

"No." I covered her hand on my arm to stop her. "Please don't."

"Then come with me."

My gaze darted beyond Charlotte to where the Winstons and their wives surrounded Raquel, and something lodged in my throat. "Charlotte," I croaked. "I really don't want to."

"You're being ridiculous and you're going to regret not going over there. As your friend, I really must insist. And I'm sure she's used to it. Come with me. Why're you being like this?" She tugged on my arm again.

I didn't budge.

She gave me an assessing narrowed glare and then turned, lifting her arm, and before I could stop her, she called across the room, "Hi! Hi there!"

Oh my God.

"Hi, I'm Charlotte. This is Jackson. You're Raquel Ezra. We're big fans!"

My gaze dropped to the floor, and I breathed in. I breathed out. I breathed in. I breathed out. I breathed—

"Hi Charlotte," Raquel's voice, made of sunshine and rainbows, called back. "Nice to meet you."

"Do you mind if we come over?" Charlotte tugged on my arm again.

I clenched my jaw, still staring at the floor, so very grateful that Charlotte was a tall woman. That's right, I hid behind my girlfriend.

"Not at all. Please come over," Raquel responded easily, and a bolt of heat shot straight to the base of my spine, making my collar feel too tight and sweat prickle between my shoulder blades.

"Come on. Don't be shy," Charlotte whispered to me, and I could hear the laughter in her voice.

What could I do? In the next moment, we were moving, walking toward Raquel. I readied myself the best I could. I worked to distance myself while on autopilot, I lifted my chin and muttered greetings to those gathered.

"Cletus." I shook hands with my friend, quick and perfunctory.

"Deputy. That's a nice suit. Did you call that tailor I told you about?"

"I did."

"Wise man." Cletus nodded somberly.

"Thank you."

He stopped nodding. "I was referring to myself."

Typical Cletus.

Next was Ashley.

"You feeling okay, Jackson?" Ashley Runous—formerly Winston—asked, pulling away after a quick hug. She always greeted me with a hug.

"Just fine," I rasped, hammering a closed-mouth smile in place. "How are you?"

"I'm okay." I felt her concerned eyes follow me as I continued shaking hands with her brothers and their wives—until I got to Jethro. He didn't extend a hand.

"Deputy James," he said flatly, his arms crossed.

"Jethro." I gave him a single nod, unsurprised by his cool greeting tonight but paying it no mind. This sort of thing tended to happen after I'd arrested someone more than once. In Jethro's case, I'd arrested him many, many more times than once, back when I was new on the force and hadn't quite topped out to my present height of six feet.

The frequent arrests paired with me being shitty to his sister in high school meant we'd likely never be friendly. But sometimes, like the handful of times I'd babysit for him and Sienna, I thought maybe we could be.

"I hope you don't mind that we interrupted your evening. I just wanted to introduce myself to Raquel, I am such a big fan," Charlotte gushed, not seeming to notice my cool exchange with Jethro Winston.

I had no idea if Raquel noticed either as I couldn't look at her. I was here with Charlotte. *I am here on a date with my girlfriend. I will not look at another woman.* But Raquel wasn't just another woman. She was . . . well, I had no idea what Raquel was.

I supposed Raquel was an idea. A memory I'd made too much out of, remembered too often, relived until the edges had grown worn and soft and frayed. Who's to say that night ever really happened? Maybe it didn't. Maybe it had been a figment of my imagination.

Regardless, she should've been nothing to me.

"Jackson is also a big fan." Charlotte pulled me forward so that I stood next to her and directly in front of Raquel. "In fact, I'd say he's probably your biggest fan. He absolutely *loves* you."

My heart stopped and then lurched painfully, and I knew—I just *fucking* knew—my face was on its way to turning a bright shade of tomato red.

"Is that so?" Raquel asked, still rainbows and sunshine.

"It is so! He owns all your movies on streaming *and* on DVD. I was a little worried when we first started dating that he'd make me wear a Raquel Ezra costume for Halloween." Charlotte laughed.

"And did he?" Cletus asked, earning him my hard stare.

Charlotte laughed harder. A few other people laughed as well. I did not.

Kill me. Kill me now. As far as embarrassing situations I'd experienced, this one ranked eleven on a ten-point scale.

"I'm honored to have such an avid fan," Raquel said. Her voice sounded a little breathless, and I knew I was being a complete ass because I hadn't looked at her yet.

I didn't want to be an ass to Raquel. My issue with her was *my* issue, not hers. She didn't deserve rudeness for being friendly and more gracious than *I* deserved. Using self-censure as a shield and a sword, I pulled my head out of my ass, took a deep breath, and finally looked at her.

Our gazes locked.

She wore a barely-there smile that looked a little uncertain, her eyes a deep, rich, dark velvet of indescribable color, and depth, and sweetness.

And just like clockwork, I felt it. The pull. The sense of everything else falling away, leaving only us. I'd felt it years ago when we were introduced at Jethro and Sienna's wedding. I'd felt it that whole night we were together. I'd felt it when I spotted her in the crowd on Saturday, at the station earlier today, and I felt it right now.

"Hi," I said, my heart racing like mad, and then suddenly just . . . slowing.

"Hi," she said, her small smile becoming a slightly bigger one. "It's good to see—uh —meet you."

"You as well."

"I hear this place is very good," she said softly. Or maybe she didn't. Maybe her voice only sounded soft to my ears.

"Depends on what you like to eat."

"Food, mostly."

"Then you're in luck. They serve food here."

She grinned widely, taking my breath away, and her gaze dropped to my neck, then to my chest. "I like this suit."

I caught myself before responding with, *If you want it, it's yours.*

It's what—instinctively—I longed to say. The easy back and forth banter at the sheriff's station earlier in the day, the way my heart beat in time with our game of verbal ping-pong, had been much the same.

Effortless. Easy. Euphoric. . . until I remembered who I was, and who she was, and who I was not. *Not anymore.*

I bit the inside of my mouth to keep from saying anything at all and tore my eyes from her face, my heart racing again.

Telling myself to snap out of it, I felt nothing but gratitude when Cletus stepped forward to say, "The suit is quite elegant, isn't it? I recommended the tailor."

"Only because Billy recommended the tailor to you," one of the other Winston brothers cut in, making everyone chuckle.

I took the opportunity to take a step back, hoping we could use the shift in conversation to make our getaway—but not because I didn't want to see or talk to Raquel. We needed to leave *because* I wanted to see and talk to her so, *so* much more than any man should when he's involved with someone else. Especially when the woman preoccupying his thoughts was engaged.

Speaking of which, every time I thought about Raquel with that cheating, scummy SOB, I saw red. It enraged me. The idea of him getting to touch her, being on the receiving end of her smiles and sweetness. It was a travesty. She deserved so much better.

So does Charlotte.

Dammit.

I am a bastard.

And that was the truth. My father had said he was proud of me, how much I'd changed, how disciplined I'd become in my personal life. I didn't deserve it—his pride or his praise—and Charlotte certainly didn't deserve to be with someone who couldn't stop thinking about someone else.

This doesn't matter. Raquel will be gone soon. She'll leave, just like before. Why would she stay? She's a huge, world-famous movie star. There's nothing of interest to her here. Charlotte and you will continue on, you'll build a life together with hard work and dedication, and none of this will matter.

"Well, we should leave y'all to your dinner." I reached for Charlotte's hand.

Charlotte pulled her fingers from mine, digging in her purse. "Just a sec. Before we go—do you mind if I take a picture?" To my horror, Charlotte had retrieved her phone and addressed her question to Raquel.

"Sure. Absolutely. No problem." Raquel readily agreed, and before I could think to object, Charlotte bent close to her, lifting the cell up as though to take a selfie.

"Please, allow me." Cletus stepped forward, taking the phone from Charlotte. "I can't abide two-person selfies. One person's face looks like a billboard, and the other looks like a doll head."

The women grinned, and Cletus snapped several shots. "Y'all want to do some poses?" he asked. "Sienna, jump in there and do that Charlie's Angels thing."

"Oh! Good idea." Sienna grinned, jumping in and bringing Cletus's wife and Ashley along as well.

"Any other poses?" Cletus turned to Jethro and then me, as though to solicit ideas. "Maybe—"

"No more poses," I said, giving my head a little shake.

"Having a bad day, Jackson?" Jethro's voice spoke from somewhere behind me. I ignored his question.

Cletus stared at me for a tick, a look that might've seemed harmless had I known him any less, and then said, "Jackson, do you want a picture with Ms. Ezra?" all curious innocence and solicitousness. So, in other words, he was being sneaky as hell.

I glared at him. "No, thank you, Cletus. I'm sure Ms. Ezra would prefer—"

"Come on, Jackson!" Charlotte marched over and moved behind me, pushing and steering my body until Raquel's shoulder brushed my arm. I sucked in a breath.

"There." Charlotte stood back, grinning at us. "Give me your phone, Jackson. I'll take the picture."

"Here. Use mine." Suddenly, Cletus had his phone out, unlocked, and in front of Charlotte. "I'll send it to him later." Eyes on me, a sinister smile curving his lips, barely noticeable behind his bushy beard.

But I saw it. And I knew what it meant. He had plans for that picture. It's a good thing I'd taken the time to become friends with Cletus Winston over the last several years, because if this is how he treated people he liked, I shuddered to think what he did to those folks he didn't.

"Thanks, Cletus," Charlotte said cheerfully, accepting the offered phone, once more oblivious to anything other than what was right in front of her.

Meanwhile, I stared stiffly forward, trying not to breathe. I could smell Raquel's perfume, floral and sweet, and the scent brought everything from our night together rushing back. *This is torture.*

"Raquel, is it okay with you if Jackson puts his arm around your shoulder? No pressure." Charlotte pointed between the two of us.

"Charlotte," I grit out, glaring at my friend—I mean, my girlfriend. "I'm sure Ms. Ezra doesn't want strangers touching her."

"No. No, it's good." Raquel encircled my wrist with her fingers, lifting my arm over her shoulders and stepping closer, the whole of her luscious body tucked against the side of mine before I'd had a single second to prepare for the scalding contact.

I felt Raquel's chest expand, press against my torso as she breathed in deeply, and I grit my teeth harder. I wanted to imagine myself taking a swim in the Artic Ocean but couldn't quite manage it, instead sending a prayer upward that this elegant suit I wore hid the less than elegant erection in my pants.

Instinct kicked in, and I breathed out, separating myself from where I was, who I was with, and the cluttered chaos of my mind.

Relax, I told myself. *Slow it down. Go somewhere else.*

I suspected any kid who has been bullied in school, any boy who was small and scrawny for his age, anyone who felt awkward and ugly growing up, learns how to do this without trying. It was an innate skill I now used whenever I found myself in a dangerous or uncertain situation at work, when tensions and adrenaline were running high.

I told myself to slow it down. Slow my mind down and pretend I was an observer, a bystander not in the thick of the action. I didn't have to feel scared or shitty about myself if I didn't wish to. I could simply pretend.

Just pretend, for a moment, that you're watching from somewhere on the other side of the room, what do you expect to see? You expect that Jackson James has never met Raquel Ezra before right now. Pretend you don't know she loves to fish, and that her favorite ice cream flavor is mint chocolate chip, and that she's great at chess, and is funny and charming and kind.

Pretend for a moment that Jackson James is meeting one of his favorite actresses for the very first time and he has no idea what her warm, soft body feels like curled

77

against his while he sleeps, the sound of her laugh, the texture of her skin, how she tastes, how her body tenses and flexes when she comes, the sweetness of her touch.

Just . . . pretend.

I breathed out. I relaxed.

"There. That looks nice." Charlotte beamed at us both and sing-songed, "Smile!"

Then it was over, and I pulled away. I turned to Ms. Ezra, movie star, and without meeting her eyes, I said, "Thank you. Goodbye."

I nodded to each of the Winstons and their significant others, waving politely as I pulled my girlfriend toward Hannah Townsen at the hostess stand. We needed to sit down and get on with the rest of our evening.

And I needed to get on with the rest of my life.

CHAPTER 8

JACKSON

"Everywhere in TV and films, actors who become mothers are treated differently. Suddenly, people will be like, 'Oh, she's a mom, so she can't play a sex symbol role.'"

— KASHMIRA SHAH (AKA KASHMERA SHAH)

I would've gotten on with my life, and happily too, if Charlotte had stopped talking about Raquel Ezra for one single second.

"Oh my gosh, she's so awesome. Did you smell her? She smells amazing. I wonder what kind of lotion she uses. I'll message Sienna and ask. Do you think Sienna would mind if I ask? I only have her phone number because of her eldest's birthday party last year. Nah. She won't mind." Charlotte skipped on the sidewalk in front of her house, doing a little twirl.

Dinner was over. Soon the evening would be over too. I couldn't wait.

"And so nice. So, so nice. I just knew she was nice. No one can act that well. Sienna's so nice, but the papers say she's nice, so I wasn't surprised. But Twitter—are you on Twitter?—folks talk about Raquel like she's a slut or something, like a man-stealing tart. She didn't give me that vibe at all." Charlotte leaned against the closed passenger side of my truck, making no move toward her house.

"I'm not on Twitter."

"What a thrill, you know? It's so great having Sienna Diaz in town when all her movie star friends visit. And Sienna is so great, I just love her—what I know about her. We're not close. I just, you know, I'm sure everybody wants to be friends with her. I haven't really approached her, we got kids the same age, so maybe it would be okay? What do you think?"

"Maybe—"

"You're right. I'll give her a call. See if she wants to have a playdate."

I closed my eyes against the threatening headache. "You should."

Charlotte was blessedly silent for a moment, and I gathered a deep breath.

"Jackson?"

"Hmm?"

"You were quiet during dinner."

A smile curved my lips, a real one. "When would I have spoken?"

"I guess I did talk a lot." She chuckled lightly, but then was quiet again.

I opened my eyes when her silence stretched and found her staring at me—studying me—with a troubled-looking knot between her eyebrows. "What? What is it?"

"Did I embarrass you?"

I didn't answer right away, but I knew I needed to say something based on the hint of worry behind her eyes. "What do you mean?"

"Kevin always said I embarrassed him, whenever we went out. That I . . . didn't act like a mother should, like a lady."

I'd known Charlotte for a long time, so I'd been there when her husband walked out on her. The man was a giant asshole—an elephant-sized asshole—in my opinion. And he acted like he had something perpetually stuck up that elephant-sized asshole, likely his own mouse-sized dick.

"Absolutely not. You didn't embarrass me." At least, she didn't embarrass me the way she was asking about.

Yes, I'd been embarrassed. Yes, she'd pushed me into doing something I *really* didn't want to do. But that was just Charlotte. She pushed. I'd known from the start of our relationship that she was a pushy person.

"I think you're lying." She gave me a wry smile. "You were bright red when we made it to the table, and I'm sorry. I did not mean to embarrass you."

I felt like she'd punched me in the stomach. If anyone should've been apologizing, it should've been me. "You—you didn't. I promise." I shook my head emphatically.

"I know I did."

"No. I was embarrassed, but definitely not in the way you mean. I was embarrassed, but not embarrassed of you. Never of you."

She screwed her mouth to the side, her gaze flickering over me like she wanted to believe me.

So I added, "It was an overwhelming experience, is all."

Inspecting me for a moment longer, she nodded, finally accepting my words. "Okay. I believe you."

"Good." I breathed out my relief, setting my hands on my hips. That settled, I looked over her shoulder at the moon, already high in the sky. It wasn't late, but I was exhausted.

"Do you want to come inside?" she asked, drawing my attention back to her. "Have a drink? The kids should be in bed."

"But they won't be asleep, and tomorrow is a school day."

Charlotte lifted her chin, the knot between her eyebrows returning, like I'd said something significant, and it irritated her.

"What?" I looked to the left and then to the right, looking for the source of her sudden ire. "What is it?"

She crossed her arms, the set of her mouth more defensive than friendly. "Tell me honestly, Jackson. If I were Ashley Winston, and she'd invited you in, would you come in tonight?"

I made a face. "No. Because that would never happen, and she's married."

"But let's say she wasn't married, okay? Let's say Drew, I don't know, they split up, he was abducted by aliens or something, leaving her with two little kids. Let's say she wasn't married and the two of you had been seeing each other for months. Let's say she invited you in. What would you say?"

My mouth worked, and just like before, no sound came out. *What the hell—*

"I knew it!"

"Knew what? What do you know?"

"You waited too long to answer the question."

"I was thinking! I shouldn't be penalized for thinking."

"If you were over her, you wouldn't need to think."

I couldn't help it, I laughed. "I am most definitely over Ashley Winston. That was a long, long, long time ago."

"And yet, if she'd asked you over to her house to fix a pipe in the middle of the night, I bet she would've gotten laid."

I flinched, honestly shocked. "Charlotte!"

"Oh, don't you Charlotte me. You know I'm right. And here you are, treating me like a lady."

"You are a lady."

"And you're a gentleman, and—I'm sorry—but I don't want a gentleman."

Wait.

Wait, wait, wait.

What is happening? How did I get here?

"You don't want a gentleman?"

"No!" She threw her hands up, rolling her eyes. "I mean, yes. Okay, of course I want a gentleman. But I want someone who at least has to *try* to be a gentleman with me. I want it to be difficult for a man to always be a gentleman with me, I want him to —to—to—"

"Not always be a good guy?" The words and thought slipped out of me at the exact same time.

"Yes! Exactly. And, Jackson, I adore you, I really do, but you . . . you never have to struggle against any ungentlemanly impulses with me, or *any* impulses. We have no chemistry."

Chemistry. She wanted chemistry? What the hell was I supposed to do with that? How did I make chemistry appear out of thin air when we'd only been on four dates as of tonight?

"You don't have to say anything." She sounded remorseful yet firm, but also deflated and sad. "Truth be told, I think I made up my mind before dinner. I think I made up my mind on Monday night. But I didn't want to send you a text to call things off."

"Made up your mind about what?" I was so lost. What were we even talking about?

"I really like you, Jackson. And I know there's going to be a bunch of people who will call me crazy for doing this, but—honey—we're breaking up."

I stared at her, disbelief a heavy veil obscuring my vision. "Charlotte. What—"

"You're a good man with a steady job and income, from a nice family who likes me. You're handsome, you take care of your body. You laugh at my jokes, and you're kind. So, so kind. And who am I? I'm a single mother of four kids. I should be grateful, right?"

Reflexively, I stepped forward and took her hand. As her friend, I hated the desolation I heard in her voice. "No. God, no. You're amazing, Charlotte. I'm the lucky one." Maybe society would have her believe that kind of shit, but it wasn't true.

She sniffed, shaking her head. "No. Neither of us is the lucky one, not in love. Because I don't see myself falling in love with you, Jackson. I don't see us loving each other like anything more than good friends."

My stomach had tied itself in knots while she spoke, and I squeezed her hand. I wasn't ready to concede defeat, not quite yet. Friendship was a good foundation, that's what I'd been told by everybody. Charlotte and I had a great friendship. There had to be something I could do.

"Charlotte, what can I do to make this right? I really, *really* like you."

She huffed a watery chuckle. "It's for the best, and you know it. You deserve to be crazy about someone, I want that for you. And I deserve for someone to be crazy about me. That's what I want."

"But—

She pulled her hand out of mine. "You said it yourself, you really, *really* like me. But you're not crazy for me. I was wearing nothing under my bathrobe on Monday—trying to force some chemistry—and you didn't even notice because it never occurred to you to take a peek. Admit it. You know I'm right."

I closed my eyes, the headache I'd been fighting all night crawling from my neck to my jaw to my temples and throbbing behind my forehead.

"We—we'll still be friends, all right?"

I laughed. It sounded sour. I had *a lot* of female friends. I had so many female friends. Boone and I may live together, but he wasn't the talkative type. My former partner and I had been friendly for a time, but ever since he and his girl got together, he didn't have much free time. All the friends I actually had real conversations with —other than Cletus Winston—were women.

Point was, I didn't want any more female friends.

But Charlotte had been a friend before we'd tried being something more, so I reckoned there was no reason we couldn't be friends again. Nothing had really changed. She wasn't breaking my heart, and I wasn't angry. I was . . . *disappointed.* Now I'd have to start all over with someone else.

"Jackson?"

"Yes. Yes, we can be friends. Come here." I reached out and pulled Charlotte forward into a hug. Wrapping her tightly in my arms, I felt her body relax on a big exhale.

"You give good hugs," she said, her voice muffled.

"So do you," I said, resting my cheek against hers.

She tucked her chin on top of my shoulder. "And you're welcome to hugs anytime you want, okay? You can come over and hug me all day if you need to."

I laughed, rolling my eyes at the very thought, knowing she meant the offer sincerely but also knowing it would be impossible. She had too many demands on her time to spend more than a minute or two giving me hugs in any given week.

"Same. And if you ever need anything." I pulled back, looking her in the eyes. "I mean it, if you need anything, don't hesitate to call."

"Anything?"

I released her arms. She caught my hand before I could step away.

"Anything at all?" Her tone sounded funny, determined as she peered up at me.

I nodded again. "Of course."

"What if I wanted . . ." She breathed out, gulped noisily, and then said on a rush, "What if I wanted to get laid?"

I blinked, my mouth dropping open as a puff of a laugh erupted from my chest. "Wait, I thought we just broke up?"

"We did, and we are. Believe me, I do not want to date you. But—now that we're not dating—there's no reason for you to be a gentleman all the time."

Oh my God. She was serious.

"We could meet up once a week for lunch. Your truck is nice and big." A pleading note entered her voice.

"Charlotte."

"No feelings would be involved. I promise. I just—God, I just miss it. So much."

I laughed, then sighed, then laughed again, pulling her in for another hug, doing my best not to laugh some more—not at her, never at her, but definitely at the situation. "You do not want to sleep with me."

"You're right, I don't. I hate sharing a bed. I could never sleep with Kevin when we were married. I used to leave every night, once he was snoring, and slept on the couch. I don't want to sleep with anyone. I want to have *sex*. God, Jackson, I want to have sex so bad. I want to be touched and petted by something I don't have to plug into a wall."

Now I did laugh.

She pulled away, her face grumpy, but her eyes were full of self-deprecating humor. "I'm serious. Do you know how many vibrators I have? I can't stop buying them, always hoping I'll find one that magically sprouts hands and hairy thighs. Is it weird that I miss the feel of hairy thighs?"

"I can't say as I rightfully know." I pressed my lips together, knowing it was ungentlemanly of me to keep laughing. Even so, I kept on laughing.

"I do." She made a grunting sound, and I knew she didn't take my humor the wrong way. "And the feel of a hairy chest against my—"

Enough. "I'm not having sex with you."

"Fine!" She heaved a sigh, slouching forward. "I already knew you'd say no. Mostly, I just wanted to complain to a *friend* about my lack of a sex life."

A twinge of something uncomfortable, a sense that I'd failed her in some way, settled at the base of my throat, made it ache. Despite the unease, I welded a small smile and walked her to her door. We shook hands, and she laughed, the sound blithe and good humored. She blew me a silly little kiss and walked inside, leaving me on her porch.

I waited until I heard her bolt lock, as I always did, before turning back to the street. My smile dropped, disappointment settling like a heavy stone in my chest. *I lost.*

I didn't like losing. I don't think anyone likes losing, but if life had taught me one lesson well it was the value of losing gracefully. Charlotte didn't want to make things work between us. I would not push her to reconsider. This wasn't like quitting, where there's still hope.

No. When you lose, you wish the person well and you walk away, and so that's what I did.

With each step toward my truck, I replayed her words, filtering through them to figure out where I'd messed up so bad that I'd lost Charlotte and the future I'd been hoping for with her, so that next time I took a chance on someone, I wouldn't end up as a loser.

* * *

You deserve to be crazy about someone.

Sitting in my cruiser, in a rainstorm, on the side of the road while I struggled to concentrate on paperwork, this was the part of my conversation with Charlotte that plagued me the most.

I shook my head for maybe the tenth time in the week since she'd called things off, frowning at my laptop screen while I tried to focus. What Charlotte didn't seem to realize was that being crazy about someone wasn't a good thing. It ultimately ended in a world of hurt and heartache.

Love—the kind of love my parents shared, the kind of love I wanted—required work. Charlotte wanted to skip all the work, all the hard stuff, all the foundational glue that held a couple together through thick and thin, and just hope everything worked out because of *chemistry*.

No.

Anything worth having, any relationship worth keeping, it took time, patience, and—most of all—hard work. Being crazy for someone wasn't anything but smoke. Crazy didn't hold your hand when you were sick. Crazy didn't comfort you at the end of a long day. Crazy didn't pay the bills and pitch in and ease your burden.

So, yes. She'd been right to break things off with me. We wanted two different things. She wanted crazy and easy, I wanted nothing to do with crazy *or* easy.

My phone rang, and I glanced at the screen. I didn't make a habit of accepting calls during my shift, but I always checked the number. Sometimes my father or Florence —that is, dispatch—called instead of using the radio.

Sure enough, it was her.

"What's up, Flo?"

"Jackson, we got a problem," she said, sounding grim.

That's how she always started things when she got me on the phone. On the radio, where everyone could hear, she was usually facts. But on the phone, she was opinions.

"How can I help?" *Please don't let this be another of Daisy's pie emergencies.*

"I know it's almost the end of your shift, but we've had two calls from several bank chains in and around Merryville and as far north as Townsend about a woman stopping by their ATMs and withdrawing the maximum amount of money. The sheriff had me call Mr. Leffersbee in town, and he confirmed from looking at their security footage that a woman matching the same description was also at his place, doing the same thing."

"Do we have a name on the account?"

"Let me finish. It's not an account with any of them, some national chain, not local."

"What about—"

"Jackson, just listen. I'm calling you specifically for a reason, but you need the background first. We got a match on the license plate—she's not hiding what she's doing —and the car is your sister's."

"Excuse me?"

"The woman is using Jessica's car. The blue Mustang, the one Duane Winston—"

"Yes, I know the car."

My sister's husband had given her the car when they were first dating, but she'd left it behind in Green Valley—years and years ago—when they left to travel the world. If you knew my sister, it would make sense. Anyway, they'd left the car at the Winston Brothers Auto Shop as a sort of advertisement, hoping to lure folks in to check out the other classic cars the shop refurbished and sold.

"Did you call Cletus? Was it stolen from the auto shop?"

"No. Cletus said the car is being loaned out, but he wouldn't tell us who it's being loaned out to. He suggested I call you, said you'd know what to do."

I rubbed my forehead, instantly knowing who was taking out the money from the ATMs and driving my sister's old car.

I hadn't seen Raquel since last week, but that just meant I'd been looking for her everywhere I went. A few times I'd caught sight of a random woman with long brown hair and tan skin, and my heart would seize for a moment. But it was never her. I'd wondered if she'd already left.

"Cletus told you to call me?"

"Yep. So now you understand. We got several banks here, waiting for us to make an arrest. Not sure how to tell them that it's okay, just Raquel Ezra the mega movie star making maximum withdrawals from ten banks."

I sighed. "Why not just call Sienna Diaz?"

"Not sure how that will help. Plus, her number is unlisted. You got it?"

"I mean, have Cletus call her. Then Sienna can call Raquel."

"No, won't work. Cletus says Ms. Ezra has her phone off most of the time. It's been mostly off since she arrived in town Saturday. There's no calling her."

"Then how's she navigating the back roads? She's got to be using her phone to navigate."

"I have no answer for you, just what Cletus told me. But listen, from the pattern of banks hit, it looks like Ms. Ezra is moving toward the city." The "city" meant Knoxville, and they had their own city police force, which meant the banks in Knoxville were not in county jurisdiction.

"Nothing she's doing is technically illegal, Flo."

"Yes, I know that, Deputy James. But if the pattern made it onto our radar . . ."

She had a point. Once Raquel started withdrawing money at banks in Knoxville, things might get messy for her with the city PD. At the very least, they'd stop her and question her because who goes to ten ATMs instead of walking inside to withdraw a lump sum?

An easily recognizable movie star with odd logic, that's who.

Even on a sunny day traveling with five friends, being stopped and questioned by law enforcement could be scary for most people, which I'd always considered a bit ironic—since our job was to protect and serve—but, hey, I definitely understood.

I'd seen enough panicked looks and frightened expressions to last me a lifetime. My father impressed this fact on all his people, telling us to approach every single citizen, no matter the reason, with compassion first and foremost.

"Anyway." I heard her heave a sigh. "I asked the sheriff if we should do something or just—you know."

"You know" meant a worst-case scenario of allowing Raquel to be arrested by Knoxville PD, then maybe someone would alert the press once they realized who they'd arrested, then maybe let Raquel's lawyers clear up the confusion while her publicity people dealt with the fallout. Something like that.

"The way people read only the headlines these days, I can see the papers now." Florence's dry comment was followed by a snort. "'Raquel Ezra caught on video, arrested for fraud. Still sexy as hell, even in jail!'" Florence cackled at her rhyme of *jail* and *hell*. I didn't point out that those two words only rhymed when spoken with our accent.

I pressed my lips together, trying not to laugh, despite the situation. I'd known Florence my whole life. She and her longtime girlfriend both had a little crush on

Raquel Ezra, even though they were old enough to be her mother. I'd discovered this fact one of the times I'd dragged my former fake fiancée—and good friend—to a Raquel Ezra movie on opening night.

Which was why I'd been so surprised when Florence had been cold to Raquel at the station last week. Upon consideration, I'd chalked it up to how protective everyone was of Charlotte Mitchell. Ever since Charlotte and I had started dating, every other woman in Green Valley had given me a wide berth. Charlotte was certainly beloved.

But more than that, after how her no-good husband had treated her, I worried she was pitied too.

Starting the engine, I flipped on the wipers. "What was her last known location?"

"Wait, don't you want to know what the sheriff said? How he wants to proceed?"

"You can tell me after you text me the address." I couldn't decide if I wanted to see her or not. Last night had been embarrassing on a number of levels. But mostly it had been torture, the bad kind and the good kind.

How many times over the last five and a half years had I thought about having just another five minutes with her? What exactly I thought I'd gain, I had no idea. But I'd craved it—her—anyway.

Florence chuckled. "I'll radio Monroe, ask him to cover your area."

"Thanks, Flo."

"Also, I heard about you and Charlotte."

About to pull into traffic, I paused, frowning out the wet windshield. "Excuse me?"

"Charlotte told Simmons's sister at the school, and Chris told everyone here. When did it happen?"

I hissed out a breath through my teeth, rolling my eyes to the ceiling of the car. "Y'all are a bunch of gossips."

"No." Flo sniffed, sounding affronted by the label. "We were all rooting for you two and so we're disappointed, is all. What happened?"

. . . You deserve to be crazy about someone.

"We wanted two different things. Sometimes it just doesn't work out."

"Is it true that she was the one to call things off with you or—"

"I got to go, Flo. Text me the address. Driving now. Bye." I hung up, turning the cruiser toward Knoxville and what would certainly be another tortuous experience. But at least I was getting my wish, another five minutes with Raquel Ezra.

Hell, maybe this time there'd be a miracle and I'd get a chance to kiss her goodbye.

CHAPTER 9

RAQUEL

"Save a boyfriend for a rainy day—and another, in case it doesn't rain."

— MAE WEST

𝓙 pulled into the parking lot of the next—and last—bank on my list after circling the building once. No drive-up ATM that I could see, and a line three people deep waiting to use the machine by the front door, meant I could either wait in the Mustang or in the rain.

I chose the Mustang. Obviously.

Engine off, I wiped a fat drop of water from my forehead, residual moisture from the three times I'd been forced to leave the car prior to now, glad I hadn't put any makeup on. By now I would've looked like that creepy girl from *The Ring.*

The day had been quite an adventure, taking this beautiful vintage muscle car on the twisty mountain roads, encountering only three or four stop-and-go lights, following the downloaded map on my phone.

My only source of frustration was the heavy rain. A light, mild rainfall would've been fine. But this had been a deluge, all day, heavier in the valley than in the hills. Most of the banks were in the valleys. I didn't mind how my clothes stuck to my body, the inescapable humidity, or getting wet every time I left the Mustang.

I minded the lack of visibility. I'd wanted scenery, dammit!

Beautiful summer vistas of green trees threaded with mist, blue skies kissing the horizon, a sunset painting the heavens shades of pink, purple, and orange—views I'd been promised in the Great Smoky Mountains brochure I'd discovered on a book-shelf at the carriage house earlier in the week.

I'd been given mist, cloudy skies, and no color other than gray. Oh, the humanity.

But! It was fine. Driving the car had been fun. I'd filled "her" with premium, as requested. My journey neared its end, just a few hundred away from the $5000 I planned to leave in the glove compartment tomorrow for the Winstons as a thank you, and I felt content.

FYI, $5000 all in tens and twenties looks like a crazy amount of money. It's a big pile of money. I almost felt compelled to cry myself to sleep on the big pile of money just to be able to say I had done so at one point in my life.

The person at the front of the line finished their business with the ATM and the second person, holding an umbrella, stepped up and under the awning. From where I sat, the awning appeared to have space for only one customer at a time. I didn't have an umbrella. I'd assumed all the ATMs would be drive-throughs. Waiting in the car meant I couldn't hold a spot, so I hoped no one else would show up and make the line longer.

But even if someone else did arrive and made the line longer, it wasn't a big deal. I would simply wait, enjoying my last few hours as the master of my own destiny.

My spur-of-the-moment vacation had been a success. Yes, I'd ignored everyone and everything from home, and I'd probably have a ton of catching up to do when I touched down tomorrow, but I felt so much more relaxed. Sienna had been right, I'd needed time around fun people, nice people, who had no expectations. And I'd needed privacy.

I'd texted Sasha last night and told her to send a car to LAX along with a security detail to meet me at the checkpoint past the gates, which was where the paparazzi usually lurked. She'd responded with a snarky text, which after two weeks of being Sasha-free, had really rubbed me the wrong way. I'd have to reacclimate to her personality at some point. Tomorrow, it would be back to my mansion-bunker in the hills, with all my employees.

And no friends.

I bit my lip, absentmindedly twirling a long lock of my wet hair around a finger, asking myself what it would've taken for me to stay in Green Valley for the whole summer. Sienna had offered multiple times and the answer eluded me now just as it had every time she'd asked. Maybe if she let me pay rent?

But no. *He* was here, Deputy Dreamy, living his adorable, picturesque small-town life with his adorable, statuesque small-town girlfriend. Even now, a week and a day after seeing him at the station and then unexpectedly at the restaurant, I didn't want to see him. I didn't like how I still *wanted* him. It made me feel shitty about myself. I knew he was with someone else, someone awesome, and yet I wanted.

Not that it mattered that she was awesome, he was with someone else, and that was that. I didn't want to run into them again, which—if last week had been any indication—I definitely would if I stayed with Sienna for the summer.

Whatever. I needed to get back to LA. My real life was there, even if no friends were. Green Valley, as restful and restorative and private as it had been, was not my real life, and—

A sudden knuckle rap on the passenger window had me jumping in my seat. My head hit the ceiling as a loud scream ripped from my throat.

"Raquel." A face lowered to peer in the window, the sight giving me another shock. "It's okay. You're okay," he said. "It's—it's Deputy James."

"Oh my God." I pressed my hand flat over my chest against my thundering heart, a relieved and self-conscious laugh bubbling out of me. My wits were completely scattered. "Oh my God, you scared me."

"Apologies," came his muted reply. "Do you mind if I . . ." He motioned to the door.

Wordlessly, I sprang into action, reaching to unlock the door and push it open. He held an umbrella—which he closed carefully before sliding in—and wore a wide-brimmed tan hat. And that's when I realized he was in his deputy costume.

No. Not costume, Rae. His official uniform.

I had no time for the sardonic voice in my head, I was too busy looking my fill and storing this sight of Deputy Dreamy all decked out in his law enforcement regalia . . . for reasons.

He shut the door, muffling the sound of the heavy rain, and turned toward me. His mouth was open like words were on the tip of his tongue, like he had a statement prepared. But once his eyes met mine, they seemed to soften, widen, and warm—just like they'd done at the station, and just like they'd done at the restaurant.

I'd reflected often over the last week that the way he looked at me was completely and utterly intoxicating. Partly because his eyes rarely seemed to stray from my face. Partly because it was him, my dreamy deputy.

"Hi," he said.

"Hi," I said. A tremor of nervous excitement—that I immediately felt guilty about—pulsed through my body. And it was the guilt that had me lowering my eyes from his handsome face and clearing my throat.

You are a mess, Rae. But you're not a terrible person. You're a good person. And you don't make moony eyes at someone else's boyfriend.

"What's—why are you here?" I studied the stick shift. *Reeeeaaaally* looked at it.

I heard him expel a loud breath. "I'm here for you."

My head snapped up. "What? You are?"

"Yes." His eyes moved between mine. "You see—"

"I want to apologize," I said, the words bursting out of me.

He flinched, rearing just an inch back, and frowned. "Apologize? For what?"

"For coming to the station last week and bringing you that pie. I'd promised you—if you recall, but totally fine if you don't remember—that I wouldn't bother you after that night, that night we, uh, the night we were together. I said no strings."

He stared at me, and his chest rose and fell a few times before he replied on a rasp, "I remember."

The cadence of his two-word answer paired with how he was presently looking at me made goose bumps prickle along my neck and chest. *No. Bad body. Bad involuntary reaction!*

"Anyway." I crossed my arms, hating and therefore ignoring the way my stomach twisted and coiled, because now I really felt shitty about myself. "I said I'd leave you alone, and that's what I should've done. It was inconsiderate to show up at your place of work, and I'm sorry."

"You don't need to be sorry."

"Regardless, I am."

His expression seemed to soften further, and I felt myself melting beneath his gaze. "I wish you wouldn't—"

"You have a girlfriend!" I tore my eyes from his, angry with myself and with him. Why was he here?

"Uh, I—"

"Having a former one-night stand show up at your work must've been awful. I'm sorry if I made things difficult for you or caused a scene." My words were clipped and edged with anger. I held on to my indignation with both hands, wanting to make it a wall between us.

"You . . ."

I waited for him to finish the thought. When he didn't, I peeked at him. He stared at me for a long moment, his gaze inscrutable, and then he shook his head. "You're not making things difficult for me."

"I had no idea you have a girlfriend. I would never, ever have talked to you at all if I'd known."

"Raquel." He lifted his hands. "It's okay. Please. Don't worry about it."

"It's really not." How could he not see that? Then again, he didn't know I'd gone there to proposition him. But still. "I just show up at your job and bring you pie and —who does that? Who—"

"Charlotte and I split up," he blurted, lifting his voice to speak over my deluge of guilt mongering and shame peddling.

Now I flinched. And I blinked. And my mind blanked.

"Please." He pulled off his hat, running his long fingers through the thick tuft of hair on top of his head. "Don't trouble yourself. You did nothing wrong."

"You broke up with Charlotte?" I liked Charlotte.

"Last week. And I didn't break up with her. She was the one to call it off." A small, dry smile tugged at one corner of his mouth, like his thoughts were occupied by something both funny and not funny.

"I'm—I'm sorry." I was . . . actually . . . a little sorry.

I hadn't talked to Charlotte for very long, but she seemed awesome and funny and vivacious. Seeing Jackson with her, and that he'd chosen someone so great, made me feel like I'd been right about him all along. His legend status had been more firmly cemented.

But on the other hand, how awesome could Charlotte possibly be if she'd let Deputy Dreamy go? Was she *insane*?

"It's fine, I'm fine." He waved away my concern. "It wasn't meant to be. I wish her well."

I couldn't tell if he was telling the truth about being fine and wishing her well, or if he simply had exceptionally good manners and control over his emotions. After some internal debate, I assumed it was the latter.

He must've read the doubt on my face because his earlier smile spread, his eyes crinkling with amusement. "You don't believe me."

"Sienna said you'd been together for months."

"We had." He nodded, his eyes dropping to his hat. "But we've been friends since we were kids. I saw more of Charlotte when we were just friends than when we were . . ." Deputy D—I mean, Jackson—breathed out an audible sigh, and when he glanced up his eyes were clear, free of post-breakup pain. "Anyway. Like I said, it wasn't meant to be, and it was never going to work. We want two different things."

"What do you want?" The thoughtless, invasive query burst from my mouth like a projectile.

He stared at me like my question had caught him completely off guard, like he felt caught, or put on the spot.

I rushed to correct my thoughtlessness. "You don't have to answer—"

"No, it's fine." He cleared his throat before saying softly, "I want to settle down, for good. I want someone who is ready to put the effort into a relationship in order to make it work in the long term. I want someone who is dedicated to seeing things through, no matter how difficult."

Effort. Work. Dedicated. Difficult.

My nose wrinkled. "Why do you—" I paused to consider what question I wanted to ask first, and opted for, "Why does it have to be difficult?"

His eyebrows lifted. "Pardon?"

"You make it sound like long-term relationships are akin to climbing Mount Everest."

"Aren't they?"

I honestly didn't know. I'd never settled down because I'd never been in love, not how people described it or portrayed it in books or the movies. But I wanted to think, with the right person, it wouldn't be all effort, work, dedication, and difficulty.

"Yes, there will be some work involved. But shouldn't it also be—" I moved my hands in front of me as I searched for the right word "—fun?"

"Fun?"

"Yes. Fun. I think being in love should be fun. And then wouldn't dedication also be easy? With the right person."

Jackson's eyelids lowered by half, his expression losing some of its softness, as did his voice. "Is that what it's like between you and Harrison Copeland? Fun?"

My lips parted as realization slowly dawned, and I felt more than a little idiotic. Jackson thought Harrison and I were together, because as far as the whole world was concerned, Harrison and I were engaged.

Jackson's lips twisted into a smile that didn't look very friendly. "Does dedication come easy to Harrison, do you think?"

Oh. Wow.

I knew *exactly* what Jackson meant by that, and his meanness was completely unexpected. The fact that my engagement was fake might've been a secret, but Harrison's supposed cheating wasn't. Maybe Domino was right, maybe Harrison's exploits did make me look pathetic.

Hearing this suspicion confirmed by my dreamy deputy sliced deep.

I must've made some sort of face, or maybe my silence betrayed me, but not a split second later, the deputy closed his eyes and inhaled deeply. "I'm sorry. That was rude."

"No, it's—it wasn't." I shook my head, still stunned and processing his statement, which—*wait a second*—had been rude. How dare he!

Had this conversation occurred two weeks ago, I probably would've let his comment go. But, I don't know, I felt different after my two weeks alone and with Sienna's family. They were all so darn nice to each other, and they'd been nice to me.

"Actually, yes. It was rude," I corrected. I made a promise to myself to start calling people on their rudeness from now on.

"I don't know you very well." What I could see of his expression looked grim and contrite, his attention back on his hat.

"No. You don't." I crossed my arms again, feeling oddly lost, and more hurt than I should have.

"Maybe this is wrong of me, seeing as how you've been engaged to the man for going on four years. I don't want to push, but—" He lifted his eyes to mine, they were imploring. "Raquel, you deserve so much better than someone who cheats on you."

I mashed my lips together while my brain sorted through all the pros and cons of admitting the truth to Deputy James.

Why tell him the truth? *Because he thinks you're pathetic.*

Why does it matter what he thinks? *I don't know, but it does. It matters.*

He wasn't finished. "We spent just a couple of hours together, years ago, and even I —a country nobody from nowhere—knew you were something special. And not 'cause you're famous or beautiful or talented. I suspected—I suspect—those things are the least of who you are."

"Oh yeah? Who am I then?" I said on a dull laugh so my voice wouldn't waver. He'd touched a nerve, one that left me cold. I didn't know who I was. I had *no idea* who I was. So how could he possibly know?

But he answered using his authoritative tone. "You're funny. Sweet. Generous. Clever. Smart. You're good. You're a good person." He huffed a laugh, adding under his breath so I almost didn't hear it, "You're sunshine and rainbows."

But one of his adjectives in particular stuck out like jean shorts in a costume drama. "Smart? Yeah right." I couldn't ebb the flow of bitterness. Smart wasn't a word often used to describe me—by me or others.

"Yes. Absolutely. Yes." He nodded adamantly. "Who thinks of something like Vegas Chess off the cuff? I know you made that up, right on the spot. And you're witty—which I guess is what clever and funny are when they get a chance to hang out. But it was your—your sweetness that got to me most."

He paused, frowning, looking frustrated and anxious. "You're still sweet. And I know I don't have any right to say so, but you deserve better than Harrison Copeland. *So much better.* You deserve—"

"What?" I couldn't bear to look at him.

"Everything," he said, the word a scrape of gravel and sand.

My frown turned upside down as his words gradually fell over me, warming my earlier frigidity. But also, my eyes stung. I had to sniff and firm my chin to keep the tears from falling. What was this? Was I sad? Did his words make me sad? I had no idea. I was all mixed up.

I felt his gaze on me as he spoke. "I'm not—this isn't about me, okay? I know we had that one night and only that one night. Fine. But Raquel—"

"Call me Rae," I said, blinking rapidly and wiping the back of my hand under my nose.

He snapped his mouth shut and frowned, like my request had interrupted his train of thought. "Uh, okay. Is Rae your name?"

"It is. It's—" I needed to swallow around the emotion at the base of my throat before I could continue "—it's what my friends call me."

"Rae."

I nodded quickly, peeking at him.

"Suits you." I watched his lips curve into a coaxing smile, the warmth returning to his gaze.

"Thank you," I managed, acutely breathless.

"Only name that would suit you better is Sunny."

I laughed, rolling my eyes. "Not Rainbow?"

"Good point. You are colorful."

"Well, I think your name suits you too." I laughed again, then added in a quieter tone that might've verged on shy, "I've always thought so."

We locked eyes for another moment, my earlier cold and dull unsteadiness trans-forming into something else, something hot and sharp and equally unsteady.

He doesn't have a girlfriend, Rae. He's single, Rae. You're here for another twenty-four hours, Rae.

"Well." He pulled his gaze from mine and gave his head a little shake. "I've said my piece. I am sorry if I upset you."

I noticed the beading of sweat at his temples. It was hot in here, stifling.

"You . . ." I was about to say *You didn't upset me,* but that wasn't true. He'd upset everything. I'd made peace with him being unobtainable, happy with someone else.

If possible, I wanted him more now than I had before. Parts of me ached, imagining what it would be like to watch him strip off that sexy uniform and—

Whoa. Wait.

Even though he was single, he'd *just* split from his girlfriend. He probably needed time before jumping into bed with me, or anyone.

Orrrrrr—and just think about it, no need to make any rash decisions—maybe now is the perfect time for him to jump into bed with you. You're leaving tomorrow. You could be his rebound one-night stand. No strings. Again.

He seemed to be waiting for me to finish my thought. But competing desires made it impossible for me to make the words and say the thing. And how would I even bring it up? How would I ask?

Just . . . ask.

I nibbled my bottom lip, uncertain.

It can't be that easy.

His gaze dropped to my mouth, grew dazed.

Try it. What do you have to lose?

"Rae, the reason—"

"Will you spend the night with me?"

CHAPTER 10

RAQUEL

"It's not true that I had nothing on. I had the radio on."

— MARILYN MONROE

His eyes shot to mine, wide with shock. "What did you just say?"

I balled my hands into fists, my heart racing, there was no going back now. "It's just—and I know this might change your mind about me being a good person—but I need to be honest with you. You were honest with me, and now it's my turn."

Jackson held perfectly still, like he might be afraid to move.

I reached for a lock of my hair and twisted it around my index finger. "Hollywood can be crazy. Nothing is real. What's in the papers and all the gossip magazines? Half of it—at least—is the marketing machine, publicists, agents, managers, trying to give their clients a leg up, an advantage."

"O-kaaay." His eyes narrowed and lost focus, maybe trying to figure out what the Hollywood machine had to do with us spending another night together.

"Here's the truth—" I released my hair and clasped my hands in front of me "—I'm not engaged to Harrison."

"You're not engaged."

"No. It's fake." Bracing, I fought the urge to close my eyes, but I did scrunch my face while I waited for his verdict. Would he call me crazy like Sienna had?

I tried to take a deep breath, but the air was too thick and heavy, the windows completely fogged over. God, it was hot in here. My clothes were mostly dried of rainwater but were still plastered to my body. Sweat trickled between my shoulder blades and between my breasts. I scratched at my neck, my fingers coming away damp.

My gaze snagged on his temples again, watching a drop of perspiration roll down his cheekbone and disappear in his beard. Another trailed down his neck and into the white T-shirt he wore under his uniform.

If I was hot, he must've been suffocating. And yet, despite the small outward signs he couldn't hide, he didn't seem at all bothered by it.

More seconds passed, his gaze now sharp, but a whisper of a smile tugged at his mouth. "You and Harrison Copeland aren't together? You're not engaged? Just to be clear, you were never engaged?"

"That's correct." I winced. "And I know it sounds crazy—"

"Not that crazy." Jackson chuckled, facing the fogged-up windshield and rubbing his forehead.

"It's just how things are there. So many relationships are for the purpose of publicity, to get more attention, more coverage. It was for my career, to raise my profile." Ugh. The reasoning sounded even more paltry this time.

"I get it." He nodded. "I *really* get it. You don't have to explain."

"You do?"

"I do." He glanced at me out of the corner of his eye. "Now I'm really sorry I said anything about Harrison cheating on you. You must think I'm an ass."

I grinned, so incredibly relieved, and then I laughed. "No. No, I don't. Not at all. Not even a little."

He lifted an eyebrow, and the look on his face was so disbelieving and therefore charming that I laughed harder. "I promise. I wouldn't have asked you to spend the night with me if I—if I thought you were . . . that." I swallowed the last word, the nervous flutter of excitement returning ten times ten. And this time, I didn't feel guilty.

If this conversation were measured in heavy stares, this one would've weighed a ton. His deep-set eyes—his *bedroom* eyes—heated, scorching me with their abrupt intensity and the mystery of all the thoughts they concealed. The interior of the Mustang felt downright cool in comparison.

The tension between us grew unwieldy in the prolonged silence, the humid air thick with electricity. For some reason, a quote from Pythagoras—one of my mother's favorite philosophers, and something she'd said often to me growing up—floated through my mind, *Be silent or let thy words be worth more than silence.*

I felt like I couldn't catch my breath, this silence intensified and roared, and I became acutely aware of my labored breathing.

Eventually, I couldn't stand it. I decided I would have to make my words worth more than the silence. "Jackson—"

Tearing his gaze from mine, he closed his eyes. "God, but you are temptation," he growled, his jaw tight.

His statement and voice made my lungs feel too small, my heart race, and a sharp twist of an ache in my abdomen had me pressing my legs together in anticipation.

I licked my lips, saying on a rush, "It could be like before, no strings. Once we do the deed, I'll disappear. And this time I promise I won't show up at your work with pie. I *promise.* This time I'll leave and never come back, I'll—"

Abruptly, he opened the passenger-side door, stepped out into the pouring rain, then shut the door, leaving both his umbrella and hat behind. I was suddenly and thoroughly overheated. With embarrassment.

That went well, Rae. So much for not coming across as desperate. Gold star.

I was still processing the impressiveness with which I'd crashed and burned when my door opened, revealing a stern—and very wet—Jackson James.

"Grab the umbrella, and please come with me." His tone was remote, official, and broke no argument.

It took me a moment to work out that he hadn't left me, and another to process what he'd said. I reached for the umbrella, and he stepped back so I could open it. Leaving the shelter of the car, I shut the door and turned to him.

Glaring over my head, he gestured to the building and ushered me forward. "Let's go."

He steered me to the front where there was no longer a line for the ATM. He didn't join me under the umbrella as we crossed the parking lot, but instead held himself away, the rain pelting his grim face and uniform.

I was so confused. What were we doing? Was he going to escort me to the ATM so I could finish up collecting the cash and then we'd—what? Leave? Go back to his place? My place? Or would he then drive off and leave me?

Before I could open my mouth to ask, we'd made it to the awning. And instead of moving to the ATM, he pulled me toward the double doors leading to the bank's interior lobby. "The real reason I'm here is because of your ATM withdrawals," he ground out.

"My . . ." I glanced at the cash machine to our left. "What do you mean?"

"You've visited more than ten local banks today and withdrawn the maximum at each ATM. This set off some alarm bells with the banks, and they called the station for us to investigate." He wiped his face of rain.

"Oh. I see." I didn't know how to feel about this information. That must've been what he meant when he'd said *I'm here for you* upon first sliding into the passenger seat.

"Usually, folks walk into a branch if they want to withdraw more than $300 and do it all at once. Multiple visits to ATMs in the area is unusual behavior unless the person has a stolen card."

"I didn't want to go into a bank."

"Why?"

I thought about telling him I'd wanted to give myself a tour of the area and used banks as my excuse but decided against it. Instead, I told him the other reason I hadn't withdrawn all the money at once. "I didn't want to draw attention to myself, walking into a bank and taking out thousands of dollars. Am I in trouble?"

"No. But I'm here to escort you inside so you can withdraw whatever amount you need." His tone was all business, and when he lifted his gaze he focused it over my head again, like he didn't want to look at me.

My heart sank. "You don't need to do that."

"I don't mind."

"No. I mean, I'm almost done. This is the last stop. I only need another $200."

"Oh." His attention flickered to me and then away. "Okay then." He looked a little lost, or maybe I was misreading him and projecting my sense of lostness on him.

Unsure what to say—because what else was there to say?—I turned from all-business Deputy Dreamy and stepped up to the cash machine, pressing my lips into a line as I navigated through the screens on autopilot.

You are temptation, he'd said. That meant he wanted me, right? Or he was tempted at least. But something held him back?

I wish I knew what it was that held him back from giving into temptation.

If you knew him better . . . if you stayed for the summer.

A bitter kind of amusement had me shaking my head. Here I was again, considering an extension on my time in Green Valley, Tennessee, all for a man who didn't want me enough to do something about it. I'd offered myself to him that night, so long ago. He hadn't taken me up on the offer then, and clearly he wasn't going to take me up on the offer now. So why stay?

The machine beeped at me, and the screen came into focus. I'd been lost in my thoughts and hadn't realized it had already withdrawn the money. It sat there, spit out of the feeder, waiting for me to collect it and leave.

Sighing, I grabbed the bills and stuffed them into my back pocket. And then I turned to Jackson, giving him a closed smile, and said, "All done."

His eyes were on me now, narrowed in a glare, his forehead creased with lines. "Rae. I want you."

I straightened, my lips parting. "You do?"

"Yes." He stalked over to me suddenly.

Surprised, I backed up a step as he advanced, but then I held my ground. *Don't back up! Stay right where you are. This is what you want.*

His rough palms slid against my cheeks, cupping my jaw, and he tilted my head back. "I want you, Rae. Very, very badly. You've taken up a lot of space in my thoughts for a lot of years."

Oh.

I opened my mouth to express some sentiment, probably happiness or curiosity about the location of the nearest hotel, but he wasn't finished.

"But I'm trying to be a better man. I want to be a better man, a serious man. Reliable. Consistent. Trustworthy." His tone brusque, his expression severe, I got the sense he needed me to understand this, that this was very important. But I also got the sense he was saying all this out loud to remind himself. "Someone people in this town and county take seriously. I've drawn lines in the sand, and I don't cross them. Ever. Because what is the value of a man who doesn't even keep his promises to himself?"

I swallowed thickly, my eyes darting between his.

"I don't do no-strings, not anymore. That's one of those lines. I'm all about the strings. So, no. I will not be spending the night with you, and this is goodbye."

Ugh. Crushed. I felt crushed. But I began to nod, because I respected his reasons, and so be it, but I was *crushed.*

But then he stepped closer, lowering his mouth to just a hair's breadth from mine. Gasping, I gripped his wrists.

"But there is something I want, something I've wanted from you for a long time."

"What's that?" I whispered, telling my hot and needy body not to arch and press against his despite all the instincts and reflexes and impulses demanding that I do.

He brushed his lips against mine, just the barest touch. My breath shuddered out of me.

"I want a kiss goodbye. I want to kiss you goodbye. Please."

Oh God, I wanted that. I lifted my chin, holding my breath, my lips parted in offering. Yet he hesitated, like he was waiting for permission and needed more than physical cues.

So I said, "Kiss me."

No sooner had the words left my mouth than he was on me, around me, surrounding my body with his strong arms, turning and backing me into the ATM machine. His mouth on mine, a deep, tortured groan rumbled from his chest.

OHMYGOD!!!

His *tongue.* His blessed, miraculous kraken tongue. I'd missed it. So long and perfect, stroking the inside of my mouth with masterful skill, somehow both wild and controlled, starving and satiated, the hot slide of it turning my center to liquid fire. I felt the kiss in my toes and—I swear—in the tips of my hair. I loved how tightly he held me, his hands roaming from my torso to my backside, grasping, pulling me closer, and stepping between my legs.

He lifted me, and I automatically hooked my ankles behind his back. Jackson rolled his hips into the apex of my thighs, and I gasped. *So good.* Panicked he'd use the brief separation to end the kiss, my fingers grabbed the front of his uniform for purchase as I returned to refasten our lips. We fit perfectly, and this felt so good, and hot, and we were both so wet, and hot. And I never, *ever* wanted it to end.

But it will end.

He softened the kiss and, dammit, I whimpered. Unwilling to let him go, I twisted my fingers into his shirt, anchoring myself. And still he softened the kiss, retreating, his movements and strokes becoming languid, drugging, making me dizzy and breathless until his lips were just a tease. A soft, barely-there touch once more.

I could've cried, except I needed to catch my breath first.

He pulled away, his gaze on mine, and if I didn't believe him before, I believed him now. He *wanted* me. Badly.

"I need a minute." Jackson closed his eyes.

"Me too." The crown of my head fell back against the alcove of the ATM, and I witnessed him struggle, his jaw tense, his breath sawing in and out.

I believed him about his reasoning for not spending the night with me. He wanted something real, not temporary. What I wanted was similar, something real with someone real. I understood, and I couldn't fault him, but couldn't he make just one tiny exception?

For me?

Oh please oh please oh please.

His eyes opened to slits, but they affixed to the ATM behind me as he stepped back, letting me go completely. My feet touched the ground. On unsteady legs, I cleared my throat and pushed away from the ATM alcove. Slowly, still breathing hard, Jackson paced to where I'd left the umbrella open on the ground by the double doors.

He picked it up, paused, his shoulders rising and falling, and then he brought it to me. "Here. Please keep it."

I nodded, not about to turn the offer down. Maybe I was being silly and sentimental, or just strange, but I wasn't going to turn down any part of himself he offered, even if it was just an umbrella. I'd keep this umbrella forever.

"Thank you," I said, surprised to discover it was still raining, maybe even harder than before. As soon as he'd charged toward me, everything else had disappeared. But now the roar of the storm filled my ears, a crack then a flash of lightning creating a sudden and brief strobe effect.

"I'll need my hat," he said gruffly, glancing over at the Mustang and frowning. "Do you mind if I walk you to your car?"

"Not at all," I said, wondering at him. He was so incredibly polite, all the time. What would it take to make the good deputy forget his manners?

Debating this, I lifted the umbrella such that he could fit under it and we could walk together.

He shook his head. "No, thank you. No need. Please." He gestured toward the car, careful not to touch me.

I nodded, licking my lips as soon as I turned and stepped off the curb. How long would I taste him there? My chin wobbled because this felt so wrong. Just like that night, when I'd left him asleep in the bed, that had felt wrong for days and days after.

But what was the answer? Stay in Green Valley like Sienna and see if things worked out with my dreamy deputy? Move here and give up on my life in LA? Sienna was the exception to every rule. She'd maintained her success, her status.

We made it to the Mustang, and I stood at the driver's side as Jackson walked around to the passenger door. He opened it. I watched as he retrieved his hat, and I reflected on how much different my path had been from Sienna's. I hadn't written screenplays for my movies. I hadn't won an Oscar. I'd lost out on roles in the last year because I was now twenty-eight instead of twenty-one; and I'd lost the only role I'd been excited about in years to a more serious, acclaimed, *respected* actress; and I continued to be typecast.

If I left LA, I'd probably fall out of the A-list in no time. My career would suffer . . . *but would that be so bad?*

I shook my head, not liking that I was actually considering this to be with a *man*. Even if things did somehow miraculously work out with Jackson and me, what next? Sienna's husband was a stay-at-home dad with a big family living locally. He gave up his own career to support hers, raised their kids, flew to her filming locations, followed her around the world just so they could be together.

How many men would do that for their wives? My dad wouldn't, and hadn't. He'd wanted to marry my mother, but he'd also wanted her to drop out of her PhD program and support his career.

"How much longer are you in town?"

I blinked, finding Jackson had walked around to the driver's side and currently stood directly in front of me, but not under the umbrella. He squinted against the rain, his eyes on me.

I took a deep, bracing breath. "Until tomorrow."

"Of course." He chuckled, the sound without humor. "Of course you are."

"Jackson—"

"No. It's okay." He nodded, taking a step back. "It's for the best."

I caught his arm before he was too far away, gripping his wet sleeve and pulling him under the umbrella. "Why?" I asked, searching his face. "Why is it for the best?" I didn't feel like it was for the best. How could he kiss me like that and then say, *It's for the best*?

"Because." He wiped off his face and then placed his hat on his head, not that it did any good. He and his hat were completely soaked.

"Because why?" I pushed. I couldn't be the only one who was having crazy thoughts, could I? Would he ever consider something real between us? Something that lasted longer than one night?

"Because it's impossible," he said, his voice deep with calm resignation, which also echoed in his gaze. He lifted his hand to my face, his thumb whispering against my cheekbone, slowly trailing down to my bottom lip and dipping just the tip inside my mouth, his eyes following the progress as though fascinated and completely transfixed.

I wanted to speak, offer to stay, but instead I caught his thumb with my teeth and gave it a little bite.

His grin dawned softly, those bedroom eyes returning to mine and twinkling, full of wistfulness and longing. Or maybe that was me.

Jackson's parting words were nearly lost in the sound of thunder and rain as he backed away. "It isn't meant to be, Rae." He smiled wider, adding, "But it sure was fun."

CHAPTER 11

RAQUEL

"I was in Asia and people asked me about being considered sex symbol. I don't know if that's good or not, because where I come from, sex isn't something you're allowed to talk about."

— BAI LING

a sound I couldn't fully incorporate into my sex dream (about Jackson) woke me up. Someone was knocking on the front door.

No. Wait.

Someone was pounding on the front door. Groaning, because the dream had just been getting to the good part, I rubbed my eyes and squinted at the clock on the night-stand. 6:17 AM. Other than the one time I'd been invited over for family dinner, no one had knocked on the door to the carriage house.

"I'm coming!" I called, searching the room for the bathrobe Sienna had loaned me. It wasn't dark, the sun had risen already, but since today would be my last in Green Valley, I'd planned to sleep in. There would be no sleeping in once I returned to LA. My trainer typically had me up at 5:30 AM every morning for my first workout.

I'd continued working out here, just at less sadistic times of the day.

"Rae! It's Sienna. I'm so, so sorry to wake you up so early. But this is important!" I heard her shout, spurring me to move faster.

"Is everything okay?" Forgetting the bathrobe, I jogged to the door and swung it open wide, finding Sienna fully dressed, a cup of coffee in one hand and her phone in the other.

She lifted up the cup of coffee. "This is for you."

"Uh, okay. Thank you." I accepted the mug.

"You might want to take a drink before I show you my phone."

"Why? What's wrong with your phone?"

Her expression was pained. "Just drink. Please."

"Did something happen?"

She put her fingers on the bottom of the mug I held and encouraged me to lift it to my lips. Huffing, I complied, prepared to take just a sip. But the coffee wasn't too hot and tasted wonderful, so I drank a gulp instead.

"Happy now?"

"No. Because now I have to show you this." Sienna stepped inside and next to me, holding the screen of her phone up so we could both see it, and pressed the play button over a paused video.

And. I. Gasped.

"Oh my Gooooood!" I bent closer, gripping her hand holding the phone. "How—where—how—"

"ATM machines have video cameras, Rae. It's everywhere, and I do mean *everywhere*. It was posted last night on EMZ. Even the big papers' gossip sections picked it up."

I watched in a mixture of horror and fascination as the video footage of Jackson's excessively thorough goodbye kiss played on the screen. I couldn't believe what I was seeing.

Also, and I know this helps nothing, Rae, but you two look really hot together.

Ugh. I just couldn't with my inner dialogue right now.

"I'm so sorry, but I had to wake you up." She handed the phone over to me and stepped fully inside, closing the door behind her. "This is bad."

Tearing my eyes away from the video, I gaped at her. "Bad?"

"Yes. Bad."

I looked at the screen again. The video had no sound, but I knew this was the part of the kiss where I'd whimpered because he'd started to pull away. "It's not a great copy, I admit. The video quality could be better, but—"

"Not the video quality, Rae! I'm talking about Jackson." She paced away.

"What about Jackson?" My initial shock upon seeing the video had begun to dissipate, but at her words I tensed again. "This is bad for Jackson?"

"Yes. It's clearly him in the video. He's in his *uniform*."

Oh shit. Sienna was right. He'd been there in an official capacity. I'm sure kissing the hell out of a civilian wasn't on his list of primary duties.

She lifted her hand toward the phone. "And he just broke up with Charlotte."

"She broke up with him."

"Whatever! It doesn't matter. Because now it looks like they broke up because of you. People here are going to talk. This could be bad for him. Very bad."

I took another gulp of my coffee, staring at her, my mind spinning. *What can I do?* "Can we get the video down? Before it—"

"No. Like I said, it's already everywhere. That's not an option." Sienna grimaced. "I know it wasn't your intention, but this just made his life more difficult."

"I didn't do this on purpose! I'd given up on asking Jackson if we could be photographed together. I've given up on the whole stupid plan and fake engagement with Harrison." I hadn't explicitly made the decision about Harrison until just now, but it felt right. I was calling off the fake relationship. And I wasn't going to quit acting, I was just going to quit pretending. My time in Green Valley, the few stolen moments I'd had with Jackson James, they'd been so essential.

Now that I'd had a taste of something real with someone real, I wasn't willing to fake it anymore.

"Sienna, I was going to leave today, talk to Domino tomorrow and tell him I want out of the arrangement. I didn't even think about the camera at the ATM. And Jackson kissed me. I didn't know he was going to kiss me until it happened."

"I know. I know you wouldn't do this to Jackson on purpose, just like I know *now* that he never would have agreed to it. Jethro told me this morning that Jackson has been trying to clean up his image for the last few years, and he plans to run for sheriff when his dad retires. I do wish Jethro had told me before now, but this—" she gestured to the phone "—could derail all of that."

My stomach hurt. The last thing I wanted was Jackson hurt. Even if everything between us ended forever, he mattered to me. Yes, I know that made me a little crazy, I barely know him, we'd spent less than twelve hours in each other's company total, but still. He'd helped me see that I wasn't willing to settle for pretending anymore. He mattered.

And even if he hadn't mattered, I didn't want to hurt anyone.

"And it's not just Jackson I'm worried about. Rae, his father and mother and sister Jessica—who, as I've mentioned, is also my sister-in-law—will be upset, they're all very close. I was just talking to Jess last night and she was so excited for her brother and his campaign."

"Campaign?"

"Jackson's dad plans to retire in three years. Maybe it'll all blow over by then?"

Crap crap crap crap.

"Sienna." I placed her phone and my coffee on the console table near the door and rushed over to her, grabbing her hand. "What can I do? What can I do to help? There has to be something. Please."

She squeezed my hand. "Jethro has an idea."

"Jethro? I thought Jethro didn't get along with Jackson?"

"He doesn't. Kinda. They—it's weird. Men are weird and complicated. He wants to help, though. But first we need to call my sister."

"Marta?" Marta had been Sienna's manager since she'd started in the business and was a PR genius. "You think she can help?"

"I do. I want to run his idea by her. This is small-town politics we're dealing with. Jethro is better at this stuff than me. But I feel like Marta will help us fine-tune the plan."

"Okay. Okay. Sounds good," I said, panicked. *Calm down, Rae. Focus on helping Jackson. There's a plan.*

"Hey." She gave me a sympathetic smile. "Get dressed and come up to the house in about an hour. We'll all call Marta together."

"Right." I shoved my fingers into my hair before I remembered how knotty it would be.

"And Rae."

"Yes?" I spun around to face her.

"Cancel your flight and have Sasha come out with some clothes and things. You'll need to be in Green Valley for a while longer. At least a month."

* * *

I quickly showered and dressed, braiding my hair in two long ropes instead of taking the time to blow-dry the thick mass straight. Then I powered on my phone, intent on calling Sasha, but paused when I caught sight of the time. LA was three hours behind Tennessee, 6:40 AM here was 3:40 AM there. She'd definitely be asleep.

But maybe Domino isn't?

I received calls and texts from my manager at random odd hours, day or night, weekend, holiday, vacation, it didn't matter. It was like he had no concept of time. On a hunch, I texted him:

Raquel: I know I was supposed to come back today, but I have to stay for a month longer. There's a video that Sienna said is everywhere already. It is me in the video, and it's not fake, but don't provide any comment to the press. Call me when you get this, I'll have my phone on.

I always used proper grammar when texting, a habit my mother—a tenured classics professor at a super exclusive private college—had hammered into me when I'd received my first phone.

"If you use *U* instead of *you*, or *R* instead of *are*, then you'll only be allowed to text in Latin. And no emojis. Ever. Those aren't language," she'd said. I knew not to disobey. My mother never bluffed, and she always threatened me with Latin.

Not three seconds later, he texted me back.

Domino: I can call you now. I have news. Give me a minute to find someplace quiet.

Pacing into the kitchen, I set the phone down on the counter and crossed to the coffee maker. Before I had a chance to do much of anything, my phone rang. I didn't even glance at the screen.

"Domino?" I heard club music playing in the background.

"Raquel."

"What are you doing up so early?" *Is he at the gym?*

"I haven't gone to sleep yet. Obviously."

Yes, obviously. "Listen, the text message said it all, and I don't have a lot of time to talk right now, but I wanted to let you know what's going on. I won't be back for a month." This was true, but it was also a lie. I had more than a half hour to talk. But in Domino's world, a half hour always turned into two hours.

"Fine. I can work with that." I heard a door close, and the club music faded. "I've been giving you your space, but I have news, and you're going to be happy. First, totally great if you want to stay at the Pepperidge Farm a little longer. And I've seen the video. I think it's fabulous. A sheriff? Hot." He over pronounced the *t* at the end of hot.

I tried to frown. I failed. And so I made sure my voice sounded extra grumpy. "He's a deputy sheriff, not a sheriff. What is this news you want to tell me? The clock is ticking."

"Okay then. I see you've recovered your spark. Good to know. Now, Gavin and his people called late last night, when the ATM footage broke of you with not-the-sheriff."

What? Gavin Sidorov was the director, producer, and writer of *Midnight Lady*, the film I'd been replaced on by my ex-BFF, the role I'd been excited about, the reason I'd escaped to Green Valley in a fit of temper and despair.

"Why would they call you?"

"They want to replace Lina with you."

"What?" I had to shake my head, because . . . *what?* "First of all, why aren't they calling John?" My agent handled all contract negotiations for film and worked in tandem with Domino. Whereas Domino was my manager and publicist. He managed my career from a holistic perspective—appearances, interviews, product sponsorship, guest spots, etc.—not just film.

Domino hesitated, making a weird stalling sound, and then finally admitted, "They tried calling him, but he wouldn't take their calls. You know he didn't want you in that role to begin with. He doesn't want you playing a prostitute or location filming in Cuba. There's still controversary about filming in Cuba at all."

I growled, *so frustrating.*

"He's only looking out for you," Domino coaxed, ever the politician.

"He's only looking out for himself." Gripping my forehead, I glared at the kitchen counter, debating my options. *No, I only have one option.* If I couldn't trust my agent, then he wasn't going to be on my team.

"Hey. I don't want to get in the middle of this." Domino sounded anxious. "I've always got your back, but I have a good relationship with your agent."

"Fine. I'll talk to him." Meaning, I'd have to think about firing him.

"And there's something else."

"What?"

"Harrison. Have you talked to him?"

"No. Not recently." It felt like a confession. Harrison and I usually touched base every few days. These past few weeks, even before staying with Sienna, I'd been avoiding him along with everyone else.

"Did you know he's been lobbying for you to get the role back? He offered to attach himself to Gavin's next project if they 'corrected their grievous error.' That's what Gavin said."

"No. I had no idea."

That sweet, stupid, high-handed man. He drove me crazy, mostly because I had no idea if Harrison was actually trying to be helpful or if he was somehow using me as

119

leverage to get something he wanted. Being on my own with my own thoughts made me realize that I couldn't trust Harrison either.

I straightened from where I'd been leaning against the counter. "You know what though? Forget it. I don't want the role, not if they're giving it to me because of Harrison."

"Gavin wants you back because he believes deeply in his soul's soul that you're the right person for the role *and* he wants to replace Ralph with Harrison. Gavin got more funding, and so now he's rethinking the project. He thinks you as the Italian prostitute and Harrison as the military traitor would be magic. The parts are completely out of your wheelhouses, anti-typecasting, and now he's obsessed."

I frowned at the ceiling of the kitchen. "Domino—"

"I'm not finished. And this might explain why Gavin felt like he could call me. His new backers also love the idea, they're also obsessed. You two haven't done a film together since *Tabitha Tomorrow*. And—and don't freak out—they'd like you and Harrison to get married during production."

"What?!" Here I was, shouting in Sienna's carriage house kitchen early in the morning. This was *insane*.

"They want the publicity for the movie. Their investment is a big one, and they think that if you and Harrison secretly-not-so-secretly tie the knot during filming, everyone will come out to see you two on the screen."

"No. Nope. This is crazy. I don't want to do this."

"Don't say no. Think about it. Talk to your boy."

I shook my head even though Domino couldn't see me. "I don't need to talk to Harrison, and he's not my boy." I loved Harrison, but I could now see that even our friendship—such as it existed—hadn't been healthy for me. "The answer is no."

"Think about it."

I laughed despite myself. "Domino, you are . . . *assillante*." I said this last part under my breath. I must've been really mad even though the tenor of my voice was calm; I'd resorted to one of my mother's Italian insults. "The answer is still no."

I took a moment and thanked my lucky stars that I'd taken this trip. If this idea had been proposed two weeks ago, I likely would've agreed to it since I'd wanted that role so much. I still desperately wanted the part, but not enough to continue pretending with Harrison. I could see clearly now, I'd started to disappear—the real me—under the weight of other people's expectations and demands.

"Just think about it."

"I'm hanging up now."

"Wait! Do you want the role? Can I call Gavin back?"

I jabbed a finger in the air. "I don't care if Harrison takes the role or not, we are not getting married, do you understand? And I don't want to start filming for another month." Goodness. It was amazing what time away from LA and being Raquel Ezra had done for my assertiveness. I hadn't felt this focused on what I wanted in ages.

"It'll be September at the earliest. Maybe even October. Production is shut down, he pissed off the union."

"Then you know I can't take the part. I have that romantic comedy." I hadn't technically signed the contract yet, but now that I was feeling more focused, I decided I would sign it. My panicked thoughts about retiring from acting felt so distant and faraway.

"Funny you should mention that. I gave them a heads-up that they might need to film around you until November. And they're both studio projects, so you'd be on the same lot if they *really* needed you for a scene."

"I thought Gavin's film was on location in Cuba?"

"It was. But like I said, he pissed everyone off."

I closed my eyes, crossing an arm over my stomach, feeling overwhelmed. "Dom, this is a lot. I'll need to see the script again before I'll agree to anything. And I want to see production notes on the set changes."

"I'll have Gavin's people send you all the details ASAP, and also send the new contract directly over to legal for their review, you just have to promise that you won't tell your agent I was the one who did it. I don't want him thinking I'm working around him with his clients."

"That's exactly what you're doing."

"Yes, you sexy Cleveland flower, but I'm only working around him because it's what's best for you. If he'd picked up Gavin's call—because he *knows* how much that part meant to you—then I wouldn't have to work around him."

"Fine. Send it to legal. If they think it looks good, I'll consider the role—but *no wedding.*" My agent had me convinced for years that I couldn't negotiate my own contracts, but I wasn't so sure anymore.

The thought made me feel like a traitor.

"And thank you for looking out for me," I added. Even though Domino was pushy, he went around my agent because he knew this role had been important to me.

"You are so welcome. You know I always have your back. Now have fun in hillbilly town."

"It's not like that. It's really nice here."

"Oh no. Not you too. Please tell me you're not going to marry a park ranger and move to Appalachia for good."

I rolled my eyes. "If I did, you'd be the first to know."

"What is in the water there? That all these gorgeous women can't seem to leave once they've been mounted by a Mountie."

"Wrong country. Mounties are in Canada." I glanced at the clock above the stove, just after 7:00 AM. I still had time before I needed to be at Sienna's. "Wait, Domino."

"Yes?"

"What time are you going to sleep?"

"Maybe six."

"Could you call Sasha before you do? Ask her to fly out here with—uh—Dave and Miguel?" Dave and Miguel were my favorite bodyguards. They made me laugh and never voiced opinions about what I wore or what I did unless they were teasing (the good kind of teasing).

Also, Dave used to be Sienna's guard years and years ago. He knew the area better than anyone else on my team because he'd been here before. Yes, Dave and Miguel made the most sense as my traveling security team for now. "Tell her to bring clothes and things for me to stay another month."

Being out here for another month without security would be just plain dumb. Two weeks, mostly anonymous, staying on Sienna's property was one thing. But word of my location would be all over social media by now. All the crazies would know I was in Green Valley, and only two of my restraining order nuts were currently in jail.

"Yes. Sure. No problem. I'll call Sasha."

"But only after six your time. Don't wake her up. And have Dave and Miguel pack for a stay of at least a month. Please."

"You got it, boss. By the way," I heard the smile in his voice, "you sound great. Clearheaded, focused. Like a badass. Whatever is in that Mountie water must be agreeing with you."

I ended the call rolling my eyes at his silliness, but also grinning, and I marveled at the change in me. I couldn't remember the last time I'd ended an industry call with a smile on my face. Perhaps the water in Green Valley was magical.

Or maybe I was smiling because I had a second chance at that role I'd wanted so badly, assuming Gavin hadn't substantively changed my character. My heart buoyed, and I felt like if I didn't tell someone the good news, I might burst.

You should call Jackson!

The odd thought flashed through my mind, completely unbidden, and I dismissed it immediately. He wasn't my . . . well, he wasn't my anything. An acquaintance I *really* liked, a man I happened to admire and was breathlessly attracted to, but not the first person I should be thinking about when I had good news to share.

And, you know, he probably wasn't in any mood to speak to me about anything at present.

Picking up my phone again, I called my mom. We didn't talk often or with any regularity, just once every other a month or so. She often traveled for speaking engagements. Syncing our schedules had become difficult once my acting career had taken off.

The phone rang and rang, and I bit the inside of my lip. I hoped she wasn't in Hawaii or Alaska or someplace like that, where the time difference meant it would be the middle of the night. Second-guessing myself, I was just about to hang up when she finally answered.

"Raquel! What a lovely surprise. Hello!"

"Hi, Mom." I smiled. A surge of homesickness sent a stinging rush of moisture to my eyes, and I laughed at myself.

"What's so funny?"

"Nothing. It's just so good to hear your voice."

"You too. What's up? Why are you calling your mother? Not that I'm complaining." The sound of people speaking in a different language came through the line. It was muffled and distant, and I couldn't quite place it.

"Where are you?"

"I'm in Italy."

"What?" This was a surprise.

"For work. We're in Rome."

"Oh. Will you see—"

"It's a work trip. They don't know I'm here."

"They" referred to her parents, my grandparents. I'd met them only a handful of times as they lived in a north Italian village that made Green Valley look like a metropolis. We'd visited for the last time when I was twelve and things had been *tense.* Since I didn't speak Italian, I had to rely on my knowledge of Latin—which I'd never spoken, only read—to follow the heated conversations.

"Oh. Okay." I didn't want to talk about her parents with her. The only subject that made her angrier was my father. "Are you having a good time?"

"Yes. Very. But I want to hear about you. You sound great!"

"Thank you. I feel great." I floated over to the couch and sat. "I took a vacation."

"How wonderful! Good for you! You work too hard. No wonder you sound so relaxed. Did that Sasha come with you?"

"No. Actually, no one did."

"Raquel, what about security?" A frightened edge entered her voice. "After that man last year—"

"It's fine. For the last two weeks, I was on my own. I'm staying with a friend, Sienna Diaz. I don't know if you've seen any of her movies." My mother had no interest in film or television, preferring to debate the writings of people who'd been dead for three thousand years.

When I talked about modern remakes of the classics, she always assumed I meant the writings of Empedocles and Plotinus. This also meant she remained one of the three people on the planet who didn't recognize Sienna Diaz by name.

"I'm sorry. I don't know who that is. But you're staying with your actress friend and it's safe? She has guards too?"

"She basically lives in this huge compound," I hedged, quickly adding, "And my security team is flying out tomorrow. Dave and Miguel will be staying with me for the next month while I'm here."

"Where are you?"

"In Tennessee, but that's not why I'm calling. I have good news." I shifted forward on the couch until I sat on the edge of my seat, resting my elbow on my knee.

"Oh! I love your good news. Tell me."

"You know that film part I told you about? The period piece about the prostitute?"

"Yes. You were very excited about the part. How is it going? Did filming start?" My mother sounded eager for information.

When I'd originally told her about the role, I'd been worried she would hate me playing a prostitute. She hadn't. She'd loved the idea. She loved that I'd be playing a role about a woman who lived life on her own terms and exploited men's desires to get what she wanted.

"Well, at the end of May, they called me and told me I'd been replaced by Lina."

"What? Lina?" She sounded confused.

"You know, my friend from—"

"WHAT?!" she roared, and then started speaking in Italian. Rapid, angry Italian. I caught a few curse words and insults—*cretino, coglione, che testa di cazzo*—and I had to press my lips together to keep from laughing. My mother might've felt constricted by her upbringing, but when she was angry, she fully embraced her roots.

"Wait, wait. There's good news."

"There is? Please tell me you've cut that Lina out of your life. I never liked her. She . . . I feel she gives you *Il Malocchio*. She's jealous. I hope her family is cursed with brittle teeth." She muttered another insult or two.

Her vengefulness warmed my heart. *I love my mom.*

"My news is that they dropped her, and the director wants me back in the role. They started preproduction, but it wasn't working out and he realized his mistake. So now the part is mine if I want it."

She didn't respond right away. I could almost hear her thinking. "Raquel." She sounded hesitant. "You know you are wonderful, don't you? You know you are a very good actress."

"Thank you." My mother rarely praised me for anything, least of all my job. But I knew where she was going with this, so I let her talk because I felt she needed to.

"Why do you let this man treat you this way? If he dropped you so easily before, what keeps him from doing it again?"

"We're drawing up a new contract. It'll be ironclad this time. I'm using just my lawyer. My agent won't be part of the negotiations."

"I remember you said that man, your agent, he didn't want you to take the role."

"He . . . it's complicated. I don't think he liked the idea of me playing a prostitute. He doesn't want to jeopardize my marketability. He likes the parts I'm usually offered and likes that they make him money, and so he doesn't want me acting in this movie."

"But he works for you. And you want the part."

"Exactly."

"Ironic then, that he doesn't want you to play a prostitute, because that's how he's treating you."

I sucked in a breath, surprised by her retort. But in all honesty, I shouldn't have been. I should've been used to it.

My mother was brilliant, she had a wickedly sharp mind and a tongue to match. We'd settled into a pretty good relationship, but she had *no time* for entitled, bossy men— or men she perceived as being bossy. Once, a visiting adjunct professor interjected while she'd been giving a lecture and tried to explain the significance of Socrates on Alexander the Great's military campaigns. To her. In front of her class.

He was lucky he'd left the room with his balls intact; his pride had not fared as well.

I heard her release a loud sigh. "I didn't mean—"

"I know." I rubbed my forehead, trying to push past the initial sting of her words for the truth behind them.

"Sorry. I just—I don't like that he works for you, and he's telling *you* what to do. He is your subordinate. He treats you like you are there for his purpose, to make him money. This is not the right way. As Plato said, 'The heaviest penalty for declining to rule is to be ruled by someone inferior to yourself.' You are so good at managing people, I am surprised you would put up with this. He is there for your purpose, to make you money. You should fire him, find someone who can take orders."

Standing, I paced back to the kitchen. "It's really okay. I understand what you meant." I didn't add that I'd had similar thoughts, just not quite as cutthroat. "It's not a done deal yet. They've updated the script, and I want to see it before I sign or agree. But, anyway, I'm still really excited about the part."

"If it makes you happy, it makes me happy." She sounded far from convincing.

"It does make me happy. I'm excited."

"When does filming start? Will you have to be on location, or will you be in LA?"

"It'll mostly be shot in LA, but I might have to go to Cuba to do some pickups, and—"

"Wait. Wait, wait, wait. Cuba?"

"Yes. They moved the majority of filming to—"

"Raquel! Is this—are you playing a Cuban?"

Oh. Shit. My stomach lurched as I quickly pieced together what she must be thinking. "No, no," I rushed to correct her misassumption. "I told you. The character is Italian."

"Is this about your father?" she whispered harshly, sounding overheated and upset. "Is this about *him?*"

"What? No!"

"Is that why you want this part? Because I will tell you the truth, no matter what you do, no matter if you are the perfect daughter, embrace his values, he will never want to know you."

"Mom." I rubbed the center of my chest, her words like tiny knives being shoved into my heart. "I know. And this isn't about Dad."

"You should not call him *Dad*. He is a stranger, he is not a part of who you are, and that was *his choice*. Think of Plato. Think of the Republic. The family serves no purpose but to confuse and distract from our goals, to pull us in directions away from our purpose. *That* is who your father is. A destructive distraction so blinded by his traditional views on the world and himself as the center of it that he ruins everything he touches. If you think going to Cuba, trying to be Cuban, will make him want to—"

"Mom! Listen to yourself. It's just a movie role. That's it." I tried to swallow but couldn't, because her words had shaken something loose inside me, and I wasn't finished though I didn't know what I was about to say. "And I hate to break it to you, but I *am* Cuban. I'm just as much Cuban as I am Italian. And I'm an American. And I'm an Ohioan. If I want to go to Cuba and learn all about that side of myself, then I will. And if I want to go to Miami and meet my half-siblings, then I will."

"You will regret it. Those people aren't your family, and they are all the same. He rejected you. *They* rejected you. I will never forgive him, and you shouldn't either. They are bad."

"No. NO! Grandma and grandpa weren't bad. They loved me. And I loved them."

She was quiet, but I heard her release another heavy sigh.

"And who do you think my father is? Was he voted by all Cubans as the most quintessential Cuban person in all the world? Because, if he was, I missed the election. Not that I could've voted, because I don't know what it means to *be* Cuban! I grew up near Cleveland. I know more German than Spanish."

More silence, but I wasn't finished ranting. "Dad is a *person*, Mom. One person. He is not representative of an entire people. So, yeah, maybe I do want to know that side of myself. Maybe I feel so lost because half of who I am was never revealed to me. Maybe while I'm in Cuba, I will look up that side of *my* family."

I sensed her withdraw with each word out of my mouth, but I hadn't been able to stop. And by the time I'd finished, I felt exhausted. But also surprised by my words. I didn't know I'd felt this way.

Do I feel this way?

"You do what you want. You are a grown woman, not a child." She made a sniffing sound, or something like it, but her voice was cool as granite. "I have to go. I am working and have to get back to work."

I nodded, saying nothing, my eyes flooding with tears. Whenever I did something that hurt her, she pulled away like this, reminding me I was responsible for myself. It made me feel so alone.

"Goodbye, Raquel. I . . ."

I waited. Rolling my lips between my teeth, I looked up at the ceiling. It blurred as I waited for her to tell me she loved me. Sometimes she would, but not always.

"Goodbye," she said.

And then she hung up.

CHAPTER 12

JACKSON

"If you're going to do something wrong, do it big, because the punishment is the same either way."

— JAYNE MANSFIELD

For maybe the tenth time so far this morning, I caught myself daydreaming about my kiss with Rae. I had no regrets about turning down her offer. A one-night stand, even with the woman of my figurative and literal dreams, wasn't something I wanted for myself anymore. I wanted permanent, not temporary. I wanted real, not fantasy.

That said, I had no regrets about the kiss either. I knew I'd come crashing down from this high at some point, but that point wasn't now. Hopefully, the high would last a good, long while.

It'll have to. You're never going to see her again. At least, not in person.

I frowned at the thought, immediately pushing it aside, and taking another sip from my thermos of coffee. It wasn't a thermos brand container, but some hoity-toity version that looked sleek and kept my coffee hot for hours. My sister Jessica had sent it for my birthday along with two bags of coffee from Italy. She, her husband Duane, and my nephew Liam were now living there full-time, until Jess got the travel bug again and they went somewhere else.

She was an odd one, my baby sister. But I liked the cup she'd sent. *You should get one for Rae.*

Now that odd thought had me frowning again, and I decided to refocus my thoughts elsewhere. Like on work.

My eyes lifted to the horizon, expecting to find an empty expanse of road beyond the cruiser's hood, but that's not what I saw. Man, I really must've been distracted if I'd failed to notice Cletus Winston pull up in his Geo in front of me. Mind, he didn't park directly in front of my car, but rather some fifty or so feet further down.

Unbuckling my seatbelt, I brought my fancy coffee container with me as I left the car and walked toward him. "Hey. What are you doing here?"

"I came to see you, my friendly, local public servant." He also carried a coffee container, a pink and purple Hello Kitty thermos. Within, I knew he'd doctored his coffee with blackstrap molasses and apple cider vinegar. Since we'd become friendly, he'd made me taste it every so often, swearing that one of these days I'd come around to his coffee recipe.

He was wrong. It was disgusting.

"How did you know where to find me?"

"This is your area, isn't it?" He motioned to the empty road.

"Yes. For today."

"Well then, you just answered your own question."

"Cletus." I halted, not wanting to be out of earshot of the radio. "My coverage area stretches for miles. How did you know precisely where I'd be?"

He walked past me toward my cruiser. "You might as well ask me if I know where JT MacIntyre's stolen gold coins are."

"Wait. Do you?" I followed him.

"That's a silly question."

"I'm suddenly thinking it's not so silly."

"No. It's definitely silly. Silly to ask, I mean. But maybe not silly in general. However, I'm not here to debate the silly quotient of questions with you. I'm here to deliver a warning and an invitation, but not in that order." He stopped at the hood and leaned back against it—half sitting, half standing.

"An invitation?" I didn't move to recline next to him, but instead stopped four or so feet away.

"Yep. To the jam session tonight."

"Oh. Yeah. I was planning to go." I sipped my coffee.

"I'd like your word, if you please." He lifted his thermos toward me. "That's a nice coffee carafe. Where'd you get it?"

"Jess sent it to me for my birthday. You want my word?"

"I'd like you to promise me that you will attend tonight's music-making merriment, come what may." He scratched his beard, which was always kept bushy and full. "My birthday isn't until December. Do you think she'd send me one of those for Tracky Dack Day?"

"I just said I was going to the jam session. And what is Tracky Dack Day?"

"It's an Australian holiday for pants. And now I'd like you to promise that you're coming to the jam session."

Confused—*a holiday for pants?*—I scrunched my face and shook my head. Cletus was always having two conversations at once. "Fine. I promise. I'll go."

"Excellent. Now to the warning." Cletus drew in a deep breath, pushed away from the hood of my cruiser, paced to me, and placed his hand on my shoulder. Looking me square in the eye, he said, "Jackson James, everyone in town hates your guts."

I reared back. "Excuse me?"

"Wait—" He let go of my shoulder and pulled out his phone. "I brought visual aids."

I stared at him, waiting while he unlocked his phone, navigated to something he clearly wanted me to see, and then shoved his phone at me.

"Watch this."

Moving my frown from him to the phone, I pressed the play button. It took me a few seconds to understand what I was seeing, and a few seconds more to understand where—and how—the video had been made, and less than a second after that to lose my breath with the weight of what it meant.

"Fuck."

"No. I think y'all stop before that happens."

I passed his phone back to him, not needing to see it again. Not now. My chest filled with lead. My stomach hurt. I needed to . . . I needed to think. *Think.*

"Jackson, I know you're having a bad day, but now might be a good time to inform you that all ATMs have cameras."

"Yes, Cletus! I know about ATM cameras. I knew we'd be recorded, but I wasn't thinking someone would take the recording and share it!"

"Why not? You were kissing a world-famous actress. They probably got enough money from the sale of that video to quit their job for a while. Maybe a whole year's salary."

I'd known about the camera, and I'd dismissed it as inconsequential in the moment. All I'd been thinking about was kissing Rae.

"Jesus." I covered my mouth with my hand, staring at the sky and the end of my career in law enforcement. How could I have been so monumentally stupid?

"I don't think he can help much with this now. This video is up everywhere—the Twitter, the Facebook, the Tikety Tok—but I've found it never hurts to ask."

I'd be fired. I'd definitely be fired. Wearing my uniform, while on duty, indecency, conduct unbecoming an officer of the law, all caught on the camera of an ATM. What had I been thinking?

You weren't thinking. Your dick was.

I shook my head. No. That wasn't true. I had been thinking.

Yes, there'd been a fair share of dick-thinking involved, but I'd been thinking with my brain too. It's why I hadn't kissed her in the car. If I'd touched her in the car, we would've ended up doing a lot more than just kissing.

She'd asked me to spend the night with her, and I'd wanted to say yes—my God, I wanted to say yes so badly—but I knew, somewhere deep down, spending the night with Rae would absolutely wreck me and I'd feel nothing but regret after. I didn't *want* to be that guy anymore. I didn't want to just take whatever was offered and be passed around for a good time, but never for a real, lasting, *permanent* time.

Not just that, but I'd spent years trying to push Rae from my mind. If I slept with her? If I had that memory? I'd never be able to move on with someone else.

And I . . . *I care about this woman.*

I barely knew her, but I wanted her happiness even if I wasn't meant to be the source of it. Sitting in the car with her, talking about things that should've been awkward and difficult but had felt so effortless, so easy, *fun*—that was Rae. That was all Rae. That's how things were with her. *Fun. Easy.* Which should've been a big red flag. Nothing easy lasts. Except I was blind where she was concerned.

I'd meant what I'd confessed, Rae was sweet. Sunshine and rainbows. If caring could be measured in time spent thinking about somebody, she was probably the most important woman in my life.

That just makes you sad, Jackson. I nodded because, yep, that was probably true. But who was I except the guy who fell when I should've stayed upright?

And so I laughed.

"Something funny?" Cletus's question was low, quiet. I barely heard the words.

"Oh. Just everything."

"What happened?"

"You saw what happened." I continued chuckling, opening the lid on my coffee container and dumping the contents on the ground. My mouth tasted like ash. "It's all in the video."

"I mean, what happened with Ms. Ezra? How long have you two been keeping in touch?"

I gave my head a subtle shake, glancing at Cletus briefly over my shoulder. "We haven't."

"Well. That's a flagrant lie."

"It's not."

"As you may recall, I was present when you met. I provided the introduction."

"Yeah. But we didn't keep in touch after that night."

Cletus seemed to grow mighty still. "Y'all didn't speak again after sleeping together?"

"No. We didn't."

He made a choking sound that had me looking at him again. His eyes were wide, his mouth open.

"What? What is it?" I asked.

"You just admitted to sleeping with *Raquel Ezra.*"

"I didn't—I . . ."

He dipped his head, his eyes wide with meaning.

I cursed. "You tricked me."

"I certainly did. Who else knows?"

"Absolutely no one." I sliced my hand through the air, my temper rising. "And we didn't—we didn't—it's none of your business what happened, but it's not what you think."

He straightened his spine, standing at his full height, which for the record was the same as mine. "Are you telling me that you've kept this secret for . . ." his eyes moved up and to the right "—five and a half years?"

"Yes," I ground out. "And I don't want you saying anything."

"I shan't tell a soul. Except for my Jenn. Because she shares my soul."

"Cletus!"

"But you do realize this makes you one of—how many brothers do I have?"

"Five," I grumbled. "Which you well know. And I don't want you telling Jenn. Tell no one." Jenn was his wife and a lovely woman, but I didn't even want Cletus to know.

He ignored my order. "This makes you one of seven men on the face of the earth who would've kept this secret." He nodded somberly and then stepped forward. "I'm ready to share the plan, Jackson." His words were a riddle.

"Plan? What plan?"

"The plan to rescue your career and reputation."

"How're you going to manage that? I was on duty. I deserve to be fired."

"Nah." He shrugged, his eyes on his phone screen. "You deserve no such thing. Not for kissing your woman."

"I was on duty. And Rae is not my—" I rolled my eyes. There was no use arguing with Cletus.

"No, you weren't on duty. And yes, she most certainly is."

"I'm not talking to you about Rae anymore, but I should know whether or not I was on duty."

"No, you weren't." He lifted up his cell and showed me the paused screen. "Doesn't your Thursday shift end at four?"

"No. Not if I—"

"Yes, it does. Yesterday, it did. You clocked in at six, that means—collective bargaining rules—your shift ended at four."

I closed my eyes, trying to think. "No. Cletus. I was there on a call."

"Were you? There's no official log of it. Nothing on the radio—according to Flo. Your shift ended and then you kissed your woman."

"You're being too literal with the rules. That's not how things work."

"But that's how your representative at the Association sees it."

I reared back. "You talked to Mike?"

"I did. I work on his old Toyota Celica. He loves that car. I called him to check on the engine work I'd done and to give him a heads-up about the video and about how your ten-hour shift had ended. And he's already called your father."

"My father." I groaned, pushing a hand through my hair, pain radiating outward from my chest. *What must he think of me?*

I'd made some dumbass, careless choices regarding public displays of affection with women when I was younger, but nothing like this. Nothing caught on video and broadcast everywhere.

"Anyway, the Association has your father's hands tied."

"He wanted to fire me?" I croaked, turning over my shoulder to peer at Cletus.

He looked at me for a stretch, gathering a deep breath before saying, "I don't rightly know what the sheriff wanted to do. But I do know, you don't wish to let your father down."

Cletus didn't usually point out the obvious unless he was setting a person up to take a verbal journey through his train of logic. I gritted my teeth and glared at him, waiting for the lecture I knew was coming.

Sure enough, he said, "You are your own man, Jackson. I freely admit—" Cletus lifted his hands, palms out as though to stop any argument I might launch "—I hero-worship the man too. Half the men in this town do. And none of us are his son. But you can't make Jeffrey James happy one hundred percent of the time. It's your life, not his. Mistakes will be made." A hint of sympathy entered his voice. "But they're your mistakes. They belong to you. Not to him."

I released a shuddering sigh, the pain in my lungs persisting. "He's my father, Cletus."

"I know, Jackson."

"I feel like—" I had to draw in another breath, working to release some of the tight-ness in my chest "—I'm never going to live up to him."

He frowned. "You think it's your job to be your father? You think that's what sons are supposed to do? You live up to Jeffrey James, I live down to Darrell Winston?"

"No." I shook my head, staring at the mix of grass and gravel under my boots. "Course not." I knew I was lucky. Folks never let me forget it.

"Anyhoo. Now you know what's up and can mentally prepare for tonight."

"Tonight?" My gaze shot to Cletus.

His eyebrows were suspended on his forehead. "Did you already forget your prom-ise? The jam session?"

"Are you kidding? I can't go now." I paced back over to him gesturing wildly in the general direction of the Green Valley Community Center. "I can't show my face there. It's not just bringing shame to the county office that I'm talking about. Charlotte just broke up with me last week, now everyone is going to think it's because of Rae. They're going to think I've been stepping out on her."

I'd have to call Charlotte and explain about Rae somehow. Without divulging too many details. I knew she'd forgive me, she'd probably even laugh about the whole thing. Except, she wouldn't be laughing when folks started asking her how she was doing and whether she was *hanging in there*, like they'd done after Kevin left. Their pity pissed me the hell off, and just the thought made me sick to my stomach. She already had enough shit to deal with.

"You promised you'd come tonight." Cletus held up a warning finger. "And besides, it's phase two of the plan."

"What plan?"

"You'll find out tonight. Just. . . dress nice. But not too nice. And do your hair, but don't make it stiff. Make it look done, but natural."

"No one is going to care about my hair!" I yelled, feeling myself edge closer to losing my temper.

"I care about your hair, Jackson," he said stiffly, lifting his chin like I'd offended him. "See? You're wrong. I. Care."

I narrowed my eyes on Cletus as he marched past, his boots crunching the gravel underfoot. I may have been at my wit's end, but that didn't mean I had a call to be rude.

After swallowing around stones in my throat, I hollered after him, "Hey. Thank you, Cletus."

"For what?" he asked, still marching.

"For interceding with Mike. For having my back. For helping me." *For being a good friend.*

"I just pointed out the obvious to Mike, which made his job easy and saved him a lawsuit. Oh. And one more thing." He turned to walk backward. "They're releasing a joint statement, and you'll be censured—or reprimanded or whatever it's called—for wearing your uniform in public while off duty. And that's about it. So get back to work."

That would not *be it*, as Cletus well knew. Maybe that'd be the official word on the subject from the department, but it was unlikely I'd be forgiven by anyone at the station for a while, and there was *no way* this would be forgotten.

Don't get me wrong. People in Green Valley and the surrounding county were good folks. But the only thing that lasted longer than grudges around here were memories.

CHAPTER 13

JACKSON

"If one person in a thousand criticized me while all the others cheered, I didn't hear the cheers."

— DOROTHY DANDRIDGE

J pulled up to the community center at exactly 7:30 PM. I parked, I exited my truck, and I walked toward the entrance.

On the way over, I'd decided to rip this bandaid off. I would not wallow or wait, I'd accept the cold shoulders, snide comments, and trails of whispers—as was my due.

I'd just come from the disciplinary meeting with Mike, acting as my Association representative, and my father, acting as my sheriff. Maybe this explained the intense determination I currently felt to slather myself in punishment and condemnation.

During the meeting, I'd told them the truth of what had happened insomuch as I deemed necessary while also protecting Rae's privacy. I'd explained that Ms. Ezra and I were acquaintances. I'd informed them that the kiss hadn't been premeditated. Mike had asked if it had been reciprocated and whether the sheriff might be expecting a complaint from Ms. Ezra. I'd told them that it had been reciprocated but suggested they reach out to Ms. Ezra to confirm. Mike had said that they would, thanked me for my candor, and reiterated for us all that I'd been off duty at the time.

It was at this point that I'd interrupted. "Mike, while I appreciate what you're trying to do, I was there on a call. I was on duty."

"There's no record of a call coming through dispatch or on the radio, son. And you couldn't have been on duty because your shift ends exactly ten hours after you clock in." Mike had given me a patient, paternal smile at this point and then slid his gaze to my father. "And I know the sheriff isn't making calls over unofficial, untraceable channels. Furthermore, I know the sheriff would *never* expect his hard-working deputies to exceed the hours allowed by our collective bargaining agreement. Isn't that right, Jeff?"

My father—leaning back in his chair, his elbow propped on the arm of it, his index finger along the side of his face, his thumb under his jaw, the rest of his hand covering his mouth—had stared at Mike coolly, but he hadn't said a single word.

"Well. There you go, Jackson. We all agree. You were off duty."

I didn't agree.

I'd done it. I'd admitted it. And I was willing to take responsibility for it—all of it— and I'd hoped that counted for something. But watching my father watching me, disappointment heavy behind his gaze, I knew it counted for nothing.

Presently, as I crossed the parking lot of the community center, ready to be ostracized by everyone, I couldn't shake the ache in my chest. I knew from experience that it would be a while before it would ease, and even longer before it dissipated completely.

But I also reminded myself that I'd gotten off easy. I told myself that if I didn't want the ache, if I didn't want folks treating me like the town pariah, if I didn't enjoy being labeled as the town player, maybe I ought to stop acting like one. Maybe I should—

"Psssst! Jackson!"

Coming to a stop, I twisted to the left and right, scanning the parking lot for the origin of the sound and ended up stumbling back a step when I saw her. "Rae?"

She stood at the corner of the building under a floodlight, wearing a long, flowy orange dress with thin straps. Her hair was in braids, her features bathed in bright light, and she was waving at me to join her. "Come over here!"

I didn't think about it. I jogged over. As soon as I made it around the corner, she took a step backward, her eyes big and searching.

"Hi," she said, a small smile playing around her full lips.

"Hi," I said, out of breath, and not because of the short jog.

Then an odd thing happened. For maybe the first time in my life, knowing I'd done something to disappoint my father, the thought entered my mind, *It was worth it.*

Kissing Rae had been worth it. More than worth it. Even if I'd been fired, the kiss would've been worth it. My father would eventually forgive me, I could always get another job, but there'd never be another Rae.

Suddenly, she threw her arms around me, pressing all the generous curves of her body against mine. "I'm so sorry. I'm *so, so, so* sorry."

Instinctively, my arms came around her. She felt so good, warm and soft and right. "You don't need to be sorry." The ache in my chest I'd been carrying all day alleviated, just simply dissolved, and I set my chin on top of her head, inhaling her sweet floral scent. "You didn't do anything wrong."

"Neither did you." She clung to me tighter.

"Hey." I stroked her hair at the back of her head, pulling my fingers along her braid. "Are you okay? What's wrong?" This seemed like more than being worried for me or upset on my behalf.

She sniffed, shaking her head against my chest. "I'm just so sorry."

It was clear, whatever she was dealing with, she didn't wish to discuss it. Or maybe she wasn't ready. I tried to think of something that would make her laugh.

Tugging on her braid, I said, "If you're sorry, then maybe if you kiss it, you'll make it all better."

She laughed. *Mission accomplished.*

Withdrawing just a bit, she tipped her chin back to look up at me. "Hmm. Maybe later."

"I'll hold you to it."

"You're holding me to it right now."

"So I am." I grinned, admiring the curve of her smile.

Rae seemed to shake herself, blinking rapidly. "What was I saying?"

"You said you're okay, and you don't think I did anything wrong."

"Yes! I think—I mean, I don't think you did anything wrong. But Jethro explained how people will say you did something wrong, and so I accept that's what they'll say, even though you did nothing wrong. Are you okay?"

I'd barely caught any of her words because my mind finally caught up with where I was, and who I was with. How was it that she was still here? "What are you doing here? Shouldn't you be back in LA by now?"

"I'm staying."

"Staying?"

"I'm here to help you."

"Help me?"

"Yes." She linked her hands behind my back and peered up at me like she thought my parroting questions were cute. "I want to help, and Sienna told me that it would be best if I stayed for you—and Charlotte—so I stayed."

"But what about . . ." *Her life? Her career? How could she just blow off all her obligations and stay?*

"I'm here for you." She used her arms around my torso to give me a little shake. "As your friend."

"As my friend." Apparently, at present, I was only capable of repeating words she'd already said.

"Yes." Rae nodded, her smile falling just slightly, her eyes darting between mine. "I don't have many friends," she said, like it was a confession. "Please, let me help."

I stared at her, my brain having trouble forming anything akin to concrete thought, and I realized I couldn't think very well when we were standing so close, when my hands held her body and her lips were only inches from mine.

I released her and backed away, shoving my fingers into my back pockets, and frowned at the pavement. *She's here to help, as a friend.* "What is it that you think you can do?"

Rae balled her hands into fists in front of her, her gorgeous eyes wide with hope. "We have a plan. It's all worked out."

"Cletus said something about that. Okay. Tell me the plan."

"We talked to Marta—Sienna's sister? She's also her manager—and she helped us think through damage control. There are a few issues, as I understand it. First, you don't want people to think that you and Charlotte broke up because of us—I mean, me. But after the pictures and video, that's what it looks like."

I was nodding before she'd finished. "Right."

"I'm here to make nice with Charlotte."

"How do you mean?"

"Charlotte and I are going to hang out tonight, in front of the whole town, and get along famously. Then no one will think I'm the reason for the split."

"Does Charlotte know this?" I'd been trying to reach Charlotte all day, and she hadn't picked up or returned any of my texts.

This was ironic because almost every other woman I knew had called me—Zora Leffersbee, Angela Jones, Darlene Simmons, Patricia Robillard, Nikki Sadler, Carmen . . . *you get the picture*—and I'd sent their calls to voicemail. The only person's call I had accepted was my sister Jessica's, and I got the sense she'd mostly called just to tease me.

Anyway, I'd started to worry that Charlotte was mad since she hadn't returned my calls or texts.

"You betcha! Charlotte knows, and she's fully on board Operation Friend Pretend."

"Pardon?"

"It was Sienna's idea. She likes to name her plans. You're lucky you didn't hear the other ideas. Anyway, you'll be with us tonight—with Charlotte and me—for part of the time."

"I will?"

"Yes. The three of us will be seen together, laughing, talking, generally enjoying each other's company—like pigs in shit."

I involuntarily made a sound, surprised by her choice of words.

She winced. It was *adorable*. "See. I can't say that. Jethro said it, and it made sense when he said it. But I'm from Cleveland. We can't say 'pigs in shit' because I'm pretty sure people start picturing stinky pigs in actual feces. But I can say 'You betcha!' and 'Tough tomatoes!' and no one bats an eye."

The sound of laughter hit my ears before I realized it came from me.

"You're laughing at me." She lifted her hands up and then let them fall against her thighs with a smack, adding robotically, "I'm a comedian."

"Yes, you are. You're hilarious."

"This is what I get for trying to steal local colloquialisms. What if I said, 'You, me, and Charlotte can be like three peas in an escape pod'?"

"That works." I'd half forgotten what we were talking about. All I knew was that— whatever it was—I hoped we'd be talking for a while.

"Thank you. Anyway, for the rest of the evening, various members of Jethro's family will also be lending their support, making sure you're never alone."

That surprised me. "Jethro? He agreed to this?"

"It was his idea. Well, mostly. Marta and Sienna contributed."

Huh. *Why would Jethro want to help me?* "And y'all think this is going to make a difference?"

Rae's lashes fluttered and a soft, hazy smile curved her lips. "I love it when you say 'y'all.'"

I pressed my mouth into a line so I wouldn't answer her smile with one of my own. We needed to stay focused, but staying focused around Rae was difficult. She was just so stinking fun. And sweet. And funny and kind. And—

"Rae," I said, needing to say something, otherwise I'd be here all night, swapping stares and admiring all the ways she was special.

"Yes! Sorry." She clapped her hands together. "That's the other part of the plan. You and I are going to make it clear that we're just friends. Just. Friends. And that you were helping me get out of a bad situation."

Just friends? "Is that so? How's that going to work?"

"You, Sienna, and Charlotte will tell people the whole thing was staged. That I asked you to help me because I wanted to break things off with Harrison, and I asked if you would help. We're taking the whole, 'Harrison and Rae have a toxic relationship, she's looking to break free, and Jackson's helping her out' approach."

I'm sure my face betrayed my disbelief. "That sounds absolutely, batshit crazy."

"Yes. I know. But people will buy it."

"Then they're batshit crazy. No one is going to buy that."

"Maybe so. In any case, I'm going to stay in town and help sell the story until everyone buys it, or at least rents it."

That had me coming to attention. "You are?"

"Yes."

My heart wanted to gallop, I reined it back. "How long?"

"I don't honestly know." She twisted her fingers in the fabric of her skirt. "At least until gossip about you and me and Charlotte dies down, and people lose interest. Why?"

I shuffled a step closer to her, compelled. "You can spare the time?"

"Actually, yes."

"You don't have a movie to film? An interview to give?" If she could spare the time, then why had she been planning to leave in the first place?

Why—

Why couldn't we—

Why had she only asked for one more night together?

"No. I, uh, was going to film a movie this summer but—" She huffed, shaking her head, a flash of irritation or pain or something like both behind her eyes.

"What?" Unthinkingly, I reached out and encircled her forearm, a shock of awareness and heat traveling up mine at the contact. "What happened?"

"Remember my friend Lina?" She slid her arm through my fingers until our hands met, held. "From the wedding reception?"

"Lina Lestari? I know her. I mean—I don't *know her* know her. But I've seen her movies."

"She stole the role."

I flinched. "No!"

"Yes."

"That's reprehensible."

"Right?" Her hand tightened around mine. "I—I trusted her, you know? I told her about it, how excited I was for the part. Then she did some maneuverings behind the scenes and got me ousted."

"You deserve better friends than her."

Her gaze flickered over me, one of her eyebrows lifting a scant inch.

"Wait. Not that you need me to say that." *Oh, damn.* First I'd lectured her about Harrison, now her choice in friends? I rushed to try and fix my misstep. "I value you as a person and as a woman. I know my opinion isn't one you need or want and what I say doesn't—and shouldn't—have any bearing on—"

"You're wrong."

"I know. I always get it wrong." I shoved my fingers into my hair, frustrated with myself and my big mouth.

"I mean, you're right, but you're wrong." She drifted closer. "I don't need your opinion. But I do want it. I value it."

"You do?"

"I do."

"Why?"

She cocked her head to the side, her eyebrows pulling together. "I don't know."

I chuckled. "Good enough for me."

She grinned, dazzling me while she adjusted our hands such that our fingers threaded together. "Thanks Jackson."

"For what?" I had the overwhelming urge to touch her cheek, so I did.

She leaned into my touch, closing her eyes. "For accepting my help, I guess. For being you."

I loved this, being connected to her, touching her, talking to her. "Thank you, Raquel." The words slipped out of me, unpremeditated.

Her lashes fluttered open, her soft smile returning. "For what?"

"Oh." My eyes dropped to her mouth, to the slight part of her lips. "Things."

"Things?" Her voice low, she tilted her head back and pressed closer, an invitation.

I slid my thumb along her jaw to just under her chin, angling it up for my mouth. I was going to kiss her now, and I would think about the wisdom and repercussions of it later. *Much, much later.*

"Yes. Things," I whispered, lowering my face, brushing my lips against hers. Hot. Soft. *Sweet.*

She shivered at the contact, letting go of my hand, her arms coming around my neck, the front of her body aligning delectably against mine. "What kind of things?"

"All good things," I said, licking the—

"There you are! I've been—*aaahhck*!" Sienna Diaz's yelp was like a bucket of ice water and a punch to the kidney.

Rae and I jumped apart, withdrawing from each other, and faced Sienna. And Jethro. And Cletus. And Jenn. And Charlotte. Everyone but Sienna and Cletus seemed to be wearing their unique version of a smirk.

"You two are not supposed to be kissing right now!" Sienna stomped forward and grabbed Rae's hand, sending me a glare the whole time. She paused just in front of me, lifting a finger. "We are trying to help you. Please. *For once*, keep your hands to yourself."

I nodded, hoping I looked contrite instead of massively disappointed. "Yes, ma'am."

Her usually pretty eyes narrowed into dangerous-looking slits, and in the next second she was gone, dragging Rae behind her. "Come on, Charlotte. Let's get started."

I met Charlotte's gaze. She still wore a smirk.

"Charlotte!"

"Coming!" With one more cheeky glance at me, she quickly walked to catch up with Sienna.

"Seriously, Rae? Seriously? What kind of silver tongue does Jackson James have?" I heard Sienna ask.

Rae made a choking sound and then began to cough. Charlotte, meanwhile, laughed hysterically.

Jenn—Cletus's wife—walked over to me and patted me on the shoulder, giving me a sympathetic smile and leaning in to say, "Cletus told me everything. Y'alls secret is safe with me."

I fought a sigh, deciding to give her a closed-mouth smile and a tight nod. She was kind and trustworthy, but I was irritated that Cletus had told her.

"Ready?" Jethro drawled, drawing my attention to him.

His arms were crossed, and he looked intensely amused, though his smile was small. Somehow, the man had always been able to convey complete ease, confidence, and utter lack of concern in any and all situations by wielding only his small smile. Even while being arrested for grand theft auto. *Several times.*

"Why're you doing this, Jethro?" I asked, needing to know. What would compel the oldest Winston brother to help me? The "punk" who'd mistreated his sister and arrested him countless times?

The older man shrugged, almost like he found my question boring. "Oh, you know. I reckoned that watching you squirm might be an entertaining way to spend an evening."

CHAPTER 14

RAQUEL

"I think it's really unfair men or people in the world think you can't be both – you can't be a sex symbol and a serious businessperson. Who says I can't be both?"

— EVA LONGORIA

*a*s far as I could tell, the evening appeared to be a smashing success.

"I need some water. Anyone else want something? Wine?" Sienna spun around her kitchen, her eyes on the cabinets, clearly hunting for something.

"No, thank you." I shook my head, taking a seat at Sienna's kitchen table and stretching my toes.

I didn't want any wine. I still felt a little raw from the conversation gone awry with my mother earlier in the day as well as seeing and kinda kissing Jackson before walking into the jam session with Sienna and Charlotte. I hadn't meant to kiss Jackson when I'd called him over. I didn't think he'd begun the conversation expecting to kiss me.

And yet, that's what happened.

"I'll have a half glass of whatever red you've got open. If nothing is open, I'll take water. But then I need to grab my kids and go." Charlotte sat next to me, leaning her elbows on the table.

Sienna had arranged for two sitters to come and watch the seven children—three were Sienna's, four were Charlotte's. As it was just past 10:30 PM, all of the kids were currently asleep.

"No. Leave them, Charlotte. Let them sleep. Just spend the night. We have tons of room." Sienna grabbed a wineglass from a cabinet and poured much more than a half glass of wine. "And look at that. I accidentally poured too much. We don't waste good wine in this house."

"Fine. Twist my arm." Charlotte lifted her hand to accept the heavy pour and sighed. "I am tired. I don't think I've been up this late in twelve years, not since before Kimmy was born. Hey, how do you think it went?"

"Great." Sienna sent us both a grin. "Really, really great. You two convinced me."

I sent Charlotte a small smile. "Charlotte made it easy."

When people had spotted me and Charlotte together, arms linked and laughing, they had appeared taken aback at first. But once Sienna spread it around that Harrison and I were breaking up, and Jackson had gallantly agreed to provide media cover for me —because why else would Jackson kiss me in front of an ATM camera? I mean, come on! We knew it was there the whole time—ruffled feathers had begun to smooth.

"Are you kidding? You made it easy." She lifted her wineglass toward me. "I forgot we were pretending most of the time."

I had too. Being around Charlotte was fun. She was just so . . . out there. Over the course of my life, I'd often faked being bold and brash to cover for nervousness or uncertainty. But Charlotte *was* bold and brash. She was herself. She really seemed to know herself, who she was.

I envied her.

Sienna filled a cup with water, then crossed over to the table to join us. "I don't think there was much pretending going on tonight, except the line we told about Rae and Jackson being 'just friends.'"

"Oh, yes. I was hoping this would come up." Charlotte pushed her wineglass aside and leaned toward me.

I fought the urge to cover my face, shame sweeping through me and making my voice tight. "Charlotte, you are a much better woman than I, helping out your ex after he—"

"Jackson and I were never together, not really." She flitted her hand through the air. "Yeah, we both wanted the same things, but it never would've worked out. He was too much of a boy scout, and he only eats boring food."

"Boring food?" Sienna lifted an eyebrow.

"Yeah, he's got some health things and that means he's real strict with his diet. But it's not just his food that's boring. Jackson works all the time—*all* the time—and he volunteers his time to various do-gooder causes, and he exercises, and he fixes his boat, and that's it. I feel like, deep down, I knew from the get-go we weren't right for each other long-term."

Sienna seemed intrigued. "Then why did you agree to date him in the first place?"

"Like I said, we both wanted the same thing."

This surprised me. Jackson had said he and Charlotte didn't want the same things. So I asked, "Which is what? What do you want?"

"I'd like to get remarried, and he said he was looking to settle down. But we didn't have any spark. I thought, hey, he's kinda cute, you know? Maybe I just needed to give him some time to woo me. Then maybe I'd feel more than friendly about him. Plus, I'd heard some stories." She wiggled in her seat, her eyebrows bouncing. "An acquaintance of mine had 'dated' him." She put air quotes around *dated*.

"What kind of stories?" Sienna propped her chin on tented fingers, fluttering her lashes.

I sank deeper into my seat, dread a wispy, swirling chill. I didn't want to hear this. But I also *did* want to hear this. The thing about being around women who were truly bold and brash was that my real nature tended to surface. If you're keeping score, my nature leans more toward clumsy than confident.

Which is likely why I said, "Campfire stories?

Sienna barked a laugh.

"Uh, no. *Bed*time stories." Charlotte winked, her grin so saucy, I wanted to call it marinara and put a label on it. "According to my friend, Jackson has a really long tongue."

"What?" Sienna reared back, then looked at me as though to confirm.

I wiped my face of all expression.

She gasped. "Rae!"

"I said nothing."

"But you knew!"

I shook my head, covering my face. "I do not feel comfortable talking about this."

"Then I'll talk about it." I felt Charlotte nudge her fingertips against my forearm. "Jackson James. He has this—like—ridiculously long tongue. And he knows how to use it."

Inwardly, I groaned and died a little, thinking about Jackson using his sexy kraken tongue on or with Charlotte, or anyone else but me.

But then she added, "Or so I've heard. He was a puritan the whole damn time we dated. I'd held out for months, for a glimpse of that thing. Nothing. Not a single sighting."

Relief flooded through me. *I'm a bad person.*

"My friend talked about him like he was this magical fish who grants wishes. Except they're all sexy wishes. And then, you know, once you're done, you just throw him back in the ocean. If he'd actually granted any of my wishes, I wouldn't have thrown him back."

I winced at the description. Did a group of men exist out there that talked about me this way?

"Like, how long is this tongue?" Sienna sounded totally absorbed.

"Really, really long." I sighed, then slapped a hand over my mouth, an *ope!* slipping out.

I stared at Charlotte. She stared at me.

And then she laughed. "Oh dear me! You naughty, naughty woman. Now you have to tell us everything."

I shook my head, my hand still covering my mouth.

"No, Rae. No. You can't stop there." Sienna wagged her index finger in the air. "That's like saying you received a fantastic dick pic from a stranger where the balls don't detract from the image and then never sharing it with your girls."

Charlotte hooted. She *hooted.* And this made Sienna laugh hysterically.

"I can't. I'm sorry, I can't," I said from behind my hand.

"Well, why not?" Charlotte looked to Sienna, appealing to her. "Don't tell me you caught feelings for the man after knowing him for—for—" She blinked, frowning at Sienna, then at me. "Wait a minute. Just how long have y'all known each other?"

I crossed my arms on top of the table and lowered my forehead to them, my stomach suddenly hurting.

Sienna whispered, "They slept together at my wedding."

"We didn't sleep together!" I groaned. "I mean, yes, we fell asleep. Together. But we didn't have sex."

"Then how do you know how long his tongue is?" Charlotte sounded honestly curious.

"Because—ahh! Don't make me talk about this. Please don't. I—I don't want to."

"I'm beginning to think she has feelings for him," Sienna whispered again. "Deep feelings."

"Oh," Charlotte said, then paused like she was thinking matters over. "Ohhhhh! But what about Harrison?"

"Harrison and I aren't really together." *Great, Rae. Tell everyone why dontcha?* "So that part was true. My relationship with Harrison is toxic, it just also happens to be fake. And it's not what you think about Jackson." I sat up, mentally imploring Charlotte not to hate me. "Jackson and I were together—we spent time together—just the one night. I liked him so much. He was just so polite. And patient. And he actually asked me what I wanted. And he asked questions and listened."

"See, those are the things I wasn't attracted to." She shook her head, giving me a sympathetic look. "If I wanted warm affection, I'd get a dog."

"Except, it didn't feel warm. Things between us, they felt *hot*. Even now, every time he looks at me, I feel like I might combust. Or melt. Or evaporate."

"Nice dialogue, Rae. You should write that down. We should write a script." Sienna nodded toward me before taking a drink of her water.

Meanwhile, Charlotte was shaking her head, her lips twisted to the side. "Nope. Not me. I think once, we might've almost approached tepid? That's the closest we got to hot. So—" Charlotte set her chin on her palm, her gaze wide and interested "—what happened next?"

"And then I left. And we didn't talk. We didn't keep in touch at all," I said, the words just as sad as I felt. "But I haven't been able to stop thinking about him."

"For five and a half years?" Her eyebrows flew up. "You've been pining for Jackson James for *five and a half years*?"

"Yes?" I balled my hands into fists.

"Well. Good Lord. That's a long time." Charlotte looked to Sienna, clearly wanting to confirm if her assessment of the situation was accurate.

"But I didn't really know him, did I? He was this—this idea of a guy. Someone who treated me well and didn't seem to want anything from me except to make me feel good."

"He made her feel good," Sienna said, her smile small wistful. Then she stood suddenly. "Just a sec, I need to go check on Jet. I'll be right back."

We watched her go, leaving through the kitchen door that led to the living room. Charlotte turned back to me, and I met her gaze, still sending her mental requests not to hate my guts.

"Oh, honey. Relax. I'm not mad at you."

"You're not? Because if I were you, I'd want to impale me with a butter knife."

She chuckled, picking up her wine and taking a sip. "No. Like I said, Jackson and I weren't suited." She paused, her eyes drifting over my shoulder. "Maybe when he was younger. He was fun then. Although, he wasn't looking for anything long term in those days. But I guess, neither was I."

"You weren't?"

"No. But I got pregnant. Pregnant girls get married around here. Or at least in my family, twelve years ago, that's what happened. I married the guy, got pregnant three more times, and he left me, and that is that."

I wondered at Charlotte and the way she matter-of-factly recounted her past, like she was sharing a recipe rather than painful details.

My mother couldn't talk about her past with my father. Just thinking about him made her irrationally angry. I cringed, thinking about our call earlier, and shied away from the memory again. I wasn't ready to think about that yet.

But I did wonder why Charlotte could be so pragmatic and dispassionate about her ex, whereas my mother could not. Maybe the failure of Charlotte's marriage had played a part? My mother hadn't married my father. She'd rejected his proposal, not even when her family threatened to cut her off completely would she agree. She'd wanted to live her life on her own terms.

And so she has. . . Huh.

One of the things I loved so much about acting was the potential to inhabit two completely different characters reacting to the same situation. Both Charlotte and my mother had become pregnant unexpectedly. How they'd reacted to it, the choices they'd made, spoke volumes about who they were. I couldn't say one reaction was better or more valid than the other.

They were simply choices. And those choices ended up defining a life.

I want to be Charlotte's friend.

"What?" Her eyes cut to me and then away. "Why are you looking at me like that?"

Ask her.

Can it be that easy?

You asked Jackson for a night together and he gave you a kiss you will treasure until the end of your days. Ask for what you want, Rae.

"Charlotte." I reached for her hand. "I want us to be friends. I don't have many friends. I'm not great at making friends. I don't want to pretend with you. Will you be my friend?"

157

"Of course." She turned her hand palm up and squeezed mine. "I thought we were friends. Or starting to be."

I huffed out a grateful breath, leaning closer to her. "Thank you."

"For what?"

"For being wonderful. And real."

"Honey, I don't know how else to be."

I chuckled, and so did she, and that's how Sienna found us, gazing into each other's eyes with mutual like.

"Oh no. Does this mean you, Charlotte, and Jackson are having a three-way?"

"Ew!" Charlotte wrinkled her nose, but then her eyes narrowed. "Now wait a minute—"

Both Sienna and I busted out laughing, and I knew my face had turned bright red.

"Don't take this the wrong way, it's not you, it's me," Charlotte said, not quite making eye contact, and—unbelievably—her cheeks had turned a little pink. "A three-way is too many arms and legs. It would remind me too much of playing Twister with my kids. What I want, what I need, is someone's undivided attention."

"Hear, hear!" Sienna raised her glass of water, clinking it against Charlotte's wine. "I'm starting to feel similarly about working with these big studios. It's like, someone is getting fucked, and it feels like it's always me."

"Oh no. What happened?" I straightened in my seat.

"I just got a text that Paratune Studios pulled out. See? It even sounds like an unsavory three-way. Anyway, they pulled out, and now I have to find a new home for my next script."

"You should just start your own studio, Sienna." Charlotte took a gulp of her wine.

Sienna snorted. "I know, right? Then I wouldn't have to deal with making films by committee. That sounds like heaven."

"How would that even work?" Charlotte leaned back in her seat, crossing her arms. "Do you need a license or something?"

"A lot of money, clout, and contacts," I said dryly. "And investors, so you diversify your risk. Also, a good sense of what's on trend, what's making money."

"Is there much overhead? With your own company?" Charlotte asked.

"No. There doesn't have to be," I said. "I've seen production companies that were just two people and a small office in Beverly Hills. The producer and the admin, that's it. Everyone else is hired on a project-by-project basis as contractors, or for a percentage of the profit."

Charlotte pointed at Sienna. "You can do that. You got money, clout, and connections. And I'm sure finding investors wouldn't be a problem. Heck, you got an investor sitting right here." Charlotte shifted her finger from Sienna to me.

"That's . . . true . . ." Sienna frowned at Charlotte, her gaze moving to the wall behind her. "Wait. Wait a minute."

Charlotte and I traded a quick look. *She couldn't possibly—*

"Oh my God, Charlotte!" Sienna half stood, reached across the table, grabbed Charlotte's face, and kissed her right on the mouth. "Charlotte, yes! Yes." Sitting again, she smacked the table. "Yes, that's exactly right. That's exactly what I should do."

"What is the commotion?" Jethro popped his head in. "We got sleeping kids upstairs."

"Sorry." Sienna winced.

"Are y'all okay?"

"Yes. But I kissed Charlotte."

"Well. I'm sorry I missed that," he said, sounding and looking sincere.

Charlotte laughed, covering her eyes. Once more, her cheeks had burned pink. *Interesting.*

Sienna jumped up and skipped over to her husband. "Guess what?"

"You want another baby?" He stood straighter. "'Cause, if so, we should go upstairs. The kitchen is occupied." He moved like he was going to leave and take her with him.

"No!" She laughed, hitting his shoulder lightly. "I'm starting my own production company. No more business meetings picking apart my scripts. All my movies will be made and managed by me from now on."

"Oh. That's great." Grinning widely—and looking at his wife like he was absolutely crazy about her, like she was magic—he pulled her forward by the hips and kissed her, just once. It was a congratulations-for-being-wonderful kiss, and the sight made my heart ache so much, my palm reflexively lifted to press against my chest.

"It is great!" Sienna beamed.

"Let me know how I can help," he said, then added quieter, "I'm so proud of you."

Charlotte wrinkled her nose, looking at me and whispering, "They're gross. I'm jealous."

"Agree." I nodded, unable to curb my smile as I watched Sienna with her Jethro. And I knew, with a certainty deep inside—to the center of my very being—*that's what I want.*

I wanted someone who supported me like *that.* Who, no matter what, believed in me. Someone who looked at me like I was magic.

* * *

Our little party dispersed around 11:30 PM. Charlotte stayed over at the main house, and Jethro insisted on walking me the short distance to the carriage house. I had to smile at his excessive manners. Did all Southern men behave this way? Or only the bearded, handsome ones?

He paused at the door after doing a quick sweep of the interior. "Now lock up and use the alarm. Folks outside of Green Valley know where you are now. I'd prefer if you stayed at the house with the rest of us—at least until Dave and your other guard get here—but understand if you need your privacy."

"Thank you. I will lock the doors and turn on the alarm."

"Okay, then. Good night." The tall man nodded once, smiling tiredly, then walked toward the big Victorian farmhouse, leaving me standing just inside the door.

But before he was out of earshot, I whisper-shouted after him, "Hey, Jethro."

"Yep?" He turned.

I took a step past the threshold. "Why don't you like Jackson?"

The side of his mouth curved upward. "Who says I don't like Jackson?"

"Sienna."

"Did she?" He sort of chuckled. "I reckon she thinks I don't."

"What did he do?"

"He arrested me."

My mouth dropped open. "He what?"

"Don't be mad at him. I deserved it. All twenty times."

"Whoa!"

"But don't tell him I said that. The statute of limitations on grand theft auto in Tennessee is fifteen years, I think."

My eyes widened.

He laughed at my expression—a belly laugh—and sent me a wave. "'Night, Rae."

"Good night," I croaked, closing the door and locking it.

Grand theft auto? Twenty arrests? *Uffdah!* I decided I wouldn't ask Jackson about it. Scratching the back of my neck, I crossed to the alarm panel and typed in the code, then walked to the kitchen, randomly in the mood for tea.

Also, Sienna had been right, men were weird and complicated.

Just like people.

Just like relationships.

I'd just placed the kettle on the stove and pulled out a tea bag and mug when I heard a light rap on the door. I stiffened. *Who could that be?*

Turning off the kettle, I walked back to the foyer and eyed the panic button. "Uh. Who is it?" I moved my thumb over the red rectangle.

"It's Jackson."

"Oh!" A pulse of excitement raced through me. I immediately disarmed the alarm and bounded back to the door, flipping the lock and opening it. "Hi!"

"Hi." He was standing farther away than I expected, at least five feet from the house. "I don't want to keep you. I just wanted to stop by and see if you were okay."

"I am. I'm okay. Are you okay?"

"Yeah." He gave me a short nod, taking a step back. "Actually, I am. Things tonight worked out better than I thought they would, I guess." He looked confused. Perhaps he didn't know how to feel about the success of Jethro's plan. "Anyway. I'll just be—"

My heart leapt to my throat. I didn't want him to leave. "You should come in. Come in." I rushed forward and grabbed his hand, pulling him back toward the carriage house.

He dragged his feet. "No. No. I don't think that's a good idea."

I stopped pulling and looked at him over my shoulder. "Oh. Do you have work tomorrow?"

"No. It's my day off."

I turned for the house again. "Then you should—"

"Rae. It's late."

"I know, but—"

"Rae," he ground out, using my hold on his hand to bring us back to a stop. I faced him, my stomach erupting in uncertainty butterflies as I encountered the stern line of his jaw and the glittering, frustrated spark behind his eyes. "We need everyone to believe we're just friends, right? And if we go inside the house, I don't think I'm a good enough actor to pull that off."

My mouth formed an *O*, and I released him, folding my arms over my chest while I wrestled with a strange combination of disappointment and pleasure at his words. I wanted to spend time with him, talk to him, get to know this mystery of a man so I could understand my feelings better.

But . . . I conceded his point.

We couldn't seem to be around each other without kissing. Bringing him inside a dark, empty house in the middle of the night was something better left to my fantasies.

For now.

Oh really, inner voice? Now you're impudent? Now?

He exhaled a short breath, it also sounded frustrated, but his tone was soft as he said, "Hey."

I placed a tight smile on my face, it was the best I could manage. "Hey."

Jackson seemed to be considering me, debating what to do next. He didn't take too long. "Do you want to go for a drive?"

"Yes," I said immediately. "Yes, I do. Let me grab a jacket."

"Okay. I'll wait here." He shifted his weight to his back foot and hooked his thumbs in his jeans pockets.

I wanted to take a picture of him like this, all handsome reluctance and sexy self-control. *This man*, he just did something to me. I couldn't explain it.

But maybe if we took this drive and spent some time together talking—just talking—I'd start to figure it out.

CHAPTER 15

RAQUEL

"I don't want to be known as a sex symbol. There's a great stigma that goes with that tag. I want to be a Sam Elliott."

— SAM ELLIOTT

I rushed into the house, snatching up my lightweight jacket from a chair where I'd left it, took a moment to turn on the alarm, and left. As promised, he'd waited right where I'd left him. We didn't touch as we walked to his truck. He opened the passenger door for me and helped bring all of my maxi dress into the cab before shutting me in.

An intense sense of déjà vu settled over me as I watched him walk around the front. We'd been here before, kinda. Except this time the coat on my shoulders belonged to me and therefore didn't smell like him.

Darn it. I should've left right away and then asked for his jacket once we were on the road.

Also, the last time I'd sat in this spot, waiting for him to take me on a drive, I'd been stunned by the fact that his people called a knit hat a toboggan.

Jackson soon settled in his seat and turned the engine, putting the truck in reverse. Then he paused, his attention focusing on something beyond the windshield. Frowning, he lifted a hand. I followed his line of sight and found Jethro on the porch, a shotgun in his hands. It was pointed at the ground, and his features were relaxed. Sienna's husband lifted his chin, turned, and walked back in the house.

"Good to know he's a light sleeper," Jackson said, his voice tinted with wry amusement.

"Why is that good to know? So you know how much noise you can make when you sneak in my window later?" I asked, then pressed my lips together, hoping my voice had sounded curious instead of hopeful.

He turned to look out the back window of the cab as he backed up. "Well, obviously. But it's also nice to know he's looking out for you."

I lifted the cuffs of my jacket to my mouth to hide my smile. "I'm sleeping in the back bedroom. The windows are quite large."

"Are they?"

"Yes. Big enough even for someone as tall and broad as you."

"You should probably measure them, just to make sure."

"I don't have a measuring tape."

"Then I should probably come in and measure them with my measuring tape."

"Yes. I would appreciate that. Then we'll know for sure."

"They always say, measure twice, cut once."

"Who? Who are *they*?"

"Carpenters."

This reminded me so much of the night we met, the back and forth, the flirting, the butterflies in my stomach, and how oddly easy it was to just be with him, to talk to him. "I knew it."

"What? What did you know?"

"Two hardware stores. This town has a wood culture."

"Yep. *Biiiig* wood culture."

I giggled at our banter, sneaking a peek at him. "This is fun. You're fun."

"So are you," he said in that easy way of his.

Feeling dreamy and loose, excited and nervous, just like I always did around Jackson, I crossed my legs and faced him. "Where are we going? Do you still have those keys? Shall we get ice cream?"

"I thought, hot chocolate."

"That sounds nice. I haven't had hot chocolate in forever." I didn't mean for the words to come out so melancholy, but they did.

"Do you like it?"

"Yes."

"Then why don't you have it?"

"Don't let anyone in Hollywood fool you with talk of eating bagels. No one eats what they want and stays camera-ready. The life of a lead actress—unless, of course, you are Sienna Diaz or a select few who can get away with it—is a broccoli and cauliflower filled landscape."

This earned me a smile, but no comment.

I continued, speaking stream of consciousness, "But you know, I don't mind. It's part of the job. And eating that way does make me feel good. But sometimes . . ."

"What?"

"Sometimes I get this urge to sneak out, buy a chocolate cake from Fred Meyer—not a frilly chocolate ganache confection of locally sourced, organic, and GMO-free ingredients from a couture patisserie, but a legit, processed sugar and wheat and dairy and trans-fat-full pile of carbs with no redeeming nutritional value—and eat the whole thing."

"Sneak out? Why would you have to sneak out?"

It was interesting to me that this was the part of my admission he took issue with. "Well, because my chef and nutritionist would be pissed. So would my trainer. And I tremble to think of the judgmental eyebrows Sasha would send my way."

"Who is Sasha?"

"She's my PA."

"Personal assistant," he filled in.

"Yes. She manages my calendar, appointments, correspondence."

"Your fan mail and such?"

"No. That's someone else. I have a social media account manager, and she has a team that works specifically on each platform."

"How'd you mean?"

"Take Instagram, for instance. They have posts, but then they also have stories, and reels. We post on all three to maximize engagement. It's important to keep the content fresh and interesting. So we have a strategy meeting every month to . . ." I frowned, inspecting his profile. "Is this boring?"

"No. Not at all." He glanced over at me, and I saw he was telling the truth. He didn't find this boring.

"Why isn't this boring?"

"Because."

I twisted in the bench seat to face him. This was the second time he'd responded to a question with "because." The first time he'd done it was on Thursday afternoon, after we'd kissed, when I'd asked him why me leaving Green Valley was for the best.

"You know what I think?" I asked.

"Probably not."

That made me smile. I placed my arm along the back of the bench seat and bent it at the elbow, resting a cheek on my hand. "I think when I ask a question, and you answer with the word *because* and nothing else, it means you don't really want to answer."

His lips twisted, perhaps hoping to camouflage a smile. "That may be."

"You are a man of mystery, Jackson James."

His mouth dropped open, and he quickly turned his head to look at me, like he thought my statement was preposterous. It was super adorable. "Me? Mysterious? I'm an open book."

"Then read me a page. Tell me about yourself. But first tell me why you don't find my descriptions of social media management boring."

"Okay, fine." He cleared his throat, adjusting in his seat and shifting the placement of his hands on the steering wheel. "I do not find your descriptions of social media management boring for a few reasons. First, I'm interested in the subject. I'd never thought much about how social media might be something to manage. The sheriff's department has social media pages and accounts, but we don't really manage them, not like how you're describing. We don't worry about engagement; they're used as a tool to broadcast information. But I've been thinking, it might be good to actually *manage* them, the way you're talking about."

"Why?"

"Well, it's about building relationships, isn't it? That's what you're doing with your pages. And relationships need good communication. How can folks know we're doing a good job, thinking about their safety and welfare, if we're only posting updates about road closures and bear sightings? Sometimes, I think, when you're communicating and want to present an accurate account of yourself, you have to brag a little."

His point was a good one. "Otherwise, how will they know what you've done and how much you care?"

"Exactly."

"Hmm." I mock-squinted at him. "Okay, what are the other reasons for not thinking I'm boring?"

"You could never be boring."

"I don't know. Just wait until I tell you about how we edit our TikTok videos. Spoiler alert, we follow a template."

He chuckled, ending the short laugh by biting his lip and sending my gaze right there. *I wonder if we'll get a kraken sighting tonight.*

"No, that's one of my reasons," he said.

"Huh?"

"You could never be boring, that's reason number two why I don't find your descriptions of social media management boring. Reason three is, I like your voice."

"Oh. I see." I cleared my throat self-consciously, and that pulled another small smile out of him. "Well, I guess—"

"And reason four is because I like hearing you talk about different facets of your work. You're very . . ."

"Titillating?"

His eyes cut to mine and then away. "I was going to say knowledgeable. Competent."

"Wait. When have we discussed my work prior to now?"

Jackson seemed to grow very still.

"Jackson?"

"We haven't. But you give interviews. I've seen some."

This, unsurprisingly, thrilled me. Without thinking too much about it, I poked his arm. "You've been watching my interviews?"

He said nothing, just smiled his enigmatic smile. I seemed to recall debating the nature of his smile the first time we met and deciding it wasn't enigmatic at all but rather shy. I decided now that it was both. And I decided I loved it.

A slow-spreading warmth unfurled in my stomach as I continued staring at his handsome profile—the not-quite straight line of his nose, how the curve of his bottom lip was fuller than the top, the strength of his cleft chin, the angles of his jaw and cheekbone, temple and forehead—thinking I could spend my evenings like this and never tire of it.

Content, silence fell between us with a certain decisiveness. We were done talking.

For now.

* * *

The smell of warm, delicious Jackson woke me up. Lifting my head, I peered down at the body I lay completely atop and had to blink to make sure I wasn't still asleep. Then I pinched myself just to make doubly sure.

But no. I was still here, and he was still here, his features bathed in pale, dwindling starlight and early dawn light.

We'd driven around for a while, engaging in bursts of comfortable conversation followed by periods of comfortable silence. Sometimes we'd flirted. But mostly we'd asked each other questions and volunteered bits and pieces of who we were.

I'd told him why I'd wanted to become an actress—I loved inhabiting the life of someone who wasn't me, and making people believe fictional stories were real.

He'd told me why he'd become a deputy sheriff—he felt he didn't have a lot of innate talents except for being patient with both people and process. According to him, law enforcement was all about patience with people and process.

"You don't think you have a lot of innate talents?" I'd wrinkled my nose at this. "How can you say that?"

"Because it's true. I know what I am, and I know what I lack."

I'd stared at him, chagrined. Nothing about his statements had struck me as self-pitying, nor had he said the words in order to fish for compliments. Jackson had been all matter-of-fact, that-is-that. But this view of himself irritated me since it was clear he believed what he'd said.

Jackson had then changed the subject before I could push the issue, asking me which of my film roles had been my favorite experience so far.

Starlight Express was the clear answer—I'd enjoyed being involved with the editing —and he'd told me some of his more humorous anecdotes about being in law enforcement, like the time he'd been called to a nudist colony to deal with a petty theft incident. Gross spoiler alert: the woman had placed the money in her no-no hole.

"How did you—I mean, how did you figure it out?" I'd asked, repelled and enraptured.

"We knew it was her. It couldn't have been anyone else. And there were only so many places she could've put it. So through a process of elimination—" He'd shrugged.

"Oh snap! Please tell me that pun was intended."

He'd thrown his head back and laughed so hard, I thought we were going to have to pull over.

We didn't. He'd kept driving.

But when the subject had turned to our families, I'd deflected artfully, turning the conversation back to him. If he'd noticed, he hadn't said anything and he hadn't pushed. It was at this point that I realized how much I appreciated this about Jackson, he never seemed to push me.

Even when he'd brought up Harrison on Thursday, pointing out that I deserved better than someone who cheated on me, he hadn't pushed.

In my life, so many people pushed me. My mother pushed me to do my best. My father pushed me away. My trainer pushed me toward peak physical fitness. My chef pushed me to eat meticulously. My agent pushed, Harrison pushed, Sasha, Domino, they all pushed. And I pushed myself, to be more successful, to be better at my craft, to be a more giving and generous actor, to stay at the top of my game in all aspects of fame, publicity, marketing, and exposure.

But not Jackson. He seemed content to just let me be.

Comfortable conversations followed by comfortable silences must've led to me falling asleep and him pulling over.

With a regretful sigh, I pulled my admiring gaze from Jackson's sleeping face and looked through the window. I concluded it was close to dawn due to the grayish color of the horizon, but I wasn't sure where we were. We seemed to be surrounded by trees on all sides.

Jackson stirred, making me regret my movements. I thought about quickly resuming my position, placing my head back on his chest and pretending to still be asleep so we could snuggle a while longer, but his eyes opened. He blinked at me. And he smiled.

"Hi," he said.

"Hi," I said, my fingers moving into the thick tuft of blond hair on top of his gorgeous head. "This truck has an impressively huge bench seat. I love it. Did you sleep well?"

"Definitely." His gaze felt dreamy, and not just from sleep inertia. "But probably not enough. I love this truck too. And this seat."

I grinned, instinct telling me to memorize this sight of him as my heart pinged with regret. If I'd stayed all those years ago, I would've seen him like this. Hazy and loose, just waking up.

Jackson's hands lifted and slid from my hips to my waist. "Do you want some coffee?"

I placed my hands on his chest to keep him from getting up. "You have coffee? How is this possible?"

"I stopped by a drive-through and had them fill my thermos." He turned his head to one side, talking around a yawn.

"When was this?"

"Hours ago." He shook his head, facing me again, his eyes glassy. "But it stays hot in there."

"It sounds magical."

His mouth hitched on one side, his attention traveling over my face in a way that made the uncertainty butterflies erupt. "You're magical," he muttered.

Pleasure and warmth and happiness and sugar and spice tackled me, making my breath catch. I wanted to tell him that he was magical. I wanted to tell him I must've been crazy, because I was absolutely *crazy* about him.

But a vise of emotion closed around my vocal cords while the interior of the truck seemed to heat abruptly. My attention dropped to his lips, and I swallowed against a rising tide of urgency and want.

Oh no. We are going to kiss again.

On the other hand, *AWWW YEEEEAH! WE ARE GOING TO KISS AGAIN!*

But we didn't, because Jackson's hands moved from my waist to my shoulders and gently lifted me, his attention moving all around the truck but never settling in one spot.

"Let me see if I can find that coffee. . . " His voice was roughened with sleep, but there was something more there too. A thickness, like he found speaking difficult.

I watched him dumbly, feeling like I'd been set away, feeling like the two and a half feet he'd placed between us represented a vast expanse, warning of additional prickly rejection should I attempt to cross it.

But . . . *hadn't he just called me magical?*

This felt like mixed messages, and I was confused. *So* confused. He knew I'd be in town for a while. We'd just spent hours last night talking, getting to know each other better, laughing, sharing companionable silence. So why was I being pushed away now?

Ask.

Was it that simple?

Yes. How many times do I have to tell you this? JUST ASK FOR WHAT YOU WANT.

So I asked, "Did I do something wrong?"

His attention flickered to me and then away. "No. Not at all."

"Then why am I over here and you're over there?"

Jackson pulled a tall coffee carafe from behind his seat and unscrewed the lid. "Because."

I threw my hands up, then crossed my arms over my chest. "Here we go again with the 'because.'"

His smile was quick and struck me as a little sad. "Because, Rae. We're friends."

"Yes, and?"

"And, like I said last night, we need everyone to believe that, not just for my benefit but also to save Charlotte from the tongue waggers and folks in town."

Ignoring the obvious double entendre I wanted to make about tongue waggers, I turned my head left and then right, making a show of scanning the trees that surrounded us. "Are the townsfolk also the trees? Are you people Ents? Is that the secret of the Smoky Mountains?"

Jackson laughed again, and this time it was full of humor. "No."

"Oh. Wait. Is Smokey Bear actually a bear-shifter? And these woods are full of bear-shifters?"

"Yes. I'm so glad you saved me from that awkward conversation."

Now I laughed and he laughed and we laughed.

But then—*grrrr*—he said while grinning adorably and taking a sip of coffee, "Rae, I think we should try to be just friends."

He offered me the carafe, holding the side his mouth hadn't touched toward me. I shook my head. "No thank you. Is that what you want?"

"I think it's best."

"We're going to be friends? *Just* friends?"

"Yes." He screwed the lid back on and returned the carafe to its place behind his seat.

I nodded distractedly, even though the idea of putting the word *just* in front of any description related to Jackson James felt wrong on a visceral level and made me feel like organizing a protest. With signs.

As I stewed in my discontent, I randomly remembered a story Nico Moretti—you know, the comedian?—had once related to me in the greenroom at his talk show. We didn't see each other often, but I'd always felt comfortable with Nico. Whenever we talked, the subjects were always real and deep and personal, never chitchat. Perhaps we'd connected because we both shared Italian ancestry. Or perhaps Nico was just one of those people who excelled at getting others to open up. I don't know.

Anyway, we'd been discussing boundaries, and he told me about how he'd carried a torch for a woman. She'd said she wanted to be just friends with him. So he'd asked her, "Where do your friends kiss you?" Because he wanted to kiss her everywhere, but also wanted to ensure he didn't cross any of her boundaries. They're married now, and I think they have at least one kid.

That story gave me an idea. "Then let's talk about how this works."

"How what works?"

"Being friends. As you may recall, I told you I don't have many."

"I remember." He looked me over, like he found this information unlikely.

"You and I, we'll be friends . . . who are hot for each other?"

He shifted in his seat but continued to meet my eyes. "Something like that."

"Then take me through friend touches."

He quirked an eyebrow. "Pardon?"

"As friends who are hot for each other, it may be difficult for me to read your phys-ical cues, and I don't want to cross any boundaries. Your boundaries might not be the same as my boundaries."

He seemed to think about this for a few seconds, and then nodded slowly. "Okay. Go on."

"I think we should review what is and isn't appropriate friend touching." Without thinking too much about it, I pulled my legs under me and knelt on the bench seat. Then I skootched closer to Jackson, placing my hand on his broad shoulder. "Is this a friend touch?"

His lips twitched and his eyes danced. "Yes. That is a friend touch, Rae."

"Okay. What if I put my hand on your chest?" I did. I placed my hand over his heart.

He nodded, his eyes still on mine, still amused.

"How about your stomach?" Trailing my hand lower, my fingertips brushed downward along the front of his T-shirt to his abdomen, and lower—

He caught my hand, repressed laughter in his voice. "Maybe stop there."

But this was serious, so I treated it seriously. I withdrew, holding my palms up and out. "Okay. Good to know. Now what about your knee?" I settled my hand on his knee.

"That's fine."

"Upper thigh?"

He cleared his throat. "Fine."

"What about—"

Jackson caught my hand again before I could move it higher, his lips pressed together, his eyes shining with humor.

Once more, I removed my hand, but I caught one of his as I withdrew. "I'm sensing a pattern."

"Are you?"

"Yes. Now, let me show you my boundaries."

I pushed my messy braids behind me, leaving the front of my dress free of my long hair. I then placed his hand on my bare shoulder, and his eyes cut to the spot, some of his amusement fading.

"You can touch me here—" I slid his palm down my arm and then lifted it back up to slowly trace over my collarbone, my neck, my cheek, pushing his fingers gently into the hair at my temples, then—closing my eyes—taking his knuckles and brushing them against my lips.

"Rae—"

"I'm not finished." Keeping my eyes closed, I used his hand like I might a soft cloth. Except, his hands weren't soft. They were calloused, and the friction felt quite nice as I moved it along the other side of my collarbone, and down my other arm, and then straightened one of my legs and lifted my skirt.

His breathing now audible in the cab, I let my lashes flutter open and unhurriedly slid his big, rough palm from my ankle to my knee. He didn't look at all amused now. His jaw tight, his attention transfixed to where he touched me. Those intense, deep-set eyes had turned from their usual rich brown to a much darker shade.

"This is still a friend touch," I whispered, bringing his fingers up to my mid-thigh, pushing the skirt as we went. Then, I stopped. Because now I was feeling breathless too.

He glared at his hand on the skin I'd revealed, the muscle at his temple jumping. His eyes cut to mine, and a shock of *oh-shit-I-think-I-pushed-too-far* made the very center of my body twist and ache with anticipation.

"What about this?" he asked gruffly, an edge of something deliciously dangerous behind the question as he slowly, so very slowly, skimmed his fingertips higher, nudging my leg wider. "Does this feel friendly?"

"Very friendly," I said, meaning it as a joke, but something got lost in translation between my brain and my mouth because his eyes flared, and then his fingers were pushing my skirt higher to reveal the waistband of my underwear.

And then his fingers were inside my underwear.

And then I shuddered, sucking in a shocked breath, my hands spasming as they searched for something to grip, and the blunt tip of his middle finger circled my clit.

"And this?" His voice a growl, he shifted closer, pulling the straps of my dress and bra down my arm. Lowering his mouth to my neck, he placed a hungry, wet kiss there, his tongue licking the skin beneath my ear before trailing down to my chest, all the while giving me the gentlest strokes between my legs. "Is this how friends touch you?"

Unable to form words, I gripped his shoulders for purchase because, even though I couldn't really go anywhere, I felt like I might fall.

He tugged harder on the strap of my dress and bra, sliding his fingers into the cup and pulling it down, his hot kisses moving over the tops of my breasts, but then he paused at my nipple, withdrawing an inch or two. His glorious tongue slid out of his mouth and painted a tight circle around the stiff peak. Everything in me coiled hot and needy at the sight.

Why must he be so fucking sexy all the fucking time?

Laving a firm, wet lick over the straining center, he caught me in his teeth. At the exact same moment, he slipped two fingers inside me, and I cried out.

"I don't think I like the thought of other friends touching you this way," he grunted, withdrawing his fingers from my body and hooking them into my underwear.

"Maybe you and I could have a—a special friendship." My retort pitched high with not a small amount of desperation.

Maneuvering me up, he firmly pulled the triangle of fabric down my legs, and then grabbed my hips, bringing me across his lap such that I lay between him and the steering wheel, my back to the driver's side window, and the hard press of his erection under my bottom.

Bunching up the skirt of my dress to my stomach, he bared all of me from the waist down, his elbow against the interior of my knee, holding me open.

Grabbing my hand, he demanded, "Look at me, *friend*."

So I did.

And then—*oh God*—and then, holding my eyes like he dared me to look away, he brought the index and middle finger of my hand to his mouth and slid them inside, tangling them with his tongue. A shock of arousal so intense speared through me, I had to bite my lip to keep from moaning. Finished torturing me, he took my hand and lowered it between my open legs, encouraging me to touch myself.

I whimpered. I was so slippery, and sensitive, and I *ached*. I didn't want my touch. I wanted his. But his hand splayed unmoving on the inside of my thigh, the tips of his fingers less than an inch from where I played with my body, his eyes on my movements. The slick, wet noises the only sounds in the quiet dawn other than my frantic, gasping breaths.

Leaning forward, he caught my ear between his teeth and whispered, "Do you know why I'm making you do this?"

I shook my head, unable to speak.

His hips shifted restlessly, rolling beneath my backside. "Because, in the future, whenever you touch yourself in this friendly way—" he nipped at my ear, his tongue licking the lobe and sending a cascade of acute shivers racing over every inch of my skin "—I want you to think about this moment, and how much I enjoy watching you play with your pretty pussy, and our special friendship."

That did it.

My head whipped back as my body began to come apart. Mouth opening on a silent scream, Jackson finally, finally pushed his long fingers back inside, hooking them up, touching the sweetest of spots, pumping into me quickly, massaging mercilessly.

I remembered this about him, and the memory hadn't been overexaggerated. He'd been exceptionally skilled at finding and stroking my G-spot *precisely* where and how I needed—then and now. I grabbed his wrist as I rolled my hips and clenched around his fingers. Bowing forward, instinct had me trying to squeeze my legs together. But I couldn't. His elbow at my knee kept me open to his gaze.

It was too much. The way he watched me, like he was in a trance. The way he touched me, like I belonged to him. My chest heaved and, even as stars continued to burst behind my eyes and the pleasure explosion radiated from my center and tremors wracked me, I curled toward him, needing his warmth and closeness, needing to bury my face in his neck and feel the hard planes and strength of Jackson hold the soft contours of me. Needing his delicious scent in my lungs and the taste of him on my tongue.

Needing *him*.

We kissed, our mouths fusing as he wrung another orgasm out of my body. His lovely thumb—the very one he'd parted my lips with outside the bank on Thursday afternoon—rubbed my clitoris in time, his rough, unyielding fingers at my entrance.

My lungs ached for air, and eventually I was forced to turn my face so I could breathe. He kissed my cheeks, my neck, and my shoulders, biting my skin and soothing it with languid strokes of his tongue. Soft, deep sounds reverberated from his chest, like he found me tasty, and he was famished.

Little by little, I returned to reality. Eventually, he stopped attacking me with his hungry kisses and simply held me tight. Everything that had come before now had been mind-blowingly amazing. But this, feeling vulnerable and being held, being caught in his solid, certain grip, felt like heaven.

I loved it. I didn't want the moment to end. I knew it would, but I hoped this would signal a beginning for us. I hoped he felt the same.

But you don't know if you don't ask, Rae.

Suddenly anxious, I shifted in his arms. He loosened them so I could see him. Features unsmiling, he gazed at me. I detected something hard behind his eyes. My stomach fluttered with nerves.

"Hi," I said.

He said nothing.

I licked my lips, trying to read his mood while my dumb mouth spoke without taking the time to deliberate the wisdom of my words. "I just want you to know, I really value our special friendship."

He laughed. But it was tight, and short, and now I recognized that the hardness behind his eyes was hunger. As he glared down at me, his palm slid into the bunched fabric of my dress, caressing and massaging one of my breasts with touches that felt both light and possessive. He couldn't keep his hands off my body, apparently.

I felt my smile dwindle as I studied the tired lines etched into his forehead. In that moment, he looked a little wild, his hair askew, his usually well-kept beard longer than I'd ever seen it.

But it was his dark eyes tracking my movements, like a predator unwilling to look away from its prey, that gave me the courage to ask, "Would you consider coming back to the carriage house now?"

He stared at me, still saying nothing, and the wild light flared into something that felt feral.

"You didn't get much rest." I tried to sound calm, reasonable, even though the way he watched me set my heart galloping. "We could just sleep, if you want."

"I'm not going to want to sleep," he said, his voice a scrape, his erection nudging insistently against my bottom. "And I think you know that."

A thrill raced down my spine and pulsed between my legs, and I hoped—*oh I hope I hope I hope*—I was reading him correctly. "I don't want to sleep either," I said.

Jackson placed his knuckles under my chin, tilting my face up and placing a hot but sadly closed-mouth kiss against my lips, saying as he lifted his head, "Then let's go not sleep together."

CHAPTER 16

RAQUEL

"Mistakes are part of the dues one pays for a full life."

— SOPHIA LOREN

$\mathcal{W}$e didn't speak on the drive back to Sienna's house. He'd pulled me close after buckling himself in and starting the truck's engine, kissing me and making me dizzy all over again before saying, "There's a center seatbelt."

I took that to mean, *Stay right here.*

Once I'd finished strapping into the lap belt, he'd put his arm around my shoulders, tugging me against his side and encouraging my cheek to rest on his chest. His scent surrounding me, soft and fluffy feelings followed, and I discovered how much I loved being held while in a truck, next to Jackson, on a drive.

Fluffy feelings weren't why we didn't speak, though. I could guess why Jackson wasn't in a chatty mood, probably something to do with the persistent outline pressing against the front of his jeans.

My bout of silence, on the other hand, had everything to do with crazy ideas and irrational internal musings.

No rule existed that said I could only act in movies. Maybe I would start taking stage roles, in Knoxville, if the local theaters were interested. Or I could get a different job, start a new career. I didn't have a college degree, but I could go back to school. I could become one of those legendary stories talked about at Hollywood parties, the A-list actress who dropped off the face of the earth, went back to college, and became a . . .

I could become a . . .

Maybe I could go back to school and major in . . .

My mind blanked.

I'd never wanted to be anything but an actress and work in film. When other kids in high school were going to football games and getting drunk at bonfires afterward, I'd been making movies, figuring out camera angles and line of sight logistics, recording myself running through monologues, critiquing my performances, using makeup to turn myself into an elf, or an ogre, or a 1920s flapper. And then trying again the next day to do everything better.

You don't have to figure this out right now.

Jackson's body shifted as he turned the steering wheel. I felt the flexing and roll of his muscles beneath my side, and I tucked all my worries and planning away for later. Much, much later. Tomorrow morning maybe, after Jackson and I spent all day and night in bed together. Then we'd figure it out. Because, short of an act of God, Jackson and I were definitely having—

"Oh my God. What is that?" Jackson pressed on the brake.

Frowning, I lifted my head, and I saw it. *Them!*

"Oh no!" I lowered immediately to his lap, hiding from view. Cars were parked up and down the two-lane road for what looked like miles. Clustered in front of Sienna's long driveway and along their fence was a giant swarm of paparazzi.

"Keep driving. Don't slow down, just keep driving. Drive past them."

"I can't. They're blocking the road." He sounded irritated. "This is a safety hazard. All these cars need to be moved."

"Jackson, listen to me. You have to keep driving."

He didn't accelerate. "There's a bunch of people up at the main house too. Like ten limos."

I groaned, covering my face. "Oh no."

"What? What's wrong?"

"That must be Sasha. But why are there—she wasn't supposed to—dammit!" I didn't have my phone with me to call her. Jackson's phone wouldn't help because I didn't have Sasha's number memorized.

"Wait!" I pulled my hands away from my face. "Where's your phone?"

"In the glove box."

"Can I use it?"

"Yeah. Yes." He honked his horn. "I'll give you the password." Glaring out the windshield, I suspected he was giving someone—or a few someones—a dirty look. "This is a mess."

Hurriedly, I pulled Jackson's cell from the glove box, typed in the password he dictated, and scrolled through his contacts. "Do you have Sienna's number? Or Jethro's?"

"No. But I have Cletus's."

"Yes, I see it." I typed out a message.

Jackson: Cletus, this is an emergency. I need Sienna's phone number. (This is Raquel Ezra using Jackson's phone)

Cletus: What kind of emergency? And how do I know you are who you say you are? Tell me something only Raquel Ezra would know.

Despite the situation, a shocked laugh burst out of me.

"What did he say?"

I read Cletus's message.

Jackson, pressing on the accelerator, growled. "Call him. Put it on speaker."

The phone rang four times before a voice picked up. "Ahoy, ahoy."

"Cletus! This is Jackson."

"Ah-ha! I knew it was you. Why're you pretending to be Ms. Ezra?"

"I'm also here," I said dryly, still laughing for some reason.

185

"Oh. Well, in that case, let me text y'all Sienna's number."

"Thank you," Jackson ground out and then gestured that I should hang up. But then a few seconds later, he added thoughtfully, "He is being particularly ornery recently. He must be worried about something."

Sienna's number came through with a chime, and I immediately texted her. "Have you and Cletus been close for long?"

Jackson: Sienna, this is Rae. I'm on Jackson's phone. Please call me.

"Only a few years. He used to not like me much." Jackson flipped on his turn signal.

"Why didn't he like you? Did you arrest him?"

This earned me a quizzical look. "No. I wasn't very nice to his sister when we were in high school. All the Winston brothers disliked me because of it."

"Ashley?"

"Yes. Ashley."

I'd met Ashley at dinner last week when we'd all gone to The Front Porch. She'd been absolutely lovely. "What happened?"

He made a face of concentration, taking a curve in the road carefully. "It's a long story, but here's the short version: We were best friends growing up, I fell for her, she did not feel the same way, but we were each other's firsts. I thought that meant we were going to get married. Upon hearing this, she panicked and admitted that my feelings weren't reciprocated. She wanted to go back to being just friends."

"Just friends, huh?"

That earned me a quick, narrowed look. He continued like I hadn't spoken. "I was mad, hurt, so I told everyone our senior year that I'd slept with her and then dropped her. I spread the nasty rumor, trying to tear her down and make myself feel better about being unwanted. Instead, all I did was show everyone why I wasn't good enough for her and why she was right not to want me."

I felt my eyebrows inch higher as he spoke. "You—that wasn't—what a dick move!"

"Correct. It was shameful and petty and small, and I learned my lesson."

"What was the lesson? Don't be an asshole?"

He nodded, flipping on his blinker again and taking a right turn. "That was certainly one of them. But there were others, such as: How you treat others defines you more than how others treat you. There's no such thing as convincing someone to love you, you can't push a person into reciprocating feelings. No one owes me anything I haven't earned. Sometimes wanting a thing is bad for me, it makes me a worse person; no matter how much I want it, if it doesn't make me better, I should let it go. And lastly, give grace when asked sincerely for forgiveness, even if the person's behavior was shameful, petty, and small."

I exhaled a long breath, frowning at the stark lines creasing his features. Just like during our drive late last night, when he'd said matter-of-factly that he didn't have many innate talents, he'd recited the story and his list in a blunt, monotone voice. I got the sense he probably still beat himself up about decisions he'd made in high school.

"That's a lot of lessons."

"Yes." He slowed the truck around a corner. "I'm just sorry I had to learn them at Ashley's expense."

"How old were you?"

"Seventeen. Old enough to know better because my parents had raised me better."

The phone in my hand rang before I could process all of Jackson's story. I stared at the screen of the cell, frowning. *This isn't my phone.*

"Pick it up, that's probably Sienna."

"Oh!" I answered it, remembering why I'd been waiting for her call.

"Rae?"

"Yes. What is going on? Why are all those cars at the house?"

"You tell me." She laughed, sounding more bemused than frustrated. "I woke up to this. I think your entire staff is here. We have a butler, a nutritionist, two physical trainers, a—"

"Dammit Sasha!" I whispered harshly.

"Yes. She is here too. And she brought some people for you to interview for her personal assistant? What? Why would your personal assistant need a personal assistant? Tom Low's former PA had PAs, and it always seemed crazy to me. And why would she fly them out to Tennessee?"

I sighed heavily, anger swelling in my chest. Sienna's questions were more than valid. Why would Sasha do this? Why would she bring *everyone*?

"They're all inside the carriage house," she continued. "Jethro turned off the alarm and made them some coffee. Charlotte left her kiddos here and went to Daisy's to grab some doughnuts for everyone."

"Thank you. That was nice of him and kind of Charlotte. I'm so sorry about this."

"Don't worry about it. Hey, don't come in the front driveway off Moth Run Road, it's blocked by the paps."

I hazarded a peek at Jackson. His features were tense.

"Yes. We saw." I rubbed my forehead. "Is there another way in? A different road we can take?"

"It's kind of hard to explain. Ask Jackson if he knows about it."

He'd been listening in, so he shook his head. "No. I don't know what she's talking about."

"Can you meet Charlotte at Daisy's? She knows the backroad behind the house." I heard Sienna turn on a faucet and some dishes clink together; one of her sons asked for juice. "Just a minute, baby. Rae, listen, the family has it well camouflaged. If you don't know it's there, the road is impossible to see."

My heart stuttered, and Jackson glanced down at me, saying in a voice just above a whisper, "We're past the paparazzi. You can sit up now."

I nodded, sitting up and feeling sad. And disappointed. And irritated. And helpless. I considered immediately evicting all of my employees from the carriage house and locking them out while Jackson and I spent quality time being friendly. Or asking Jackson to take me back to his place.

But I wasn't that person. I couldn't leave Sienna and Jethro and Charlotte to deal with my mess. If I'd called Sasha and talked to her directly instead of sending a message through Domino, then I wouldn't be dealing with this circus now.

"I know you don't have your phone, but Jackson knows how to get to Daisy's. Call Charlotte and let her know you're coming," Sienna added, likely misinterpreting my silence as worry over locating Daisy's.

"Okay. I'll use Jackson's phone to text Charlotte. See you soon."

"Sure, sure. No problem. And don't worry. It was honestly kind of funny waking up this morning to eight limos in the front yard. Why didn't they just rent a passenger van?"

Good question.

I clicked off, swallowing thickly as I navigated to Charlotte's contact information in Jackson's phone. She wasn't labeled as *Girlfriend*, or *Ex-girlfriend*, or *My Love*, or anything like that. He had her labeled simply as *Charlotte Mitchell*. Just her name.

I thought about looking for Ashley's entry, to see if he had her contact information at all and what he'd called her, but immediately pushed the impulse from my mind. That would be an invasion of privacy.

"Are you texting Charlotte?" Jackson asked. "Tell her I'll call the station and have some guys come out to clear the street. They can't park along that road."

Smiling pensively to myself, I sent Charlotte a quick text, explaining the situation in as few words as possible, asking her to wait for me at Daisy's, and then navigated back to Jackson's contacts.

"Did they recognize you?" I asked, typing in my unlisted, impossible for anyone to find phone number. "The paparazzi, I mean."

"They didn't seem to," he grumbled distractedly, glaring at the road like he was deep in thought. "We're almost there."

After typing my number, I navigated to *Add contact* and paused, thinking back to his story about Ashley. A chill traveled down my spine.

"Jackson?"

"Yes."

"How many people did you tell about our night together?"

He frowned, looking unhappy. "Just Cletus. I didn't tell him, he guessed that we'd spent the night together after he introduced us. I didn't share any details, none at all.

189

And I'm sorry he found out. Cletus, he can be sneaky. But I should've been more guarded."

I relaxed, the chill disappearing, replaced with the warm hum I usually felt whenever we were together. *One person and no details? That's actually not bad.*

"When did you tell him?" My thumb still hovered over the button that would save my number.

"Yesterday."

"Yesterday?" I gaped at him. "The first time you told someone was yesterday?"

"Yes. And I apologize." His voice had deepened with regret, and when he looked at me, I could see he was sorry. *Very* sorry. "I want you to know, I told him nothing. I would never betray your privacy like that."

"Jackson, no. I know you would never betray me. I'm just—" I was going to say surprised, except I wasn't. The Jackson I knew was circumspect and responsible, diligent and hard-working, and *fun*. HE made me feel comfortable, safe. As I reflected on it, I would've been surprised if he had told more people. "It's okay."

"No, it's not."

"No. It is. I told Sienna." I hesitated, thinking, then added, "And Charlotte."

He muttered a curse word under his breath, his forehead coming to his hand. "You told Charlotte?"

Yikes.

The anxiety in his voice gave me heartburn. "No details—not really—just that we'd hung out one night, years ago, and that we didn't have sex. But she brought up your legendary tongue." *Oh God.* Shit.

Now I felt like a jerk.

"I see . . ." He squirmed in his seat, his jaw tight.

I am such a jerk. "Are you angry with me?"

He shook his head. Then he glanced at me and gave me a smile that didn't reach his eyes. "No. Course not."

I didn't believe him, and the tempo of my heart increased. "Jackson, please don't be upset. I really didn't say much." *Just that I've been pining for you for over five years. Other than that, not much.*

We drove in silence for a while. I fretted, and he stewed. Unlike last night, this silence wasn't as comfortable. Staring at the screen of his phone, I debated whether or not to add my number. Would he even want it now?

Clearing my throat, my eyes on the *Add contact* button, I asked, "Have you done anything like that to anyone else?"

"Pardon?" I'd obviously pulled him out of some pretty deep thoughts.

"What you did to Ashley in high school. Have you treated anyone else that way?"

"No." He heaved a sigh, his tone solemn. "I don't do that kind of thing."

"What kind of thing?"

"I don't push anyone for anything."

I looked up from the phone and studied the side of his face, noticing how—since I'd asked him about Ashley—he'd pushed himself against the driver-side door, leaning his arm against the windowsill, sitting as far away from me as possible in the small space. We weren't touching anymore. The realization unsettled me.

"And—" he swallowed, looking pained "—I've been the subject of gossip. At first I didn't mind, I leaned into it. I was flattered, even. But then I learned having a reputation as a playboy can get you laid, but it doesn't get you a date to a wedding, or anyone's respect."

Ugh. I understood exactly what he meant.

"Folks around here, they get an idea in their head, and it's hard to modify it. Someone who sleeps around might be an honorable, respectable person, but it doesn't matter. That's all people see. It's just as hard to alter an idea as it is a first impression." His voice barely above a whisper, I surmised he was speaking to himself more than to me. "I might change, but that doesn't mean I can change people's minds about who I am, because the idea persists, even if it's faulty. My father has a saying, warning about this."

"What does he say?"

"It's something like, 'Your mistakes and missteps will reinforce people's unflattering ideas about you, and your good deeds will be explained away by nice weather.'"

I wanted to reach out and touch him, hold his hand, or squeeze his leg—or better yet, wrap him in a hug— but he was so far away and turned in on himself. I hesitated.

Picking my words carefully, I said, "You know, it's okay to want things. To want people to see you clearly, for who you are."

Wow, Rae. That's some good advice. Perhaps you should take it.

"I know," he said.

I didn't believe him, so I pushed the issue. "There's a difference between fighting for something you want and pushing another person to do something—or be something —they don't want."

Look at you, Rae. Wisdom-ing your wisdom all over the place.

He nodded, flipping on his blinker again and pulling into the parking lot of the diner. "We're here," he said, cutting the engine, unclicking his belt, and pulling the driver's side latch. "Let's go find Charlotte."

Jackson was out and had shut the door before I could respond.

My stomach sank, and I studied his phone screen, the cursor waiting for me to label myself in Jackson's phone. Hurriedly, before he finished walking around the front of his truck, I finally clicked *Add contact* and labeled myself as *Sunny*.

* * *

Half of my staff left Sunday, another quarter departed Monday morning. Praise be, only Sasha, Dave, and Miguel remained by Tuesday.

But after a week of putting up with constant whining, doors being slammed, and crap left all over the place, Sasha and her attitude were tap dancing on my last nerve. No wonder I needed a butler and cleaning staff in LA! I was convinced the woman used an inordinate amount of toilet paper. And she couldn't change a toilet paper roll if a lifetime supply of designer purses were on the line.

"Are you sure you like this color? Because I think people are used to seeing you in shades of red." Sasha picked up the red swatch I'd already discarded in favor of the pink. As far as I was concerned, the matter had been settled over an hour ago. One red carpet event of me wearing pink instead of red wasn't going to make or break my acting career. I honestly didn't care either way. Red, pink, purple, black. Whatever!

This was her job. This was why I paid her, so I wouldn't have to think about every single tiny detail.

Has it always been like this with her? Yes.

How did you put up with it for so long? Maybe I thought mean equaled smart?

I felt like I'd been sucked into an alternate dimension, where I was now viewing myself from the outside—or the old version of me—and I found her exhausting and boring.

"I really think you should do the red." Sasha picked up the pink swatch, tossed it into the pile with the rejects, and put the red down next to the sketch of my dress.

No. Wait. Scratch that. I find Sasha exhausting and boring.

"Hey, hey, hey! I brought lunch," Charlotte's cheerful voice called from the front door. I leaned back from where I sat at the kitchen table and relief washed over me at the sight of my friend. Who I liked. And who was nice to me.

Jumping up, I left my PA and her pushy opinions behind, walking over to take the bags from Charlotte. "It's so good to see you."

I lifted up, she bent down, and we kissed cheeks. "Good to see you too. I guess this is more like an early dinner. I just got off work and the kids are saying hi to Ben, Andy, and the baby. Jethro asked if they could stay for a bit and play, so I'm dropping off dinner. Or lunch. Depending on what you want to call it."

"Thank you. It can be breakfast, lunch, and dinner. I haven't eaten all day."

Sasha and I had been meeting nonstop since Sunday. She'd proclaimed each issue an emergency, and I'd lost count of how many times she'd said my absence had brought everything to a standstill. No one could do *anything* without me. I was *never* allowed to take a vacation again without my staff.

But once we'd worked our way through the first five items—colors for redecorating her en suite bathroom, whether to follow our standard August calendar for social media or create a new one, whether or not I should have lunch with Ana Ortega next week at the studio and what I would wear, things like that—it was clear that these were tasks and decisions she could've handled on her own and didn't merit my involvement.

Pasting on a smile, I turned to carry the bags of food into the house and called to Sasha. "Charlotte brought us food."

"What is it?" Sasha met me with folded arms and an expression that could only be described as petulant.

"It's sandwiches from Daisy's," Charlotte said, meandering into the house after me but addressing Sasha. "I brought tuna for Rae and veggie for you, because I remembered you're a vegetarian."

"A sandwich? So I guess the bread is wheat? They don't have any salads in this town?" Sasha huffed, scratching her scalp with a pencil and turning her back on Charlotte. "We should fly Marques back out."

Marques was my chef. I liked him. Probably because he didn't speak English, so we rarely talked. Not that there was anything wrong with Marques. But I was coming to the realization that most of my employees were insufferable, pushy crybabies, and I'd been bamboozled by celebrity inertia into thinking I needed them.

But the last two weeks told me differently.

"No need to fly out Marques. I'm staying. You're leaving. You'll see him tomorrow. Or maybe even tonight if we can wrap all this up." I fought the urge to tell Sasha to say thank you to Charlotte and stop acting like an entitled brat. But she was my employee, not my child.

That said, this incident was soooo going on her performance review.

Exhausted. And Bored.

Unloading the containers, I popped each one open to figure out which was one veggie, which one was tuna, and which one—

"The BLT is mine." Charlotte pointed toward the pile of takeout.

Meanwhile, Sasha dug through her purse and pulled out a one-hundred-dollar bill. I watched in horror as she marched over to Charlotte and held it out. "Do you have change for this?"

"Why? You planning on going to the Pink Pony?"

"It's for the food." She waved it under Charlotte's nose. "And do you need a tip?"

Charlotte lifted an eyebrow at my PA. "I don't think you have any tips I need."

"No, Sasha. Charlotte is a friend of mine. Remember?" I sent Charlotte an apologetic smile. This was the third time I'd had to remind my PA who Charlotte was.

Sasha looked between us. "What? Are you two fucking or something?"

Charlotte's mouth fell open, her eyes ping-ponging to mine.

"What?!" I almost dropped the takeout. "That was—Sasha. That was way over the line."

She lowered the hundred and huffed, turning to face me completely. "Sorry, okay? It's just been really stressful since you left us with a big fucking mess, Raquel! I'm so stressed." She swung her arm toward the front door. "I've been the one having to clean it up. And now I have to be out here, in hillb—"

I stopped her before she could make a hillbilly reference. "No. You don't. I told Domino only to have you pack some clothes for me and fly out with Miguel and Dave. I talked to him, and he confirmed that he'd told you exactly that."

"Domino doesn't know what it takes to keep everything running smoothly. Only I know. And I can't believe you sent back my PA candidates. You expect me to do everything! I need more help."

I jerked back, my temper rising to lava levels. "Uh, no. You haven't been dealing with anything. You saved it all for me to deal with. What have you been doing for two weeks?"

"I've been completely overwhelmed!"

"Well now you're completely fired." I said the words three seconds before they formed in my brain. Even as they solidified, I felt no remorse.

Perhaps I'd allowed Sasha to speak to me this way before, but not anymore.

She reared back. "What?"

"You're fired. I don't like how you speak to me."

It's amazing what being surrounded by kind people will do. Sienna, her family, Charlotte, and especially Jackson. They'd taught me how I wanted—how I *deserved*—to be treated, and not by pushing or bullying me.

Or perhaps being around Sienna and Jethro—and Jackson, his good manners and steady character—had made me realize that I wanted wholesome and real more than I wanted glamourous and exciting.

Or perhaps spending a few weeks on my own, making my own meals, doing my own laundry, setting my own schedule, and making my own decisions had been just what I'd needed. There's nothing like being capable to remind a person just how capable they are.

Or perhaps I've just finally grown up.

But you know who hadn't grown up? Sasha.

"Are you kidding?" she screamed. "You disappear for two weeks and now you don't like how I speak to you? And now you think you can *fire* me? What happened to you? Why are you suddenly being like this?"

Nuh-uh. I wasn't doing this. I was so done. "I'll call Domino. He will meet you at the house so you can pick up your things. I'll put you up in a hotel for one month—no expense account—so you can find a new place to live. Or you can pocket the cash and be done. But you're fired."

Sasha made a sound that resembled a chicken squawk, searching the ceiling as though passive, doormat Raquel lived up there. When she found nothing but high ceilings and crown molding, she turned, grabbed her purse, and—sending me a fiery glare—stormed past Charlotte.

"And place the credit cards on the console table as you leave, please. Call Domino. He'll help you make flight arrangements back to LA. You can pick up your last check from his office."

She paused by the front door, and with jerky movements, slapped three credit cards on the table. And then, in a very *Goodbye, Cruel World!* kind of move, she turned and shouted, "Good luck surviving without me, Raquel. I wouldn't work for you again if you begged me," slamming the door on her way out.

Wonderful silence followed her departure, during which Charlotte and I stood motionless. Eventually, I looked at my friend, she looked at me, and she said, "Since you might not survive past tonight, and this very well may be your last meal, are you still okay with tuna?"

"Yes. I feel good about tuna." God. I loved Charlotte.

She strolled over to the fridge and opened it. "What kind of beer do you have in here?"

"I don't. Sadly."

"Do you want me to go get some from the big house? Jethro has cases and cases. They keep getting it free from people who love Sienna."

I chuckled. "Sure. Go ahead. Thank you." If people in LA had offered me cases of free beer, I probably would've accepted it too.

"I'll be right back. And I'll make sure she leaves without slashing any tires."

Charlotte left me in the kitchen with my sandwich and no regrets. Yes, my life would be more difficult for a little bit . . . *but would it?*

I sighed at the thought. It would be more difficult. Sasha was exhausting, and she frequently foisted her responsibilities on me, but she'd been good at keeping track of details. Until I could get someone new hired and trained, things would be stressful. Details would be missed.

That said, I didn't want a live-in PA anymore. I didn't want a live-in anything anymore, except a dog. *Or a Jackson.*

I grimaced, shoving thoughts of Deputy Dreamy from my mind and focusing on the issue at hand. When I got back to LA, I would be making some changes. And when I hired a new PA, he or she would not be living with me. I'd grown addicted to privacy and autonomy here, and going back to the way things had been ceased to be an option the moment I stepped off the plane in Green Valley three weeks ago.

While I waited for Charlotte to return, I placed the veggie sandwich in the fridge, figuring I could eat it for lunch tomorrow, and poured us both a glass of water. I was just setting the table for two when Charlotte burst back in, carrying six cases—yes, SIX cases—of beer.

"Rae! Come quick."

"Oh my God! Do you need help?"

"No. I work out. Plus, hefting around four kids means I'm strong as a bull. But—get over here!" She set the beer down by the door.

"What? What is it? What happened?"

197

"Nothing bad. And your little friend is gone. A taxi already came and went—which is basically a miracle. Taxis usually take forever to arrive. But enough about that. Guess what's pulling up the driveway?"

"What?" I scooted around the stools at the kitchen island and rushed to where Charlotte was unloading her burden.

"It's a cruiser. From the sheriff's department."

"Oh!" My heart leapt, and I pressed my face against the window that looked out onto the driveway. I hadn't seen or heard from Jackson since Saturday, and I'd been kicking myself for not entering my number in his phone under my real name—or, you know, my stage name.

"Is it Jackson?"

"I don't know." She squinted out the glass, then cocked her head. "Oh. No. That's not Jackson. I think that's Boone."

"Could Jackson be with him?" I did a dance of uncertainty in the foyer, not sure if I should run into my bedroom and change out of my frumpy clothes, or if I should watch from the window, or if I should go open the door.

"I don't think so," Charlotte said softly, and then to herself, "Where the hell is that dummy?"

My heart dropped, and I pressed my hand to my chest, rubbing the ache. I agreed with Charlotte. Where the hell was that dummy? Whatever he'd done Saturday to get the paparazzi moved away from Moth Run Road had worked. And the paps hadn't returned to line the road, but they did materialize whenever I left Sienna's property.

Maybe the paparazzi are why he's staying away? Or maybe he's mad that I told Charlotte about our night together? I hated that he was so hard to read. What was I supposed to do? Should I get his number from Sienna and call him? I felt like . . . no. He should call me, right? Or check on me? Or should I check on—

A knock shook me out of my never-ending loop of questions, and I calmly walked to the door and opened it.

Before me stood a man who looked a lot like a young Derek Luke, dressed in the same uniform Jackson had been wearing when he'd found me at the bank over a week ago. "Hello, Ms. Ezra. I'm Deputy Boone."

"Nice to meet you." I held out my hand for him to shake. "Won't you come in?"

"No, ma'am. This shouldn't take long. I just have a few questions. Do you mind coming out here?"

I glanced at Charlotte. She shrugged.

"Suuuure." I followed Deputy Boone outside. He didn't take me too far from the house, just three feet or so.

"I'm here to check up on you, and make sure everything's okay after the events of last Thursday."

"The . . . events?"

"Yes, ma'am. We're doing our due diligence. Just wanted to check in and make sure you didn't have any complaints against the department, or Deputy James."

Crossing my arms, I allowed my confusion to show on my face. "Uh, no. Absolutely no complaints. Except, you know, I haven't heard from him." I chuckled.

"Uhh. . ." Deputy Boone did not chuckle. He was all business. And I could see that what I'd said confused him.

"Sorry. That's not—sorry. No, no, Jackson was a perfect gentleman, and I do mean perfect."

He reached into the front breast pocket of his uniform. "Here's my card if you have any questions or something occurs to you that you'd like to talk about."

I accepted the card, not looking at it, and anxiety climbed up my throat because I could see Deputy Boone was finished and ready to leave, so I blurted, "How is he?"

"Who, ma'am?"

"Jackson." I fiddled with the business card I'd just been given. "Do you know him?"

"Yes. We work together." He said this very slowly, like he wasn't used to answering questions.

"Is he okay? Does he have any . . . complaints? About me?"

More confusion flickered over his features, and he responded to my question with one of his own. "Ms. Ezra, do you know how to reach Deputy James?"

"Yes. I mean, I don't have his number." I snorted, then regretted it when his eyebrows jumped. "Sorry. I regret that snort. I have snort lament. Charlotte has Jackson's number, and I see her basically every day, so, *yeeeeah.*"

"I also happen to have Deputy James's card." He pulled out a business card holder, this time from some unseen pocket on his person, and thumbed through several business cards, eventually handing one over to me. It was Jackson's. "If you feel like you need to reach out, you should."

I looked at the card. I gazed at it, the black lettering on the white, thick paper that read Deputy Jackson James. I still loved his name.

"I don't want to bother him."

I glanced up and found Deputy Boone inspecting me, like he was working really hard to figure out what to say, or how to say it.

"Do you think I should call him?" I asked. "Do you think he wants to hear from me?"

His expression unreadable, he tucked away his notepad and pen. "If you have a reason to call Deputy James, then you should. If you don't, then don't." The words sounded a bit like a warning, and they were definitely a riddle. "Have a nice day, ma'am."

He turned. He left.

And I don't think he heard my belated, "You too," as he drove away.

CHAPTER 17

JACKSON

"It is better to be looked over than overlooked."

— MAE WEST

I saw Rae and Charlotte together everywhere. I saw them at the park, playing with Charlotte's kids. I saw them downtown, grabbing lunch at The Sandwich, Soup, and Salad Stop. I saw them in the Piggly Wiggly, grocery shopping. I even saw them at the station, bringing in treats from the Donner Bakery for all the deputies and staff.

I'm sure they would've said hi if I'd given either of them the chance. I hadn't. This was for four reasons:

First, the paparazzi. Green Valley had some experience putting up with the paparazzi. Sienna Diaz being a big movie star meant we usually had a photographer lurking about in town at least three or four times a year. When Sienna first arrived in town, things had been pretty bad. But not like this.

This time they'd descended like a swarm of locusts. All the restaurants ran out of food. They didn't just want photos of Rae, they wanted photos of Rae with *me*. I lacked the motivation to provide any of these antagonistic scavengers with a meal ticket.

Luckily, pictures of me on my own had lost their allure after the first week post-ATM-gate, but several photographers continued following me around anyway, taunting me, perhaps hoping I'd forget I was being followed or hoping to make me lose my temper.

Being followed meant the sheriff had pulled me from the field and placed me on desk duty until further notice. I wasn't much use to the community as a deputy, being trailed by paparazzi all day, making citizens nervous every time I answered a complaint or call.

Second, seeing Rae and Charlotte all around town together would've been disconcerting enough—especially now that I knew Raquel had told Charlotte about us—but in addition to the paparazzi, Rae's newly arrived bodyguards followed them constantly, two hulking shadows trailing their every move and keeping everyone else —and I do mean *everyone*—at bay.

According to Flo McClure, Karen Smith had tried to walk over while they were at the playground and the guards wouldn't let her within a ten-foot radius. I imagine this made Charlotte happy. Karen Smith was widely recognized as one of the town's main gossips and had perpetuated the idea after Charlotte's divorce from Kevin that Charlotte was someone to be pitied.

Cletus had told me in passing that most of Rae's entourage had been sent packing to LA after three crazy days, everyone except the two guards and her PA. I hadn't seen the PA, and I didn't know why the sight of the two men grated, but it did. Did they sleep at the carriage house with Rae? Was she ever alone? I wanted her to be safe, protected, looked after, but how could she live like that? Being followed everywhere she went sounded terrible. Didn't she have any privacy?

But then, I'd broken my own rule for the first time in over five years and Googled Raquel Ezra, searching for articles on when she'd started using bodyguards. A whole slew of truly disturbing stories popped up—like one about an intruder who'd brought rope into her house and she'd burned him with a curling iron, and another guy who'd followed her around Sunset Boulevard, flashing her, and another guy who'd tried to climb the gates of her current residence—and suddenly I didn't mind the guards' presence anymore.

If anything, I felt a bit angry with her that she hadn't seen fit to bring them with her to Green Valley from the get-go.

"Bad day, Jackson?" Flo asked, tossing a file on my clean desk, it landed with a *smack.*

"No. Day's been fine. How's yours?"

"Okay, I guess. This is the paperwork for that overdose two days ago, the one at the hotel, not the one at the residential address. The family is asking for a more detailed report."

I picked up the folder and issued her a tight smile. "I'll ask Boone if he has anything to add, go back over what I wrote, see if I can provide more detail."

Third reason I'd kept my distance, a random string of opiate overdoses, a kidnapping victim found dead in the park, and a slew of domestic abuse calls during the last week and a half. Since I was stuck in the station, I'd been the one typing up the reports, acting as the secretary for everyone else. I didn't mind the assignment, given what my thoughtless (and yet worth it) actions had brought me, and I wanted to help, but there was a reason I hadn't become a coroner.

Each of the deaths struck me as more depressing than the last. Being the conduit through which needless, seemingly endless death was described for official purposes and consumption hadn't done much for my state of mind.

Flo nodded, studying me. "Seriously, you doing all right, Jackson?"

"Just fine, thanks." I flipped open the folder and pretended to scan the intake form.

"You—uh—had a chance to catch up with your Ms. Ezra yet? How is she holding up? Did she and that Harrison fella finally call it quits?"

I gathered a deep, silent inhale through my nose and forced a bored, even tone as I replied, "I haven't spoken to Ms. Ezra. I imagine she's fine. Maybe call Charlotte, she would know."

Which brings me to my fourth and final reason for avoiding Rae—Ms. Ezra—I was determined to think of her as Ms. Ezra from now on.

I could not be trusted around her without losing every stitch of my good sense. Let me clarify that: I did not trust *myself* around Ms. Ezra. She wasn't the problem. I was the problem.

Taking her on that drive had been a mistake. Kissing her, touching her, making her come in my arms had all been grievous errors in judgment, and I didn't like myself much afterward. I'd been pushy. When she put my hand on her body, it was like I'd lost my mind.

Point was, being around Ms. Ezra made me someone else, someone thoughtless, reckless, someone who cared only about feeling good in the moment rather than staying focused on my worthwhile goals for the long term. Being with her was as easy as breathing. Her presence made my head swim and my heart light, but it did not make me a better person.

For example, being with Ms. Ezra had me considering absurd ideas, like quitting my job here and looking for a position with the LA County Sheriff's Department, moving out to California so we might be able to . . .

What? What exactly do you think a movie star wants with someone like you?

She wanted a fun time. Following her to Los Angeles just to be her fun time would be crazy. And foolish. And a waste of all the hard work I'd been putting in here. I wanted to be sheriff of this county, but more than that, I wanted to *deserve* the job.

I needed to push her from my mind. I walked the other way whenever I spotted her, determined to stop being an idiot, determined to stop thinking about her because I knew reaching or pushing for someone so far above my level would eventually come with a hard, painful fall.

Stay upright, Jackson.

Flo loitered for a long moment and then left, her feet scuffing against the linoleum floor as she went. Karen Smith may've been the town gossip, but Flo McClure was usually the source of it. The less I said to Flo, the better. I didn't wish to provide any additional fodder.

Surprisingly—and I wasn't complaining— I had not been at the center of Karen Smith's or Flo's gossip mill these days. Sienna and Jethro's plan to save my reputation had worked. Mostly.

Folks in town were quick to eat up the story Rae, Charlotte, and Sienna had spread around at the jam session, that I'd been off duty and doing Rae a favor, offering to help her break free from a toxic relationship.

I couldn't believe it. This explanation for our kiss in front of the ATM made absolutely no sense. But what did I know? People apparently found the story easier to swallow than the possibility that Raquel Ezra wanted to be with me.

Most folks even felt sorry for me and had told me as much. I'd done Ms. Ezra a favor and ended up with a parade of photographers tailing me everywhere I went. With the townsfolk, I'd come out of ATM-gate smelling like a rose. A sad, inconsequential rose, but a rose nonetheless.

My work colleagues seemed more skeptical. Maybe because some of them were present when Rae had shown up with that sour cherry pie? Regardless, no one had come out and asked me what happened—in fact, most everyone had given me a wide berth—but I got the sense they knew there was more to the story.

The sheriff, meanwhile, would have none of it. And he obviously didn't wish to discuss it. We hadn't spoken in private since the meeting with Mike. In front of my coworkers, he'd been the same as he usually was—professional, thoughtful, respectful—but if my father had more to say, he'd kept those thoughts to himself.

My mother, on the other hand, stopped by my house in the evenings unannounced when I was working on the boat, bringing my favorite dinners and offering to do my laundry. She'd say, "Hang in there, baby." I knew she was referring to the strained relationship between me and my father, not the paparazzi.

She'd also say, "I don't want to pry, but if you need to talk about anything, you let me know."

My mother had recently—within the last few years—retired from teaching elementary school, but she still volunteered as a teaching assistant three days a week. She was basically MacGyver, Martha Stewart, and Captain Marvel all rolled up into one woman. Janet James could turn dirt and a paper clip into a winning science fair project, bake ten dozen gluten-free, dairy-free cupcakes while grading assignments, making dinner, and checking in to ensure my sister and I had finished our homework, washed our hands, and eaten our vegetables—all without breaking a sweat or displaying a single crack in her outward calm.

She was basically the most competent, capable, supportive, kindhearted, no-nonsense person on the planet.

I wasn't going to talk to her about anything, least of all the ways I'd failed to live up to my father's expectations.

I rubbed my forehead and flipped through the file on the overdose. These were printouts of documents that existed in the online system, but Florence and the rest of the administrative staff liked their paper files for recent cases.

"Is that the overdose the Nelson family keeps calling about? Or is that the FBI file for the kidnapping?" my father's voice asked from somewhere behind me.

My instinct was to stiffen, which I did, but I also managed to nod. "It's the overdose. I'll add more details." I'd finished with the kidnapping file hours ago, but I still couldn't get the crime-scene images out of my mind. What I needed was to go on a long, punishing run; or maybe spend ten hours working on the boat.

I'd often wished I was one of those folks who could get drunk, but drinking more than three beers just bought me a cluster headache and a world of hurt.

"I read the report you and Boone put together on that overdose. Not sure how much more detailed y'all can get." His hand came to my shoulder, gave it a pat. "They're not going to be happy, no matter what you say. Sometimes there are no answers that will satisfy. Best to tell the truth and move on."

"Even so . . ." I flipped to the third page, bypassing a picture of the young woman lying on the floor of a hotel room, a crime scene photo taken before the death had been ruled an overdose.

I sensed him hover behind me while I pulled out my notepad and jotted down a few questions for Boone. We'd been thorough, but maybe there was something we could add that might lessen the Nelsons' grief, even a little.

"I understand you wanting to do right by the Nelsons, but there's more than enough work to do, Jackson," my father said finally, his footfalls carrying him away. "Don't spend too much time weeding an empty garden."

* * *

My father's comment about weeding empty gardens came from his father. His father —my grandfather—had been a farmer, and all his sayings seemed to revolve around dirt and plants and weather, but it also reminded me that this Saturday was my day to visit the plots.

I'd been roped into adopting plots by Ashley and her husband Drew. Ashley mentioned a year or so ago that the park rangers needed more volunteers for their adopt-a-plot program. Normal, nonscience folks like me would take time out of their schedules to collect seasonal biological information about designated areas inside the Great Smoky Mountains National Park, like when wildflowers bloomed, which kinds, how many; changes in the tree canopy; changes in the surround foliage. That kind of stuff.

Charlotte and her kids had come out with me a few times. Documenting the flora had always sparked some interesting conversations. I had four plots, two along Cooper Road Trail and two about a hundred yards from the parking lot at Cades Cove—one to the north, the other to the south. Even though less monitoring was required during June and July, I wanted to make sure I did my due diligence.

Saturday morning, after a quick breakfast and coffee, I set off for Cooper Road Trail with my notebook and pen. Once I'd finished investigating and writing down all the relevant information, I hiked the rest of the trail and did my best to enjoy the unseasonably cool summer morning, ready to turn my mind to something other than images of overdoses and violent death.

I then set off for Cades Cove, realizing once I'd parked that the day had gotten away from me. It was now just past 4:00 PM, and I'd missed lunch.

My notebook and pen in hand, I jogged toward the first plot. I thought maybe I heard someone call out my name and looked over my shoulder, but I didn't slow. If I neglected to eat soon, I'd be in danger of a cluster headache. I needed to make quick work of it and get back home.

When I didn't immediately notice anyone who might've been shouting my name, I continued toward the plot, not seeing the big man in dark sunglasses and a dark suit until I was almost on top of him.

"Hey. You. Stop," he said, stepping in my path.

I did stop, drawing up short and frowning at the granite set of his jaw. I recognized him. This was one of Rae's—I mean, Ms. Ezra's—bodyguards. Which meant—

"It's okay, Dave! This is a friend," a voice full of sunshine and rainbows called out, and I caught sight of her a split second before my lungs seized. Rae waded through the tall grass of the prairie and wore tight yoga pants—or something like them—a fitted plain white T-shirt, and a baseball cap. She came from the direction of my plot.

I swallowed both my surprise and a rush of chaotic sentiments, taking a step back at her approach, my brain telling me to turn around, go home, eat some food, and check on the plot next weekend. But the rest of me rebelled. I stood rooted in place, ensnared by the vision of Rae.

"Hi." She walked right up to me and gave me a big hug. "I—uh—I missed you."

I stifled a groan, closing my eyes and bracing too late for the impact of *her.* Even surrounded by the earthy smells of the grasses, trees, and prairie, her scent enveloped me. I breathed in, my lungs hot and aching, my arms coming around her body, holding her.

Jackson, if you are photographed with her, it will be—

Worth it. So, so worth it.

"Hi," I said, breathing past the spiky heat in my chest and relaxing into her embrace. Since the hug was already happening, I might as well surrender to it.

We stood there like that for a time. I honestly have no idea how long. She readjusted her head, placing her cheek against my heart and pulling in a deep breath just to let it out on a big sigh two seconds later.

"Sorry I smell like bug spray. It's good to see you," she said, her voice quiet and shaded with sadness.

"You too." It was good. *Too good*, my surly brain warned.

I pulled back, releasing her completely and stepping out of the circle of her arms. "What are you doing here?" Turning my head to glance at her guard, I gave him a short nod which he returned. I couldn't see his eyes, but I wouldn't have been surprised if they'd been narrowed to threatening slits.

Her eyes moved over me, her stare feeling somehow heavier than before, weighted with something I couldn't place. "I'm supposed to meet Charlotte and the kids for a picnic here. Or, not here, but over there." She twisted at the waist and pointed behind her.

Right at my plot.

CHAPTER 18

JACKSON

"A sex symbol? A symbol of sex? I don't think that I am a sex symbol, although it's very flattering. I'm 59, now, so I think I'm possibly past my sell-by date. I think I am."

— LIAM NEESON

"She sent me GPS coordinates and said it was important we meet precisely there because she had something to show me, but now she's late." Rae pulled her phone out of some unseen pocket and scrolled through a few screens. "She hasn't texted, but I'm wondering if maybe my reception is spotty. Except my phone has full bars. I don't know."

"I see," I drawled, my attention snagging on her second guard. He wasn't as conspicuous as the first guy, turning his head this way and that as though scanning the horizon, but I felt his attention on me.

Perhaps discerning the direction of my thoughts, Rae gestured to the big guy first and the smaller guy second. "Jackson, this is Dave and Miguel. Dave, Miguel, this is Jackson."

"Oh. You're Jackson," Miguel said, his posture immediately relaxing.

I walked over to Dave first since he was closest, extending my hand. "Yep. I'm Jackson."

Dave took it, gave me a firm shake and another head nod. "Nice to meet you, man. Charlotte talks about you *a lot.*"

Miguel called over, "She's not the only one."

I looked between the two men, my eyebrow raised in question. I wanted to thank them for looking after Rae and keeping her safe, but I wasn't certain how my expression of gratitude would be received. She wasn't mine to fuss or worry over. *Even so . . .*

"They're hilarious," Rae said. I found her blushing but not smiling. "And they're both under an NDA, so they shouldn't be volunteering any unnecessary information." Unless I was mistaken, this last part sounded like a legitimate threat. I'd never heard her voice so stern.

Bemused, I walked over to Miguel. He grinned widely at me. Or maybe he grinned widely at Rae's threat.

As we shook hands, he leaned close and whispered, "I'll tell you later."

"I heard that!" Rae marched over and grabbed my arm. "Ignore them. We're ignoring you!" she hollered.

Chuckling at this exchange, I allowed myself to be pulled behind her toward my plot and a red and white checked tablecloth spread on the ground. To one side of the circle sat a giant picnic basket.

"I'm so sorry about them," she said on a rush. "They like to gossip."

"Hey, Raquel," Dave called òver.

"I said we're ignoring you!"

"We got company. Do you want me to stop them?"

We both turned and searched the prairie for newcomers. It took me about three seconds before I recognized the four women, all of whom were waving gleefully at us.

"Jackson!" Darlene Simmons—a tall redhead with whom I'd spent more than one enjoyable evening many years ago—sing-songed my name. "Yoo-hoo! Jackson! Didn't you hear me calling your name in the parking lot?" Darlene was a medical doctor now.

Next to her were three more of my—ahem—conquests. Although, in retrospect, an argument could be made that I'd been a conquest for each of *them,* not the other way around. I'd never pushed, only taken what they'd freely offered.

Regardless, none of the ladies had been left unhappy by our arrangements, nor had they been left with a broken heart. I'd never shied away from greeting any of them if we'd happened to run into each other. Until now.

This cannot be happening.

I felt Rae's eyes on my profile as she called to Dave, "It's okay. Don't stop them."

"Right-o," he said, sounding cheerful.

"*Friends* of yours, Jackson?" Rae moved like she was going to drop my hand.

I squeezed her fingers tighter, some base instinct within me not letting her withdraw. My eyes slid to hers. "From a long, long, *long* time ago."

"How long?"

"Before we met."

"That long?" She stepped closer, her voice dropping, "Anyone since me?"

"Not that I can recall at this moment," I whispered, my brain telling me to shut up as my heart egged me on. "But that might be because, when I'm with you, all I see and can think about is you."

She stared at me, unsmiling. "You say pretty things."

"I say true things." My thumb moved over the back of her hand but, despite wanting to, I didn't bring her knuckles to my lips for a kiss.

Dave's "Hellooo, ladies. Having a nice day?" met my ears, and I released a silent sigh, remembering that four of my ex-flings were at this very moment parading a path through the prairie to say hi.

Rae unleashed a dazzling smile as they approached. "I can't wait to meet them."

"You won't have to," I grumbled, turning to face my past. "They're here."

"Haaaay y'all." Darlene lifted her hand to wave in that weird way some people do, opening and closing their fingers like they're trying to catch a mosquito. "Whoa. I'm out of breath. Dear me."

Still holding on to Rae, I gestured to the three women, each in turn by lifting up my notebook in their direction. "Raquel, this is Angela Jones, Darlene Simmons, Jessica Molina Ramirez, and Patricia Robillard." An odd combination of apprehension, ingrained good manners, and a sense of duty making it so I wasn't quite certain where to look. "Ladies, this is Raquel Ezra."

"It's so nice to meet you!" Darlene enthused. "I am such a fan. You are amazing."

"I'm also a fan," Angela said, reaching out her hand for a shake, necessitating that Rae drop my fingers.

"It's nice to meet you," Rae said, and she sounded like she meant it.

Angela, expression hazy, added, "I've seen *Starlight Express* twelve times. I might have a problem."

Rae chuckled, and Jessica stepped forward, wearing a huge grin. She started speaking in Spanish, her tone equally gushing and effusive.

Rae's grin wavered, her forehead knitting together, and she covered Jessica's hand with hers. "I'm sorry, I don't—" she looked at me anxiously, her tan cheeks rosy with a pink blush "—I don't speak Spanish. I'm so sorry."

"Oh! No, I'm so sorry!" Jessica shook her head quickly, looking mortified. "I'm sorry. I just assumed. And you know, I don't even realize I'm speaking it sometimes, especially when I'm nervous. Sorry."

"No, don't apologize. I never learned. My mother—who is from Italy—didn't even want me to learn Italian. I picked up a little bit though, despite her best efforts, especially when she cussed."

This made everyone laugh, and I could see Jessica relax, the matter forgotten.

Darlene launched into a monologue about how brave she thought Rae's acting choices were. This lasted for several minutes, and I began to feel light-headed. I still hadn't eaten. Even though we stood beneath one of the big oak trees and in the shade, the heat of the late afternoon began to wear me down.

Eventually, Darlene paused to take a breath, and Angela—who had been Darlene's roommate in college, which was how we'd met—grabbed her friend's hand and spoke before the redhead could, "Anyway! Thanks for letting us interrupt your date. We just wanted to say hi."

"Oh, this isn't a date." Rae waved a hand through the air as though dismissing the idea. "Jackson and I are *just friends*."

A shard of something cold and painful slithered from the base of my skull downward at the way she'd said "just friends."

"We're waiting for Charlotte Mitchell and her kids." Rae laughed, all smiles. "Jackson and I ran into each other by accident. This isn't a date."

My stomach soured, and suddenly I was no longer hungry. But I grit my teeth. *No one to blame but yourself, Jackson. If you hadn't been such a fuckboy in your early twenties, none of this would be happening now.*

"O-okay," Angela said, her eyes flickering to mine and then back to Rae. "Sounds good. We'll just, you know, get going. Good to meet you."

"Bye Jackson." Patricia sent me a cheeky grin. "Let me know when you're in Knoxville. We'll have lunch."

I nodded politely, saying nothing, because I suspected no matter what I said, it would be the wrong thing.

Soon the women were on their way, taking a moment to speak with Dave as they went. As soon as they were out of earshot, Rae turned abruptly and marched over to the blanket and sat. I followed slower, studying her as I approached, and taking note of her erratic movements.

She withdrew her phone. She glared at the screen. "Charlotte is going to be another half hour," she grumbled. "She said she fell asleep on the couch."

That sounded like Charlotte, she was always taking catnaps.

"She probably wanted some alone time," Rae said wryly. "I think she's getting sick of my company."

My eyes flickered to Miguel and Dave twenty paces back, the suits and dark sunglasses a jarring sight against the tranquil backdrop of the national park.

"Are you hungry?" Rae asked, her eyes flickering to me just briefly.

I debated how to answer. I wasn't hungry, not anymore, but I needed to eat. "I could eat."

"After meeting your fan club, I'm not sure I have much of an appetite. But I have this picnic basket full of food. Do you . . .?" She motioned to a spot on the blanket across from her.

"Thank you." I crossed to the place she'd indicated and lowered to my knees, setting my notebook and pen to one side as I watched her struggle to open a bag of chips. "Hey. You might want to—Rae. You're upset. Stop a minute." I reached over and covered her hand.

She closed her eyes, shaking me off. "I'm not *upset*."

Oh. Yeah. She's upset. I wasn't going to tell her to calm down. Telling a woman to calm down was like throwing gasoline on a tire fire.

I glanced around us. We were surrounded by a tall, thick wall of prairie grasses and reeds. How we were sitting, not even Dave or Miguel could perceive what we were doing. Unless there were paparazzi in the sky, no one could see us.

She huffed, opening her eyes and glaring at me. "I should be able to speak Spanish."

Uncertain where she was going with this, I asked, "Why is that?"

"I'm half Cuban. Did you know that? I'm fifty percent Italian, fifty percent Cuban, and one hundred percent midwestern." I would've taken her statement as a joke—a play on words—except she sounded brittle. "But my problem is, I'm really ten percent Italian, ten percent midwestern, and eighty percent I-have-no-idea-who-I-am." She sighed, the sound so melancholy, I had to fight with myself not to reach out and pull her into a hug.

"I wish I knew how to speak Spanish." She stared at the tablecloth, sounding thoughtful and distracted. "I think—I think I'm going to learn. I'm going to learn. And then I'm going to Miami. And Cuba."

"You should," I said softly.

Her eyes cut to me, then narrowed, glittering angrily. "Oh? You think so? You don't think that might be *pushy* of me?"

I held still, watching her. At some point, if I was patient enough, she'd tell me what I'd done to upset her. I just needed to wait.

"No response to that? I guess saying *because* isn't an option right now, is it?" she hissed, dropping the bag of chips and folding her arms, her features tight. "'In anger we should refrain both from speech and action.'"

She sounded like she was quoting someone, but I had no idea who.

She must've seen my confusion because she grumbled, "Pythagoras. Some Greek dude who lived thousands of years ago and my mom—whatever! Forget it. I want to ask you a question."

"Sure. You can ask me anyth—"

"Did you have sex with all of them?"

Maybe I should've been shocked or offended. I wasn't. I absorbed her question and the anger behind it, doing my best to reach inside her mind and attempt to read her thoughts.

She's . . . jealous?

"Yes. I'm jealous!" she announced, like I'd asked the question aloud. Rae waved her hands wildly in the air. "But, you know, it's not even about them. They were delight-ful. Absolutely delightful. Fine. Have sex with hundreds of women. Fine. But am I an idiot? Just tell me." She jutted her chin out, eyes flashing.

"No. Of course not—"

"*When I'm with you, all I see and can think about is you, Rae,*" she cut me off, mimicking my words from earlier and punching the chips next to her. "I don't believe a single thing you say."

"I have never lied to you." The words came out rough, my throat full of gravel and my chest full of lead.

She ignored me, ranting like I hadn't spoken. "I promised myself I wasn't going to do this. I promised myself that if I saw you, I would be friendly but cool, since we are *just friends*. Obviously, if you wanted to be more than just friends, if our little car trip had meant anything at all to you, you would've called me."

I didn't try to offer the excuse of not having her number. I didn't have her number, but I could've asked Sienna for it a hundred times now that her cell was in my recent calls history. But I did say, "You know you mean something to me."

She scoffed. "Whatever. I don't care. I should just get over it." Rae flicked her hands in the air like she was flicking the idea of me away. "I really should. But then your harem shows up, and I don't know, I guess I'm jealous that you wanted all those women more than you wanted me."

A surge of anger had me gritting out, "And what would be the point of wanting you, Rae? Are you planning to stay in Green Valley? Are you moving here?"

"No. Because I have no reason to stay, do I? No one wants me here." She laughed, sweeping her arm out. "Listen, there is one more thing I want to know. I understand that you've changed"—she said the word *changed* like it was the dumbest word in the English language— "and you want a long-term relationship with a nice, dedicated, hard-working, struggling, unfun woman. But this is what I don't get, why didn't we have sex that night when we first met? According to everyone , you were Mr. Funtimes back then. Why didn't you want me?"

Her accusation landed right in the center of my chest, unleashing my temper. Acting on instinct, I encircled her wrists with my fingers, hauling her up such that we were both kneeling, just inches between us. "You think I didn't want you that night?"

"No. I don't." She pushed against me but didn't try to break free. "You could've taken my bishop *at any point!"* The end of her sentence was whispered harshly, like maybe she wanted to yell but knew she couldn't.

I followed suit and lowered my voice to a harsh whisper. "You told me, when we were at the overlook that night, the minute we had sex, I'd be—and I quote—'dead to you.' I thought—" I shook my head at the memory, at the burst of panic I'd felt when she'd said those words, and the stupidity of my hasty, desperate logic at the time. Swallowing thickly, I forced myself to even my tone, loosening my grip on her wrists. "I thought, if we didn't sleep together—if we didn't have sex that night— then maybe you'd be open to seeing me again. Maybe it wouldn't count as a one-night stand."

Her lips parted in surprise and most of the anger drained right out of her.

"But to your original question, the answer is no, Rae. I haven't had sex with all those women. Just two of them. But I did mess around with the other two. They all went to college together, and I happily took whatever they offered. Because I didn't care if I saw them again, and they didn't care if they saw me. I messed around a lot when I was younger, and it was all fun and it was all easy. And none of it lasted or mattered.

I didn't expect it to. I didn't spend nights aching for any of *them*, wondering what they were doing, wondering if they'd be open to seeing me again, wondering if they still remembered me or ever thought about me."

Her beautiful brown eyes were unguarded, searching, and she seemed to be holding her breath, waiting for me to finish.

"I could've asked Sienna for your number, you're right. I thought about it a thousand times. But I didn't because I am blind when I'm with you. I'm not sure I can be a good man when I'm with you. I'm not sure I can trust myself not to push you for more than you want to give me. And that's on me. That's my failure. So, yes. I could've called. But I'm crazy about you, and being crazy about someone isn't good for me. Or them."

"Oh, Jackson."

"And just like everything I've ever said to you since the moment we met, that's the God's honest truth." I said through gritted teeth, letting her go and moving to stand.

"No. Wait. Wait a minute." Now she reached for me, dragging me down and keeping me on my knees—figuratively and literally. "I wish you had said something to me back then."

"Why? Would you have stayed?" I spat, angrier than I had a right to be.

"Yes. I would have!" She nodded earnestly, closing the distance between us to tenderly cup my jaw between her hands. "I wanted to stay that night. I wanted to get to know you. I wanted you to take me fishing. And if you'd asked, I would have stayed."

What? I shook my head, ingrained instinct telling me to reject her words.

Rae leaned forward to kiss me, a short, urgent press of lips before wrapping her arms around my shoulders and placing her cheek next to mine. "I don't know what to do," she said, squeezing me tightly. "I've never felt like this before. I don't understand it myself, and I know it doesn't make sense, because we barely know each other, but I want a shot at being your nice, dedicated, hard-working, struggling, unfun woman."

What is happening?

My brain couldn't keep up. But my body, my hands in particular, seemed to know exactly what I wanted. I twined several locks of her long, thick hair around my fingers and pulled gently, forcing her chin back. I looked down at her, at the uncertainty, the hopeful vulnerability written all over her features.

Something too big to contain or measure swelled within me, a feeling, a sense, an emotion I couldn't name, but it was fierce, and it turned my heart into a wild drum such that I heard nothing else. My mouth was on hers then, claiming the sweet sound of her surprise as I laid her back on the blanket and tasted her tongue, settling myself firmly between her open thighs and rocking forward.

She moaned. Her fingers clawed at my shirt to lift it, to reach inside and touch my skin, branding the expanse of my back.

Her nails dragged around my side, scratching my stomach as I feasted on her neck and pushed up her white T-shirt. I wasn't thinking about anything—not where we were, not who stood nearby, or who might happen upon us. Making Rae feel good, making Rae come, making Rae beg—*whoa, not sure where that one came from*—occupied the entirety of my thoughts. Kissing and tasting every square inch of her body, listening to her sounds of ecstasy, feeling her muscles lock up, the intensity surprising her, just like I'd had the honor of doing twice upon a time.

But this time, I wanted inside her, my name on her lips when she came, and after she came, and then the next day. I wanted one night after another, waking her up to satiate my need and waking her up to satiate hers. I wanted mornings and afternoons too.

"Hey, Raquel!"

Someone's voice penetrated my single-minded concentration, but just barely. Not enough to stop me from pulling down the cup of her bra and swirling my tongue around the stiff center of her breast.

She panted, watching my tongue circle her. Her hips shifted, rubbing impatiently against the erection barely contained behind the fly of my jeans. I shuddered, drawing her nipple into my mouth.

"Raaaaqueeeel?" the voice tried again.

"No, no, no," Rae whimpered, grabbing fistfuls of my shirt as I began lifting myself up. "Ignore him."

"Charlotte is here. And she brought the *kids*," the voice said, an unmistakable hint of urgency behind the words.

I stiffened, reality crashing around me as the blanket and the picnic and the crushed bag of chips came sharply into focus.

I looked at Rae. She looked at me.

"So whatever you two are doing," a second voice added, "you might want to put it away."

CHAPTER 19

RAQUEL

"Everything you see I owe to spaghetti."

— SOPHIA LOREN (ATTRIBUTED, BUT LATER DENIED)

"Jackson James! Well, what a surprise." Charlotte said this around the world's largest, most self-satisfied smirk in the history of smirking. "What are the chances?"

"Charlotte," he responded evenly in his delicious voice, but his eyes told a different story. His hands were stuffed deep in his front pockets and his shirt was untucked.

I knew—if he felt anything like I did—he was in a fair amount of pain. The pain of a frustrated, unmanifested-yet-definitely-imminently-possible reconciliation.

As soon as Dave mentioned the kids were present, Jackson and I had jumped away from each other, frantically working to straighten our clothes and hide all signs of hanky-panky. I experienced trouble switching over from Jackson-reconciliation-hopes to Charlotte-and-the-kids-fun-times. I knew I looked at him hungrily, because I was currently calculating how long we need to be sociable before we could leave.

And then what, Rae? This was the question.

We still had a lot to talk about. I'd told him how I felt. I'd told him I wanted to try being together *for real*. He hadn't responded with words. Getting busy on the picnic blanket hadn't been my intention. But it seemed like every time we were alone, we made out instead of making up.

"Has it been a bad day or a good day, Jackson?" Charlotte asked lightly, looking like she couldn't be more pleased no matter how he answered.

He didn't answer.

"Are you here to check on your plot, Jackson?" Kimmy Mitchell wandered over to the blanket and plopped down, picking up the bag of chips I'd assaulted earlier.

"Your plot?" I snuck a glance at him, but his eyes were narrowed on Charlotte.

She was still smirking. "Oh! That's right. I'd forgotten all about your plot. How silly of me. And what a coincidence that it's right here, where we are standing, right now." She wasn't even trying to lie believably. She looked like she was trying not to laugh. "How are your plots, Jackson? All my plots are going swimmingly."

"What's blooming?" Joshua Mitchell, the second oldest and a sensitive, sweet soul, took the bag of chips from Kimmy and gently opened it for her.

"Wait, what plot are we talking about?" I addressed this question to the kids since I wasn't sure Jackson was capable of conversation yet. His body had been *quite* primed for other activities when we'd been interrupted.

"Jackson watches over the land for the rangers and takes notes about the plants and such." Joshua opened the picnic basket and riffled through it as his baby brother toddled over.

"You do?"

He gave his eyes to me, the heat behind them tempered but still present, and I longed to pull him away from here, someplace private, for hours upon hours so we could figure things out between us. Maybe we needed to be placed in cages so we couldn't touch each other.

Great. Now I'm going to have cage fight sex fantasies about Jackson tonight.

"Something like that," he finally said, a barely-there smile softening his features and making me melt.

Note to self, buy a cage.

"Nonscientists, or future scientists—" Jackson absentmindedly ruffled the toddler's hair and then helped Frankie sit as he knelt next to the basket "—can adopt plots of land in the park. All you have to do is stop by every two weeks between spring and late fall, write down what's there, keep track of the tree line, the foliage."

"It helps the rangers understand how the weather makes the plants grow." Joshua handed a plate to Kimmy, then to Jackson, then to himself. "Momma? Are you eating?"

Charlotte grabbed her second youngest, pulling the ponytail out of Sonya's hair and redoing it. "No baby, we're not staying long."

"Oh? That's too bad," I said. It wasn't too bad. It was great news. And now I felt like a jerk. I lowered to my knees, accepting a plate from Joshua.

"Yes!" Kimmy—who had just spotted the main course in the basket—sent me a hopeful look. "Is this for us?"

"What is it? What did she make?" Charlotte, looking undecided, hovered at the edge of the blanket.

Kimmy turned over her shoulder. "Pesto primavera," she announced, pronouncing the words perfectly.

"Then I guess we will be staying after all." Charlotte immediately sat and reached out a hand. "Gimme two plates, Josh. One for me and one for your little sister."

"Pesto primavera?" Jackson's eyes skimmed over me. "What's that?"

"It's a fancy name for spaghetti with this green slimy sauce and vegetables, and you haven't lived until you've eaten Rae's pesto primavera." Charlotte raved, and I knew her compliment came from the heart. The last time I'd made my mother's recipe for her, she'd eaten three servings. "Wait a minute. Haven't you been to Italy, Jackson? And you've never heard of pesto primavera?"

"We didn't eat out much, and I was only there for a short trip to see the baby," he replied, passing out the forks and napkins to the kids. Frankie sat down on Jackson's lap, like it was the most natural thing in the world, as he directed his next comments to me, "My sister lives there for now, and we all went out when my nephew was born."

"Does your sister work outside the home?" I asked, realizing I didn't know very much about Jackson's family.

"Yes."

"What does she do?" Kimmy reverently passed me the container pesto primavera, and I peeled back the lid.

"She's an heiress," Charlotte said matter-of-factly.

Jackson sent her a flat look. "She teaches. She's a math teacher. Wherever she goes, she teaches at a local school."

"She's an heiress," Charlotte whispered loudly. "That's how she can afford to go wherever she wants."

"Anyway." Jackson cleared his throat, setting down the toddler's food to cut the pasta and vegetables into little bits. "Where'd you pick up this recipe?"

"It's my mother's recipe."

"She's from Italy," Charlotte said around a mouthful of food. "And if vegetables in Italy tastes like this, I want to become an heiress and move there like your sister."

I felt Jackson's eyes on me, so I gave him mine.

"You don't talk much about your family," he said softly, like he was just realizing this.

"We don't always talk when we're together," I whispered.

"What do you two do if you're not talking? Do you play?" Joshua asked, looking honestly curious.

Charlotte choked on her food, and I set Jackson's plate down to hand her a bottle of water. "Are you okay?"

"Fine. Just fine," she rasped, gulping the water. She breathed out, then in, then said, "Jackson, why don't you tell Rae more about the plots? That's a nice, normal, uncomplicated subject."

"I would like to hear about them." I finished heaping a serving onto his plate and handed it back to him.

"Sure. But let me eat for a minute first. I skipped lunch." He accepted his plate and promptly picked up his spoon and fork. Twisting to the side to maneuver around the toddler, he pressed the tines of his fork against the curve of the spoon to painstakingly twirl the noodles, meticulously coiling them until none dangled. The sight made me smile. He was so careful and thoughtful, even with spaghetti.

Making myself a plate, but momentarily forgotten, I watched as he brought the bite to his mouth, and I knew the precise moment the sauce hit his tongue because his face contorted with pleasure, and he groaned.

"Oh my God."

Goose bumps spread over my arms and neck at the sound of his enjoyment. My mouth watered. I felt a little dizzy.

"Say *Oh my goodness.* Not *Oh my God,*" Kimmy instructed, cutting through my daze.

I redirected my eyes to her and discovered she'd already finished eating, her plate completely clean.

"That's right, Kimmy," Charlotte said around her own bite, then gave Jackson a meaningful look. "What did I tell you? Isn't it *outstanding?* I'm just saying, Rae. If that whole acting thing doesn't work out, you should open an Italian restaurant in Green Valley."

"This is—" Jackson shook his head, drawing my attention back to him and his facial expressions of ecstasy. "Rae, this is the best thing I've ever eaten."

"Ever?" I asked, the word slipping out before I could stop myself, and a spiky wave of mortification rushed up my neck and cheeks.

Rae! What is wrong with you? There are children present!

Jackson grew very still, his eyes fastened to the plate in his hands, his mouth paused mid-chew.

And Charlotte, chuckling heartily, stacked her plate with her kids' plates and stood. "Well. I think that's our cue to leave."

I sighed, also standing. "I'm sorry."

"Don't you apologize." She pointed at me, giving me a warm grin as she leaned in for a hug. "You just fed my kids dinner. You're officially my favorite person. Come on everyone. Let's get going. Come on."

With Jackson to help wipe off the youngest's face and me stacking the dishes, it took several minutes before the children actually vacated the blanket—because somehow Kimmy had taken off her shoes, and then lost a shoe, and then Joshua wanted to try on Jackson's shoes, and, and, and—and then they were gone.

Jackson stood at the edge of the blanket, watching them go while I knelt, figuratively sitting on the edge of my seat, wondering—worrying—what would happen next.

"Do you want kids?" he asked, twisting to look down at me. "And what was your childhood like? In all your interviews, you don't talk about it."

Neither of these questions had been expected. It took me a moment to recalibrate the direction of my thoughts, and a few more to find the words. I decided to answer the easy question first.

"I don't know if I want kids, honestly." I peered up at him. "I don't know if I'd be a good mom."

He made a small sound, turned completely, and sat on the grass. "What is your mom like?"

A light laugh escaped me. "She's very smart."

"What does she do?"

"She's a classics professor at a small, private liberal arts college."

"Hmm. So, Latin and such?"

"Yes. She actually made me learn Latin."

"How'd you like that?"

I opened my mouth to complain about it, but then stopped myself, really thinking before answering. "At the time, I mostly hated it. But Latin is not like learning other languages. The pronunciation is extrapolated based on current related languages, so I didn't speak it. I learned to read and write it, though."

"Why 'mostly'? What did you like about it?"

"The examples, in the textbooks, are always very gruesome and funny."

"How so?"

"Uh, like, they all have to do with murder and insurrection."

226

He laughed. "Really?"

"Yes. I guess because you're never going to have to ask someone where the bathroom is in Latin, they skip over all the conversational stuff."

"I don't know, depends on the conversations you're having, I guess." The side of his mouth curved upward. "So, she's smart. And she's got good recipes." He reached over and picked up his plate, bringing it back to where he sat on the grass. "What else? Was it just the two of you?"

"Yes. Just the two of us."

He seemed to study me before saying, "Do you not want to talk about your family?"

"I don't." I never did.

"Okay. That's fine. But then maybe, could you tell me why?"

I smiled at his cleverness. "I see. You're not going to push me to talk about my family. But then you ask why I don't want to talk about them, which means I'll have to talk about them."

"Is that what I'm doing?" He ate another bite of his pasta, his tone light and conversational. This was so nice.

I chuckled and crossed my arms. "Fine. I don't like to talk about my family because I feel like I don't have one."

He frowned, lowering his fork, his eyes wide with concern. But he didn't ask me to elaborate, which was probably why I did.

"My mom left Italy for the States over strong objections from her parents. They're still in Italy, and I've only met them and my aunts, uncles, and cousins a few times. We're not close. When she moved here, it was on a student visa, and she met my dad in Miami—she didn't go to school down there, she was on summer break. She then got pregnant with me. He wanted to get married, she didn't, and so she raised me on her own."

"What about your dad? Do you see him?"

I shook my head. "I've met him nine times that I can remember, and not since I was eight. He doesn't want to know me."

"He said that?"

"Yes."

Jackson winced. He set his plate down and crawled over to me. Pulling me into a hug, he reclined onto his back, bringing me with him. My cheek pressed to his chest, his arms around my body, and I closed my eyes.

"It's his loss. I can't imagine meeting you and not wanting to know you," he said firmly, making my insides feel warm. "Did your biological father have any more children?"

I expelled a heavy sigh. "Yes."

"How old are they?"

"I don't know. I think the youngest is nineteen or twenty."

Jackson's fingers began stroking my upper arm in a way that felt absentminded. "What are they like?"

"I've never met them."

His fingers halted. "Really?"

"Really." I frowned at the sky, my heart pinging, and muttered, "I'm not even sure they know I exist." My stage name was different from my real name, Raquel Ezra instead of Raquel Zanella. But even if I used my real name, I had no reason to believe my father had ever told them about me.

"They're over eighteen. Have you ever thought about reaching out?" His absent-minded touch started up again, the gentle strokes lessening the dull ache in my chest that typically accompanied any thoughts about this subject.

"I have, but . . ." But what would I say?

Hi. I'm not Troy McClure, I'm Raquel Ezra. You may know me from such films as Starlight Express *and* Tabitha Tomorrow. *I also happen to be your half-sister. Want to grab a coffee?*

And what if they said no? What if they—like my father—didn't want to know me?

"But?" he prompted when I didn't continue.

"Can we talk about something else?" I snuggled closer to his warm body, leaving the disturbing thoughts behind by draping my leg over his hip and an arm over his chest.

Touching him made everything in me soothe and settle. "What about your family? Your dad is the sheriff, right?"

"He is. He's. . ."

"It's okay." I gave him a little shake. "You can talk about your family, you're not going to upset me if they're awesome. I wouldn't have asked if I didn't want to know." Lifting my head, I twisted and placed my hand on his chest, pushing up so I could see his face. "I want to know about you."

He gazed at me, and I felt his fingers sift through my hair as he admitted, "They are awesome."

I smiled, turned, and resettled against him, gazing up at the blue sky. "I figured they were."

"Why?"

"I don't know. You're just—I don't know. You seem so well-adjusted. Almost *too* well-adjusted."

"You make well-adjusted sound sexy or something." He laughed, and that made me smile wider.

"It is. It's so sexy. And your manners. Politeness is sexy to me. You're . . . grounded. You seem to really know yourself."

His chest rose and fell with a deep breath, and then he tugged on me, changing our positions so we rested on our sides facing each other, but not touching. His handsome eyes moved between mine, like he was searching for something there. "Did you mean what you said?"

"You mean about being your nice, dedicated, hard-working, struggling, unfun woman?"

He grinned, but then quickly tried to arrange his mouth into a serious line. His gorgeous bedroom eyes gave him away, though. They continued sparkling with humor. *I love his eyes.*

"Yes, Rae. Do you really want to be with me? For more than one night?"

"Yes. Absolutely. I do. I want many nights. I want to give this a try, for real." I nodded, my hand moving with a mind of its own to grab the hem of his shirt. "Do you want to be with me?"

"Yes. Very much," he said, his voice a tad rougher than before, and my heart swelled. *THIS IS HAPPENING!!!*

But then Jackson's gaze narrowed. "If you don't, at any point, all you have to do is tell me. I'm not ever going to push you into staying with me or doing something you don't wish to do."

That made me smile wider. "I know that. You're a little infuriating that way."

"Infuriating? How so?"

"Because it makes you hard to read. Most people, when they want something, they push, or they ask. But not you. I think maybe you see even the act of asking for something you want as pushing." My hand slid to his and I threaded our fingers together. "I want to be with you, Jackson. I want to give this a try. But I need to trust that you'll tell me what you want, or you'll ask, and not believe yourself to be pushy, or impolite, or a bad person just for asking. There's never any harm in asking, it's not you imposing your will on me. I'm a big girl. I can say no."

Jackson frowned, his eyes dropping to the vicinity of my chest. I knew he wasn't staring at my boobs but rather considering my words.

"And," I added, "I'll let you set the pace. I can be patient. We can take things as slow as you need. I'm in this to win this."

Abruptly, he said, "Okay," giving me back his gaze. He looked determined. "Okay, I'll try."

"Good." I gave his hand a squeeze. "From now on, I will assume you are asking for what you want and know I won't go running to the high hills in terror should you make a request."

He squeezed back, chuckling. "And on that note. Rae. Would you like to go fishing with me on my boat this Wednesday, because I would like to take you fishing."

I was nodding before he'd finished his sentence. "Are you kidding? Yes, yes, yes!" Flinging myself at him, I ended up lying on top of his body as his back rolled to the blanket. Since I had him in such a delightful position, I peppered his face with kisses and straddled his hips.

His big hands slid to my waist and held me still. "Wait, wait a minute. I have some rules." He lifted his head to steal a kiss from my lips, then held himself away.

"Okay. Tell me." *FISHING!*

"No touching."

I immediately stilled. And then I lifted myself up, straddling his hips, and crossed my arms. "What?"

"As I've said, I'm crazy about you. And every time we're together, we end up—"

"—almost having sex."

His long body seemed to stretch and tense under me, his hips shifting restlessly. "Yes," he said, his voice roughened. "I'd like to get to know you, just be with you, talk. I know there's this—"

"—pull between us."

"Exactly. And I want to—"

"—get to know me better without thinking about sex the whole time. I feel *exactly* the same way."

"Great." He squinted at me. "Are you going to keep—"

"—finishing your sentences? No. But I am enjoying the fact that I can totally read your mind."

Laughing, he slid his fingers from my jaw to my temple and into my hair, guiding my mouth down to his and kissing me sweetly. I gripped the front of his shirt, wishing he'd kiss me less sweetly, but knowing it would be a bad idea. Things between us tended to spiral out of control quickly. And we were in a field. In public. We'd be lucky if some paparazzi a-hole hadn't filmed us already using a camera drone.

Lifting me slightly away, he gazed up into my eyes, giving me that hazy, happy look of his, and my insides turned to melted crayons, a permanent mess.

"Finish this sentence," he whispered, his attention trailing down to my lips. "I love it when Rae . . ."

Hmm. "When Rae?" I shook my head. "I don't know. You tell me."

He wore the small, secretive (and shy) smile I loved so much, pulling me down to whisper in my ear, "Guess you can't totally read my mind."

I dipped my mouth close to his ear and finished his sentence, "—yet."

CHAPTER 20

RAQUEL

"I think Mick Jagger would be astounded and amazed if he realized that to many people he is not a sex symbol, but a mother image."

— DAVID BOWIE

"I'm starting to understand what you meant about Jackson being a boy scout," I whispered, smearing suntan lotion on my face and neck in front of my mirror.

Nor, apparently, could I read his mind.

Charlotte stood behind me in the doorway to my bedroom, a coffee mug in her hand, and I met her eyes in the mirror. She and the kids had spent the night. The kiddos were at the main house, Charlotte had slept with me in my bed, and Miguel slept in the second bedroom that had become his room. Dave slept on the couch in the living room, he said he preferred it.

I was currently getting ready for my fourth fishing date with Jackson. Every Wednesday morning at 5:00 AM, he picked me up in his truck, hauling his beautiful boat behind him, and we drove over to a big lake. He'd told me the story of the lake on our first date, some sort of old gold mine that the locals filled up with water. Now it was a huge fishing spot but also quite secluded; the lake could only be accessed by those who had property around it. Jackson used a friend's property, backing his truck up to their boat launch.

Anyway, we would launch the boat, he would park in front of his friend's house, we'd get on the boat, and we'd spend all day fishing and just generally having *the best* time talking about anything and everything. But no touching. Like, never. Never ever. And it was driving me *ca-ray-zee.*

"I warned you." Charlotte sent me a sympathetic look, her voice raspy with sleep. She'd woken up around 4:30 AM, even though summer school was now at an end and she could sleep in if she wanted.

"You didn't warn me, it's not something to warn me about. It's—" I huffed, turning and motioning for her to come inside my room and shut the door. I didn't want Miguel or Dave to hear this. One of them would be getting up soon to follow me to the lake. They didn't come on the boat with us, but they parked in front of the empty house and waited for us to finish fishing.

At first, I'd felt bad. But then Dave told me to get over it. "It's my job, Raquel. I don't want you feeling bad about me doing my job. If I didn't like this job, I'd get another job."

Dave was good people.

Charlotte closed the door and crossed to the bed, sitting on the corner of the mattress. "If me telling you that Jackson is a boy scout wasn't a warning, then what was it?"

"It was two friends talking about their dating experiences and preferences." I stood in front of her, spreading the extra suntan lotion up my arms. "Jackson is wonderful."

"Yes. He is. But he was a boy scout with me for months, we had no spark at all." She took a sip of her coffee, inspecting me. "But I thought things were different with y'all. I've seen your chemistry firsthand, I figured you'd been using that boat as your love shack. It's got a bed, right?"

"It does have a bed," I said, the words coming out like a wistful lament. "It has a double bed, and he keeps it covered with a tarp, and on top of the tarp he's placed supplies."

"You mean he's gone and put a chastity cover on the bed?" She chuckled, shaking her head. "He's reverting to his puritan ways. You need to do something about it before the time finally does come and he keeps a sheet between your bodies when you have sex."

I rolled my lips between my teeth to keep from laughing, but it didn't help. I still laughed, my shoulders shaking.

She wasn't finished. "Then he makes you wear a scarlet—"

"Okay, stop. Just, stop and help me figure this out." I sat next to her on the bed.

"I'm happy to help, but first you have to tell me what's going on. Or, you know, what's not going on." She gave me a meaningful look.

I knew exactly what she meant. I'd been tight-lipped about stuff with Jackson. I felt certain he didn't want Charlotte—or anyone else—to know the details of our relationship. But I needed to talk to someone. Surely it was okay to speak in generalities?

She must've seen my reluctance because she sighed, setting a hand on my knee. "Listen, I don't need details. In fact, I don't want them. But if you have a problem and you need help, you should be able to talk to someone about it. If you don't talk to me, who can you talk to?"

"Sienna?"

"And?"

I shrugged.

"Oh, baby." She patted my knee. "Then just talk to me. You know I won't say a word to anyone."

"Do I know that?"

Her mouth dropped open.

I rushed to explain, "You and Sienna were gossiping about Jackson that one night, and although none of it was bad, per se, I know he doesn't want to be the subject of any gossip. I know it bothers him. I also realize you would be doing me a favor, helping me think through this, but I need your promise that whatever I say *never* leaves this room. You will tell no one."

A frown of concern appeared between her eyebrows. "It bothers Jackson? That the womenfolk talk about him and his legendary sexual prowess? I thought guys ate that kind of stuff up."

235

I shrugged again, not willing to divulge more on this specific subject. She didn't need to know the depth of Jackson's aversion to being gossiped about, or why he felt so strongly about it. Just that he did.

"Okay, yes. Absolutely. You have my promise. I will say nothing. And I'll shut down talk when I hear anyone else gossiping about him. I'm—I'm sorry."

"It's okay, it's in the past. Now you know. Don't beat yourself up."

"I'll try not to. I care about him, you know. He's always been one of the people around here who has never pitied me—for what happened with Kevin. He's a good friend. So, I'll be a better one." She wore a self-deprecating smile, patting my knee again. "Now, let me help. Tell me what the issue is."

"Jackson won't touch me." The words burst out, and I covered my face.

"Like . . . at all?"

I shook my head.

"But I thought—wait a minute. Y'all were missing from the group Friday at the jam session. Sienna found you all flustered with your shirt untucked."

"Okay. Yes. You're right. There was that one time." I dropped my hands from my face.

In addition to our fishing excursions, I'd also seen Jackson sporadically over the last month. Sienna had invited him over for dinner a few times, we'd run into each other downtown while I was with Charlotte or at the community center for jam sessions on Friday nights.

The instance to which Charlotte referred had occurred less than a week ago and caught me completely off guard. Jackson had pulled me into a dark room with absolutely no warning, away from everyone, covered my mouth with his and feverishly kissed me everywhere my skin was bare, giving me two orgasms with his fingers before Sienna and Dave had shown up calling my name.

We hadn't talked about it after. He'd behaved like a gentleman the rest of the night, but he did leave early, explaining that he had to work on his typical Saturday off. I'd expected him to text me or call me and talk about it. But he didn't bring it up during our text exchanges, and now I was left wondering if I'd imagined the whole thing.

"But, Charlotte, other than this past Friday, the only time he touches me is to either give the back of my hand a kiss or to hug me from behind—" *and then he always places a lingering kiss on my neck that gets me hot but gives me no relief*"—and I've been counting the hugs. He's given me seven. Total. AND he only touches me if no one is around, which is basically never."

"Rae, both y'all are still followed by photographers. Of course he's not going to touch you in public. He's trying to be respectful of the gossip you have to deal with too." She seemed to reflect for a moment, then added, "And me, for that matter. I think he's being careful about showing too much interest in public because he doesn't want anyone in Green Valley to think the kiss at the ATM was real, because then folks might start feeling sorry for me."

"Okay, that makes sense." And that actually made me feel a little better.

"And if he found a way to give you two some privacy at the jam session last week, enough to get a few decent kisses in, then he might be feeling just the same as you—frustrated and wanting more."

"That's a good point." I nodded, thinking back to our hot encounter on Friday. "But what about the boat? No one is with us on the boat. And whenever I invite him over here, he declines."

"I have no idea why he hasn't made a move on the boat. But, honey, you got a full house here. Dave on the couch, Miguel in the other room. You might not mind getting busy with your man with two bodyguards nearby, but Jackson is old-fashioned that way."

I nodded, this all made sense, however— "Then why hasn't he invited me over to his house?"

"Probably because Boone is there." She twisted her lips to the side thoughtfully. "But you should ask him about the boat. Ask him why he won't make a move on the boat."

"Wait. Back up. Boone? Who is Boone?"

"Boone is that hot deputy that came here over a month ago asking if you had any complaints about Jackson. Remember? It was the day your little assistant rage quit. Or, you fired her. Anyway, Boone is Jackson's roommate."

I thought back. "What? Jackson has a roommate? Why didn't I know this?"

Charlotte shrugged. "I don't know. Boone is kind of quiet. I imagine living with him is like living with a ghost. He moved into Jackson's house over a year ago. I think he rents out his old place and runs a few other rental properties. He takes after his uncle Trevor that way, real good with money."

I was having trouble following Charlotte's train of thought since I remained focused on just one part of it. "I feel like the fact that Jackson has a roommate should've come up before now."

"Have you and Jackson talked about all your roommates in LA?"

That had me pausing. "I guess, no. No we haven't. But they're not my roommates. They're staff I pay to—"

"—live with you." She nodded, wearing a small smile. "You and Jackson only get Wednesdays to be together privately. I don't figure he wants to use the time to discuss Boone, just like I don't figure you want to use the time to discuss the people who live with you."

"That's true."

"So—" she sipped from her mug, eyeing me over the brim "—go ahead and ask Jackson today why he hasn't made a move on the boat."

I twisted my fingers. "I don't want to ask him."

"Pardon me?"

"I told him I would trust him to tell me what he wants—or ask for what he wants—and that I'd let him set the pace. I told him I would be patient." I winced, bracing for her reaction.

"Well." Charlotte shook her head, pity in her eyes. "That was a mistake."

"I know that now!"

"I mean, yes. You should trust him to tell you what he wants, that part was good. But you should never—and I mean *not ever*—tell a man that you're going to let him set the pace. Either they're too fast or too slow. There's no in between with men. Feast or famine."

"What do I do?" I covered my face again. "I told him I would be patient, but ever since Friday—especially since Friday—I feel like I'm dying here. I want him so much. And he's just . . . gah!"

Charlotte made a considering sound, and I felt the mattress lift as she stood. I peeked at her between my fingers and watched her pace the room, her expression thoughtful as she muttered, "We'll just have to make him lose control somehow." Her attention flickered over me. "Is that what you're wearing?"

I glanced down at my green capris and white UV filtering shirt. "Yes?"

"No." She set her coffee cup down on my bedside table. "You got a—a—swimsuit? Better yet, a bikini?"

"Jackson said it's not a good idea to go swimming in the lake when it's this hot."

"Who said anything about swimming? Just tell him you're working on your tan." She wagged her eyebrows. "You're wearing a bikini, if you got one. And those cutoff shorts. Oh! And that white halter." She opened the drawers of my dresser and started rummaging around. "What time will he be here?"

"In fifteen minutes." I pulled off my capris, jumping into action. I wasn't certain her plan would work, but what did I have to lose? Wearing a bikini didn't seem unreasonable, wearing a bathing suit on a boat was perfectly normal behavior. And what was the worst that could happen? Maybe he wouldn't notice. Maybe I was overthinking this. Maybe—

"Fifteen minutes is plenty of time."

I hesitated, my fingers twisting in the hem of my shirt. "Charlotte, is this dishonest? Or am I—I don't know—playing games? I don't want to play games with Jackson."

"What? No! You're putting on a bathing suit and hoping for a reaction. Show me a woman or a man who doesn't dress a certain way hoping for a reaction from the person they like, and I'll show you a naked gorilla. There is nothing wrong with wanting your guy to admire you. Even married people do this. Stop fretting and go put on this bikini." She held up a black string bikini that still had tags attached.

I walked over and accepted it, not yet convinced. "I'll need to put on more suntan lotion."

"No! Don't you dare. Make him put it on you," she said, then she chuckled to herself. Evilly. "That should do it."

* * *

239

Dave—already awake, dressed, and drinking coffee in the kitchen—lifted his hand in the air as I walked out of my bedroom, "I promised Domino I'd ask you these five questions. Number one, have you called Harrison back?"

"Yes. We're playing phone tag." This was the longest we'd gone without talking in four years, but I'd finally called him back this week.

Unlike my first two weeks in Green Valley, I hadn't been avoiding him purposefully this last month. But with Sasha leaving, I'd been working eighteen-hour days trying to make sense of her organizational structure, follow up on items she'd neglected, and undo damage caused by some super rude emails she'd sent to people over the two weeks I'd been gone.

Eventually, I'd reorganized her entire system, migrated all appointments onto a shared calendar, moved tasks into an app called Trello, and then—finally—worked through the tasks, answering all emails myself.

As of two days ago, everything outstanding had been completed, and my days settled down.

"Okay, thanks." Dave lowered his thumb. "Number two, did you like any of the candidates he sent for Sasha's replacement?"

"I did, and I have a draft email on my computer with the names I'd like him to interview."

"Great." He lowered his pinky finger. "Number three, did that salon work out? Were you happy, and do you want his people to schedule another appointment?"

"Yes. They were great." Things had been getting hairy, and the salon had me feeling smooth and silky again.

"Good to know. Number four, did you look at the new script from Gavin for *Midnight Lady,* and what do you think?"

I heaved a sigh and covered my face. "Ugh. I looked at it. I hate it." I didn't know what to do. I thought about sending back extensive notes and rewrites, but I doubted Gavin would listen. And now I didn't want the part at all. I wished there were a way for me to have the final say on the scripts and creative direction of my films.

"You'll have to tell Domino that yourself. And, last one, when do you think you'll be done here?"

For some reason, I glanced at Charlotte. Her eyes were lowered to the carpet like it was the most interesting carpet she'd ever beheld.

"I'll be another month, at least."

"Fine." He lowered his hand, his eyes sweeping down and then up my body. He looked at Charlotte. He looked at me again. Then he said, "I'm guessing I shouldn't go today."

"Probably a good idea," Charlotte answered, pushing me toward the door, grabbing the cooler we'd prepped last night. It was my turn to bring the food.

Once we made it to the front door, she put a bag on my shoulder that contained sunscreen, sunglasses, my wallet, my phone, and a change of clothes. On my other shoulder she placed the strap of the cooler. "Too bad you didn't make any sexy food, like banana pops or something."

"Or ice cream," I said.

She gave me a look, like I was weird, then stepped back and studied me. "Stop stressing. You don't have to take off the white halter or shorts if you don't want to. But if you do, and this bikini doesn't do the trick, there's no hope for Jackson James."

I laughed outwardly even though I felt stressed on the inside. I'd already tried the skimpy-clothes approach when I'd first arrived in town and brought him that pie for Operation Deputy Distraction. Then again, he'd been dating Charlotte at the time.

And yet, what I wore didn't seem to make any difference to Jackson the times he'd hauled off and kissed me with little or no warning.

Jeans and a sweatshirt the rainy day of the ATM kiss. My orange maxi dress the night we drove around and he'd been . . . friendly. Black yoga pants and a T-shirt the afternoon at the picnic. I'd worn all of those outfits since, and they hadn't elicited any particularly amorous reaction from him.

But then last Friday for the jam session, I'd put on a white and pink gingham summer dress, and he'd lost his mind. See? No correlation.

Charlotte held my gaze, her expression encouraging. Before I could articulate doubts, I heard the sound of Jackson's truck pull into the drive, and my stomach went crazy with nerves.

"It'll be fine. It'll all work out. You just concentrate on having a good time and let him concentrate on you. Okay?"

I nodded, turning for the door and opening it. I stepped out, looking up to find Jackson jogging toward me, wearing what he usually did for our boating trips: cargo shorts and a long sleeve UV shirt. This one was light blue and fit him verra nice, showcasing the narrowness of his hips and tapered waist. He was so handsome even in the dim light.

"Hi," he said, eyes on mine, gaze intent and happy.

"Hi." I swayed toward him, momentarily forgetting that I was supposed to be worried about something.

"Ready to go?" He reached for both of my bags, pulling them from my shoulders and walking next to me as we crossed to the truck. "Where's Dave? Isn't it his turn?"

Oh yes. Now I remember. "He's not coming today. Neither is Miguel."

"Oh. They sick or something?"

"No." Darn it. I couldn't think. What could I say about Dave and Miguel staying behind that didn't make everything about my outfit seem obvious?

Luckily, Jackson sent me a small smile and said, "I guess it makes sense for them to stop coming. That lake is as secluded as they come, and I imagine it's pretty boring, sitting in a hot car all day."

I stood to one side as Jackson opened the door of his truck and placed my bags in the cab. The July morning was already hot. Even so, I fought a shiver. Finished loading my items, he turned and held out his palm to help me up into the truck. This was the point at which he would usually kiss the back of my hand—if he were going to kiss it —so I'd learned to pause and wait a second before stepping up into the truck.

But once I fit my fingers into his waiting hand, his smile waned slowly as he finally seemed to look at me. And what I was wearing. And what I was not wearing.

After a protracted moment, Jackson's eyes cut to mine, held. My stomach threw a dinner party and only invited anxiety.

"Are we going swimming?" His voice deepened with the question.

"No," I croaked. I cleared my throat as I stepped up into his truck. "I thought I might work on my tan." *UGH!* The words.

They were the wrong words. They were Charlotte's words, not mine, and they tasted wrong in my mouth. Perhaps Rae from two months ago wouldn't have minded. She was used to pretending every day, playing a role wherever she went. And Rae from our first night together would definitely not have minded. She was used to faking boldness.

But current Rae, the person I was now, didn't want to play pretend and didn't want to fake it. Especially not with Jackson. Yes, I wanted him to notice me and think lusty thoughts about me. I wanted him to do wonderful things to my body and let me do wonderful things to his, but I also wanted to be honest.

I turned to look down at him, to find different words, but my mouth dried up and my tongue felt useless as soon as I caught his hungry stare on my bare legs.

Or, maybe, just this once, I'll suck it up and play pretend.

CHAPTER 21

JACKSON

"A sex symbol becomes a thing. I just hate to be a thing."

— MARILYN MONROE

I don't have any condoms.

The words were a mantra as I drove to Bitty Johnson's house on Bandit Lake to launch the big boat; and when I parked my car in Bitty's driveway; and when I jogged back to the lake and hopped on board. *I don't have any condoms. I don't have any condoms. I don't have any condoms.*

Technically, I did have one condom. It was in my wallet and had lived there for going on three years. It was probably expired. Therefore, for all intents and purposes, I didn't have any condoms. And lack of condoms would (. . . should) keep me from doing something stupid, like breaking the rules of our agreement.

Much like the ride over from Jethro and Sienna's property, Rae and I were silent as we moved around the boat. She knew where I kept everything, and we fell into the routine we'd developed over the last few weeks. Usually, during this time, we'd be laughing and joking and flirting.

I didn't much want to flirt with her right now. There was only one thing I wanted to do with Rae at present, and *I don't have any condoms.*

My mother—*yes, good idea, think about your mother*—had often said that most humans were visual creatures. She'd follow up this statement by reminding me and my sister that, since humans were visual creatures, they were also ultimately responsible for how they reacted to what they saw.

"Control yourself," she'd lecture. "Look away if you must, but never act in lust."

This saying had always made my rebellious sister snort-laugh, and I'd chuckled along. At the time.

But right now? Sitting in the captain's chair with the awnings all the way down, steering us out to the center of the quiet, secluded lake while mist rose around us and the colors of sunrise streaked across the sky, but I didn't even notice because *RAE!!!*

My mother's words struck a new chord.

"Jackson?"

I pulled in a deep breath, not looking.

Over a month ago, Rae and I had agreed that we wouldn't touch each other during our Wednesday fishing trips. Each week had been more difficult than the last, but I'd taken measures to reduce the chances of breaking our agreement.

First, I'd filled the cabin in empty boxes and unnecessary supplies. Second, I'd taken myself in hand several times a week to take care of business solo. And third, I'd learned early on to excuse myself and take a breather whenever her company—something she inadvertently did or said that just felt irresistible—became overwhelming.

But seeing Rae this morning, after weeks of getting to know her better, being around her not often enough, and falling deeper every day, dressed like she was, so much of her skin visible to my eyes, I hadn't been able to draw a full breath since helping her into the truck.

"Jackson?"

"Yes. Sorry." I shook my head as though to clear it. "I was just thinking about something. Are the awnings okay? I pulled them all the way down, but I can lift them up to get some air."

"They're fine. I like the privacy, for now. So what are you thinking about?" In my peripheral vision, I saw her slip into the seat nearest to mine and cross her legs toward me.

"Just—uh—things my mom used to say when Jess and I were teenagers." We weren't yet close to the center of the lake.

"Like what?"

Uhhh . . .

"Are you okay?" she asked, an edge of worry in her tone.

"Sorry. I'm hot. Is it hot?" I pulled at the collar of my shirt. I felt hot. And itchy. And uncomfortable. I'd noted the muggy, oppressive quality to the July morning before driving over to get Rae, so I had doused myself in bug repellant. Presently, I felt like I might be crushed by heat, and the sun had just risen. "Maybe we should head back. It's only going to get hotter."

Rae breathed a laugh and muttered something under her breath that I didn't catch.

"Pardon?" I asked.

"I said, 'I sure do hope so.'"

"You want to head back?" Boone would be gone to work by now, we'd have the house to ourselves. *And I can get condoms on the way. You know, just in case.*

"No. I meant about it getting hotter. I hope it does get hotter."

I frowned. "You do?"

"Yes."

"Why?" Why would anyone want it to be hotter than this? I was so hot, I couldn't think.

"Because, Jackson, I—would you look at me? Please?"

Attempting to fill my lungs again to no avail, I braced myself as best I could, brought the boat to a stop, and faced her.

Her eyes were wide and, if I wasn't misreading her expression, she looked anxious, maybe a bit scared.

My ungentlemanly thoughts were eclipsed by concern, and I reached out, grabbing her hand. "What's wrong?"

"I'm wrong," she said, standing from her seat and stepping closer. "And I'm sorry."

"What do you have to be sorry for?"

"Because—and here is a peek into the ridiculousness you've signed up for—I am wearing this outfit with hopes of seducing you."

I'm sure my eyes bugged out of my head as I stood and faced her. "Come again?"

"I wore this outfit"—she swept her hand down the front of her body—"hoping that I'd be able to seduce you. Today. On this boat."

My attention dropped to the top she had on. The fabric was white and see-through to the smooth skin of her torso and the tiny triangles covering her breasts. *It was a string bikini.* I swallowed thickly as blood rushed south, because I'd thought maybe it was, but I hadn't looked long enough to confirm one way or the other.

Ladies, here's a tip. If a man is into you, and you're in the mood to get laid, wear a string bikini for him. Doesn't matter where—a beach, a pool, a shower, your bedroom, the family room, even the laundry room—doesn't matter what's going on —you're cleaning the house together, you're pregnant and cranky, he's cooking dinner, he's watching a game on TV—he'll stop whatever he's doing and take great pleasure in pulling those strings. Satisfaction guaranteed.

"And I'm sorry," she concluded, like she'd been speaking, but I'd been too busy thinking about divesting her body of the tiny bathing suit.

That had my stare returning to hers. "I have some thoughts," I admitted, my voice uneven as some wonderfully dirty visions of us together, *imminently together,* filled my mind. "But first back up and explain again why you're sorry."

"Because I told you I'd let you set the pace, and here I am trying to rush things along. But Jackson—" she shuffled a step closer, and I placed a hand on her waist "—I'm having a difficult time here. It's been a month, and we only seem to be alone on Wednesdays. And then with what happened on Friday, I can't stop thinking about you."

We'd drifted closer, her head tilted back, her lips inches from mine. I played with the tie holding her top in place, working to bring my heart rate back under control before I made a move. Because I would be making a move. The awnings were down, concealing us from all sides except the front, but the reflective glass of the exterior windshield took care of that angle. We weren't in the center of the lake, but we were far enough away from shore that no one could hear us as long as we weren't too loud. *But I don't have any condoms.*

If I didn't hurry and settle down first, I'd be totally fucked. *And so will she.*

"Rae," I said, her name a scrape. I had to clear my throat before continuing. "If you want to change our agreement, then I am all for it. Just say the word."

Her forehead wrinkled in confusion. "What agreement?"

"That we don't touch on Wednesdays, that we use the time only to talk."

She wrinkled her nose. "Is that what we agreed? I thought the no touching thing was just for the first Wednesday."

My nod was immediate and forceful. "Okay. Yes. Motion passed. New agreement is now in place. All touching is allowed."

A grin split her face, something like dawning realization behind her gaze. "Are you telling me that I've been suffering for no reason because of a miscommunication?"

"No." I lowered my head, stealing a too-short kiss. I couldn't wait to taste her. *Everywhere.* "I'm telling you we've both been suffering for no reason because of a miscommunication."

As I spoke, my fingers twisted into the tie holding her shirt and I paused, rethinking my strategy. Sliding my hand beneath the thin fabric, I pulled the string holding her bikini in place, a pulsing, insistent ache in my groin momentarily clouding my vision.

Rae laughed at my words, the sound absolutely magical, her arms coming around my neck. "What are you doing? Are you trying to take off my bathing suit?"

I nodded, incapable of speech as the string went lax around her back. Holding her gaze, I devoured the sight as heat and haziness replaced the laughing brightness in her eyes.

"Jackson . . ." she whispered, angling her chin in offering.

Not yet.

I lifted my head just an inch away, wanting to see her face, her expression as I touched her. My only regret after making her come on Friday at the jam session had been the dimness of the backstage area. Forced to fumble around in the dark, I'd wanted to watch her then, starving for the sight of her face as I made her come. I loved watching her.

I was, after all, a visual creature. I wasn't about to miss a single second now.

Lifting my hand, I pulled the last string around her neck. Her lashes fluttered, but she held still as I fisted the scrap of fabric and pulled it from beneath her shirt. I dropped it somewhere behind me and leaned back, my gaze trailing to her neck, then lower to the shape and outline of her perfect breasts visible beneath the gauzy fabric of her top.

My mouth flooded with saliva, my dick shoving against the interior of my shorts. Licking my lips, I didn't miss the way her body shivered, and my eyes cut back to hers.

I felt desperate, but obviously so did she. I paused to grin, loving how she looked at me. "Do you miss it?"

"What?" she asked breathlessly, her eyes on my lips.

"My tongue."

She shivered again, nodding, her nipples pebbling, straining, and ripe for my mouth. I bent, sucking at the center of her breast through the inconsequential barrier, palming her other breast and massaging, loving how she squirmed and panted as I leaned away and admired the evidence of her arousal.

I need a condom. Fuck. I. Need. A. Condom.

I'd never had sex without one. Back in my wayward days, I used to keep dozens in my glove box, replacing any spares every two months. I'd never considered this paranoid behavior but rather responsible behavior, *honorable* behavior. Using a condom meant I wasn't a bad guy, I wasn't what other people said about me. I was responsible, diligent, safe, thoughtful—even when no one else thought so. But I'd emptied that glove box years ago.

There's only one thing to do.

"Rae." I slid my hands down her back to her bottom, giving it a rub and squeeze, because I couldn't help myself. Now that I was allowed, I wanted to touch her every-where at once. But I was on a mission. Moving my fingers to the button of her shorts, I said, "This is what we're going to do. First, I'm going to—"

She grabbed my face and kissed me, her tongue searching for mine and moaning deeply when she found it. Her body arched, rubbing along my torso, and all my plans and thoughts flew straight out of my head.

I unbuttoned and unzipped her shorts. I shoved them down her legs. I reached inside her bathing suit, and I separated her with my finger, groaning when I felt how wet she was. How ready. And my mind filled with visions of how great she'd feel once I had her beneath me and I pushed inside her body, how I'd love watching the heat build behind her eyes as I moved and filled her.

But her being ready and willing and me being mindless didn't change the fact that I still needed a condom I didn't have.

So as gently as I could manage, despite the pain it caused me, I pushed her away. "Wait. Wait. God—oh fuck, just wait."

Breathing hard, her hands grasping, she let me set her back. Her eyes pleaded, her expression a little crazed. "What? What is it?"

"I don't have a condom."

She shook her head. "It's okay, I'm on birth control. And I'm clean. Are you clean?" Her fingers gripped my shirt tightly, like she wanted to rip it.

"Yes. But, Rae, I . . ." My throat was so tight, and the urge to just do it, to just give in and fucking finally take her, crushed me. Almost. "Rae. It might not make sense, but I need a condom if we're going to do this."

She gaped at me for a long moment, but then she nodded and closed her mouth, like she didn't trust herself to speak. Her eyes told me she didn't understand, but that she accepted my words.

"I have to go get some." I grabbed her arms and guided her back to the seat she'd occupied earlier, not trusting myself to put my hands elsewhere. "But before I go, I want—I need—to do something."

She continued nodding, looking like she was ready to burst from frustration. The sight was both arousing and amusing. Apparently, she couldn't read my mind. Yet.

Careful not to touch her hip, I pulled the string there, and she looked down, confusion on her features. "What—?"

Before she finished her thought, I knelt in front of her, grabbed the backs of her thighs to hold her in place, spread her legs, and licked.

Her whole body convulsed, a shock of curse words flying out of her mouth, and her hands grabbed fistfuls of my hair. "Jackson!"

Fuck. Yes. I'd wanted this. I'd missed this. I *needed* this. The feel of this soft, delicate part of her on my tongue, the taste of her, the velvet texture of her legs. Lifting her knees over my shoulders, I pressed harder, tonguing her tight entrance, but not expecting her to come yet. Which is exactly what she did.

If I'd been in a different, less tortured state of mind, I might've been amused by the expediency of her orgasm. Less than thirty seconds had to be a personal record for me. Acting quickly—relatively speaking—I slid my fingers inside her already clenching channel. She covered her mouth with both hands, holding the scream inside.

I looked up, wanting to see her loss of control, and our eyes collided. Her whole body shook, her powerful legs squeezing but then easing, like she worried I couldn't breathe; her hands gripping the seat behind her as she struggled not to make a sound, like she didn't trust herself not to fall. And she closed her eyes; like she found the sight of me still licking and sucking and kissing that sweet spot between her legs overwhelming.

But she should've trusted me. I would never let her fall. And when she lost her grip on the chair, I caught her. Sadly, it was before I felt my job had quite finished—she had two or three more orgasms in her yet—but she straddled my lap and wrapped her arms around my neck tightly, her breath still gasping.

"I can't—I can't take anymore. I can't."

"Shhh . . ." I stroked a hand over and down the back of her head, holding her just as tight until her breathing evened, and her grip loosened, and her heart slowed.

Exhaling a loud sigh, she pushed just far enough away from me so we could see each other, but she kept her seat, her eyes searching mine. "Jackson," she whispered. "I—I don't know how to ask this."

I swallowed around a building thickness, saying nothing. *Please don't ask me to make love to you without a condom.*

"Can I . . ." She shifted back a bit, and I had to grit my teeth at the feel of her body. She then reached down, her gaze on mine, and cupped me over my shorts.

I hissed, closing my eyes, my hips instinctively jutting forward. "Please, don't."

She removed her hand immediately. "I know you want to use a condom. And—yes. We should. For sex. Absolutely. But do you also use a condom for blow jobs?"

Oh. Damn.

I shook my head, forcing the words out. "No. Rae. I've never done that."

Her sharp intake of breath had me opening my eyes. Hers were wide with shock. "What? Never? Never *ever*?"

"No." I threaded my fingers into her long hair, pushing it away from her face. "No one ever offered."

Her mouth wide open, a number of emotions flickered behind her eyes too fast for me to catalogue given how close we were and how great she felt in my arms.

Eventually, she said, "Oh, Jackson," and pulled me into an even tighter hug than before. "I offered, if you remember. I put my queen right in your path during Vegas Chess. I wanted to. I wanted you."

My jaw hurt from gritting my teeth so much. "I remember," I said, not adding that I hadn't trusted her then. I hadn't trusted that she actually wanted to do it.

"Then why didn't you take me up on it?" she asked.

If no one had offered before, not in all the years of my exploits, how could I trust that Raquel Ezra had actually wanted me in that way?

I shook my head, not wanting to explain something that seemed so obvious. My friends—my female friends—had always talked about blow jobs like they were a chore. Even my married female friends, like the act was a favor they did for their husbands on special occasions or to pacify them. They'd compared it to having a hairy, sour Twinkie in their mouth if the guy was soft, or a hairy, sour tree branch if the guy was hard.

Women had always wanted me to go down on them, and they'd often wanted sex. I'd never met a woman who wanted to give me, or presumably anyone else, a blow job.

"This isn't a conversation I want to have right now." I glanced at the horizon through the windshield. The sun had risen above the tree line, and that was good. The convenience store closest to the lake opened at 6:30 AM. *I need to go.*

"Fine." She placed a kiss on my neck, sucking my skin into her mouth, her hands— both of them this time—lowering to the front of my shorts. "I don't need to talk about it, if you don't."

I caught her wrists, losing my breath for a moment. "Whoa. Wait. I need to go get—"

"Later. I *need* you in my mouth, right now."

I'm sure I made some sound, probably nonsense, and my hands released her wrists because my body demanded that I do so. Actually, it was my dick. Just my dick. My dick vetoed every other voice and crushed any doubt or dissention.

Shut the hell up and don't ruin this for me, Jackson. You'll thank me later.

She placed persistent kisses along my neck and jaw, biting at my chin as her hands reversed course and shoved my shirt up, her hands sliding over my chest and stomach. "You have an incredible body," she said on a sigh. "I can't wait to see and taste all of it. Stand up."

In the next moment, she'd pulled my shirt completely off, and in the next, I stood before her. Kneeling, Rae leaned back as her gaze traced from my shoulders to my abdomen. She placed a biting kiss on the spot just above the waistband of my shorts while her fingers unbuttoned and then unzipped my fly.

My hands opened and closed at my sides, my breath catching in my lungs, and I didn't—I didn't know what to do. I felt like I should be doing something, somehow making this good for her.

What can I do to make this good for her?

"Relax," she whispered, maybe reading my mind, slowly pulling my shorts down my legs and tugging my boxer briefs along with them. A bolt of panic closed my throat at the sight of her full lips so close to me.

What if she hates this but doesn't feel like—

"Jackson."

I blinked, telling my wild mind to concentrate, and I brought her back into focus. She gave me a soft smile, but her eyes were dark as midnight, hot and greedy. "Trust me. I want this. I cannot wait to have you inside my mouth." Her gaze lowered, and she licked her lips. "You are so perfect."

And then I was in her mouth and—

Sorry. That's all I got.

I think I grabbed the steering wheel of the boat. . . maybe? And her hands came around, palming my backside to hold me still at some point. . . perhaps? But I do recall for certain that she moaned, and it was one of those good ones, not like she was in pain and not a fake-pleasure one. She may've been a world-class actress, but in this regard, I had some expertise.

What she was doing, it felt like heaven, like ecstasy, like incandescent perfection. It felt so amazing, it almost hurt. And I knew I was about to lose myself in her mouth if she didn't stop. My eyes were shut tight. If I looked at her now, it would all be over. Another personal record for me, but this one was embarrassing.

"Rae—Rae, I'm—it's—" My brain was full of nothing but profanities, and so I didn't trust myself to speak. Instead, I reached for her to communicate the urgency of my crisis, wanting to take over rather than come in her mouth.

"I want you to," she said, her hand replacing her tongue and giving me a rough pull. She bit one of my fingers playfully, and then brought me back inside the hot, wet paradise of her mouth.

I came.

I just—all over her—in her—and she—and I—and it happened. I opened my eyes, needing to see her face, to make sure she was still there with me. I watched as she wiped her mouth as she stood and retied the one side of the bikini string I'd pulled at her hip. She grinned like the sight of me tousled and spent satisfied some cavernous need within her.

Her hands came to my chest, and her attention followed, her palms moving along my breastbone, lower to my ribs. "I've wanted to see you like this for a very long time." Her words sounded distracted, faraway. "I've had countless fantasies about it. You, naked. Me, dressed."

That had me quirking an eyebrow. "I may be naked, but you're not wearing much."

She shrugged like this was no matter, her attention still transfixed to where her fingers touched. "I know we need to leave to get condoms, but could we—"

"No. Not we. *I* need to leave to get condoms." I stepped back and around the captain's chair, hunting for my clothes. "You're staying here." As much as was possible while wildly aroused, I'd already thought through the plan. "We can't be seen together somewhere buying condoms. I'll go and come right back."

I felt her gaze on my bare back a moment before her hands settled on my bottom. "Jackson James, you have a very bite-able ass."

I chuckled, but fire filled my lungs. *I need to hurry.* "You can bite it all you want when I get back."

Her movements felt reluctant as she released me, and I heard her sigh. "I will miss you."

"I'll miss you t—"

"I was talking to your butt."

Laughing, I turned around and pulled up my shorts, inspecting her. "Is this how it's going to be now? You're going to be like everyone else and start missing my body more than me?" I'd meant it to be a joke, but she—and I—heard the edge of truth in them before I realized what I'd said and how it sounded.

She stared at me, her features growing sober. But not shocked.

"God, Rae. I'm sorry. I was—sorry." I glanced heavenward, trying to think of a way to put us back on the playful path, because that had been a monumentally stupid thing to say after she'd just given me—

"Never." Rae stepped right in front of me, grabbed my face, and forced my eyes back to hers. "Do you hear me? *Never.* You are magnificent, Jackson. In every single way."

Blinking against an odd rush of something stinging my eyes, I needed her to let me go so I could leave, and we could forget my misstep.

But she wasn't finished. "Yes, your body is beautiful. But it is nothing—and I mean *nothing*—compared to this." Rae threaded her fingers into my hair at my temples. "Your brain is beautiful. Your honor is beautiful. Your dedication and hard work is beautiful. And this—" Her hands lowered to the left side of my chest.

I found I couldn't swallow as I waited for her words, nor could I breathe.

Her touch gentle, her gaze imploring, she whispered, "This heart is stunning. It's my absolutely, without a doubt, favorite part of you. And when you're gone, when we're not together, this is the part of you I will always miss most."

CHAPTER 22

RAQUEL

"I'm a modern woman in the sense of I take care of myself, I'm fiercely independent, and I'm really ambitious. Yet I have these old-school thoughts in my mind."

— EVA MENDES

*W*hen Jackson said he would leave me on the boat and head over to the store, I thought he meant we would return to his friend's house and he would head out from there. That is not what happened.

One minute, I was telling him how special he was to me, and we were kissing, and touching, and hugging. And in the next, he'd climbed down into the water.

"I thought you said we couldn't swim in this lake?" I whisper-shouted after him, squatting low at the side of the boat.

He flipped his hair back, wiping his eyes. "No, I said it's not a good idea when it's this hot. There could be an algae bloom. Or snakes."

SNAKES? "SNAKES?!"

He laughed. "Nah. There might be snakes, but they keep clear of swimmers."

"Jackson! Get out of there!" I whisper-shrieked, reaching my hand over the side, knowing my voice would carry across the mostly calm surface if I raised it any louder.

Treading water, Jackson began to drift further from the boat. "I haven't seen any algae this summer, and I'm in a hurry. Without Dave or Miguel keeping an eye out at Bitty's, this is the safest place for you while I'm gone. I'll be back in a jiff." He turned toward the house where we'd launched.

"Wait! You're swimming over there? Why don't you just drive over in the boat, and then I'll drive back here, and—"

Jackson twisted around. "I don't want anyone seeing you driving this boat out here without me, knowing you're alone. I'll take Bitty's Rambler, leave my truck, and be back soon. If you have time, fold the boxes up in the cabin. Or I'll help you when I get back."

"Fold the . . .? You mean all those boxes covering the bed are empty?"

Grinning, he winked. It was as adorable as it was sexy as it was infuriating. Then he left, swimming in the lake I'd been told we weren't supposed to go swimming in.

I stared after Jackson, unable to believe what had just happened. And I was left astounded by how fast and strong a swimmer he was. He'd probably make it back to the launch faster by swimming than if we'd used the boat at no-wake speed. I watched his figure disappear into a thicket of trees, camouflaged to anyone looking in that direction.

Clutching my forehead, I glanced down at myself. The girls appeared to be just as confused as me. One minute we're all over each other and they're having the time of their lives, the next he's gone, swimming away at top speed, and leaving all of us wishing he were still here. *I need to find my bikini top.*

Locating the top didn't take long. I opted to peel off the halter in the privacy afforded by the awnings before securing the triangles in place and retying everything. Taking the short stairway down, I ducked as I entered the cabin and glanced around, frowning at the pile of cardboard boxes. Poking one, it tumbled over and fell at my feet.

That sneak.

He'd covered the bed, and I could guess why, especially now that I knew and understood him better. Charlotte's guess had been correct, the empty boxes on the bed were a chastity belt. For him. Or me. Or both of us. Whatever. He'd been trying to be honorable, follow the rules he thought we'd both agreed to back at the picnic.

Picking up the first box, I untucked the flaps holding it together and flattened it. I then made quick work of the entire pile. There weren't many, just enough to cover the surface of the tarp and make it appear as though we couldn't access the bed. The boxes broken down, I turned and opened a drawer in the kitchen to look for string, or tape, or something to bundle the cardboard.

I had much to do. The tarp needed to go, and sheets and pillows needed to be located for our love nest.

At least a half hour later, and feeling like a hot and sweaty mess, I surveyed my progress and eyed the AC unit. Jackson had told me on one of our previous excursions how he'd found the boat, that he'd been lucky to get it for a good price at an auction.

But it was Charlotte who'd provided the real story.

"It was a mess. I mean, it looked like a heap of garbage when he first got it. Holes everywhere, the cabin destroyed, the decking ripped up, no motors, no upholstery, no chairs, no nothing. The only thing that the weirdo previous owner had left alone was the controls—you know, the computer and navigation panel." Her face a grimace, Charlotte had taken a deep, gulping pull from her beer before continuing. "I told Jackson he should've just built a boat from scratch instead. But no, he was determined. That's Jackson."

That's Jackson.

I caught myself smiling at the beautiful interior cabin, admiring the careful craftsmanship, blood, sweat, and tears that had likely gone into Jackson's boat.

This kind of weekender fishing boat, decked out like he had it—with an AC and a built-in head/shower combo compartment, kitchen with a fridge, sink, microwave, flat-screen TV over a convertible couch to queen bed—cost somewhere in the neighborhood of $800K new. Even used, these boats held their value.

I could afford several if I wanted, no problem. I'd call Domino and he'd call someone else—my finance lady, I think her name was Mackenzie—and *bam,* I'd have a boat.

But it wouldn't be this boat.

Jackson's hands had repaired everything I could see. All the blood, sweat, and tears had been born out of determination, hard work, dedication, struggle, and probably some fairly unfun times. And now, she was absolutely gorgeous. Stunning. One of a kind.

This boat would last, because he'd built it to last. He'd done the work. No wonder that was the kind of woman—and the kind of relationship—Jackson thought he wanted.

Emotion clogged my throat as I folded the tarp around the tied cardboard boxes and then smoothed my hand over the fresh sheets. Bed made, I shut the upper door. I flipped on the AC. I prepared a snack just in case he might be hungry. I took a shower. I slipped into the bed, naked, and I waited for him.

When he returned, I wanted everything to be just right. I wanted Jackson to be comfortable. I wanted him to be happy. He worked so hard, and he deserved someone to look after him. Someone to take care of him. To work hard beside him, with dedication. To share his burdens—even when they were a struggle, or unfun.

More than anything, I wanted that person to be me.

* * *

I woke up surrounded by a sleeping warm man. *Jackson.*

I smiled. I hadn't meant to fall asleep, but that's what getting up at 4:30 AM will do. Inhaling his scent, I turned carefully and slowly in the bed to face him. His arm tightened around me, but he remained in dreamland as I came to rest on my other side, admiring the lines of his face.

He must've returned a while ago and taken a shower. His skin smelled like soap, not lake water, and I kicked myself for missing a Jackson James shower show. *Next time.*

Damp hair curling on his forehead, I wanted to pet it, and the short beard on his face. My gaze lowered to his lips, and I just barely restrained myself from kissing the bottom one, promising myself I would, just later.

Wait, is this creepy? I frowned, debating the question. Was it creepy to watch someone sleep if you're in love with that pers—OH MY GOD!

I sucked in a breath, my mind a sudden riot of fear and hope and despair and *ohshit ohshit ohshit!* I was in love with him?

Yes. You're in love with him.

But-but-but—how did this happen?

Well, you see, Rae. When a man and a woman really like each other, and are insanely attracted to each other, and respect each other, and treat each other with compassion and kindness, they—

SHUT IT.

I sat up unthinkingly, gripping the sheet to my chest as his arm slid to my hip. My heart pounded, a cold sweat breaking out between my shoulder blades and around my neck. What was I going to do? I'd never been in love.

Jackson has been in love before.

The thought, completely unbidden, sent a spasm of something cold and unpleasant from the base of my spine outward through my entire body, curdling in my stomach. I immediately recognized the sensation as jealousy. Based on the pieces of the Jackson puzzle I'd been able to assemble, he'd been in love twice: once with Ashley (Winston) Runous when they were teenagers, and once with a woman named Zora Leffersbee, to whom he'd been engaged. Neither of these facts had bothered me at any point before right this minute.

His bare leg moved, brushing against mine. I held my breath. When he didn't move again, I breathed out.

Listen, I knew Jackson wanted me, liked me, respected me, appreciated me, and was *with* me. He wasn't with anyone else. Being jealous of relationships that ended years ago was silly. Logically, I knew this. And yet I was jealous.

Now that I'd realized my feelings; now that I'd named this raw, desperate wanting, and fear, and protectiveness; and especially since I didn't know whether he felt similarly, how was I supposed to behave? Did I tell him and hope for the best? Would that be pressuring him? And if he didn't reciprocate? How did that work?

Aaaaahhh! Love is stressful and scary. Plato had it right, love is a serious mental disease.

I turned my head, looking over my shoulder at him, my thundering heart stuttering at the sight of his sleeping face. How many people had loved me?

Admittedly, foolishly—before this summer, before watching Sienna with Jethro and their kids, before spending time with Charlotte and her kids, and before irrevocably falling for Jackson—I'd thought the adoration and admiration of my fans was love. It wasn't, and it isn't. It can't be love if you're always on the receiving end and never on the giving, and vice versa. And you can't love someone you don't know.

They didn't love me.

My mother did when I was younger for sure. I remembered her cuddling me and kissing me. But as I aged and tried to become my own person, I felt that affection diminish by degrees until it had become what it was now: reminders that I was my own person, that I was on my own.

My paternal grandparents had loved me, but my father never had.

Did Harrison ever? Or my high school boyfriend? . . . *no.* Nor, obviously, had Lina.

I'd never taken stock of my life this way before, not consciously. I'd never measured myself by how or whether others loved me. It made me feel small, enormously sad, and lonely—all the feelings I'd been running away from in LA. Apparently, I hadn't left them behind on the West Coast but had simply distracted myself with new scenery instead. Same feelings, different geography.

You're a mess, Rae.

Pressing my lips together, I swallowed several times and blinked the building tears away. I breathed in through my nose and out through my mouth until the wave passed. Swallowing once more with effort, I closed my eyes and slowly, slowly reclined, giving Jackson my back, acutely aware of everyplace our bodies touched. I needed to . . . chill. *Just chill.* I needed to figure this out.

So what if no one loved me? So what if I was in love with Jackson? Couldn't I just decide it didn't matter? Did being in love with someone really change anything? I didn't think so. For example, I was fairly certain I loved Charlotte and Sienna—or I was falling for them—and nothing had changed between us because of it. Perhaps I could love Jackson and not say anything. I could pretend—

No. No more pretending.

I cursed quietly, working to ignore the sharp ache in my chest.

"Rae?"

I stiffened at the sound of Jackson's sleep-roughened voice. But in the next moment, the way he slid his arm to my stomach, pulling me fully against his chest, and lifting his head to kiss the rise of my shoulder, had me melting. The tower of tension I'd been building within me crumbled, mostly, leaving only the foundation and the first floor. Basically, my anxiety lowered to a simmer instead of a boil. I didn't need to say anything now. I could figure this out later. This wouldn't be me pretending. This would be me compartmentalizing and setting aside my feelings until they could be addressed at a more convenient time and location at some point in the very distant future.

"Rae, are you up?"

"Yes?" I tried for light and carefree. Instead, the single word sounded like a croak.

"What time is it? I saw you lie back down."

Oh.

"Uh, I don't know. I didn't check." I squeezed my eyes tighter because there was something about his voice, some new weight to it, plucking different strings in my heart. It unsettled me. *Compartmentalize and set aside.*

He paused, his body still behind me. "Do you want to go back to sleep?"

"No. I'm not sleepy."

"Hey. Can you turn around?"

Uhhhh.

What if I did, and he could see that I loved him? What if Jackson could tell just from looking at my face and he didn't feel the same? That would be completely devastating. I wasn't ready to be devastated.

"Are you okay?"

Chill, Rae. Just chill. Compartmentalize and set aside.

Sucking in a deep, silent breath, I forced my eyes open and pulled slightly away so I could lie on my back. Meanwhile, Jackson placed his elbow on his pillow and propped his chin and cheek in his hand. I felt his attention on me as I settled.

I blinked once, shoving anything and everything chaotic waaay down, and then looked at him. His eyes were sleepy, but also happy, and their trademark intensity remained undiminished by either sleepiness or happiness.

"Hi," he said.

"Hi," I said, allowing myself to get lost in his closeness and warmth, and definitely not the fact that I looked at him now with the knowledge that I loved him. I was in love with him. But everything was just fine. Everything was wonderful.

Everything hurts.

"Are you hungry?"

I shook my head. How do you behave with someone when they hold your future in their hands? Obviously, you stare at them, mutely, and hope you don't fuck anything up.

"You're quiet," he whispered, his eyes moving between mine as a soft, teasing smile curved his lips. "Do you want to talk?

I shook my head again.

"Oh?" His smile grew, as did the sharpness behind his gaze, and his hand resting on my stomach moved to where I still held the covers gripped to my chest. Bending closer, Jackson kissed my collarbone, scraping his beard against my shoulder, and whispered hotly in my ear, "What do you want to do?"

My toes curled, my stomach twisting warm and tight, and I raggedly whispered, "You decide."

I didn't want to direct traffic. I didn't want to make any decisions. I felt too overwhelmed, paralyzed by how inexplicably big and important this moment felt, and how big and important and frustratingly uncontainable my feeling were. They didn't want to be compartmentalized or set aside. They wanted to become nudists, cover themselves in honey, and take a baseball bat to a wasp's nest while shouting proudly, *LOOK AT US! HERE WE ARE!*

"Whatever I want?" Jackson smiled. I felt the curve of his lips against my neck just before he placed achingly gentle kisses beneath my ear, my jaw, the corner of my mouth, making my legs tense and flex. He'd barely touched me, and I was already on fire for him.

Perhaps being in love with someone did this. Love was an aphrodisiac that sat on the backburner, waiting for Jackson's touch—and only Jackson's touch—to turn up the heat.

Jackson stared down at me, warm and hazy, yet also searching. "What's wrong?"

I shook my head. "Nothing," I said, forcing out the reply. My heart lodged itself in my throat, my breathing increased in tempo, and I told my hands to stop white-knuckling the covers.

His eyebrows pulled together, and he tugged at the sheet, slowly sliding it down the front of my body to pool at my waist. I shivered, but not because I was cold.

"Are you having second thoughts?"

A short, slightly hysterical laugh bubbled up and out of me, and inexplicably I felt like crying again. I didn't want to cry. If I cried, then I would have to tell him I loved him. And if he didn't love me, the chances of us doing anything else today dropped to a big, fat zero percent.

I grabbed his face and kissed him. He immediately responded, and the hot interior of his mouth felt like heaven, like home, fueling the fire inside me to a raging inferno and drowning out all my doubts and fears. Jackson slid his hand beneath the covers and hooked his fingers behind my knee, pulling it toward him, opening me. I was already dizzy from the mating of our mouths when he skimmed his fingertips along the sensitive interior skin of my thigh. I sucked in a breath, prickly with agonizing anticipation just before he touched me *there*.

Jackson lifted his head, his eyes seeming to ignite and spark as he made contact, circling me with frustratingly unhurried strokes. He gazed at me, like he wanted to study my every reaction, and I felt like I was being teased, fondled for his pleasure.

I didn't want to be fondled or teased. I didn't want him to draw this out. A burst of unwieldy and unsteady emotion had me closing my eyes. I couldn't watch or look at him. I couldn't talk. At most, I could only lay back and hope these feelings and sensations didn't crush me.

Whether he sensed my mood or felt similarly inclined, Jackson said nothing, but I sensed the heat of his attentive gaze move over my bare skin. The bed depressed, shifted, and I felt him climb over me, holding himself above to nip and tongue my breasts as his fingers coyly caressed between my legs. He was playing with me. At least, that's what it felt like, and my hands fluttered at his shoulders. I couldn't quite bring myself to touch him in any meaningful way, probably because I wanted to touch him so badly.

His kisses, our bodies moving against the crisp sheets, and our mingled breathing were the only sounds between us. Abruptly, he withdrew, ending his teasing, and though it had been torture, I instantly missed it.

I felt him rise to his knees. I heard the sound of foil being ripped. I bit my lip. I held my breath. And then he returned, his body covering mine, the friction of his chest and legs a sweet torment. He left no space between us. But he didn't enter me.

"Rae." His voice was a beseeching rumble, and his nose slid against mine. "Open your eyes, Rae."

I tried distracting him by lifting my chin for a kiss.

His mouth retreated but he rolled his hips, sliding his erection along my clit. I shuddered, my hand lifting to grip his sides, my fingers digging into his body, trying to pull him down.

"I want your eyes," he said, his voice more of a rumble now and less beseeching. "And I'm asking."

I wanted to say no. I didn't want to open them. If I opened them, then he would know. There was no compartmentalizing and setting this aside. I should have left when he was asleep. I should have left and returned to Los Angeles. Today. I could have avoided all of this if I'd left. *Love is the worst.*

Eventually, Jackson's hips stopped moving, and I knew he was looking at me, his waiting turning to worry. I felt the shift in him before he shifted off of me.

And then he cursed. And then he was gone.

My eyes flew open then, and I found him sitting naked at the end of the bed, his back to me.

"Jackson?"

"All you have to do is tell me to stop, Rae. I will listen, and I will stop." He twisted at the waist, his eyes locked on mine, and the self-loathing I saw there felt like a punch to my stomach.

I scrambled to my knees, reaching out for him. He stood from the bed, evading me. Acting on instinct, I chased him, grabbing his wrist, and forcing him to face me. *Thank God this cabin is so small.*

"No, no. Jackson. I didn't want you to stop. I want you. I wanted to—"

He wasn't looking at me now, and he exhaled a short, disbelieving breath. Grabbing his other wrist, I tried moving into his space to kiss him, but he lifted his chin.

"Don't," he said, twisting his arms to force my hands off.

"Jackson," I pleaded. "Wait. Wait. Just wait." He still had the condom on. He was still *urgently* hard. We could still make this happen.

He didn't wait. He turned for a drawer and pulled out a pair of boxer briefs. "I'm not angry, Rae. I promise. I just need to know that if you're not into it—"

I snatched his boxers, holding them hostage behind my back. "I am. I am so very into it. And I'd love nothing more than for us to get back to it."

"Then why don't I believe you?" Finally, Jackson gave me his eyes, and I could see that he wasn't angry. He was hurt. "Why wouldn't you look at me? What did I do wrong?"

Ugh. I tried swallowing. I couldn't. "Jackson—" *Oh no.*

I was going to tell him. I was going to say it.

Don't! Don't say it. No one loves you. He won't either. He won't—

He lifted his hands like he was going to touch my arms but then drew back at the last minute, instead wiping a palm over his face. "I need some air. Will you give me back my boxers, ple—"

"I'm in love with you!"

AAAAHHHH!!! STOP!

But I couldn't stop. Now that the words were out there and I was naked, bared to him, my feelings wanted to grab the baseball bat and knock down the wasp's nest. "I'm in love with you, and it's okay if you don't feel the same, but I'm terrified that you don't, but it's okay if you don't because that would seem to fit within the scope of feelings people have for me, so again, it's totally fine . . . if you don't."

I shut my eyes as soon as my clumsy confession lost steam. Just barely, *barely* resisting the urge to go jump in the lake and swim away from whatever the repercussions of those words would be.

He breathed out again, another short sound of disbelief, but the sound wasn't as sharp. I waited. And I waited. And I felt his gaze on me. And he said nothing.

Tears built behind my closed eyes and closed my throat. I felt my chin wobble, but I nodded. *Okay.* "Okay." I supposed that was that. No point in holding his underwear hostage anymore, so—

His hands grabbed my face and his mouth crashed down on mine, and we were kissing before I realized we were kissing. He backed me up the single step to the bed, his marauding mouth moving like a starved man, teeth and tongue and lips overwhelming my senses. His hands were now everywhere, like he didn't know where to touch first. Like he wanted to hold all of me at once.

I dropped his briefs and gripped his upper arms to keep my balance. Still connected, still kissing each other with absolutely frantic abandon, Jackson laid me back on the bed and followed me down, kneeing my legs apart. His body came over mine, and still we kissed. He reached between us, fingering my slick opening, sliding two inside with absolutely no resistance, his thumb circling me and stoking the frenzied fire higher. I moaned. I whimpered. And still we kissed.

I turned my face to breathe, but he allowed only two gasping breaths before he claimed me again, removing his hand, positioning himself, and sliding right in with one forceful thrust.

My head pressed back against the cushions at the sudden invasion, my pelvis tilting instinctively to receive him as a sense of glorious fullness coiled and uncoiled the pooling warmth in my lower stomach.

Then and only then did he lift his mouth, muttering a curse, taking the Lord's name in vain, and pressing our foreheads together as he moved with the grace of someone who was exceptionally skilled—or perhaps possessed innate talent—at making a woman lose her mind.

He didn't pound or piston into me, but stroked in this indescribable way, his pelvis reminding me of an ocean wave with each return and retreat. I listened to us, the quiet, gentle sounds we made as we joined, our kisses, his breath, my sighs.

"You feel so perfect," he whispered, his eyes closed, his mouth moved to my neck to suckle and sip. "I want to stay inside you forever."

"Please do," I gasped, trying to mimic his expert movements, but I wasn't as good at this. My attempts felt inelegant and grasping compared to the artistry with which he used his body. I wasn't going to last. This felt—this felt—

"Jackson!" My hands slid along the hard planes of his back, and I tried to stop my nails from digging into his skin, but I needed to grab something, or bite something. I felt stretched and full to bursting everywhere, like I might tear starting at my chest, and the sensations felt so painfully good, both bliss and agony.

My back arched, all the muscles in my body flexing at the same time, and my mouth opened on a soundless scream as white bursts of light blinded my vision.

Jackson shifted positions. I felt him rise up to his knees and lift my hips, widening my thighs that wanted to clamp together, and *that's* when he pounded. That's when he pistoned, hitting just the right spot over and over and over, and that's when my screams were no longer silent.

Grabbing fistfuls of the bedcover, I tumbled into complete and utter mindlessness, where I was nothing but sensation and feeling, and my body and all of it hurt so *fucking* good. This was a place I'd never visited, didn't know existed, and I knew it was no accident I'd found it with Jackson.

"I love you," I heard myself say. I couldn't keep it inside me.

Jackson came as soon as the words left my mouth, and I knew he came because his careful, meticulous movements meant to maximize my enjoyment became something altogether *not* meticulous or careful, but greedy and graceless. And yet somehow more than perfect, and so damn sexy.

He seemed to spiral down from his high all at once, returning to my body with hungry, biting kisses for my stomach and breasts, shoulders and arms. He nuzzled my neck, giving me his weight and pressing his hips forward. He was still inside me, and a growly, grumbling sound reverberated from his chest.

"We're not leaving this cabin today," he said, sucking my earlobe into his mouth, sending wonderful shivers racing to my toes. How my nerve endings still functioned after the intensity of those orgasms, I had no idea.

"We're not?" I hadn't yet caught my breath, I felt like I'd run a million miles.

"No. Not until you believe and accept how much I love you."

My body stiffened, and I pulled my head to the side, staring at him, shocked. "You love me?" My voice cracked on the question, betraying the enormity of my current feelings on the subject.

His eyes softened as they held mine. "Rae, that you even have to ask means we'll be here for a while."

This was the first time someone had touched me and it felt important. The way he looked at me, the way his eyes traced my nose to my lips. How he smiled when I smiled and frowned when I frowned. It all felt *important*. Like I should be taking notes for a later test, or filming it all for later review. I needed to keep it, hold it close, far from everyone else. I needed to keep it safe and protected. But I also wanted to take an ad out in *Variety* and scream about it from the tallest building, *I love this man, he is important to me!*

My eyes stung with a new wave of tears. I pressed my lips together because my chin had the wobbles again. "You love me," I said, trying the words on. They felt too good to be true.

"Hmm. You don't sound too certain." Jackson grinned, lifting an eyebrow, taking away the breath I hadn't caught yet. Lifting himself up, he climbed down my body, saying between kisses, "I guess I'll just have to show you again."

CHAPTER 23

JACKSON

"It's nice to look back on your life and see things as lessons, and not regrets."

— RIHANNA

*L*ife was good.

We'd spent all day in the cabin yesterday, naked, with the AC on, despite the fact that I'd started believing Rae within the first hour. She knew I loved her. She knew it and believed it and accepted it.

And yet—as I'd repeated yesterday during hour four, five, and six—one could never be too sure.

I grinned at the memory, my blood heating as visions of her carefree smiles and laugher played through my mind. It had been the happiest day of my life—so far—because Rae loved me, I loved her, we were solid, things were fantastic. Life wasn't good, life was *superb. . .*

So why had I woken up anxious, and why did I spend all day today looking over my shoulder, a sense of dread heavy in my chest, waiting for the other shoe to drop?

"Jackson?"

I shook myself, realizing I'd been staring into the past, and gave Florence my attention. "Sorry. Did you say something?"

She didn't respond right away, her dark brown eyes looking me over for a tick, like she was looking for something, or expected to discover something new about my features.

Eventually, she stepped closer, glanced over her shoulders—left, then right—and leaned close. "Have you been online today?"

Careful not to exhibit any change in expression, I shook my head. "No. Why?"

She pressed her lips together, her eyes growing real big. "You might want to check Twitter."

"I don't have a Twitter acc—"

"Fine. I'll show you." She pulled her phone from behind her back and shoved the screen under my nose, her voice dropping to a whisper. "Next time, ask me to go get your condoms. I don't mind. It'll confuse the heck out of Charles, that's for sure, and give both Nancy and me a laugh."

I couldn't focus on her words *and* what I was seeing. A picture of me at the convenience store?

"Swipe your finger to the left, there's more," she said. Flo must've been impatient because she reached over and did it herself.

The second photo showed a close-up of my hands, what I'd purchased. *Great. Now the whole world knows what size I wear.* The third and fourth photos showed me leaving the store, and the fifth through tenth were pictures of me and Rae leaving the boat together yesterday, hand in hand, smiling like lovesick fools.

Which I supposed we were.

"You two look so cute together." Flo had twisted her neck to look at the pictures with me. "Nancy told me it was going to happen, but I didn't want to get my hopes up."

I couldn't think, my heart started hammering. I mean, this wasn't good, right? Or . . . was this bad? *Will this hurt Rae?*

"And it's so nice that Charlotte and Rae have become such good friends." Flo was still talking. "Do you think she'd mind if I called her Rae? You ask and let me know. Anyway, when I called Charlotte this morning to check in on her, she sounded thrilled. Said she set the two of you up." Flo gave my shoulder a little nudge, and I looked at her. She was smiling. Gleefully.

I tried to smile but wasn't so sure of my success.

It didn't seem to matter to Florence, though. Still grinning, and looking at me like I was treasure, she took the phone from my hand and straightened. "I bet Charlotte saw the chemistry between the two of you right away, it's hard to miss, unless you're blind." She chuckled, then sighed. "I just wish we could find someone for Charlotte too. She's such a lovely girl, and so hard-working. It's a shame what that Kevin did."

"Flo."

"Hmm? Yes?"

My mind on Rae and whether or not this latest development would negatively impact her, I stood from my desk. "Do you mind if I take a minute to, uh, make a call?"

"Oh! Yeah, well. You can't." She gave me a plaintive look. "Sorry. I meant to tell you first, your father wants to talk to you. Now."

I felt my façade slip at this news, my eyes cutting to the door of his office. "Oh. Okay."

Flo patted me on the back. "Good luck," she said, then walked off, leaving me to my fate like she hadn't just dropped a bunch of bombs all over my life. *Or shoes.*

Gathering a deep breath, I walked between the aisles, taking the shortest route possible to the sheriff's office while my mind stumbled over what this might be about. *It's about the pictures, and you know it.*

Yeah, I guess I did know it. Did he think I was behaving irresponsibly? The thought made me frown, and honestly it made me mad. By the time I'd made it to his door, knocked, and he'd called for me to enter, I'd talked myself into quite a tizzy, reasoning that, although I respected the hell out of my father, his life was not my life, and I was going to love whomever I damned well—

"Momma." I stopped short because my mother stood in front of my father's desk, her hands clasped in front of her, a small smile on her face.

"Jackson," she said. "Thanks for coming. Close the door, please."

My father, who stood at his desk behind her, leaned to one side and gave me *the look.*

Now, all y'all will know this look. This is the look one parent gives their child when they're warning him or her about what's about to happen at the hands of the other parent. Typically, parent A—in this case, my dad—disagrees with parent B—in this case, my mom—but feels obligated to play a supporting role in the looming conversation.

"Take a seat," my mother said, gesturing to one of the chairs in front of my father's desk and moving to one side so I could.

On autopilot, I closed the door, splitting my attention between the two of them as I walked over. I knew better than to sit before a lady did, so I stood in front of the chair and let my mother reach up and set a kiss on my cheek. Then she sat, which was our prompt to do so as well.

"Jackson, honey, how are you?" she asked, her smile friendly and patient, her eyes a normal size. This was a good sign. I only needed to worry if her eyes grew big or small. Didn't matter which, either spelled disaster.

"Just fine," I said, my gaze flicking to my dad. He sat with this his hands folded on top of his desk. He wore a rather bland smile, not too big, not too small, not too interested, and his stare pointed forward at nothing. *Okay, well, that's a bad sign.*

"And your boat? How's your boat?"

"The boat is . . . is . . ." *Oh.*

She'd seen the pictures. My mouth went completely dry. My mother had seen the pictures of me buying condoms from Charles at the convenience store and then the photos of Rae and I leaving the boat.

Her eyes narrowed. "Jackson James, do you have something you wish to tell us?"

I gripped the arms of the chair, uncertain what she wished to hear. She'd said nothing about the video kiss at the ATM, probably because she considered the issue my father's to deal with, and probably because she—unlike everyone else—didn't believe the story that had been spread around by Sienna, Jethro, and Charlotte. Knowing my mother, she'd been waiting patiently for me to fill her in.

But now, her patience had ended.

I understood. We lived in a small town. She was the wife of the sheriff. She was a respected teacher and educator. People talked. I was an adult—certainly—but I was also a member of this family. Being a member of a family meant that my decisions didn't just impact me. The actions of one person reflects on the others. I knew my mother would support me in whatever I did—she might not always like it, yet she supported me—but she didn't like to be blindsided by gossip, especially not gossip broadcast on a national level.

I glanced at my dad. His eyes met mine and he raised his eyebrows, just once, like, *What do you want me to say?*

Thankfully, my mother gave us both the answer. "I'd like to invite your lady friend over for dinner."

"Yes!" I agreed at once, glancing at my dad again. He gave me a small nod.

"Let me know if she has any food allergies or special dietary requirements." My mother crossed her legs at the ankle, picking a piece of lint invisible to my eye from her skirt. "You know it's no trouble for me to make whatever she likes best. This woman obviously means something to you. I want to make a good impression."

"I can't imagine you not making a good impression," my father said, earning him an appreciative sideways smile from his wife.

I breathed out a bundle of nerves, nodding. "I'll find out. But I'm pretty sure she eats anything."

"Even red meat?" my mother asked with a hint of wariness.

"Yes. Even red meat," I assured her, and saw that soothed some of her nerves.

"Good. It's settled," she said, standing, which meant my father and I also stood. "We'll see y'all on Saturday." Once more, she placed a kiss on my cheek, but this time she also paired it with a hug. "We love you, Jackson," she said softly, her embrace tight. "We just want to see you happy."

"I know." I met my father's gaze over her shoulder. His smile looked genuine now. "I love you too."

* * *

"Steak?" Rae looked between me and the package of USDA prime rib I'd picked up for her. "You want me to give your mother steak? As a gift?" Her tone hinted at inner turmoil.

"Yes." I nodded just once, allowing my attention to settle on Dave for a moment. He stood next to his black Escalade, waiting for Rae and me to finish our conversation so we could all drive over to my parents' house.

"I want her to like me," Rae said, sounding and looking distraught.

"She will love you."

Rae didn't look convinced. If anything, she looked more panicked than she had on Thursday when I told her about dinner with my parents. Personally, I thought we were lucky. The fallout from condom-gate seemed minor and easily managed compared to the clusterfuck that was ATM-gate.

According to Rae, her publicist had expressed delight with the photos, especially the ones of us on my fancy boat. He'd said the boat raised my profile, whatever that meant. He'd also said something about Harrison being irritated, not that I cared what that asshole thought.

Anyway, Rae hadn't been negatively impacted. That's the important part.

I, on the other hand, received my fair share of dirty looks from folks around town on Thursday and Friday before and during the jam session. According to Flo, they felt like they'd been lied to, and considered the photos as evidence that I'd hoodwinked them all with the initial version of events surrounding the ATM video. This had been easily remedied—for the most part—by Charlotte stepping in and spreading an alternate story. She let it be known at the library, Daisy's Nut House, and the Piggly Wiggly that she'd set Rae and me up, a tale corroborated by Darlene Simmons.

Darlene was the redhead who'd monologued at the Cades Cove picnic about Rae's roles being brave choices. Darlene confirmed Charlotte's story, adding that Charlotte had mentioned to her—while Charlotte had walked into the park that Saturday and Darlene had been leaving it—that Charlotte purposefully tricked Rae and me, placing us at same the place at the same time.

And so, if you can believe it, most folks in town ended up being happy for us. Other folks didn't buy Charlotte's version, thought we'd been together this whole time, but still seemed (albeit warily) happy. I did receive a slew of text messages from ex-flings, female friends, and my sister expressing curiosity and excitement for me. None of my work colleagues seemed surprised or appeared to care one way or the other. My parents seemed fine with the idea, but—presently—expected us for dinner within the next twenty minutes.

Which brings us to now and Rae staring at me like I was nuttier than a package of trail mix.

"Not flowers? Or a nice silk scarf? Or a bottle of wine? Or an iPad? Or Swiss chocolate? Or a Louboutin Cabata tote?" She held up two giant gift bags, presumably filled with the items she had just mentioned.

I put the steaks back in the plastic Piggly Wiggly bag, tying the straps together. "You can put the steaks in the bag with the wine. But I'm telling you, there is nothing better you can give my mother than steak."

Her forehead wrinkled with deep creases of concern, her eyes searched mine, torn. "You're not playing a trick on me, are you?"

"No." I stepped closer, giving her a soft kiss and slipping the steaks into the bag I hoped held the wine and not the silk scarf. "I wouldn't do that. I know you're nervous, even though I've told you ten times you don't need to be."

She nodded, looking pained and close to tears. "Okay. Okay. I'll give your mother steaks."

"Good," I said soothingly. "Now let's go." Taking the bags from her fingers before she could change her mind, I placed my free hand on the small of her back and gently applied pressure, guiding her toward the Escalade. We'd decided to have Dave drive us tonight rather than arriving in two vehicles. I'd also liked the idea because I got the sense Rae needed to be held before and after the dinner.

When I'd told her of my mother's request, she'd freaked out.

And by that I mean, she'd *FREAKED OUT*, leaving the family room of my house— where we'd just settled in to watch a movie—pacing back and forth in the kitchen for several silent minutes, and then launching a thousand questions at me about how she should behave and what she should wear and asking me if we could write a script for the evening for her to follow.

Apparently, Rae had never been introduced to a man's parents before. This fact, plus what I knew of her own situation growing up, I understood her anxiety. But I felt confident in my mom and dad. I knew I just needed to get her there and then everything would be just fine.

I handed the gift bags over to Dave, sharing a commiserating look with the guard, then opened the back door for her. She didn't hop inside, but rather seemed distracted by the simple and modest black dress she'd finally settled on wearing.

"Is this too formal?"

"No."

"Does it make me look like I'm in mourning?"

"No."

She turned like she might walk back to the house. "I think I'll go with the blue one. I don't want them to think—"

I stepped in her path, steering her back to the car and basically lifting her into the back. I shut the door once she was inside, and I heard Dave engage the locks to prevent her from escaping. The guard and I shared another look. After what he, Miguel, and I had been through today—a ten-hour fashion show with a woman *intent* on making the perfect first impression—I wanted to ask Dave and Miguel to be groomsmen at my wedding. We'd bonded. For life.

Dave and Miguel had also spent the afternoon telling me all about Raquel's house in California, the double gates, the dogs, the bars, the redundant alarm systems, the steel reinforced entries and three panic rooms. I suspected, even after today's lengthy first-impression fashion show, the guards still preferred Sienna's carriage house to the prison-like atmosphere of Rae's place in LA. But it left me wondering if maybe Dave and Miguel should both come with us to my parents' house tonight and stay for the evening. I didn't like thinking about all the desperate and violent super fans that had made the security at her house in LA necessary.

Walking around the car, I heard the locks disengage and I opened my door, sliding inside next to Rae and her bouncing legs. She was staring forward, biting her thumb-nail, and likely imagining all the worst-case scenarios that awaited her.

Taking out my phone, I texted my mom.

Jackson: She's very nervous. Maybe have Dad make those margaritas.

Mom: On it. Double the vodka.

Jackson: Margaritas have tequila.

Mom: We'll add it all, you're not driving.

278

I smiled at my mom's response, sliding the phone back in my pocket. I then reached over and pulled Rae toward me, wrapping her in my arms as Dave turned around in the Winston's driveway.

"Buckle up," I said, reaching for the seatbelt behind her and handing it over. While she fumbled with the latch, finally managing it after three tries, I clicked mine into place.

Placing my arms around her again, bringing her cheek to my chest, I said, "Rae, I promise, they are going to love you."

This must've been the wrong thing to say because I felt her body stiffen. "You don't know that."

I sighed. I couldn't imagine anyone meeting her and not loving her instantly, just as I had. And then more and more each time we met, each interaction, each look and touch and smile.

"Would it help if I told you something weird about my mother?"

Some of the tension in her body released. "Not if it's a violation of her privacy. I don't want—"

"No. Of course not. This is something well known about Janet James."

"Oh?" She straightened and looked at me. "What is it?"

"My mother grew up on a Texas cattle ranch and feels a great affinity for supporting American ranchers."

She seemed to digest this. "That doesn't seem weird. If she grew up on a cattle ranch, her affinity makes sense."

"Yeah, but it's somewhat extreme. With my mother, almost everything else is up for discussion, but anyone who tries to convince her to stray from her beliefs on this one thing, well, she'll never look at them the same way again. She has bumper stickers on the back of her truck praising meat culture and steak in particular."

Rae gave me a little smile, like she found this delightfully odd.

Taking this as a good sign, I went on. "See, one thing I've learned over and over again in my line of work is that how a person is raised informs their convictions."

Rae nodded, leaning back in her seat, watching me.

"Their ideas about the world are formed based on their own experience and the people they know personally. Sometimes, these ideas are so deeply held that evidence and facts to the contrary feel like an attack. This is what it's like with my mother and red meat."

Now Rae frowned. "She thinks if people don't like steak, it's a personal affront?"

"No, no. Nothing like that. You can talk poorly of red meat, you can be a vegetarian or a vegan—none of that bothers her. She considers those your beliefs, your choices. Fine with her. But if you tried to change her mind, or if she sensed you were judging her belief in the importance of the American cattle industry? Don't bother speaking to her again."

"Huh." Rae's thoughtful stare moved beyond me to the window. "I guess I feel that way about certain recipes or approaches to acting. It's like, you have your way, let me have my way, and don't push me about it."

"Right, but recipes and acting approaches typically don't have an impact on the environment, health and wellness, and so on."

Her eyes cut back to me. "Have you ever argued with your mother about it?"

"Just once. I was in college and thought I could convince her with facts. I didn't want to change her mind so much as get her to admit there was a valid alternate perspective and that red meat might've been the cause for my headaches growing up."

"What happened?"

I shrugged, chuckling. "I learned my lesson."

She grinned, studying me, but then her grin waned. "And she forgave you? For arguing with her about a belief she holds so dearly?"

"Of course. I'm her son." I slid my hand from around her shoulder to her hand, picking it up to kiss each of her knuckles. "She loves me, even if I disappoint her, even when I drive her crazy."

CHAPTER 24

RAQUEL

"The American dream is a term that is often used but often misunderstood. It isn't really about becoming rich or famous. It is about things much simpler and more fundamental than that."

— ATTRIBUTED TO DOROTHY DANDRIDGE

*A*pproximately twenty minutes into the evening with Jackson's family, I felt *incredibly* silly for being so nervous.

First, his mother was just the kindest, funniest, sweetest, most patient carnivore I'd ever met. When I'd given her the steaks, you would've thought I'd given her the moon. But I understood. The steaks were my way of communicating to her that I accepted her, and her beliefs. I wasn't going to walk into her house and argue with her. I was there to build a relationship, not sabotage it before it started.

Second, Jackson's sister, her husband, and their baby surprised everyone and arrived fifteen minutes after we did. Just like Jackson's mom, his sister had embraced me and seemed genuinely happy to meet me. Initially, the surprise had thrown me for a loop. But then Jackson and Jessica had bantered and bickered—

"What are you doing here?" Jackson had grumbled after his earlier excitement when she'd walked in, putting his hands on his hips.

"I'm here for the steak. What are you doing here? And dressed like that?" She'd turned her nose up at him, giving his outfit a once-over. "Shocking."

"You know we're here to have dinner with Mom and Dad, and there is nothing wrong with what I'm wearing."

"I mean, I'm not going to be the one to tell you it's indecent, but okay. Live and let live. And are you sure your dinner was tonight? Because I'm pretty sure—"

"You are a sneak." He'd pointed at her, but he couldn't hide his smile. "What did you do? Hop on a plane as soon as you found out I was bringing Rae over?"

"No! Of course not." She'd gasped, looking exceptionally offended. "First, I rubbed some coconuts all over a banana and had myself a pina colada. *And then* I hopped on a plane. Get your facts straight, big brother."

I could guess what she'd meant by coconuts and bananas. She'd sent a wink to her handsome redheaded husband while speaking and passed the baby to him. Then, they'd kissed.

Jackson seemed both disgusted and delighted by his sister, and this dynamic persisted throughout the evening, which could not have worked out better. Jessica's—and baby Liam's—presence had pulled attention away from me, allowing me to settle in and observe first before being expected to engage.

Both Jessica's husband and Mr. James—I mean, Sheriff James—were polite, but quiet. I got the sense this simply reflected their nature. They weren't coolly polite, or distant, or unfriendly. More like, they didn't express their opinions as freely as Jessica, Janet, and Jackson.

Speaking of which, I marveled at Jackson's boisterousness around his sister. He was *not* like this with me. When just the two of us spent time together, Jackson would flirt, sure. But mostly he was serene, a little shy, funny but also intense and sincere.

Actually, his father reminded me of the Jackson I knew, the contemplative way he seemed to absorb the conversation around him, only speaking when he felt it necessary to correct a misconception or ask a thoughtful question.

It was neat to see both Janet and the sheriff's influence on their son, to spot the parts of them reflected in him.

Toward the end of dinner, whether it was my second margarita or the hint of Jackson's smile I noted in the sheriff's grin, I felt deep affection stir within me for these people I didn't know very well but felt convinced I could grow to seriously love.

"Duane, would you help me clear the dishes?" The sheriff stood, lifting his chin toward his son-in-law.

I stood before Jessica's husband could, picking up my plate and Jackson's. "Oh, let me help."

"Oh, no, Rae. You're a guest today, but next time you'll be family. Please don't worry about it." Janet sent me an imploring look, then sent the same look to Jackson, like he might be able to talk me out of clearing dishes.

"Actually—" Jess chimed in, handing her plate over to me "—let Rae and Daddy do the dishes. It'll give them a chance to talk. Y'all haven't let either of them get a word in edgewise or sideways or overwise or underwise."

"Yeah, Duane. Why can't you be quieter?" Jackson folded his arms, sending a narrowed stare to his brother-in-law.

The redhead glared at Jackson, saying nothing, a reluctant smile tugging at his mouth. It was obvious there existed a mutual respect between them, if not always a mutual like.

Jessica then launched into a diatribe about Jackson's propensity to interrupt, which Janet attempted to referee, which left the sheriff and I to clear the dishes. Smiling at the sibling's antics, I followed Jackson's dad into the kitchen and to the sink, setting the plates down on the counter. After three trips, we'd cleared the entire table.

"Let me do the dishes," I said, reaching for the first dish and searching for a wash-cloth or a scrubby thing.

"Oh, now. That's not a good idea. If Janet saw you doing dishes, I'd be sleeping on the couch tonight. Here—" he walked over to a drawer and pulled out a towel "—why don't you dry, and I'll wash. I don't know why, but in the hierarchy of chores, drying is more respectable than washing."

"Okay. Sounds good." We exchanged a friendly smile, and I accepted the towel, positioning myself next to the sink.

It was at this point I realized they had a dishwasher—which he opened and began to load.

I huffed a laugh, folding my arms. "That's—that was sneaky."

He sent me a sly-ish grin, and he looked so much like Jackson in that moment my heart jumped.

"Just keep me company. I don't want to go back out there with the loud people. I need a minute." Finished with the first dish, he bent to place it in the dishwasher, adding, "And you're not loud, are you?"

"I guess I'm not." I leaned back against the kitchen counter and allowed my attention to wander, noting all the details that made this a home instead of a film set. The paint wasn't perfect, but it wasn't messy or chipping. It was just old and careworn. Papers and newspaper clippings were stuffed in well-used cookbooks that sat beneath cabinets. A teapot with a chip on the spout. A blender that hadn't been cleaned after use. A range with one broken burner. A burn mark on the counter. Someone must've placed a hot pot on the butcher block before realizing their error.

"That was Jess."

"Excuse me?"

He tilted his head toward the burn mark. "Jess made the mark there on her last night in town. She and Duane came over and made us dinner. She put the pot in that spot, and it left a mark."

"Oh." I considered this information for a moment. "It's kind of ironic, she goes her whole life without burning the counter, then on her very last day in town she leaves her mark."

"No, no." He chuckled. "She's burned the countertop plenty of times. That one is just the latest in a long history and path of her destruction."

The way he said this made me laugh, and my laugh pulled a smile from him as he continued. "I usually remove the marks once a year or so, sand it down, polish it back up, but that one. . ." He loaded two more dishes into the washer, saying as he stood, "It might be the last one she makes in this kitchen, so I want to keep it."

My heart jumped for a different reason this time, and in a different direction. It climbed up my throat, making speech difficult. I wondered, did my father keep the marks his children made in his house? Did he treasure them? It's hard not to compare. I didn't want to compare. But how could I not?

Time to change the subject.

Clearing my throat, I walked around him to the side with the dishwasher, taking the cup from his hand and loading it, needing to do something. "So, uh, why do you think Jackson wanted to be a sheriff's deputy?"

"Have you asked him?" He set the next cup on the counter.

I placed it next to the first. "I did. He said he didn't feel like he had any innate talents except for patience with people and process."

"Ha! That's true—I mean, it's true he has an innate talent with people and process, but I take issue with him saying he doesn't have any other innate talents."

Glad to hear the sheriff's response, I nodded. "That's what I said too."

"But it sounds like Jackson."

We shared a smile that felt quiet with understanding. *Man, I really like Jackson's dad.*

"I'd say something pretty significant about himself that he left out is his—his compassion, and his empathy. He's always been incredibly empathetic, even when he was a kid. He notices things other folks don't."

"Like what?" I recognized this about Jackson as well, but I wanted to hear his dad talk about him.

"Like . . ." The sheriff seemed to think matters over for a moment, as though searching for the perfect example. "Like Jackson notices when his mother starts getting arthritis in her fingers, so she can't peel apples for apple pie anymore. He teaches himself how to peel apples faster than her. This last year, she managed just one for every four of his."

Yeah. I just fell more in love with Jackson James.

But the sheriff wasn't finished. "On a similar vein, he notices that my hands shake a little bit when I peel my eggs and end up with half the egg white and a mashed yolk." He lifted up his hands so I could see the slight tremor, suds dripping from the palms. "So once a week, I'll find ten hard-boiled eggs, all peeled, waiting for me in my fridge at the office."

Inexplicably, my eyes stung. *Jackson is getting a blow job tonight for being an exceptional human being.*

285

"Those are just two examples." He laughed lightly, dipping his hands back in the soapy water. "Of course, there's more, but I don't know if he wants me tattling on him."

I watched Jackson's father wash the next plate and the next, before something compelled me to say, "I met Jackson for the first time at Sienna and Jethro's wedding. And when we walked out of the wedding tent, he immediately put his jacket around my shoulders."

"He probably thought you were cold." He nodded, as though a man giving a woman his jacket happened every day here.

"And since we'd left before dinner was served, he took me to get food." I smiled at the memory. "Because he thought I might be hungry."

He set a new pile of dishes on the counter. "So, you see what I mean."

"I do," I said, loading the plates. "You raised an exceptional son."

He glanced over at me, pleasure shining in his eyes. "I hope I meet your mother one day."

I reared back an inch, his statement confusing and unsettling me. I searched my mind, wondering why this sweet, gentle man would ever want to meet my mom. "What? Why?"

He shrugged, like the answer was obvious, but he said it anyway. "So I can tell her she raised an exceptional daughter."

* * *

Even though Jackson had invited Dave to stay and have dinner with everyone, he'd declined. "Just call when you're ready to be picked up, or I'll be here at ten thirty, which ever happens first."

Dave's knock on the door at 10:30 PM sharp surprised me. Clearly, I'd lost track of time, and I found myself sad to leave.

"Promise you'll come back soon," Janet said as she pulled me in for a tight hug.

"Only if you let me cook dinner next time." I closed my eyes, enjoying the maternal embrace.

"When will that be?" Jess sent her brother a teasing grin. "Maybe we'll swing by."

After hugs and kisses and good wishes were passed around liberally—and Dave was given two covered plates for both him and Miguel—we departed, all of Jackson's family staying on the front porch until we turned onto the main road.

I sighed. Happily.

"Did you have a good time?" Jackson teased, his eyes full of mischief.

"You know I did."

"Hmm." Jackson picked up my hand and kissed my palm, trailing his tongue from the center of my hand to my wrist. "Maybe we could—"

The privacy screen being lowered had both of us looking at the back of Dave's head.

"Hey. Guys. I'm sorry to interrupt. But we have a situation back at Sienna's place."

We glanced at each other, and Jackson asked, "What kind of situation?"

Dave made a grunting sound, long and loud. "So, you see, Harrison is there."

"What?" I leaned forward in my seat, certain I'd misheard Dave.

"Miguel is babysitting him. He just flew in this evening and wanted to surprise you. We convinced him not to interrupt your evening with a phone call, but I promised you'd be back by eleven."

Jackson tugged on my hand, drawing my eyes back to his. "What do you want to do?"

I grumbled, irritated that after such an awesome night with Jackson's family, I had to deal with a surprise visit from Harrison. We'd been playing phone tag for over a week. I knew I needed to talk to him, to figure out how to best separate for the benefit of public perception.

"I don't know." I crossed my arms, thinking. "I guess I'll talk to him, get this worked out."

Jackson leaned closer, his voice dropping. "Get what worked out?"

"You know, how to make a clean break for the public that doesn't make it look like we've been lying for years."

This earned me a look from Dave, which I caught in the rearview mirror, and I winced.

"Sorry, Dave. It was fake. No one knew but a few people."

"Well, thank fuck." Dave shifted in his seat, bunching and releasing his big shoulders. "Excuse my French, but I never could figure out why you two were together."

"You don't like Harrison?" Jackson, seeming genuinely interested in the big man's opinion.

"I mean, he's all right. He's no *you*, but he's okay."

Jackson's pleased smile was a flash of pride, but he hid it quickly.

But Dave had more to say. "I didn't like that he was always stepping out on my girl here. She deserved better, you know? And it never seemed to make sense because, even after his cheating hit the papers, these two seemed to still get along fine. Raquel wasn't crying over him. So I thought, 'Hey. What do I know? Maybe theirs is an open relationship.' Not so uncommon in the business."

Jackson absorbed this information, bringing my hand to cradle between his. "Thanks, Dave."

"Anytime, Jackson." Dave then lifted the privacy screen, likely sensing we needed a moment to talk.

Once it hit the top, Jackson asked, "Do you want me to stay?"

I rubbed my forehead. "Yes. But also, no. I always want you to stay, I always want you with me. But if you stay tonight, then it might make things tense, and then it'll be difficult to get him to agree to what I want and leave."

He didn't look worried, but I thought maybe I detected the barest hint of jealousy glittering back at me behind his deep-set eyes. I also suspected he worked to hide it.

"Jackson, Harrison is a friend. Yes, we dated once, but that was before you and I met. He cheated on me, we broke up for good, and then I met you at Sienna and Jethro's wedding. Everything with Harrison since has been for the benefit of publicity."

"I know." His attention dropped to where he held my hand.

"My goal for tonight is to hammer out a strategy, one that both he and I can feel good about, that will allow us to split publicly without raising suspicions of our ruse or require telling any more lies. It's over, it's done, it's in the past. But . . ."

I waited for him to bring his eyes back to me before I continued. "But I agreed to this. I need to end it responsibly and thoughtfully. If Harrison had fallen in love with someone last year, while we were faking our relationship, I would hope that he would've felt the same and given me a chance to have some input on how it ended."

"I understand that. In this situation, being Harrison for the next few months will be difficult and awkward," he said, truly seeming to empathize with Harrison.

I mean, he *really* seemed to understand what Harrison's perspective might be, and that gave me pause. "I appreciate you being so understanding about this." I heard some bewilderment leach into my voice.

Jackson quirked a half smile at my tone. "Let's just say, I've been in his shoes before."

"You have?"

"Yes." His smile grew, turned into a shy one. "My ex-fiancée Zora Leffersbee was never my fiancée."

Flinching back, my mouth dropped open. "Are you—are you serious?"

"Yep. She and I were—are—good friends, and we never dated. We don't talk as much as we used to, now that's she's off with the love of her life, but we had a similar arrangement to yours and Harrison's. Except, instead of doing it for attention and publicity, we did it to avoid the attention of our families and their constant questions about our personal lives." He chuckled.

"Huh." I sat back, contemplating this change in what I thought I knew about Jackson James. "So . . . you didn't love her?"

"As a friend, absolutely. As more than a friend, no."

I don't know why, so don't ask me why, but this information felt momentous, like a huge relief. It also left me feeling ashamed. I'd been jealous of this woman and judged her, a person I'd never met, because I thought Jackson had loved her and she'd left him. I'd been hugely curious, but I hadn't wanted to bring her up to anyone —not Sienna, not Jethro, not Charlotte, and definitely not Jackson. I didn't want to listen to Jackson talk about a lost love. I'd wanted to pretend she didn't exist, that he never loved her.

And now it turned out he'd never loved her.

"Sorry I didn't mention it before," he said, rousing me from my confusing thoughts.

"No, no. It's okay." Now that I knew the truth, all the curiosity I'd been pushing from my mind erupted into an avalanche of questions. "Zora wanted out of the agreement?"

"Yes. She's a health outcomes researcher, and her family are friends with mine. We've known each other forever. They kept pestering her about settling down and getting married, much worse than mine. So one of us offered—I forget who—and we talked through it. It made sense, we got along so well. She wanted to focus on her career without being asked whether she had a boyfriend, or why she was still single, or being told she needed to adjust her work-life balance." Jackson made a face here, his eyes drifting up to the ceiling of the car. "I have similar issues."

"Similar issues?"

"People telling me I work too much, or too hard. Folks like to comment on the food I eat, how much I exercise, how many of my days off I spend at the station, following up on a case or working through lower priority complaints."

I nodded, remembering what Charlotte had said about Jackson, that he only ate boring food and that he worked all the time.

"But I like what I do," he said matter-of-factly. "I love it, actually. I like that I can draw a straight line between what I do and making a difference. I like that I solve problems and, hopefully, make this part of the world better and safer for folks. Maybe I'm boring, but I figure someone has to be, you know?"

Warm affection and admiration surged through me, and I leaned forward to press a kiss on his lips, also placing a hand on his knee. "I don't think you're boring," I said, sliding my hand up his thigh.

He didn't catch it or stop me, but rather opened his legs for my touch and returned my kiss with a hotter, more demanding one. And when his warm palm settled on my knee, following a similar path up my thigh, I decided to tell Dave to take a detour back to the carriage house.

Before I could enact this genius plan, I felt the car slow, turn, and jostle. We'd already arrived back to Sienna's. I groaned.

Jackson grinned, lifting his mouth from mine and kissing my jaw. "Call me when he leaves."

"You'll come over?" I linked my fingers behind his neck, encouraging his kisses. We still had a few seconds, I wanted his mouth on my body. *Then again, I always want his mouth on my body. Nothing new about that.*

But Jackson wanting to come over was new. We hadn't been together (other than making out at his place on Thursday) since the boat. I ached for him.

"I'll come over when he leaves." Jackson leaned back and pulled the hem of my skirt back over my knees. "I don't want to make things harder for you."

"And you'll stay the night? All night?" My arms were still around his neck, I couldn't seem to bring myself to let him go.

"I have to get up early for work, but I'll stay the night if you want."

"I do want!" I kissed him again, this time a quick, hard press of my mouth.

He grinned, undoing his seatbelt. "Come on, then. The sooner you deal with your fake fiancé, the sooner we can be real friendly."

Oh. I liked the sound of that.

CHAPTER 25

RAQUEL

"Rest satisfied with doing well, and leave others to talk of you as they please."

— PYTHAGORAS

*J*ackson was as much a gentleman with Harrison as he was with everyone. As I reflected on it—watching the two men shake hands and exchange pleasantries—I tried to recall a moment or a person with which Jackson hadn't been patient.

His sister. I smiled softly at the memory of the two of them at dinner, teasing each other. I decided his sister didn't count. He didn't need to be self-contained or controlled with her. He could let loose, say what he thought, and just be himself.

You. My smile widened. There had been a few times during these almost two months when Jackson had abandoned politeness with me. I hadn't minded.

But other than with his family and with me, I couldn't think of another instance. Even when I'd first arrived in Green Valley and he'd been covered in pie, being filmed by a stranger, he'd been polite with the man. Firm, but polite.

Same thing when I'd overheard his phone call at the station—with the reverend, about the neighbor's prizewinning roses—he'd been firm, but polite. And not mean-polite, like he resented having to be polite, but truly polite, like he comprehended and appreciated the other person's perspective, even though he didn't fully agree with them.

When four of his former flings had approached us on the day of the infamous picnic, or with Charlotte after. He'd been visibly frustrated, but he'd always been polite.

"So. That's the guy."

Presently, Harrison stood at my shoulder, and we both watched Jackson drive away in his truck, the taillights winding down Sienna's driveway toward the main road.

"Yes. That's the guy," Dave said, hovering at my other shoulder. "And we like him a lot. A. Lot."

"And he's hot," Miguel chimed in around a mouthful of popcorn. He stood next to Dave. "Don't ruin this for us, Harrison."

I nodded, saying nothing, because they really had no idea how hot Jackson was, which suited me perfectly well.

"You made popcorn? Are you expecting a show?" Dave asked Miguel.

Meanwhile, Harrison placed an arm over my shoulder and whispered, "But he's not as hot as me."

"That's debatable," Miguel tossed back at Harrison, apparently overhearing his comment. Then both Dave and Miguel turned toward the main house, continuing to bicker about popcorn, with Miguel giving Dave a shove. "What? I wanted popcorn. Stop commenting on my food."

I smiled, watching my guards for a moment before realizing they were heading in the wrong direction. "Hey, where are you going?"

"Sienna said to come over so you and Harrison can talk," Dave said, turning to walk backward. "But you only get an hour and then we have to kick him out. Jethro's orders."

I glanced at Harrison, to see how he felt about this arrangement. His face—which I used to think of as devastatingly handsome—was scrunched in a frown. I thought he must've been irritated at the time limit, but then he called after them, "It's not debatable to anyone with eyes, Miguel."

Without turning, Miguel said, "Yeah, yeah, yeah." He then added something else on a mumble that I didn't hear as the two guards made it to Sienna's front porch.

Still frowning, Harrison faced me, his arm dropping from my shoulders. "But he is hot," he said, the statement sounding like a concession. "I thought maybe he was just photogenic."

I firmed my lips so I wouldn't smile. "Nope."

"Hmm." Harrison inspected me, making no attempt to conceal his trademark swaggery grin. He had a very alluring grin—boyish and yet wolfish at the same time. "You look good, Rae. Rested."

"Thank you, Harrison. I feel good and rested."

He tilted his head to the side, indicating to the carriage house. "We should go inside before we're eaten alive. I think I've already been bitten twice. How do you stand all the bugs here?"

I stepped forward to lead the way. "I use this substance called insect repellant. Have you heard of it? You can now buy it in stores, anyone can get it."

"Ha ha. Domino warned me you were back to your old self."

"Oh? Did he?"

"Yes. He said you were cracking jokes and laying down the law every time you two talked this month."

Good. Domino, smart and talented at his job, had obviously prepared Harrison for what to expect. I wasn't a pushover anymore, allowing others to treat me like a commodity. I made my own decisions.

"Do you want something to drink?" I asked, closing the door behind us and walking toward the kitchen. I checked the clock above the stove. With any luck, I'd be able to convince Harrison to see things my way, we'd hammer out the beginning of a plan, and he'd leave before midnight.

Then, Jackson friendly times!

"No, thanks. Let me text my driver, let him know to come back and wait outside until we're done."

I grabbed a water glass for myself and filled it at the fridge, debating how best to hurry this along.

"This guy, he's a policeman?" Harrison asked distractedly.

"He's a sheriff's deputy. But you're not here because of Jackson." I turned to find that Harrison had followed me into the kitchen. He stood on the other side of the island, eschewing a stool in favor of standing, his phone already tucked away.

"I love his name, *Jackson*. It's a good name." Harrison rubbed his clean-shaven chin, the entirety of his attention now on me. I used to find his eyes—which were pure turquoise—unsettling. Now, they were just Harrison. "Do you think I should grow a beard?"

"I don't know. I imagine you're tired?"

"I am tired. I've been traveling all day." His gaze swept down and then up my body, perhaps taking note of my slouchy, sleepy posture. "Should I come back tomorrow?"

"No. Let's talk this through now, then you can get back to LA."

"Fine." He braced his feet apart, his expression carefully bored. "I know you want to call it off."

"Okay." *Good. Glad that's out of the way.* "But?"

"But I want you to consider the wedding during production of *Midnight Lady* one more time."

"No." I didn't add that, unless the script reverted to its original state, I didn't want the part anymore.

"Just, listen." He lifted his hands, palms out. "Think about it. We could do the wedding shoot, the whole nine, staring into each other's eyes. The tux, the white dress. That shit will blow up everywhere. We can sell the first photo rights for major cash, donate the money."

"I'm not marrying you." I took a sip from my water glass.

Unsurprisingly, he continued as though I hadn't spoken, "And then, two months later, messy divorce. You move out, reconcile with your hot guy here if you want, if you think that works for your goals and won't hurt your image too much. Meanwhile, I'm heartbroken, you're the one that got away. I'm this dark, brooding, sexy, sensitive loner who can't get over the loss of his soul mate. They'll let me play Batman after that." He bit his lip, grinning and wagging his eyebrows. "I've always wanted a rubber suit."

Despite myself, I laughed. "Harrison—"

"Come on, Rae." He came around the island to settle his hands on my shoulders, giving me his most beseeching, smoldering stare. "You know you want to."

"I definitely don't want to." I shook his hands off. "I'm not even a little bit tempted."

"What? Why not?"

"Because just the thought of pretending again makes me want to throw up."

"Gee. Thanks."

"Seriously. It makes me sick, what you and I did these last four years—and for what?"

"Free publicity? Great movie roles? A place in history as one of Hollywood's most epic love stories?"

"I'm done." Even now, thinking about it, my stomach soured. "The answer is no. We separate now. I promise to make everything before right now continue to look real, I promise I'll keep this secret forever, but it's over today."

He sighed, shoving his hands in his pants pockets and studying me for several seconds, his stare turning hard. "So, what? You're with this guy? This police guy?"

"Yes. Because it's the truth." I drank another sip of water.

His eyes searched mine, imploring me to rethink my decision. "Isn't it so much safer to just keep pretending? No one can hurt you if they don't really know you, Rae."

Typical Harrison.

"No. You have it wrong. No one can hurt me if I know *myself*." I managed a small smile. "So no more pretending.".

Face grumpy, eyes narrowed, Harrison made a disgruntled sound, the line of his mouth flat and severe. "And there is nothing I can say or do to change your mind?"

"No."

"Okay." Crossing his arms over his chest, his gaze turned frosty. "Then I guess we have to talk about how to extract me from this in a believable way."

"I guess we do." I nodded.

"I have another plan, and it means we end things now, but I don't think you're going to like it."

"Go ahead, what's the plan?" I asked, trying not to feel guilty, or like I was abandoning him to walk this road on his own.

"Lina reached out to me," he said, scrutinizing my expression.

Irritation flared in my chest at the mention of her name. "Oh?"

"Yes. After the pictures of you and Jackson—man, that is a great name—after the pictures of you two leaving that boat surfaced. She wanted to make sure I was okay."

I braced myself for what I suspected was coming next. "Oh, no. You didn't."

Harrison lifted his eyebrows. "I did."

I set my water cup on the island, placing a hand over my stomach. "So now you're with Lina?"

"That's the new plan, if you won't agree to my old one."

Ugh. "Does she know it's all for show?" I might've cut her out of my life, but that didn't mean I wanted her being used.

"Yes. She was the one to suggest we keep things camera-official, but open otherwise. And she wants me to lobby for her to get the role in *Midnight Lady* back."

I nodded, feeling helpless and sad for some reason. I didn't want Harrison, I didn't want to fake it and pretend for publicity, I didn't want to be friends with Lina, I didn't want to play that character anymore, so why did I feel this way?

"So, let me guess, you and Lina are going to film the movie, get married, and so forth. You're plugging her into my part."

"The part you don't want because you are *in love* with your man, Jackson. Correct."

I no longer felt guilty for abandoning Harrison to walk this road alone. I should've known better, I wasn't irreplaceable. In Hollywood, everyone and everything is interchangeable.

* * *

Harrison left at 11:30 PM. He seemed fine with the new plan, neither happy nor unhappy nor resigned to it. I wasn't particularly happy, but we'd reached an agreement, and now it was settled and done. Domino, Harrison, and I would talk through the final details when I returned to LA so facts could be spun into career gold, which would then be mined for our mutual benefit. *If possible.*

I found I didn't have much energy left to care about whether my career suffered, which I assumed it would. Or perhaps I did care but pondering the decline of everything I'd worked for depressed me. I wanted to stop pretending, stop cultivating a façade. I wanted to live an authentic life. Uncertainty and risk were the price. Maybe people would accept the real Raquel, maybe they wouldn't. Only time would tell.

As soon as Harrison walked out the door, I texted Jackson to come over and then hopped in the shower. I needed to wash off the stress and sadness before he arrived. One byproduct of Harrison's visit—intended or not—was the reminder that I would be returning to Los Angeles at some point soon. My summer here in Green Valley was coming to an end. Jackson and I hadn't yet discussed what would come after.

Turning off the faucet, I thought I heard a sound coming from the bedroom, and I frowned. Dave and Miguel weren't due back for another fifteen or twenty minutes at least, and it seemed highly unlikely that Jackson would already be here.

Except, no. . .

A cold chill raced down my spine, and I strained my ears, holding my breath and berating myself for not turning on the alarm. *Shit. Shit. Shit. Sh—*

Another sound, like a closet door sliding open, sent terror clawing up my throat. Someone was in my room, and I didn't think it was Dave or Miguel, they had no reason to be in my room. And I knew it couldn't be Jackson, he couldn't get in, he didn't have a key. I eyed the bathroom door and the flimsy, twist lock on the knob. It wasn't locked. But even if it had been, a hard kick to the door would send it flying open.

Don't panic.

I'd been in this situation once before, a few months prior to moving into the fortress I now called home in Hollywood Hills. The situation had been the reason for my move. *You were ultimately okay then, you're okay now. You just need to think.*

Whoever it was, they'd heard me in the shower. They knew I was in here. There was no hiding that. Maybe . . . maybe I could delay walking out of the bathroom? I could wait them out until Dave and Miguel returned. I could pretend I was drying my hair while I secretly hid behind the door with a weapon. I'd done something similar the last time, and it had worked.

I don't want to die.

Stop! Stop it. Find a weapon. *What can I use for a weapon?* My eyes frantically searched the bathroom as I pulled a towel off the rack, wrapping it around my body tightly. I needed a weapon, I needed—

"Hey, Rae?"

I sucked in a breath, gripping the towel bar, because that wasn't a psycho stalker's voice.

"Sienna?" I croaked before I could stop myself.

"Yeah, hey. Sorry—I just wanted to let you know I'm in here. I need something from this closet for Ben for tomorrow and—Oh my God, Rae? Are you crying?"

I nodded, another muffled sob escaping despite my best efforts to keep it in. My adrenaline crashed, leaving my limbs shaking. *Calm down. Calm down. False alarm.* I sunk to the floor.

"Rae?" She tried the door and obviously found it unlocked. In the next moment, Sienna was on the floor next to me, her arms around me. "Oh no. No, honey. It's just me. I'm so sorry. I'm so sorry. You're safe."

"Hey! Why is this door open?" Jackson's voice called from somewhere in the house, and I felt Sienna's body tense.

"Shit. I left the front door open." Hugging me tighter, she lifted her voice to call out, "We're in Rae's bathroom." Then to me she whispered, "Dave and Miguel said they were coming right behind me, I swear. I'm so, so sorry."

"You're fine. I'm sorry." I wiped at the stupid tears, sucking in a deep breath. "I don't know why I'm crying."

"You know why you're crying, you've come face-to-face with an attacker before. Oh! Jackson. Come here."

"What—what happened?"

The edge in his voice had me looking up. He stood at the doorway, his forehead furrowed with severe concern, his eyes searching my toweled form, perhaps for injuries.

"It's my fault." Sienna said, kissing my forehead.

"No, it's my fault." I sniffled, forcing a laugh. "I heard Sienna in the bedroom and got freaked out. My imagination got away from me and—"

He rushed forward, taking me from Sienna and lifting me in his arms. "I got you," he said, holding me close and carrying me to the bedroom. "You're safe, I got you."

"I was safe the whole time," I protested half-heartedly, catching Sienna's eye as she sent me an apologetic look and rushed to the bedroom door.

"I'll just leave you two. You're in good hands. I'll get the thing for Ben tomorrow. And again, I'm so sorry," she said, backing out of the door.

"You have nothing to be sorry about!" I called after her.

"Yes, I do!" she shouted from the other side of the door.

I cry-chuckled, shaking my head and closing my eyes. My chin wobbled, and I tried to breathe through the residual adrenaline leaving my system. What a roller coaster of a day.

Jackson sat on the bed, still cradling me, his lips pressed to the top of my head. And that's when I realized his heart was galloping. I tried to lean back so I could see his face, but he was holding me too tight.

"Jackson, hey. You're holding me too tight."

His arms loosened but his heart didn't slow. I managed to lean back, holding his jaw between my hands, wanting to force his eyes to mine. They were dark and wild, not meeting mine.

"Jackson? Are you okay?"

He nodded, his throat working. "I'm sorry. It's just, I've seen—" he paused, managing a swallow. But when he spoke next his voice was tight. "In my line of work, I've seen some things. And when I came in, you looked—and you were on the ground in just a towel, crying, and I thought—" His attention lifted to the ceiling. "Sorry."

I stared at him, both wanting and not wanting to know what he thought. In the end, I didn't ask.

I twisted my arms around his neck and held him back. "I'm fine. I promise. I heard Sienna in the room, and it freaked me out. That's it, that's all. I'm not hurt."

He nodded, his arms wrapping around my back. "You were crying because you were scared?"

"Yes. Before I moved into my place in Hollywood Hills, I had a—an intruder come into my bedroom while I was in the shower. I heard him moving around. It brought all that back."

Jackson seemed to stop breathing. "What happened?" he asked.

"I hid in the bathroom and plugged in a curling iron. He got tired of waiting for me to come out, and when he opened the door, I whacked him in the face with the iron, burning him, then I kicked him in the balls, then I ran out of my place into the street and screamed for help."

Jackson expelled a breath, pressing a kiss to my neck. "Thank God. Thank God you got away."

Something about the sound of his voice sent a ripple of unease up my neck, like he'd been a witness to an alternate ending and knew what happened—or what might've happened—had I not battled my way out of the bathroom.

We held each other for a short moment, and I barely had a chance to reflect on what I'd said and his reaction to it before he twisted and deposited me to the bed. He then stood, paced to the windows, and checked behind the curtain.

He mumbled something that sounded like, "I left you on that boat."

"What was that?"

"These windows are locked," he said, his voice louder. "But I don't like how big they are."

I held the towel at my chest, frowning at his back. "Maybe they should have bars."

"Maybe . . ."

I made a scoffing sound, my blood pressure rising to an unmanageable level for the second time that night. *He can't be serious.* "Jackson, no. They don't need bars, and they're not too big. The windows are fine. And I'm fine."

He turned, his hands on his hips. I flinched, shocked by how he was looking at me, like I was a problem to solve. This was the first time he'd ever looked at me like that. It pissed me off, but it also hurt.

"Rae. The door was unlocked and open. The alarm was off."

"Because Sienna was walking into her carriage house, on her property, which she owns." Was he treating me like a child? Or was I imagining it?

"But what if it hadn't been Sienna? Where are Dave and Miguel?" Jackson flung his hand toward the bedroom door, his tone anything but polite. "You're not safe here."

"I am safe here, and you are overreacting."

This statement seemed to only irritate and inflame him, and when he spoke next it was through clenched teeth. "No. You are not safe. You need more guards. Or—or you need to leave. You need to go back to LA."

I gaped at him, feeling like he'd just slapped me. "You want me to go back to LA?"

"Yes. Dave says your house out there is a fortress. You should at least think about it. You'd be safer there than here. You should—"

"I don't want to go back to LA."

"You should—"

"Don't tell me what I should do!" I said, my voice rising before I could control the volume. I stood from the bed. "*I* decide what I should do! I am responsible for me, not Harrison, not Domino, not my mother, and definitely not you!"

Now I was yelling. Great. *Just great.*

Jackson snapped his mouth shut and glared at me, the set of his jaw stern and severe. He said nothing.

I closed my eyes. I breathed in. I breathed out. I was so tired. And my nerves were rattled. And my emotions felt like one giant raw nerve. Now was not the time to discuss this.

"Listen, it's been a long night. I think it would be best for us to table this conversation until morning, after a good night's sleep."

I opened my eyes and found him still glaring at me.

"Jackson?"

"You're sleeping here tonight?" he asked.

"Yes." I inspected him, looking for a crack in his armor. He looked infuriated. But behind the fury, I sensed fear. "Will you stay with me?" I asked, trying to gentle my voice but instead ended up sounding impatient and cranky. Great. *Just great.*

"Is that what you want?" he asked, his jaw ticking. "Since, you know, I don't get a say."

I barely, just *barely* refrained from rolling my eyes. "You do get a say in what *you* do. You do not get a say in what *I* do. I'm my own person, Jackson. I make my own decisions; I do not need you or anyone else making them with me or for me." I repeated the words my mother had said to me countless times. I was my own person, I was responsible for myself and my decisions. Me. Only me. Obviously.

Now he flinched, like I'd slapped him. But then he nodded, his eyes dropping, his features hardening further. "I see."

Something icy and uncertain slithered through me, settling in my stomach and making my chest feel hard and heavy. He was upset. I was upset. And I didn't know how to make either of us *not* upset. More words didn't seem likely to help, so I stepped forward, reaching for him.

He took a step back, out of my reach.

My hand dropped, and so did my stomach. "Jackson—"

"I'll just get out of here so you can change," he said, tossing his thumb over his shoulder before turning and walking for the door.

"Wait." This was dumb. What were we even fighting about? I darted over to where he was and wrapped my arms around him, pressing my chest to his back. "You don't need to leave. Stay. Stay and be with me."

He didn't touch me, and his body felt so stiff and distant. "I need a minute," he said quietly. "But I'll be back."

Letting my arms slide away, I watched him leave the room. Without looking back, he shut the door behind him.

CHAPTER 26

JACKSON

"I wasn't a sex symbol, I was a sex zombie."

— VERONICA LAKE

"*B*ad day, Deputy James?"

"Not at all." I lifted my head and glared at Boone. He stood at the edge of my desk, sipping a cup of coffee even though it was just before 6:00 PM. A few weeks ago, during one of his rare conversational moods, he'd been complaining about not being able to sleep at night. I'd told him to quit drinking coffee after 3:00 PM.

"It's almost six, Boone," I said, returning my eyes to the file in front of me, if not the whole of my attention.

"It's decaf, James. And why're you in a shit mood?"

"I'm not."

I was. But Boone and I didn't talk much even on his chattiest days. This wasn't a conversation I wanted to have with anyone, least of all at work, two hours past the end of my shift, with a roommate who barely said hi and goodbye.

I'd gone for a walk last night, and then I'd returned and laid next to Rae on her bed. She'd slept fitfully, but I hadn't been able to sleep at all. I kept thinking about all those people who were obsessed with her, trying to break into her house, trying to get to her.

In particular, I thought about the man who she'd fought off with a curling iron. I'd looked him up. He had an arrest record three miles long. He'd brought rope and zip ties to her house. Chief among his charges were domestic abuse and sexual assault, and I could not stop thinking about it.

And then I thought about what she'd said, that her decisions were her own.

You get a say in what you *do. You do not get a say in what* I *do.*

I didn't know how that worked. My parents didn't love each other that way, neither did Jess and Duane from all outside appearances. They were partners, they made room for each other, they took each other's wishes into account. Could I be in love with someone and not have a say in their life, their safety? Would I be okay with that? I didn't think so. I wanted a say. And I wanted her to have a say in my life too.

Flipping through the file in front of me, I grimaced as my eyes moved over the image embedded in the printout. More tragedy today, and on a Sunday too. God rests, but death doesn't. A multicar accident with one casualty, all because some teenagers were trying to pass a Toyota Corolla on a switchback.

Boone didn't leave my desk right away. I sensed his loitering presence, heard him sip loudly from his cup of coffee. But eventually, he drifted, leaving me to my notes from Deputy Evans's brief description of the event during our phone call. He'd been the first officer on the scene, which meant he was also on his way over to Mr. Rossi's house right now to break the news about the man's youngest daughter.

I swallowed around a lump, thinking about my sister Jess and her husband, Duane Winston. I still couldn't believe she'd married him. He was . . . reckless. When they lived here, he drove too fast and had always pitched a hissy fit whenever I'd pulled him over for speeding.

Rather, for Duane it had been a hissy fit. The man didn't say much, just glared like his eyeballs were made of lasers and my face was the target. But maybe, if he'd seen what I'd seen, if he'd been privy to the mountain of tragedy caused by taking roads too fast, he would be more careful, especially with my sister and nephew in the car.

306

I hope he's careful now. I hope he keeps them safe. And I hope Jess lets him.

For the millionth time since leaving the carriage house before dawn, my thoughts turned to Rae. She wanted us to be people existing adjacent to each other with no overlap. She wanted easy and fun, a love affair without investment, without making room for each other, without compromising, without all the difficult work that built a foundation and helped it last. But I'd suspected this from the beginning, hadn't I? Being with her was too easy.

This isn't going to work.

Just the thought made me feel like I couldn't breathe, yet it was the truth. This was what I'd been trying to avoid. But now I loved her, and I didn't know how to stop or what to do. I wasn't going to push her into making room for me in her life if she didn't want to. She had to want me there. And she had to want a place—a say—in my life too.

Falling when I should've stayed upright.

We'd drift apart, I knew we would. There was nothing anchoring us together, nothing—

"Jackson James."

I blinked, my eyes coming up to find Cletus and Jethro Winston standing where Boone had been just moments prior. *Wait . . . that was a few moments ago, wasn't it?* What time was it?

I frowned, checking my watch, surprised when I saw the time. "It's past seven."

"So it is." Jethro plucked the file from my hands, closed it, and set it on the desk. "Let's go, James."

I glanced between the two of them. "Where are we going?"

"We're going for a beer," Cletus said, giving me a somber nod. "But you should probably change first, seeing as how your shift ended three hours ago. You don't want another violation thingy for wearing your uniform while off duty."

* * *

I changed out of my uniform, but I had no intention of grabbing a beer with the Winston brothers. I thanked them for their offer and begged off, claiming it had been a long day. Once we were in the parking lot, they watched me walk over to my truck, slide inside, and attempt to start the engine. It wouldn't turn over.

That's when Cletus moseyed up and asked if I was having car trouble.

And now here I was, forty-five minutes later, sitting in Genie's Country Western Bar, at a booth, Jethro and Cletus Winston staring at me from the other side, and I could not have been more surprised or perplexed by the evening's events.

"How was work, Jackson?" Jethro asked. It was the first time he'd spoken since approaching me at the station. Like usual, he wore his smirky, careless, ghost of a smile.

"Fine," I said, not wishing to discuss work with Jethro. I didn't imagine he had much respect for law enforcement if his prior arrest record was anything to go by. "Why am I here?"

"Glad you asked." Cletus pushed his beer to one side and placed his arms on the table, leaning forward. "We will now discuss your relationship with Ms. Ezra."

I'm glad I wasn't drinking anything as Cletus spoke, I'm sure I would've spit it out. "Excuse me?"

"You are excused."

"No, Cletus." My eyes cut to Jethro's, then back to Cletus. "What—why would I be discussing Ms. Ezra with you two?"

He cleared his throat. "Firstly, in our culture, traditionally, men do not discuss the trials and tribulations of their romantic relationships with other men, not like the womenfolk do. I believe this leads to unnecessary angst, heartbreak, and the blockage of essential harmonizing hormones which aid mental wellness. You should talk to someone, and it should be us."

"Oh really? Why you?"

"I was just getting to that. Secondly, you should discuss the matter with me because I have superior deductive reasoning skills. You should discuss the matter with Jethro" —he lifted a hand toward Jethro, like I couldn't see the man right in front of me— "because he has expertise in the field of study you wish to traverse, wooing and marrying a Hollywood starlet and keeping her in a state of perpetual bliss. And you should discuss the matter with *both* of us because we have an excellent and proven track record maintaining healthy relationships with exceptional women, and also because you have no brothers."

"I have no brothers," I repeated flatly.

"Exactly. We have brothers. We are brothers. And therefore, we have a built-in support system of men we trust to tell the truth, but who also break it kindly. You have no similar support system that I can deduce. As such, seeing as how I am generosity personified and Jethro didn't have plans tonight, we are offering to fill the void."

"What happened?" Jethro asked, bringing my attention back to him. To my surprise, the ever-present smirky smile had been replaced with a sober stare. "She's been crying all day. What happened?"

Ugh. His words were a sucker punch, and I momentarily lost my breath. "Is she okay?"

Jethro shrugged, and he seemed to be gritting his teeth. "You tell me."

I closed my eyes, leaning back in the booth. "It was stupid. I should apologize." The words felt and sounded hollow, likely due to the fact that I didn't believe them.

It wasn't stupid. I didn't wish to apologize. She'd made it clear I had no say or vote when it came to her safety, or her life, or any of her decisions, and that too, had felt like a sucker punch.

"Please elaborate on 'stupid,'" Cletus said.

I opened my eyes and stared at my beer. My eyes were too tired to focus, so I rubbed them with my fists. "It was never going to work out, and I was stupid to think it would."

"Why was it 'never going to work out'? Do you have access to a prophesy on the subject? Did a soothsayer approach you on the ides of July?" Cletus asked.

I chuckled, but the sound lacked humor. "No, Cletus. It's like . . ."

"What?" Jethro tapped the table, bringing my attention back to him and his sober stare. "What is it like?"

"It's like, she's too easy."

The Winston brothers frowned in unison, then looked at each other, then looked at me. But it was Cletus who spoke. "Did you just call Raquel Ezra 'easy'?"

"Not like that. I mean, being around her feels easy, effortless."

Cletus stroked his long, bushy beard. "I fail to comprehend the problem. Are you saying that Ms. Ezra is too accommodating of your personality failings and therefore you feel she isn't worth knowing? That seems like what the kids these days would call 'problematic.'"

"That's not what I said."

"You called her 'easy.'" Cletus gave me a meaningful look.

"What I'm saying is, being with her feels natural. She never asks for too much from me." I went to drink from my beer but found the bottle empty. "Like I don't have to watch my words, I don't have to change anything about myself, I don't need to make room for her or think about what I say before I say it. There's no compromise, no give and take. She's easy to be with. We click. We have fun."

"And you don't trust easy?" Jethro guessed, no judgment in his tone. He twisted in his seat to gesture toward Patty at the bar for another round.

"No. I guess I don't. Everything I have worth having, everything that's lasted, I've worked hard for. I'm not—" I had to clear my throat before continuing with the admission "—I'm not naturally good at anything."

"Elaborate on that," Cletus said, looking truly interested.

"Just, everything. In high school I was a C-plus/B-minus student, and I studied all the time. All the time. I practiced the oboe every day from freshman year to senior year and still sucked at it. I'm just getting passable now."

"You still play?" Cletus perked up.

"Course I do."

"Huh. How come I didn't know this?" Cletus seemed to be inspecting me closer. "You should play at the jam session some time."

"Uh, no. I'm not that good, and I don't think an oboe would fit in."

"Never know unless you try," Jethro said under his breath.

"But I'm careful about what I try, Jethro. There's no use trying unless I'm committed to seeing it all the way through. I don't—can't—try unless I know I have the time to dedicate, to invest. Whatever it is, it's going to take years before it pays off, and even then, I still only get to about a B minus in skill."

Jethro stared at me for a long moment, his smirky smile returning in full force. "Jackson James, do you feel sorry for yourself?"

"No. Not at all. I just know what I am and what I lack."

"Then what the hell is wrong with you? You have an amazing woman who is in love with you. She's *in love* with you, and you're sitting here with us, whining about being a B-minus student. What is wrong with this picture?"

I also leaned forward, a sudden spike of anger making me speak before pondering my words. "I'll tell you what's wrong with me, Jethro. I walk in last night and find the door open and unlocked and the alarm off. And then I find Rae on the floor of the bathroom, crying because she thought Sienna was one of her stalkers—like the guy who broke into her old house in LA with rope and zip ties, an ex-con she barely escaped from who had an arrest record three miles long, most of which stemmed from domestic abuse and sexual assault."

Jethro leaned back, and it appeared I now had his full attention.

"And these last months have been nothing but death at work. So many overdoses, a kidnap victim found dead in the park, and today a three-car pileup with a teenager gone before her time. Do you know how many crime scenes I've been to where I find a victim crying on a bathroom floor? Hiding from their attacker? Do you know all the paths innocents take to get there? Do you have any idea what went through my mind when I saw Rae last night?"

"I reckon I have some idea," he said quietly.

"Then do you know what she told me when I asked her to consider going back to LA, for her own safety?"

He shook his head.

"She told me I had no say. She told me I was overreacting. She told me her life was hers, and my life was mine. She makes her own decisions, she does not need me or anyone else making them with or for her." I lowered my gaze to the table and found someone had placed a new beer in front of me. I grabbed it and drank it, thirstier than I'd been ten minutes ago.

"And that made you mad?" Jethro guessed. "Rae doesn't want you ordering her around and so you left?"

I got the sense he didn't quite believe his words—that I'd ordered her around—but rather was trying to play devil's advocate, help me see her side.

As such, my temper cooled, and I worked to pull in a deep breath. "No. I left because it was time to go to work. But I meant what I said, it's not going to work out between us. Rae doesn't want a say in my life either." I let Jethro see the starkness I felt about this subject. "She wants easy and fun, not hard work and not compromise, not connection. I was raised to believe a relationship is a partnership. Love means taking a person's wishes into account when you make decisions. I want to take her wishes into account, I want to change my life to make room for her. But I'm not going to push her to make room for me. I can't *make* her want to have a say in my life."

"Hmm." Jethro covered his mouth with his hand, studying me. "You make good points."

"He does," Cletus agreed. "You see now why we're best friends?"

"I do. But Jackson—" Jethro frowned at his bottle and picked the label "—what have you done to make room for Rae? How have you changed your life for her?"

I shook my head. "It doesn't matter now."

"Humor me," Jethro said, drawing my stare.

I saw he was serious, so I said, "I've been looking into the requirements for transferring or applying to LA County as a deputy sheriff."

"What?" Cletus's question was sharp. "You're leaving Green Valley?"

Jethro ignored his brother's outburst. "Did you tell her this?"

I shook my head. "What's the point? Like I said, I'm not going to force her to make room for me. She has to want it."

He paused, seemed to consider my question, then asked, "Do you love her?"

I didn't hesitate. "I do."

"Then you have to tell her all this." Jethro leaned forward, his stare intent. "You have to spell it out, just like you did with me and Cletus. You have to lay it all out and *ask* her to make room for you. You're right, you can't force it, or demand it, but you can ask. And tell her how you're making plans to make room for her."

I considered what the oldest Winston brother suggested, but before I could make up my mind one way or the other, Cletus drummed his fingers on the table to get my attention. "Let me see if I have this straight, being with Rae is easy. You feel like you don't even need to work for the grade."

"That's an odd way of putting it, but yeah. Continuing with the same analogy, being with her is like taking a college course with no papers and no exams, where the entire grade is based on participation. But, like I said, I want—"

"You want the hard stuff, the papers and the exams, yes, yes. We are aware. But let me finish this thought. Time spent with Rae is easy, and therefore it's not a grade worth earning?" Cletus asked.

"More like, it's not a grade I feel like I can trust to . . ."

"To?" Jethro prompted.

"To stay on my transcript. If I don't work for something, how can it be mine? How can I deserve it?"

A glimmer of respect shone in Jethro's gaze. "I get that," he said, and I sensed he told the truth.

"Then allow me to pose the following question—" Cletus turned to the side and said to his brother "—and bear with me, Jethro." Facing me again, he said, "Did you work for Ashley?"

"What do you mean?"

"When y'all were teenagers, was she a struggle?"

"No. Being around her was—" I snapped my mouth shut before I could say the word, gritting my teeth. In typical Cletus fashion, he'd led me down the road before I'd realized we were going anywhere.

It didn't matter because he finished the thought. "Easy, right? And she didn't return the depth of your affections."

"That's right. She—uh—didn't think of me the same way I thought of her." Man, this was not a subject I wished to discuss with Ashley's brothers, even all these years later.

"Hmm." Cletus was back to stroking his beard.

"Rae isn't Ashley," I snapped.

Cletus pointed to himself. "*I* know that. But do you? Do you really understand that Ms. Ezra is not Ashley? That you're not doomed to make the same mistakes over and over?"

I said nothing, my throat full of rocks.

He wasn't finished talking. "There are similarities, to be sure. Ashley and Ms. Ezra are both regarded as beauties, though they look markedly different. They're also both blessed with natural talent—A-plus talent, if you will—in their respective fields. Now, this next part isn't me being mean, though it may sound like it at first."

Bracing myself, I said, "Fine. Go on."

"To the casual observer, someone like Ash or Rae being with someone like you might not make much sense." Cletus stared off into the distance. "You're a sheriff's deputy in a big Tennessee county with a bunch of small towns that can't afford their own police department. You're not wealthy. You're not learned. You're not impressive. You don't eat meat. You're not showy or flashy. Your face isn't perfectly symmetrical—"

"This is you not being mean?"

"Let me finish."

"Fine. Continue," I grunted, wishing I'd never made overtures to be Cletus Winston's friend.

"I postulate that falling in love and making it last is like anything else in life that feels overwhelming when you're at the beginning of it. Saving for a down payment on a house. Writing a book. Getting one of those PhDs."

I lifted an eyebrow to show him I didn't get his point.

"Talk to Ms. Ezra. Do the work. Tell her your plans and your hopes. It might feel impossible now, but it won't always." The side of Cletus's mouth hitched with a rare smile. "My point is one I feel you already know: everything always feels impossible, until it's inevitable."

CHAPTER 27

JACKSON

"A strong man doesn't have to be dominant toward a woman. He doesn't match his strength against a woman weak with love for him. He matches it against the world."

— MARILYN MONROE

I asked Cletus to drop me off at my parents' house. Maybe it was the three beers when my system was used to zero, but I needed to talk to my father. Right now.

Rather than walk in, which was my usual practice, I knocked. I didn't know if Jess and her family were still in town. My sister wasn't great at communicating her plans. When my father opened the door on his own, he held a kitchen towel and appeared pleased to see me.

"Come in," he said, walking toward the back of the house and expecting me to follow. "I'm almost finished. You can help me dry."

I followed him through the house. It was quiet, which meant Jess had already left. Or maybe they were visiting Duane's side of the family. I dismissed that thought right away; if they'd been over at the Winston homestead, I doubted Jethro and Cletus would've taken me out for beers if they could've been hanging out with their brother.

Regardless, Jess and her family weren't here. My mother was probably in her office, preparing supplies and lesson plans for the start of school. Only a month remained before school was back in session, and she approached each year as a teaching assistant with the same gusto and planning as she had prior to her semiretirement.

Unsurprisingly, my dad led me to the kitchen, tossing me the towel. I caught it.

"Come over here and dry these." He gestured to a pile of bowls. "Your sister made pie for the Winstons, but she left some here too. We can have another slice after we're done, but don't tell your mother."

"Jess is over at Sienna and Jethro's?"

"That's right. They left around four. Why?"

I frowned. "It's just that . . ." If Duane, Jess, and Liam were visiting and available, why were Cletus and Jethro out with me?

"Jackson?"

"Never mind." Shaking myself, and tucking that mystery away for later, I walked over to the big pile of bowls and got to work.

"How's Rae? Did she have a good time last night?" he asked, scrubbing out the sink. My father had a checklist for cleaning the kitchen, one he and my mother had made years ago. She'd complained that he didn't clean the kitchen right, so they'd sat down and made a checklist. He'd wanted to do it right for her, so he'd changed. He'd made room. He'd invested.

That's what I needed to do.

When it came right down to it, I didn't know if I could ask Rae to make room for me, to invest. Truth was, I didn't want to ask. I wanted her to *want* to invest without me asking. Asking felt too much like pushing. But maybe I could show her I was making room for her. Maybe I could lead by example, and then she'd make room for me.

"I don't think I'm running for sheriff," I said, ripping the bandaid off, and facing my father. I braced for his reaction.

His movements stilled. He paused. Then he turned to me. "You're not running for sheriff."

"No." I folded the towel and set it on the small butcher block kitchen island, walking backward until I hit the counter. I leaned against it. "I'm going to move out to Los Angeles, if Rae wants me there."

His eyes narrowed, like he was working to process this information. "You're moving out to Los Angeles."

Well, now I know where I get my tendency to repeat recently spoken statements.

Ready for his disappointment, and maybe even his disapproval, I said, "Yes, and, if Rae wants me to move to LA, I'm going to apply to join the County Sheriff's Department out there."

My father frowned, his eyes dropping to the floor and studying the tiles he and I had laid there fifteen years ago. "You don't want to run for sheriff?"

"No, I do. I really do." My voice sounded ragged, so I cleared my throat before continuing. "But I need to show Rae that I'm going to fight for her, for us. That I'm invested in our future and that I want to make room for her in my life." *So she'll make room for me in hers.*

"By giving up on your dreams?"

Here we go. "Dad."

"No. I get it." He lifted a hand, a slight, curious smile on his face. "I do. Just, let me get this straight. Do you want to move to Los Angeles?"

"Yes. Because that's where Rae will be."

"But if she weren't, would you?"

I stared at him, eventually providing an answer that wasn't a surprise to either of us. "No. I wouldn't."

"You want to stay here, and run for office, and take care of the folks in this county. However, you think if you don't do something big—like move to Los Angeles and give up your life here—that you're going to lose Rae?"

"Yeah." I stuffed my hands in my pockets, not sure how I felt about any of this. "That about sums it up."

"All right. And if you weren't afraid of losing Rae, if you could stay here and be sheriff and you wouldn't lose her, would you stay? That's a slightly different question from the ones I've already asked."

I gave him a smile I'm sure looked as feeble as I felt. "Well, that's not really an option is it?"

"I'm not sure if it is an option, and I'm not the one you should be asking. Have you asked Rae if it's an option? Have you asked her what she wants? You can't know the answer to a question you haven't asked."

"Jessica said something similar to me recently."

"Jess is pretty smart. Takes after your mom that way." He smiled, his eyes dropping to the burn mark on the butcher block. But then his smile faded, and he crossed his arms, leaning his hip against the sink. "I know you're here to tell me, not ask me for advice, but I'm going to give it to you anyway, and here it is—" he lifted his eyes and held mine "—don't make any decision out of fear, if you can help it. Especially not a decision that impacts your future like this."

I nodded, feeling numb.

"If you're with somebody, and you're afraid you're going to lose them, talk to them. Tell her you're afraid. Admitting a vulnerability to someone you love and who loves you in return usually brings you closer, it doesn't push you apart."

My stomach swirled, protesting the three beers and no food. Or maybe it protested his advice, especially when he added, "Now, that's assuming she feels the same for you. That's assuming she wants to make room in her life for you. If she doesn't, well, then it's better to know sooner rather than later."

I turned, walking toward the kitchen table and grabbing the tall back of my seat, the chair I always sat in when I was a child. There were six chairs at this table, but there were only four of us.

Admitting a vulnerability to someone you love and who loves you in return usually brings you closer, it doesn't push you apart.

"Can I ask you a question?"

"Yeah, go for it." My father picked up the towel I'd left on the counter and dried his hands, then turned back to the sink to wipe the rim.

I studied his back for a moment. My father was taller than me. I'd never grown to his height.

"Why do you wish you had more kids?"

Once more, his movements stilled. He turned around and faced me. "Pardon me?"

"You've said it a couple times. More and more recently. You said it in June when we were at Daisy's for breakfast."

"So I did." His stare grew hawkish. "And I can see it's not what you're thinking."

"What am I thinking?"

"Based on the look on your face, we both know what you're thinking." My father, watching me very carefully, set the towel aside and crossed to the kitchen table, standing behind his chair which sat at the head of it. "Jackson, do you think I wanted to have more children because I think you and Jess aren't enough?"

I shrugged, spurred on by the beers. *I should never drink. It turns me into an asshole.*

He looked pained by my nonresponse. "That is not the case, son. W-we should h-have had more children f-for *you.*"

"For me?"

"Yes. You and Jess. What's going to happen to you and your sister when we're gone? When your mom and I pass away? I'm much less worried about Jess. We always knew she was going to leave and you were going to stay. Not because you don't have a big imagination and big dreams, but because your dreams are different."

I stared at my father, and for the first time in my life, I noticed he was old. His hair was grayer than blond, his forehead lined with wrinkles, and he didn't seem as tall and imposing as he once was. *My father is old.*

"And so, to the point." He scratched his cheek, his eyebrows lifting. "I've always wished that we'd given you another brother, another sister. So you wouldn't be alone. Also, because kids are great. I wish we could have had more, especially if they turned out like you and Jess."

I had to swallow several times before I could manage to say, "This was not the answer I was expecting."

"I reckon so, you look surprised." He seemed amused by the look on my face. But he wasn't quite finished with his explanation. "Now that Jess is married to Duane, she has Liam, and the Winstons are a big family. I know she'll be supported and taken care of. But, like I said, I don't like the idea of you being alone when your mom and I go. You need community, you need people. Sure, you need someone to take care of you, but I suspect—more than that—you need someone to take care of. And that's part of the reason I think you'll make a great sheriff. You'll have lots of folks to take care of."

Emotion clogged my throat and instinct had me pushing out a weak joke. "You planning on dying soon?"

"No, no." He leaned forward, his forearms resting on the back of the chair. "But look at my sister. She died of an unexpected heart attack. Tina's mostly by herself now. Sure, we invite your cousin over for dinner, but she doesn't come. She doesn't have people anymore. We try to be there for her. But watching her is like watching a lost baby bird." He paused, sighed, then added, "I don't want that for you."

"I'm not a baby bird."

"That's not what I'm saying."

"I know that's not what you're saying. But you don't have to worry about any of this. You're going to be here for a while." If I said it multiple times, I felt like I could trust it more.

"Am I? We can't know that. Look at what happened to Bethany Winston. She gets a cancer diagnosis and six weeks later she's gone, leaving all those kids without a mother."

"Dad. All the Winstons were grown when she died."

"But they're still orphans. When you lose your parents, no matter how old you are, you're an orphan. I know something about that. And I don't want you being on your own when it happens," he said, straightening from his chair and walking over to me.

"If you feel like you need to follow Rae to LA, if you think that's where you need to be, where you can do the most good, then you have my blessing. But think about what I said." Hesitating for just a split second, he set his hand on my shoulder and gave it a squeeze, his palm warm and steady. "As your grandfather used to say, 'Seeds sown in dread never bloom because fear makes for shallow soil.'"

CHAPTER 28

RAQUEL

"If you haven't cried, your eyes can't be beautiful."

— SOPHIA LOREN

I didn't call Jackson on Sunday.

If I didn't call him, if we didn't speak, then we were still technically together, and he couldn't break up with me. Also, I didn't want to make an idiot of myself and beg him to give me another chance. But let's be honest here, regardless of when it happened or how dry my eyes were at that moment, I was going to burst into tears and beg him to give me another chance.

"Are you okay?" Dave asked, holding very still at the entrance to my room, his tone cautious. "Will you eat? I think you should eat. Don't throw anything."

I pressed my face against my pillow and said, "Erm sseriefer dungth at."

"What?"

Fine. I'll lift my head.

"I'm sorry for doing that. It was highly unprofessional, and I was completely in the wrong. Please accept my apology, and I understand if you feel you need to seek alternate employment. I will be happy to offer a severance and assist you—"

"Oh, stop it. It was two throw pillows. They're literally called *throw* pillows. I mean, come on. Sheesh." In my peripheral vision, I saw Dave stroll into the room. He held a mug and a plate. "And I might've been a little bit of an asshole, so . . . truce?"

Flipping onto my side, I stared at him. "Are you kidding? A little bit of an asshole? You were a GIANT asshole."

He shrugged, taking another step inside the bedroom and sitting on the end of my bed. "Yeah. I guess I was. But somebody needed to say something."

"'Don't fuck this up, Rae. Whatever happened, I'm on Jackson's side.'" Sitting up in my bed, I deepened my voice to quote Dave's asshole statements from yesterday—when I'd woken up to find Jackson gone without a word and Miguel and Dave giving me dirty looks over coffee.

So, yes, I'd yelled at Dave. And then Dave had yelled at me. And we both made big hand movements and crude gestures. And then we'd yelled at each other, and I threw pillows at his head and slammed my door, and now here we were, Monday morning, and I couldn't seem to move. I'd spent all day Sunday in bed, hiding from the world, convinced that the moment I turned on my phone, I'd get a breakup text from Jackson.

Except, he wouldn't break up with me that way. Jackson—being Jackson—would show up in person, and probably bring roses and coffee. He would sit me down and be all gentle and kind about it, staying with me until he was certain I'd be okay. He'd probably also give me a pep talk, a motivational speech about how great of a person I was and how he'd keep me in his prayers. Then he would check the oil and tire pressure of my loaner car as he left.

He was the best. *God, I love him. PLEASE DON'T LET HIM BREAK UP WITH ME!*

Dave lifted the plate he held toward me. It contained grapes and carrots when all I really wanted was cake. A whole chocolate cake. A big, giant, double chocolate frosting laden chocolate cake with a giant glass of cold whole milk. No fork. I just wanted to shove my face in it and become one with the cake.

"Thank you," I said, taking the plate from Dave. It wasn't cake, but he was right. I needed to eat something.

"Are you ready to talk about what happened?" he asked, quickly following it with, "I promise, I won't judge. I'll just listen."

I popped a grape in my mouth, not tasting it as I chewed. "I messed up," I said simply.

I had messed up. I wasn't sure what I'd said that had made Jackson so angry and distant, that had made him sleep on top of the covers Saturday night instead of beneath, that had made him careful not to touch me as we lay together, both of us not sleeping or talking, but I must've said something.

I'd fallen asleep just before dawn. When I awoke, he was gone, and I felt certain he hadn't kissed me goodbye. *If we get through this, I'm going to institute a rule: he has to kiss me goodbye.*

"What did you do? How'd you mess up?" Dave handed me the mug.

It resembled the freshly juiced concoction of greens that my chef back in LA made me for breakfast—celery, cucumber, spinach, parsley, and ginger—and suddenly I was glad my taste buds weren't working.

"I'm not sure, to be honest. But I know I messed up." I took a gulp because I knew it was good for me even though I'd never particularly liked it.

"Okay, take me through what happened." Dave turned and placed a leg on the bed, bent at the knee in front of him. "Harrison left, Sienna came over to get something out of the closet while Miguel and I finished up helping Jethro—he was making rasp-berry jam, I brought some over—and then we walked back to the house. The next thing I know, Jackson is leaving your room looking like his world has ended."

My heart twisted. "What do you mean? You saw him? Did he say anything?"

"He said hello like always, asked how our evening had been—'cause he's the fucking politeness police—and then told us he was going on a short walk and would be back. But he asked us to lock the front door and turn on the alarm."

"And then what happened?" I was on the edge of my seat.

Dave scratched the back of his neck. "I stayed up and let him back in about an hour later. He woke me up before the sun, apologizing if you can believe it, asking me to lock the door and turn on the alarm after him. And that's it, that's all I know."

I slouched. "He didn't say anything else?"

"No. So what happened? What'd you two fight about? And what can I do to help?"

Staring at him, I made a decision. I needed to talk to someone. And yes, Dave worked for me. He was my employee. But—dammit—I needed advice. Also, he'd signed an NDA.

"Okay, first I have to tell you some background. Hold on a second." I set the plate of food aside and gulped down the juice, wanting to get something in my stomach but not wanting to chew. I was too sad to chew. *Unless it was cake.*

I then told Dave about Harrison's visit, what we'd decided, how he'd lobby for Lina to take the role in *Midnight Lady*—which was fine, whatever, I hated the new script —and how she would basically replace me in Harrison's life.

"That's . . . weird." His features were twisted with distaste.

"It is what it is. No one in Hollywood is irreplaceable. Except maybe Sienna."

"Nah, that's not it. You're not replaceable in Hollywood, but being Harrison's side-kick does seem to be a revolving door of stand-ins. Which, if you ask me, just means it's not where you belong. If you can be replaced so easily in a person's life, then you probably don't need to be a part of that person's life."

I nodded, biting the inside of my lip, his words making me feel better about the situation.

"So then what happened? Jackson came over?"

"No. Then I took a shower, and that's when Sienna came over." Even though it was embarrassing, I explained what had happened with Sienna, how I'd thought she was an intruder, how I'd freaked out and convinced myself I was going to be murdered violently.

At this point, Dave let loose a string of curses and skootched next to me on the bed, wrapping me in a big hug. "I don't care if this violates one of your employee-boss rules, but I'm giving you a hug."

"Okay. I accept." I laughed, returning his embrace. I decided then and there that I needed more hugs from more people. My life had been distinctly lacking in hugs. It would be all hugs, all the time from now on.

"Aww. You two are cute." Sienna, standing in the doorway with her hands clasped under her chin, grinned at us. "I remember Dave hugs. Those were the days."

We separated from our hug, Dave settling back next to me against the headboard. He then promptly stole a grape from my plate. "You can get some whenever you want, sweetheart. But as much as I like Jethro, he also scares me, so maybe check with him first."

Sienna laughed, drifting into the room and taking the spot at the end of the bed that Dave had vacated a moment ago. "I will check with him, but I'm sure it will be fine. And then it'll be hug time." She winked at her former bodyguard.

I frowned at the two of them. "Why would you check with Jethro before hugging Dave? Why can't you just hug Dave?"

Dave sent Sienna a look I couldn't decipher, which she mimicked, and then they both looked at me.

"Dave used to dip me when we hugged," Sienna said, crossing her legs. "Like I said, I'm sure it's fine. But it's very—I don't know—flirty? It's a respect thing."

"You don't feel like it's controlling? Needing to check in with Jethro?" I crossed my arms. "You should be able to hug whoever you want."

"I *can* hug whoever I want, and I do." Sienna sent Dave another look. "But I wouldn't want Jethro hugging someone that way without explaining it to me first, giving me the backstory. It's not controlling to take your partner's feelings into account, to listen to them and give them a chance to voice concerns before making your own decisions."

The tempo of my heart increased as she spoke, my mouth went dry, and—after spending the last eighteen hours wondering what I'd said that had angered Jackson so much—it all finally clicked.

"Oh my God. I'm such an idiot." I covered my face with my hands.

I felt Dave's tentative palm on my back, giving me a clumsy pat. "What? What happened?"

Letting my hands drop, I finished the story of Saturday, telling Sienna and Dave what I'd said to Jackson about making my own decisions and being responsible for myself.

"You didn't!" Dave reared back, his eyes wide. "You did not say that. Shut up! Not after he walks in on you crying on the floor of the bathroom."

Sienna placed a hand on my leg, her gaze sympathetic. "I understand what you meant —and he should've been more patient with you, especially after what had just happened—but you have to see how it probably sounded to him."

Dave wasn't finished. "You know he must see all kinds of stuff in his job, bad shit. And he's thinking the worst, and then he's panicking about your safety, and then you tell him he has no say in your life? That kind of thing will make a dude crazy. It's like, hardwired or something in our brains. *Me Jackson. You Rae. Must protect.*"

I groaned. "This is all so messy. I don't understand this. Aren't we all responsible for ourselves? Aren't my decisions my own?" This is what my mother had always told me.

"Yes, of course. But also, no. Not when you're in a committed relationship, no." Sienna shook her head. "For the record, I want to point out again that you'd just experienced something deeply distressing. He should have been more patient with you. And he shouldn't have told you to go back to LA, that was thoughtless of him. That said, moving forward, if you want a say in Jackson's life, then you have to give him a say in yours."

"I don't want to control him! I want him to be happy."

"But let's say he decided to quit his job and become a no-parachute skydive instructor," Dave said, stealing a few more grapes.

"Of course I wouldn't be okay with that because that would be suicide." I sent Dave a flat look. "Don't be ridiculous."

"Fine. What if he got into snake handling?" Dave took the plate and set it on his lap, giving up all pretense of sharing the plate with me. "I hear it can be a hell of a rush. Or what if he took up motorcycle racing with no helmet? Or what if—"

"Okay, okay. I get your point." I lifted my hands, my chest and neck hot for some reason. "When it comes to his safety, I guess I would want my opinion to be considered." I peeked at Sienna, then Dave. "Do you think this is why he's so mad? Because of what I said?"

Dave exhaled through his nose, his eyes unfocused as he considered my question. "You know, he didn't seem mad. He seemed . . ."

"Hurt," Sienna supplied, her expression still laden with sympathy. "I bet he was hurt."

UGH! That made me feel worse. "I need to apologize." I picked up my phone from where I'd placed it on the nightstand, navigating to the settings so I could switch off airplane mode.

"Rae." Sienna squeezed my leg, drawing my attention back to her. "Before you call him, why don't you and I go out, get some fresh air? You've been buried in here for over twenty-four hours."

I gestured to the phone. "But I—"

"Then you can think through what you want to say." Sienna sent Dave a look, tilting her head toward the door.

"Okay, that's my cue to leave. I'll just. . . " He rolled off the bed, taking the plate with him. "Let me get you some more carrots," he said, leaving the room and shutting the door.

Sienna studied me for a moment, a gentle smile on her lips. "Look, I know you're sorry. But I also know that you were overextended then and you're feeling overwhelmed now. Saturday night, you met Jackson's family and had spent the whole day tying yourself in knots with worry. And then Harrison shows up." She paused, frowning. "I'm assuming you already know, or that he talked to you about it when he was here, but pictures of Harrison and Lina are everywhere. The story of their 'romance' broke yesterday."

I snorted. "He didn't waste any time. Yes, I knew it was coming." I didn't want to be with Harrison—fake or otherwise—but it was disconcerting to be replaced so easily and by someone who'd stabbed me in the back.

But then Dave's words from earlier floated back to me, *If you can be replaced so easily in a person's life, then you probably don't need to be a part of that person's life.*

"If you can stand the paparazzi and put on a brave face, I'd like to take you out. There's a celebration thing at the Donner Bakery today, outdoors, very public. Domino called me, he'd like to see some shots of you today around town, looking happy and unaffected by Harrison and Lina's new relationship."

I rolled my eyes, huffing a laugh. "You mean, if I can fake it. If I can pretend to be just peachy, then we can go out." My less than peachy mood had very little to do with Harrison and Lina, and everything to do with missing Jackson. But still, I didn't want to pretend to be peachy.

"Yes, I guess that's what I meant." Her eyebrows furrowed. "What? What is it?"

"The whole reason I called everything off with Harrison is because I don't want this. I don't want to pretend anymore. I'm tired of faking and making brave faces. I just want to *be*."

Sienna gave me a look like she thought I was weird. "Rae, we all fake it. Every single one of us. It doesn't matter if you're in the business or not. I fake it at my kids' birthday parties. I fake it at family dinners. I fake it on some Fridays, when we go to the jam session and all I want to do is leave and go somewhere alone with my own thoughts. It's called showing up—for yourself and for others—even when it's inconvenient."

"What are you talking about? You don't fake anything. You're the least fake person in Hollywood. Look at you, you have your shit together, you know what you're doing."

Sienna shook her head the whole time I spoke. "No, baby. No. I don't have my shit together. Every day is making-it-all-up-as-I-go-along. No person alive has all their shit together."

I threw my hands up. "What? That makes me feel even worse."

"Why?"

"Because I thought—looking at you and the life you've built—I thought maybe there was a finish line. A point at which I wouldn't have to fake *everything*."

"You don't have to fake everything, but there is unlikely to be a point in your life where you'll feel like you have everything figured out. Life is a series of mistakes and missteps. If you think you're in a race, you probably are, but there is no finish line. The race never ends, not while you're alive. You can either stay in the race and keep going, faking it, day after day, or you can remove yourself from the race and take a different path—faking it only sometimes."

"I don't want to lose the race and I don't want to quit, and you're saying those are the only two options."

"No. I'm not. Because you're not in this race—or on a path—by yourself." She skootched forward, grabbing my hand. "If you feel like you're pretending all the time, maybe it's more about who you've surrounded yourself with rather than the race itself. The game is the game, the race is the race, but who you're with—your team, your family, the people you love, the people you trust—that's how you stop faking all the time. Surround yourself with people who want to be with you, the real you."

"Well, what do you suggest I do? Give up my career?" How else could I live an authentic life?

"No! No, no, no. Never. But maybe, find another way?"

Squeezing her hand back, I heaved a watery sigh. "I'm open to any and all ideas."

Sienna's sympathetic smile dwindled, and her gaze became a stare, and the stare grew unfocused. And then she snapped her fingers, her eyes suddenly sharp. "Open your own production company. Stay in Green Valley. Make your own movies, with me."

My breath hitched. "You can't be serious," I said, but my brain took off at full speed. *Can I do this? I want to do this.*

"I am. I'm doing it. *We* should do it. You and me. We'll do this together. I've already started the ball rolling."

Part of me wanted to protest—the part that didn't want to take advantage or be a bother to anyone—but the rest of me grabbed on to this idea with both hands.

"You know you can do this, Rae." She nodded, her eyes bright and excited. "You are incredible. *We* can do this. We'll make only the films we want to make, with only the people we want to work with."

"Then yes," I said, nodding, hope and dread and every single possible emotion rising up and filling me until I felt like I might burst. "Yes. Let's do this. Let's make our own movies." My voice cracked, and I don't know why, but I started to cry. It hit me like a wave. Like a big, giant tidal wave. I covered my eyes, shaking my head at myself. "I'm sorry."

"Don't apologize," she said, her tone neither sympathetic nor soft. "You cry if you need to. There may not be crying in baseball, but there is definitely crying in the film industry."

CHAPTER 29

JACKSON

"As a sex symbol, I don't know what is appealing to women. I think it's the way you treat women that makes you sexy if you like."

— RAY WINSTONE

"*B*ad day, Jackson?"

I stopped. I turned. And I looked right at Genie Lee.

She, like everyone in the crowd here, held a plate with a big slice of cake on it. The first week of August was Cake Week at the Donner Bakery. This year marked the fourth annual celebration, initiated by the head baker and Banana Cake Queen, Jennifer Winston. Everyone called her the Banana Cake Queen because her banana cake was insanely delicious.

Everyone that is except for Cletus Winston, he called her "wife."

But back to Genie Lee, her question, and her small, teasing, expectant smile. I imagined she'd asked the question figuring she already knew what I'd say. I'd say what I always said, and that would be a lie. Lucky—or unlucky, depending on how you reckoned things—for Genie, I didn't feel much like lying.

So I took a step closer to her and said, "Actually, yes, Genie. I'm having a bad day. I'm glad you asked."

Her smile fell and her eyebrows formed two arches of surprise on her forehead. "You—"

"It's been a bad, bad day. Yesterday we had that car crash, and I'm still feeling sick about it. I'm sure you've already heard. And today we had another unexpected tragedy—I'm not allowed to discuss it, but it's weighing heavy on my mind—and I feel like I can't take a deep breath, you know?" I breathed in, attempting to demonstrate what I meant. "Sometimes I feel like, what is the point? Every day, folks ignoring posted speed signs, doing drugs, hurting their loved ones, getting themselves into trouble, making bad choices. And I want them to stop. I want them to make good decisions for themselves and their families. I want them to stop being so careless and thoughtless. But there's nothing I can do. And so, yeah. I'm having a bad day."

Genie gaped at me, her eyes wide and worried. "Oh, Jackson."

"But it's okay." I lifted a hand, waving away her worry. "I'm feeling a little down about it, it feels like a lot today. But tomorrow is a new day, right?" I took a step back, giving her a small, optimistic smile. "And what does Maya Angelou say? 'Every storm runs out of rain'? Something like that. I like that quote. Well, have a great rest of your day, and enjoy the cake." I nodded, turning, and walked through the crowd.

I breathed in, hoping I'd be able to fill my lungs this time. I still couldn't. I likely wouldn't be able to take a real deep breath until I saw Rae and made things right. It had been almost two full days since our disagreement, and we hadn't spoken except through text messages.

Rae hadn't texted at all on Sunday. I'd sent her a message Sunday night after leaving my parents' house on foot, my heart heavy with uncertainty.

Jackson: Please give me a call when you have some time. I'd like to talk.

She didn't message me back until this afternoon.

Sunny: Just seeing your message. I had my phone off, I'm sorry. I love you and miss you and agree we need to talk. Sienna is taking me to the Donner Bakery for something called Cake Week. I'll be there until six, and then I'll be at the carriage house.

Sunny: Also, Dave, Miguel, and Jethro will be with me the whole time. Please don't worry. I will be safe and careful.

Her second text eased a tension I'd been carrying since Saturday night, giving me hope that maybe she'd be open to discussing her safety. I didn't want to push her, but I knew, deep down, I wouldn't be able to help myself. If she wasn't safe, if someone could just walk in and get to her whenever they pleased, I wouldn't be able to leave her side. I'd make myself crazy with worry.

I'd texted her a quick note back, letting her know I'd be at the bakery by 4:30 PM, so here I was.

The crowd was thick, but that was no surprise. Cake Week drew a big crowd. The big crowd meant I had to stop every few feet and say hi to someone, chitchat and ask about their son, or daughter, or dog, or houseplants. But then I spotted Dave's tall head by the entrance to the bakery, and I made a beeline for it, putting off folks who tried to stop me and ask after my family, my boat, and my houseplants.

With each step I took closer to Dave, my heart rose higher and higher in my throat until I almost stood directly in front of him, searching the area for Rae and not finding her.

I forgot my manners, and instead of greeting Dave like I ought, I blurted, "Where is she? I thought you were supposed to be with her?"

He grinned, reaching his hand out for a shake. "Jackson. It's *so* good to see you. Rae is in the kitchen with Miguel and Jethro. Sienna and Cletus are there too." He turned, waving for me to follow while he filled me in. "The crowd became too much, you know? She didn't want to leave. You said you'd be here at four thirty, and she wanted to wait. But, man, I hope you're hungry, because Cletus's wife made this *huge* chocolate cake, just for Rae. And it is *sooo gooooood*."

I was only half listening as we walked through the mostly empty bakery to the side door leading to the kitchen. Dave paused and knocked, saying, "Open up. It's Dave and Jackson."

Working to ready myself for the sight of her, I ignored my hammering heart as the door opened. I searched the space. And I saw her.

She hovered just behind Miguel—who'd opened the door—and her gaze crashed into mine.

"Hi," she said, her voice breathless.

"Hi," I said, struggling to remember what I'd been thinking just seconds ago.

A hopeful-looking smile curved her lips, and she stepped around her guard, hesitating for maybe a second before wrapping her arms around me. "I missed you. I'm so glad to see you." Her voice caught, snagged on the words, giving me the sense she hadn't been certain I'd show. The sound cracked my heart wide open.

"I missed you," I said against her neck, placing a kiss on the soft skin.

We held each other, and someone cleared their throat. We ignored them, clinging to each other. It felt like I had my whole world in my arms right now, and I wasn't certain I'd ever be able to release her. I wanted to stay just like this, maybe forever, and I accepted the fact that I'd never be able to walk away from Rae. She was it for me.

But then Cletus Winston's voice cut through my reflections. "You don't have to let go, but we're just going to move y'all into the room." Hands came to my shoulders and guided me into the kitchen.

I lifted my head, speaking to Cletus, "We're capable of—"

"No, no. Stay just like that," he said, encouraging us not to release each other by placing a hand on my back and a hand on hers, smooshing us together. "We're leaving to give y'all some privacy. Hug for hours if you want. There's cake for sustenance and a couch in the back for . . . other things."

While he spoke, the people in the kitchen filed out. I caught glimpses of Jethro and Sienna and their kids, Jennifer, Beau and his lady, Shelly. Miguel left wordlessly through the back door, but Dave left through the door leading to the front of the bakery. Presumably, they were each guarding an entrance until we were ready to leave.

And then the doors shut, and we were alone, still hugging each other. Rae had dipped her head back to watch the action, a smile on her face. The sight of it eased another tension, and I tried to take a deep breath again. This time my lungs almost filled, but not quite.

She looked at me and I looked at her, sad to see her smile diminish and be replaced by a line of determination and something else I couldn't place.

"Jackson," she started, her hands linking behind my back. "I am sorry."

I studied her, saying nothing, waiting for her to explain. I didn't want to make any assumptions.

Apparently reading my mind, she continued. "I'm sorry for what I said on Saturday. I know you were concerned about my safety, and you were, you know, freaking out a little. I'm sorry I said that you have no say in what I do. That's not true. You have a say, just like I have a say in your life."

"Do you want a say in my life?"

"Yes!" She used her arms around my body to give me a shake. "In fact, I demand it. I want a say."

I unsuccessfully fought a smile. "You sure?" This was exactly what I'd wanted her to say. The relief I felt in this moment was immeasurable.

She grinned. "Absolutely."

I let my answering grin free, lowering my head to hers, wanting a kiss.

She stopped me, tilting her head to the side. "Wait. First, I need to say something else. Once we start kissing, you know we're not going to be able to stop."

My eyes on her lips, my mind already halfway down that road. I hoped, whatever it was she needed to say, it wouldn't take long. I was *hungry*.

Letting me go, Rae took a step back and twisted her fingers. "There's two things we need to discuss, and they can't wait."

"Okay." My gaze trailed down her body for the first time. She wore that long orange dress I liked. I wondered what color her underwear was, she always wore a matching set. I looked to her shoulder, the strap of her bra was white.

"Jackson! Ahhh! Stop." She backed up, walking around the big kitchen island and placing it between us. "You have to stop looking at me like that or I'll never say this and then it will fester."

I nodded obediently, lifting my eyes to the ceiling. "Okay."

"You can look at me."

"Not yet. I need a minute."

She laughed, the sound full of giddy pleasure. "Fine. Then just listen. Here goes . . ." She paused, like she was gathering her thoughts, then said, "I know you were scared for me on Saturday, and I understand why, and I'm not upset about it. But you have to understand that I don't want to go back to living in a fortress."

I looked at her then, her words chasing away enough of my lust and replacing it with apprehension. "Rae, you need to be safe."

"And I will be. You and I, together, we'll figure it out. But I'm not living behind two gates with guard dogs, separate from everyone. I *hate* living that way. It makes me feel isolated and alone. I need community, I need people."

Frowning, I absorbed this information, but I didn't like it.

"I need community so much that I tried to build it with staff, surrounding myself with employees I paid instead of friendships. That's not going to happen in Green Valley. My house here will be safe, but it's not going to be a prison."

"Wait, your house *here*?"

She nodded. "Yes. I'm moving here."

I shook my head, rejecting this statement with every fiber of my being. "Rae."

"It's good. It's right for me."

Don't push, Jackson.

But I had to push. I had to push back against this. I couldn't just let her give up her entire career, all her dreams. "No, Rae. I can't let you do that."

She opened her mouth to argue, so I walked around the counter and grabbed her hands. "Please, just listen. I know your decisions are your own, and I respect that. But if I get any say in this, I absolutely do not agree. You can't make movies in Green Valley."

"Yes, I can—"

"The film industry is in Hollywood, in California. I can do my job anywhere, and I've already talked to my father."

"You can—what? What are you talking about?"

I stole a quick kiss before telling her my plan. "I've already started looking into what it would take to be a deputy with LA County, and I've already discussed it with my father. He knows I'll be moving when you go."

"Jackson!" She looked shocked, which I'd expected. But I didn't expect her to look horrified. "Please tell me you didn't do that."

"I did."

"That was—no." She pulled her hands from mine, gripping her forehead. "No, that's never going to happen. I'm never going to take you away from here. I can't even fathom it. This is where you belong, and not just because your family is here. What about running for sheriff? People here *need* you."

"But what about—"

Now she grabbed my hands, silencing me. "Listen, just listen for a minute, and stop trying to *Gift of the Magi* me, okay?"

I tried to place the reference, but before I could, she said, "Sienna and I are starting our own production company, based here, in Green Valley. She's already started the process, and she asked me to sign on as a partner. I want to do it. No! I *need* to do it. I need this. I need to get out of Hollywood. I love California, I do, but I'm ready to move on. I'm ready to be part of something real. I'm ready to take control of my career in a way that's meaningful, not chasing publicity or parts that might make me competitive but ultimately do nothing to fulfill me as an actor."

Trying to keep up, a million arguments came and went from my mind. But as I looked at her—really looked at her—I saw she was serious. She believed she needed this.

"This is what I want," she said, shifting her weight from foot to foot, her eyes darting between mine. "And I know some people might think it's a risk, but I don't. I believe in Sienna, and I believe in me, and I think—"

I scooped her into my arms, unable to think past my excitement for her. "It's going to be so great," I said, spinning her around, so proud, so happy. "You're going to knock their socks off and take over the world."

Rae's arms came around my neck and she held on, laughing, but she also sniffled. "Well, let's get a few projects rolling first."

The wobbly quality to her voice made me set her down, and I stole another kiss—this one slower, longer, savoring—before I pulled away so I could see her eyes. They were glassy with emotion.

"Hey. Are you okay?"

"Yes. I'm great. I'm so great." She lifted a hand and then dropped it, making a smacking sound against her thigh. "Everything is wonderful. You're wonderful, this thing with Sienna is wonderful—she's named it Operation Latina Domination, but I have no idea what we'll name the company—and the chocolate cake I ate today was wonderful. I'm just—"

She pressed her lips together, but she couldn't stop the shaking of her chin or the tear that rolled down her cheek.

"What? What is it?"

"I'm happy!" she said, the words bursting out of her. "I'm so happy."

"And you're afraid it won't last?" I stepped closer, trying to understand.

"No." Another tear followed the path of the first even though she wore a wide smile. "That's just it. I know it'll last. I know Sienna and I are going to be successful. I know I'll love living here. I know we—you and me—are going to last. And it feels overwhelming to know I'm at the very beginning of all this happiness."

I thought about her words until I felt the truth of them, and then I too felt over-whelmed. *We're going to last.*

She was right. We were. This wasn't temporary. We were going to last.

"Jackson," she said, her eyes soft and sweet, her hands lifting to cup my face. "I love you."

"I love you," I said automatically, still riding the wave of realization, acceptance of my good fortune.

I kissed her. She kissed me back. I touched her. She sighed, relaxing completely in my arms, like she knew they'd always be there to catch her, like she knew I'd never let her down. It felt too good to be true, but I didn't doubt it. Because I didn't doubt her.

I will see her tomorrow.

I will see her next week.

I will see her next month.

I get to hold her, and love her, whenever I want.

I knew Rae would always catch me too. Besides, it didn't matter if I fell. With her, I could be both upright and fallen, serious and fun, easy and devoted all at once. I was absolutely, over the moon and stars crazy about her, and that was perfectly fine.

Rae was magic, and I would always and forever believe in Rae.

EPILOGUE

RAE

"I'm quite cool about my sex symbol image. It's nothing to be proud of or ashamed of."

— URMILA MATONDKAR

Several Years Later

"It's okay to be nervous," Jackson whispered in my ear. "I got you."

"I know." I nodded, the movement jerky. I was definitely nervous. I couldn't remember ever being more nervous.

Facing Lina and Harrison at my first film premiere post-faux-split? Whatever.

The initial day of filming on Sunray Productions' very first project? No problem.

The red carpet Oscar walk for our first best picture nod? No biggie.

But this? I was a mess.

Behind me, Jackson placed his hands on my shoulders and smoothed them down my arms. "My mom wants you to call her when it's over."

"I know. I will." Janet and I spoke almost every day whenever I wasn't in town. Even if it was just a few text messages back and forth, we touched base. At first, it had been odd, having someone who wanted to know about me, every day, check in to make sure I was happy and healthy and didn't need a cup of sugar or a random apple pie. She wasn't pushy, not at all. Our relationship had just sort of . . . happened. We fell into the habit naturally, easily. I loved her.

I wouldn't, however, be calling my mother about this. She didn't even know we were in Miami. I wasn't keeping it from her, but I knew telling her where I was and what I had planned would only make her angry. I didn't want her to be angry.

Years ago, at the end of my first summer in Green Valley, my mom had called me when news of Harrison and Lina had made it inside her bubble of academia, several weeks after the story broke and the general public had consumed it, processed it, and wrote hundreds of op-eds about it.

She'd been furious on my behalf. I'd waited patiently for her to wear herself out, trying not to laugh at all her colorful Italian insults and phrases, before telling her the truth about my relationship with Harrison. This information had made her feel better —that I'd used him to further my career and now our agreement had ended amicably —but then I told her about Jackson and my plans to stay in Green Valley.

"I love him. I'm in love with him. I'm starting my own production company with Sienna Diaz, and I'm so happy," I'd said.

She'd clammed up, told me I was responsible for my own life and choices, made an excuse, and hung up.

Our relationship continued to follow this pattern. Sometimes we chatted once a month. Sometimes six months would go by. Sometimes she approved of my news. Sometimes she didn't, and she'd remind me I was responsible for myself.

But those words—*You are your own person, your choices are your own*—had stopped cutting like they used to, probably because they weren't necessarily true anymore. I was my own person, but I shared myself with people who loved me. My choices were my own, but I'd surrounded myself with friends who cared enough about my choices to offer their opinion and wanted my opinion on their choices.

Obviously, my mother cared about me—in her own way and always on her terms. And that was okay.

Or rather, perhaps it wasn't okay. Perhaps it was sad and unfortunate that I'd never have a real relationship with my mother as an adult. But something I'd learned from watching Jackson and his family, and from my friendships with Charlotte and Sienna and others, was that I couldn't *force* her to be more than a spectator in my life.

If my mother wanted a relationship with me—a real one, not a shallow one, not a fake one—she had to want it. I would keep the door open for her, but it was up to her whether or not she ever walked through.

And besides, I didn't want to think about her—or how she'd react—on today of all days. I was nervous enough.

A massive swarm of panic butterflies had me leaning back against Jackson's solid chest, and I searched my mind for something, *anything* to take my mind off what was about to happen.

"So . . ." I started, stopped, then said the first thing that came to my mind, "Did you buy my latest movie on Blu-ray/DVD and streaming?"

"Really? You're asking me this now?" He spoke against my ear, laughter in his voice.

"I'm trying to take my mind off my nerves. Answer the question."

"You haven't checked?"

"I didn't want to snoop."

"That's a lie. You're always going through all my drawers."

My mouth fell open with mock-shock. "How dare you. Don't make me out to be some sort of creeper. You know I go through your drawers so I can smell your clothes. Now apologize."

He didn't apologize, but he did turn me around and give me a toe-curling kiss, his lovely, long kraken tongue tangling with mine and making me breathless. Lifting his mouth, he trailed it along my jaw to my neck, swirling it against the skin beneath my ear.

"I miss you," he said, nipping at my ear. "I want to taste you."

"I want to be tasted," I said, my breath hitching as my mind tried to negotiate a new plan for this afternoon. Maybe we could find a nook or a cranny or a door with a lock and—

"They're here."

345

I stiffened, the panic butterflies swarming anew. "They're here?" I croaked.

"Yes." He straightened, looking down at me with his twinkly bedroom eyes. "How'd I do? Did I distract you?"

I nodded, now breathless for two reasons. "How do I look?"

"Perfect."

I made a face, not yet ready to turn around. "No, I mean, how do I look? Do I look desperate? I want them to like me. Should I have worn—"

"Your brother and sisters are going to adore you. And if they don't, I'll arrest them."

Unexpected laughter bubbled out of me, and I smacked him lightly on the arm. But his tactic had worked. I felt better. I'd needed that laugh.

"Okay, Sheriff James, calm down."

He grinned. "Now—" he kissed my forehead, then leaned back to give me a supportive smile "—turn around, walk over there, and introduce yourself. You know I'll be right behind you."

I didn't feel particularly brave, but I'd come this far, right? I could do this. I could introduce myself. "Okay, yes. I can do this."

We stared at each other for a protracted moment, and Jackson's smiled softened. "Hi."

"Hi," I whispered back, happiness and hope tugging at my lips.

"I'm proud of you," he said, his tone sincere. "No matter what happens, no matter who they are, no matter how they treat you, it doesn't change who *you* are."

His words—much like his mere presence and every delicious, sexy, polite, patient, *good* part of him—a balm to my soul. Gathering a deep breath, I finally felt enough courage to turn around and face my half siblings, to face the fear and hope I'd been juggling in equal measure since making that first phone call three months ago.

With Jackson behind me, I knew I could face anything.

THE END

Subscribe to Penny's awesome newsletter for exclusive stories, sneak peeks, and pictures of cats knitting hats. Subscribe here: http://pennyreid.ninja/newsletter/

ABOUT THE AUTHOR

Penny Reid is the *New York Times*, *Wall Street Journal*, and *USA Today* Bestselling Author of the Winston Brothers, Knitting in the City, Rugby, Dear Professor, and Hypothesis series. She used to spend her days writing federal grant proposals as a biomedical researcher, but now she just writes books. She's also a full time mom to three diminutive adults, wife, daughter, knitter, crocheter, sewer, general crafter, and thought ninja.

Come find me -
Mailing List: http://pennyreid.ninja/newsletter/
Goodreads: http://www.goodreads.com/ReidRomance
Facebook: www.facebook.com/pennyreidwriter
Instagram: www.instagram.com/reidromance
Twitter: www.twitter.com/reidromance
Patreon: https://www.patreon.com/smartypantsromance
Email: pennreid@gmail.com …hey, you! Email me ;-)

OTHER BOOKS BY PENNY REID

Knitting in the City Series

(Interconnected Standalones, Adult Contemporary Romantic Comedy)

Neanderthal Seeks Human: A Smart Romance (#1)

Neanderthal Marries Human: A Smarter Romance (#1.5)

Friends without Benefits: An Unrequited Romance (#2)

Love Hacked: A Reluctant Romance (#3)

Beauty and the Mustache: A Philosophical Romance (#4)

Ninja at First Sight (#4.75)

Happily Ever Ninja: A Married Romance (#5)

Dating-ish: A Humanoid Romance (#6)

Marriage of Inconvenience: (#7)

Neanderthal Seeks Extra Yarns (#8)

Knitting in the City Coloring Book (#9)

Winston Brothers Series

(Interconnected Standalones, Adult Contemporary Romantic Comedy, spinoff of Beauty and the Mustache)

Beauty and the Mustache (#0.5)

Truth or Beard (#1)

Grin and Beard It (#2)

Beard Science (#3)

Beard in Mind (#4)

Beard In Hiding (#4.5, coming 2021)

Dr. Strange Beard (#5)

Beard with Me (#6)

Beard Necessities (#7)

Winston Brothers Paper Doll Book (#8)

Hypothesis Series

(New Adult Romantic Comedy Trilogies)

Elements of Chemistry: ATTRACTION, HEAT, and CAPTURE (#1)

Laws of Physics: MOTION, SPACE, and TIME (#2)

Irish Players (Rugby) Series – by L.H. Cosway and Penny Reid

(Interconnected Standalones, Adult Contemporary Sports Romance)

The Hooker and the Hermit (#1)

The Pixie and the Player (#2)

The Cad and the Co-ed (#3)

The Varlet and the Voyeur (#4)

Dear Professor Series

(New Adult Romantic Comedy)

Kissing Tolstoy (#1)

Kissing Galileo (#2)

Ideal Man Series

(Interconnected Standalones, Adult Contemporary Romance Series of Jane Austen Reimaginings)

Pride and Dad Jokes (#1, coming 2022)

Man Buns and Sensibility (#2, TBD)

Sense and Manscaping (#3, TBD)

Persuasion and Man Hands (#4, TBD)

Mantuary Abbey (#5, TBD)

Mancave Park (#6, TBD)

Emmanuel (#7, TBD)

Handcrafted Mysteries Series

(A Romantic Cozy Mystery Series, spinoff of *The Winston Brothers Series*)

Engagement and Espionage (#1)

Marriage and Murder (#2)

Home and Heist (#3, coming 2023)

Baby and Ballistics (TBD)

Pie Crimes and Misdemeanors (TBD)

Good Folks Series

(Interconnected Standalones, Adult Contemporary Romantic Comedy, spinoff of *The Winston Brothers Series*)

Totally Folked (#1)

Folk Around and Find Out (#2, coming 2022)

Three Kings Series

(Interconnected Standalones, Holiday-themed Adult Contemporary Romantic Comedies)

Homecoming King (#1, coming Christmas 2021)

Drama King (#2, coming Christmas 2022)

Prom King (#3, coming Christmas 2023)

CPSIA information can be obtained
at www.ICGtesting.com
Printed in the USA
LVHW052118150921
697893LV00007B/1094

9 781942 874737